Praise for the Home Repair Is Homicide Mysteries of Sarah Graves

"Memorable characters and helpful household tips enhance a dark cozy that will keep the reader turning the pages until the surprising and dramatic conclusion."
—*Publishers Weekly*

"Blends do-it-yourself home repair tips into a very suspenseful murder mystery, with well-depicted characters and plenty of action. . . . Always staying one suspenseful step ahead of the deductive reader, this scary story nails it." —Fredericksburg *Free Lance-Star*

"Graves transcends the boundaries of the conventional mystery by allowing her protagonists to indulge in heroics that land them in the shark-infested waters of the thriller." —*Library Journal* (starred review)

"Reigning master of the [cozy] genre."
—*Romantic Times*

"A fast-paced tale of hide-and-seek . . . exciting and entertaining . . . If you are a mystery fan, you will love it." —*Galveston County Daily News*

"Relentless pacing, an appealing heroine and perfectly loathsome antagonists will more than satisfy series fans." —*Publishers Weekly*

"This first-rate thriller features nail-biting suspense that ensnares the reader to the final page. . . . Full of courageous women and compelling action. Highly recommended." —*Library Journal* (starred review)

"Graves provides an entertaining read sprinkled with practical tips. A recipe for success—even if it makes you want to start one of your long-overdue home-repair projects!"
—*Wichita Falls Times-Record News*

"Another well-plotted whodunit . . . I love this series."
—*Kingston Observer*

"Sarah Graves is in top form. . . . As always, Graves's trademark home repair tips add utility to fun." —*Mystery Lovers Bookshop News*

"Like the old Victorian homes she describes . . . Graves's stories seem to grow better with the passing of time. . . . Readers who enjoy solving mysteries and fixing up older homes will appreciate Jake's do-it-yourself expertise in both areas." —*Booklist*

"[An] innovative cozy series . . . Readers will relish the author's evocative descriptions of small-town Maine, strong characters whose relationships evolve, sense of humor, and, of course, helpful home-repair hints." —*Publishers Weekly*

"Offers all the pleasures of the 'cozy' subgenre . . . [with] its feisty amateur sleuth . . . [and] quirky assortment of friends and family . . . The plot is leavened with home repair passages full of detail and a nice dose of attitude." —*New England Today*

"An enjoyable read for those who like their mysteries well-built." —*Bangor Daily News*

"Graves makes rehabbing shutters and other chores suspenseful. The novels are as well crafted as the household projects are carried out."
—*The Boston Sunday Globe*

BY SARAH GRAVES

The Dead Cat Bounce
Triple Witch
Wicked Fix
Repair to Her Grave
Wreck the Halls
Unhinged
Mallets Aforethought
Tool & Die
Nail Biter
Trap Door
The Book of Old Houses
A Face at the Window
Crawlspace
Knockdown

And look for
Dead Level

Coming from Bantam in Summer 2012

KNOCKDOWN

A

Home Repair Is Homicide
Mystery

SARAH GRAVES

BANTAM BOOKS • NEW YORK

Knockdown is a work of fiction. Names, characters, places, and incidents either are the product of the author's imagination or are used fictitiously. Any resemblance to actual persons, living or dead, events, or locales is entirely coincidental.

2012 Bantam Books Mass Market Edition

Copyright © 2011 by Sarah Graves
Excerpt from *Dead Level* copyright © 2012 by Sarah Graves

All rights reserved.

Published in the United States by Bantam Books, an imprint of The Random House Publishing Group, a division of Random House, Inc., New York.

BANTAM BOOKS and the rooster colophon are registered trademarks of Random House, Inc.

Originally published in hardcover in the United States by Bantam Books, an imprint of The Random House Publishing Group, a division of Random House, Inc., in 2011.

This book contains an excerpt from the forthcoming book *Dead Level* by Sarah Graves. This excerpt has been set for this edition only and may not reflect the final content of the forthcoming edition.

ISBN 978-0-553-59342-6
eBook ISBN 978-0-440-42312-6

Cover design: Jamie S. Warren
Cover images: Shutterstock/Susan Law Cain (house); Shutterstock/LilKar (tree)

Printed in the United States of America

www.bantamdell.com

9 8 7 6 5 4 3 2 1

Bantam mass market edition: January 2012

THEN

Jacobia. **Come on now," said Victor. "Be** reasonable."

Her husband's voice on the telephone had a soothing tone, the one he used on patients who would recover if they did just as he said.

His definition of *reasonable*. Victor was a brain surgeon, and he always tried that voice on her, too, before he brought out the big guns.

Bazookas of sarcasm, rocket launchers of scorn.

But not yet. "Jake, I was here at the hospital all along. The ward clerks must not have realized it, that's all."

"Uh-huh. And they didn't page you."

She knew they had. It was nine in the morning and she was sitting on a wrought-iron café chair, on the prettily landscaped terrace of their penthouse apartment overlooking Central Park.

The café chair was enameled absinthe green. The shrubs in the huge clay pots were Himalayan forsythia and dwarf Japanese maple.

On the wrought-iron bistro table, a grease-stained paper plate holding a slice of last night's pizza sat alongside a jelly glass stenciled with the image of Yosemite Sam.

There was a bite out of the slice. In the glass was some of the two-hundred-dollar bottle of wine she had opened once it became clear that not only was he not coming home for dinner as he'd promised, he wasn't coming home that night at all.

"If they did page me, I didn't hear it. Maybe I was catching a nap in the on-call room. I don't exactly always have the luxury of keeping a normal schedule, you know."

His tone shifted to the terse, coldly annoyed one he used on underlings, nurses or junior surgeons, who hadn't obeyed an order of his quickly enough. "Some of us have . . ."

Real jobs. Ones that matter. Life-or-death occupations whose demands trump everything else.

Including you, he didn't finish, but he might as well have. But she was immune to that now. Especially since she knew perfectly well that he hadn't been at the hospital last night, as he claimed.

She drank the red wine out of the Yosemite Sam glass in a couple of swallows, refilled it, then picked up the paper plate with the slice on it and sailed it out over the terrace's railing like a Frisbee, not watching to see where it went.

"I was there," she said. "At the hospital. You were signed out."

Brief silence from Victor. From down in the street came the blare of a car horn, possibly as a pizza-laden paper plate landed on a windshield.

"What?" Outrage now. "You mean you came over here to . . ."

"Check on you. Yes. At midnight when you hadn't

shown up and you weren't answering your cell, I got worried. So I went out in my party dress and the diamond-and-platinum earrings you gave me when we got married."

She drank more wine. It was pretty good, actually. She'd have finished it the night before if she hadn't been distracted by the decanter of forty-year-old Scotch.

"To make sure that you were okay, that you hadn't had some kind of an accident on the way home, or gotten mugged. Because we had a date, remember?" she added gently, her voice breaking.

Which was silly, really. But the tears prickled in her eyes nonetheless, blurring the soft green tops of the trees in Central Park. It was spring, and the lovers down there were walking hand in hand along the paths beneath the flowering cherries.

No doubt. She swallowed hard. Probably her tears were only on account of the wine. Because she couldn't still care so much, could she?

"It was embarrassing," she said. "The ward nurses all looked at me with pity in their eyes." *Poor thing. Wouldn't you think she'd've had enough of it by now? Why doesn't she wise up?*

Why, indeed. "Yeah, I suppose it would be embarrassing," he retorted angrily. "How would you like it if I . . ."

I would like it, she thought. *If you cared enough to bother, I would like it very much.*

But he didn't. He didn't even care if she'd humiliated both of them; not really. It was only that this change of subject was convenient for him, focusing as it did on what *she'd* done instead of on what he'd been doing.

Which she also knew. Because while she'd lingered at the nursing station, waiting for them to page him even though he was signed out and then waiting some more while he didn't answer, she'd seen the nurses' schedule posted on a bulletin board.

The schedule listed who was on duty that night, and who was off. Most of the names were familiar; Victor had been a surgeon at the hospital for several years now.

But one name was new. It was also in the phone book, with an address. "I guess nurses must make pretty good money these days," she said.

"What?" he demanded in the kind of voice that meant someone was being difficult past all reason. "What are you . . . ?"

Talking about. "Monica," she said. "That Greenwich Village rowhouse she lives in? That your car was parked outside all last night? It's nice. The house, I mean."

Gotcha. Not that she took any pleasure in it. She was just tired of Victor thinking he'd put one over on her, was all.

Thinking that she was stupid. She drank the rest of the wine and resisted the urge to send the bottle over the railing, too.

"Good-bye, Victor," she said tiredly, and hung up. Probably he had an excuse for why he was at one of the nurses' homes last night instead of with her, celebrating their thirteenth wedding anniversary. But she didn't want to hear it.

Not, she reflected, tipping the empty wine bottle upside down sadly, that there was much to celebrate. The phone rang, the display showing Victor's hospital number.

Now he would try to shame her by telling her how paranoid she was, how her pathological suspicions were driving him to find solace in the arms of another woman.

Although she knew only too well that the arms weren't what interested him. Ditto the eyes, the ears, the face, or the brain.

Especially not that. The phone kept on ringing. She looked at it for a long moment, then picked up.

"Hello? Is that by any chance my lying, cheating, son-of-a-bitch husband calling me? Because if it is, listen to this."

She smashed the device hard against the terrace railing and smiled as its parts flew everywhere.

"And that goes double for your latest girlfriend, the poor little dope," she said into the phone's shattered shell.

Behind her, a blare of what at normal volume might've been music thundered through the penthouse apartment. But cranked up this way, it was more like a sound-wave-based demolition device.

She could practically feel the walls cracking. Any minute, the building superintendent would be up here. She hurried inside.

"Sam!" She hammered on his door. She'd have gone in, but he kept it locked.

He was twelve. "Yeah."

"Sam, turn it—"

The volume lowered abruptly.

"—down!" she shouted.

"Yeah."

She contemplated the door. "You okay in there?"

"Yeah."

She looked at herself in the hall mirror: showered, dressed, and with a little foundation and lipstick applied, in spite of everything. *Okay.* She'd run a comb through her short dark hair, too, and she had shoes on her feet.

Whoop-de-do, she thought bleakly, eyeing her reflection with skepticism. No beauty queen, but the navy slacks and jacket over a silk blouse were respectable enough, as were the black pumps. Luckily, she had the kind of lean, dark looks that didn't require much upkeep.

Yet. *Much more of this and I'll be laying on the makeup with a trowel just to look human.*

"Sam, I'm leaving for the office. I've got an appointment."

Brief silence. Then, "Okay."

Well, at least it wasn't *Yeah.* "You're going to school, right?"

He knew she'd call the school later to make certain he was there. The music volume went back up a little, but not as much as before.

She glanced at her wristwatch, the black Movado museum piece she'd bought for herself the first year she'd made any real money on her own.

Or what she'd thought of back then as real money. A few more minutes and she'd be late. "Sam?"

The music went up a notch. "Sam, this is your

mother out here talking to you. Now you answer me this minute or I'll—"

What? she wondered despairingly. What would she do? Summon a locksmith? Or call 911 and have the door broken down?

There was no point talking to Victor about this. If she did, he'd have a fatherly chat with their son, and after Sam fooled him again with another tale about how she was just overreacting as usual, Victor would confront her.

And she didn't want to hear that, either. Didn't know what she would do, actually, if she had to—

Sam's door opened an inch. Through the crack, her son looked out flatly at her, and even as angry as she was at him, the sight was a relief.

She managed a smile. "Hi."

Sam had dark curly hair, long-lashed eyes, and a full mouth like his dad's. She wanted to ruffle his hair, but if she tried he would probably slam the door on her wrist.

"Sandra should be here in a minute." The house-keeper, she meant. "She'll drive you to school."

And make sure you go in. Sandra was fat, fair, and forty: not Victor's type. More important, she was onto Sam's tricks.

"I left you a casserole in the refrigerator, in case I'm late." Stouffer's, actually. But it didn't matter; he wouldn't eat it.

"Thanks." Patiently, waiting for her to leave him in peace.

"Are you going out with your friends later?"

Might as well at least pretend she still had any say

in what her son did or didn't do. She thought lately he was hanging out with the Tooley boy from the fifth floor, but she wasn't sure.

The Tooley boy was sixteen and had already been in juvenile detention. Still, he was better than the crew Sam used to spend time with, shoplifting and riding the tops of subway cars at all hours of the day and night.

"Sam," she repeated, "are you . . . ?"

His door closed. The lock clicked. The music went up again, although not enough to bring the building super. It was as if Sam knew just exactly how far he could go.

What do you mean, "as if"? she asked herself bitterly as she left the apartment.

The lobby of her building on Central Park West had the kind of prewar glamour you couldn't find in new construction: art deco wall sconces, gleaming black marble floors, crystal chandeliers. Her heels clicked past the concierge's desk with the vase full of fresh florist's blooms on it, then the security guard's podium, and finally the low table spread with complimentary copies of the *Times* and *The Wall Street Journal*.

She picked up a *Journal* as she went by; she could read it as she cabbed to the office. "Mrs. Tiptree?"

Damn. She turned, trying to indicate by her expression and posture that she was late. Which she wasn't; not yet. But she did not want to talk to the building superintendent, Mr. Halloran.

Or rather, be talked to by him. "Mrs. Tiptree, I'm sorry to have to trouble you."

Have to. That was a bad sign. "But our other residents . . ."

She drew herself up. "There've been complaints?"

Her tone dared him. But of course there had been complaints. What with the threats and accusations flying between her and Victor, and Sam's music being played at volumes generally reserved for arena concerts, it was a wonder that the other tenants didn't assemble outside their apartment door with torches and pitchforks.

Inspiration hit her. "Talk to my husband about it."

"But—"

"The man of the house," she practically spat at the unlucky building superintendent. Really, he didn't deserve this.

But by now she *was* late, and anyway, there wasn't a thing in this world she could do about any of it, and especially not about the music; heaven knew she'd tried. So for now she thanked her lucky stars that Sam at least still lived at home, and not on the street half the time like the Tooley boy.

Outside, limos picking up other tenants sat idling along the curb while their drivers read the papers and drank coffee. On the sidewalks, elderly ladies in pastel Chanel suits tottered along behind tiny dogs on pastel leashes; nannies pushed Italian-made strollers and luxury baby carriages.

Changing her mind about the cab, she turned south, hoping a walk might clear her head. At this hour she could travel faster on foot than the traffic could move, anyway.

Thirty minutes later, at Madison and Thirty-fourth, the city was one part blaring cab horn, one part jackhammer, and three parts way too many people, all hustling like mad. In the deli on the corner, she got coffee and a bagel and carried them into her building, where they were nearly knocked from her hands by a man rushing past her out through the lobby.

Gray fedora, salt-and-pepper mustache, scarred face . . .

She knew him, and he must have recognized her, too, because he turned around and came back in. It was Jerry Baumann, known to his friends and associates as "Da Bomb."

She did not like thinking about why he was called this, or how she knew.

"Listen," Jerry growled, not pausing for niceties. "I went upstairs and told him the situation. It's not gonna change. He gets the money to us by tomorrow, or—" He drew a crooked finger across his throat.

"I beg your pardon?" Jake began, aware of the doorman listening with interest from his desk just inside the front door. "How did you even—"

The whole reason for having a doorman at all was that no one was supposed to be able to get upstairs without first being announced via intercom, and approved.

But when she glanced over inquiringly, he was suddenly extremely busy with some papers in one of the desk's drawers.

Come on, Jerry "Da Bomb" Baumann's face said

clearly. *You think some freakin' rent-a-cop's gonna stop me?*

"You tell him," he repeated as he opened the door to the street. The sudden clamor of noise was so loud that it was almost comical.

"Don't let him get thinkin' anything else," Jerry Baumann said, and then the door swung shut.

"Some help you are," she said to the guard, who upon Jerry's departure found his paperwork less engrossing.

"Yes, ma'am," the guard said evenly, unsmiling.

"Who's up there?" she demanded. Despite leaving home late, she'd made good time; her appointment wasn't for another ten minutes.

But just then the guard's desk phone rang, and the elevator doors opened. *The hell with it,* she thought as she stepped in, pulling the key to her office from her shoulder bag with one hand while balancing a paper bag with coffee and a bagel in it with the other; she'd find out who was there herself.

She didn't need the key, though, because the office door—no name, just the suite number—stood open. Inside, the anteroom smelled like Old Spice laced with bubblegum.

And something else. *Fear sweat,* she thought. "Hello?"

She didn't have a secretary or a receptionist. She wouldn't even have had an office, but some of her clients weren't the kind of people she wanted coming to her home.

Some of her clients, she didn't even want them

knowing where she lived, although they probably did anyway. "Anyone here?"

The bubblegum smell was getting stronger. On the tan carpet, a few grains of something granular was sprinkled, like a trail of . . . She knelt and touched the stuff, and after a moment tasted it.

Sugar. What the . . . ?

"Hello."

She looked up. A little boy, maybe ten years old, stood in the doorway to her inner office, where she met clients.

The boy, scrubbed so clean he practically glowed and with an obviously fresh haircut under his kid-sized baseball cap, wore a blue blazer. Under it he wore a white dress shirt and a striped silk tie—a real one, not a clip-on. His slacks were belted, and from the way they broke just so over his oxblood shoes, they had obviously been tailored for him.

"Hello. Who are you?" She got up, brushing sugar granules from her fingertips while the kid went on eyeing her somberly.

"Steven. My mother calls me Junior." The boy blinked once, slowly. From the white bits around his mouth, she gathered that the ones on her carpet were from something that he'd been eating.

"Are you going to let the bad men kill my father?" he asked.

His voice held an odd, remarkably unchildish undercurrent of menace. Then it hit her, who he must be. *Oh, for Pete's sake.*

She should have known; under that new haircut of his, the kid's ears stuck out a mile.

Just like his dad's.

"Hi, Jake. Sorry we're a little early."

Steven Garner Sr. appeared in the doorway behind his son. "I slipped the guy downstairs a little something; he let us up," he confided.

Unlike the boy, he did not look freshly laundered. He wore rumpled slacks over white high-top sneakers that had seen better days, a polo shirt with dryer wrinkles still in it, and a blue cotton warm-up jacket with an egg splotch on the front.

"I saw Baumann in the lobby just now," she said, and watched Garner's face tighten with anxiety.

The kid was still staring at her. "You hungry?" she asked him, despite the evidence of a recent meal—a doughnut, probably—around his lips.

The boy nodded; what little kid wasn't always hungry? "But my mom doesn't let me . . ." he began as she brought out the bagel.

"Steven," his father told him gently, "go sit down over there and eat the bagel, okay? Go on," he repeated as the boy looked doubtful. "I'll make it okay with your mom."

The boy rolled his eyes, giving Jake the idea that making things okay with his mom generally wasn't so easy. But he did as he was asked.

"And don't do anything else," his father told him, which Jake thought was a little strange. The look he gave the kid was odd, too: stern, but with a thread of fear in it. "Just sit."

"Come on," Jake said, waving Steven Sr. back into her inner office, which was even more spartan than the outer one.

The desk was a gray metal cube squatting in one corner, the chairs like ones in the motor vehicle department's waiting area, square and serviceable. No pictures or diplomas hung on the walls or stood on the desk; venetian blinds covered the windows.

All business here, the room's bare, utilitarian chill said clearly. She sat at her desk, gestured at the seat in front of it, and watched Steven Garner sink onto it gratefully.

"So. How can I help you?"

Although she already knew. His hangdog expression, a mobbed-up minion down in the lobby . . . even the security guard had known enough to go deaf and blind with Baumann around.

Garner, by contrast, was just a low-level errand boy, the kind of guy who lived for the moment he would be invited along on a truck highjacking.

And who would die waiting, because guys who were always as much in need of cash as Garner was could never be trusted. So she would be his last hope, and his next words would be . . .

"I need money." He glanced up at her. At his day job he was a school photographer, she knew.

Not exactly a big earner. "A lot," he added, "of money." He leaned across the desk. "Because they're going to kill me if I don't get it to them."

"Yeah, so I just heard. But I'm not in the business of—"

Loan-sharking. Or whatever you wanted to call it. "I help people take care of their money, you know?" Jake said carefully. "Invest it, diversify it . . ."

Launder it, get it out of the country. She'd set this

appointment up only as a favor to one of those other clients, and she was already regretting it.

"Yeah, I know," Garner conceded. "I just thought . . ."

"How much are we talking about?"

He looked up, his eyes alight with hope for a moment. But when he saw her expression, his own face fell again. "Fifty."

The amount he'd named shocked even her. "Thousand? You're into them for—"

"Yeah. Don't ask me how it happened, okay? It happened the way it always happens. You lose, you chase your losses, next thing you're on their shoot list."

Only Baumann didn't say *shoot*. "I've got a family. You saw the kid; he's a good boy."

Right, she'd seen the kid because she'd been intended to see him, maybe feel a little sorrier for Garner. She did, too.

Just not fifty grand's worth. She was about to say so when a small head peeped around the doorframe. "Dad?"

Garner frowned. "I told you, siddown out there, okay? Wait for me, I'll only be a—"

The boy didn't move. His big, not-quite-innocent eyes took in the room with its clinical lack of decoration, the metal cabinets and the shelves stuffed with file folders.

He didn't smile. He looked . . . sly. "Steven, maybe you could just sit down in the chair out there until your father and I are finished here," she said gently.

His eyes didn't change, their expression calm and

knowing. It gave her a chill, suddenly, realizing that the boy understood what his father was doing.

That he was begging for his life. But he'd come to the wrong place, because the only thing she knew for sure about Garner was that if she did lend him money, he would never return it.

Heck, he hadn't paid the mob back, and they were willing and able to kill him on account of it. So what chance would she have?

The boy went back to the outer office. She got up and closed the door. "What have you got?"

"What?" Garner looked confused. "I . . . What do you mean, what have I—"

"House? Car? Anything? A coin collection? Has your wife got any good jewelry?"

He was shaking his head. "There's the house, but it belongs to my wife. It was her parents' place, and anyway, what would you want with—"

She sat across from him again. "You're not getting it, what I'm saying to you. I don't want it. But they might."

Despair filled his face. "Just . . . you mean . . ."

He glanced at the door, beyond which his son waited. Right now the kid had a roof over his head, a place to go at night.

And tomorrow maybe he wouldn't. But his dad would be alive. "Steven, I'm suggesting you offer them something. It's harsh, I know. But it's the best I can do for you right now."

Or ever, she didn't add, but he understood. When he got up from the chair he moved like an old man.

She got up, too. "A house is a big thing, Steven. If you're lucky, maybe they'll take it."

"Yeah," he said bitterly. "If I'm lucky."

She didn't offer to put in a word for him. It wouldn't have done any good. He knew that, as well. He opened the door to the outer office, then turned.

"Listen, I was thinking I might take the kid out for lunch, maybe to a ball game. You know? But . . ."

He spread his hands helplessly.

He was tapped out, of course; his last twenty to the guard downstairs, probably. Without a word she opened her desk's top drawer and drew out five hundred-dollar bills.

She crossed the room and handed them to him. In the outer room, the little boy sat in a chair with his ankles crossed and his hands clasped in his lap, waiting. Watching.

"Thanks," Steven Garner said, stuffing the bills into the inside pocket of his cotton jacket. "C'mon, kid."

They turned to go. She followed them to the door, hoping Garner wouldn't decide to just take a flyer out the propped-open window at the end of the corridor.

He didn't. As they moved away down the hall, the little boy glanced back over his shoulder before they disappeared into the elevator. Those eyes . . .

Jake shivered, not liking the expression in them and glad when the elevator closed. And that was the last she ever expected to see of them:

Steven Garner Sr., his boy, and her five hundred bucks.

But she was only two-thirds right.

> *Remove dark stains from wooden floors by dabbing the stained area only with half-strength bleach. Rinse and repeat until the stain is gone, then recolor the lightened spot, if necessary, with wood stain and an artist's brush.*
>
> —Tiptree's Tips

Her name was Jacobia Tiptree—Jake, to her friends—and on that bright day in July twelve years after the Manhattan meeting, she was scraping loose paint off the porch steps of her big old house in Eastport, Maine, when the guy on the bike went by again.

Or she'd thought the paint would be loose, anyway. But as her son Sam always said, hope springs infernal, and the reality was something else again. Meanwhile:

Pedaling slowly, looking right at her, the guy on the bike frowned as if he'd just sniffed a spoiled carton of milk. He was decent enough looking otherwise, clean-shaven and neatly dressed.

But this was his third trip past her home in the last half-hour. And each time he went by, he'd been staring at her in that same unpleasant, almost accusing way.

Still holding the scraper, she got up, trying to recall where she'd seen his sour expression before. That she *had* seen it she felt certain, but on somebody else's face.

A *similar* face. The guy turned the corner, not looking back. She stood there another moment, wondering. But then with a mental shrug she knelt by the steps once more and returned to work.

After all, it was nearly the Fourth of July, and the remote island town of Eastport—three hours from Bangor, light-years from anywhere else—was full of tourists. No doubt the bicyclist was one of them, and she really had seen him around, somewhere.

As for his riding by so often, maybe he liked the house. She had when, upon finding Eastport over a decade ago, she'd fallen instantly in love with the old place. Now from the porch steps she pictured it as she'd first seen it:

An 1823 white clapboard Federal with three stories plus an attic, it had three red-brick chimneys and forty-eight windows, each with a pair of green shutters. Among its other selling points were a huge yard, a fireplace in every room, and original hardwood floors.

Unfortunately, it had also been a wreck. Under nearly two hundred years' worth of charm lay nearly as many of neglect; she'd had to get the wiring redone and the chimneys rebuilt, and it had needed painting.

All of which she'd had done, for an amount slightly less than it would've cost to bulldoze the place and start over. Back then, she'd known no better; nowadays, mostly from necessity, she was a halfway decent home-repair enthusiast.

But it wasn't only about money. Scrape off enough old paint, patch enough plaster, sand the wood floors and rehabilitate half a hundred antique windows plus shutters, and you too could begin feeling that maybe—just maybe—you'd rehabilitated yourself.

Too bad the half she was any good at was so rarely the half that needed doing. This time, she'd decided to paint all the parts of the house that she could reach and farm out the high work. The plan had seemed reasonable as she was formulating it.

But for one thing, the porch was massive. So there was a lot of old paint to scrape off before the new could go on. Also, the peeling bits clung like barnacles. Wielding the tool, she went at them with fresh energy; they hung on for dear life.

"Grr," she muttered, but they couldn't hear her, and even if they could it would probably only make them more obstinate.

As she thought this, the guy on the bike appeared again, pedaling along. Dark hair, striped red-and-white polo shirt, blue jeans . . . in his middle twenties, maybe, she thought.

The bike was a balloon-tired Schwinn from the fleet of them that were available for rent downtown, with a wire basket up front, fake-leather saddlebags, and a bell.

Brring! She wouldn't have thought a bike bell could be rung threateningly, but he managed it.

"Hey," she began, taking a step toward the street.

Climbing sharply from the waterfront, Key Street featured big antique houses fronted by huge maples lining each side. It was the very picture of a traditional Maine coast town's prosperous old residential area. Scowling, the guy stood on the pedals and pumped, speeding away through it.

Once more she felt she knew him from somewhere. But there wasn't much she could do about it, so when he'd gone she returned to removing a ton of porch paint one stubborn chip at a time.

Soon a warm, salt breeze, sunshine like pale champagne, and the faint cries of seagulls over the bay had all but erased her memory of the bike guy . . . until, just when she'd really forgotten about him, he came back yet again, half an hour or so later.

Using a belt sander, she was at last making progress on the job. Under the power tool's howling attack, the paint came off in clouds of sawdust.

And that was more like it. She'd finished the first step, begun on the second, and shut the sander off to replace a clogged belt when someone behind her cleared his throat meaningfully. On its own, her hand moved to grab the sharp-edged paint scraper.

"You won't need that." His voice was New York–accented.

She stood, turned, and took a step toward him, forcing him to move back fast.

"You're on private property. And I want you to leave now."

The fellow smiled at her. Not a pleasant smile. More like a baring of teeth. "Yeah, I guess you would."

Close up, he appeared clean and neat, with a careful shave and a recent haircut. "But hey, not everyone gets what they want in this world." The smile slid into a smirk.

Her heart thumped. "You've mistaken me for someone else." She took another step. "You'll have to go, or I'm going to call the police and let them take care of you."

At this he let out a laugh of genuine amusement. She was gripping the paint scraper very tightly, she realized.

"'Call the police,'" he repeated. "That's a good one."

"Okay, that's it. I mean it, you need to go."

She searched her mind for an exit strategy, not wanting to turn her back on him. Besides, the screen door at the top of the steps was locked so the dogs wouldn't barge out through it.

Oh, the hell with it. Back in Manhattan, half the pedestrians on the sidewalk were pushier than this guy. Scraper in hand, she advanced on him.

His hands went up in a conciliatory gesture. "Okay, I get the idea. You don't want to hash over old times."

She followed him to the end of the sidewalk. He got on the bike, rode it in a tight circle, then braked hard, skidding.

"I guess if I were you, I wouldn't want the past coming back to bite me, either. Not if I'd done what you did."

Speechless, she could only stare.

"But it has," he continued. "What'd it say in that famous guy's play? 'Murder will out'?"

She found her own voice. "You've got the wrong person. Now please take your nonsense and—"

His hands gripped the handlebars: smooth skin, pristine fingernails. "I know you, though. And what you did. Anyway, you've got until the fourth," he added. "When it's over, you will be, too. Over, that is."

As he spoke, a little cloud sailed across the sun and the sky darkened suddenly. The breeze stiffened, and all at once the gulls' cries sounded hostile.

"That play-writing guy had it right," said her unpleasant visitor. "'Blood shows up again. Murder will out.'"

He began pedaling slowly away. "And now," he called back as she stared after him, "right now, it's here and it's outing *you*."

Brrring!

She was still shaking when she got inside. Locking the back door, she hurried to the front to be sure the screen really was on the hook.

It was, and the bicycle guy was nowhere in sight. Her heart hammering, she checked the dogs and found them both asleep in the laundry room, the coolest place in the house.

Not that they'd have been any help. At thirteen, Monday the black Labrador was too ancient to be roused by much, and Prill the Doberman would be inclined to kiss a burglar to death.

Meanwhile, her husband, Wade Sorenson, and her grown son, Sam, were out fishing together; her father, Jacob Tiptree, and her stepmother, Bella Diamond, were away for the morning, too.

So for now she was on her own with this. Whatever *this* was; maybe nothing. But who was the guy . . . and what could he want?

Back in Manhattan, it might not've been so strange. Some of her clients there were so crooked that when their sons went to prison, they regarded it as the equivalent of graduate school.

But eventually she'd wised up, throttled down, and left the city behind, along with an ex-husband so faithless that the only thing she could depend on about him was that she couldn't depend on him.

By contrast, the old house in Eastport could be depended on for many things: faulty plumbing, a foundation that was fast rotting into the ground, and a bad fuse box, for instance.

When she moved in, the old plaster was falling down anywhere that the antique wallpaper wasn't holding it up. The floors were indeed lovely, but so uneven they resembled the heaving deck of a storm-tossed ship. The bath was a mildewed horror, the woodwork needed refinishing, and the roof leaked, so the gorgeous old tin ceilings were lacy with rust.

In other words, the place was exactly like her ex-husband, Victor, only fixable. So naturally she'd fallen for it.

Now she looked around at the big, bright kitchen with its high, bare windows, pine wainscoting, and scuffed floor. Even as old-fashioned and faintly shabby as it was, due to her stepmother Bella Diamond's efforts the room always glowed as if lit from within by the spirits of Betty Crocker and Holly Homemaker.

And the old things in it—the soapstone sink, the pass-through to the butler's pantry—just made it more familiar and comforting. But with the arrival of the bike-riding stranger, the past abruptly took on a threatening edge. And what had he meant about her having until the fourth? Had he actually been threatening her?

At the thought, her whole life here felt suddenly so fragile that it was all she could do not to rush to the cellar for one of the handguns she kept there, locked in a weapons box.

She knew how to shoot them, too. Half Wade's courtship of her—besides being Eastport's harbor pilot, he was a crack shot and old-weapons expert—had happened on the town's firing range.

But wanting a gun now was surely overreaction. The guy on the bike was no one to worry about, because real threats didn't advertise, did they? They crept up on you. They—

The back door opened behind her. But she'd *locked* it, she had definitely—

She was halfway to the cellar door, thinking, *Key, lockbox, Smith & Wesson .342 Special,* when the familiar voice stopped her.

"Hello? Anyone home?"

The breath went out of her in a whoosh as she recognized her best friend, Ellie White. "Ellie. I thought you were a—"

The dogs scrambled from the laundry room. Even Monday, her whitened face sweet with an old-dog smile, could always manage a welcome for Ellie.

Laughing, Ellie began dispensing dog biscuits, then froze when she caught Jake's look. "Everything okay?"

Ellie was tall, slender, and redheaded with pale green eyes and freckles like gold dust sprinkled across her nose. Today she wore a white smock, a bright patchwork skirt, and sandals.

Jake sighed. "You startled me, is all."

Ellie had house keys. "I knocked," she explained, "but . . ."

But Jake had been preoccupied. Now she busied herself making coffee, trying to cover the fact that her hands were trembling.

Ellie wasn't fooled. "Speak," she ordered as the dogs went back to the cool room.

"It's nothing. Really, I just . . ."

Since the day they'd met—Jake the newcomer in town, Ellie the native Eastporter—they'd been practically inseparable. Now, without asking, Ellie began making lunch.

Soon sliced bread, butter, and honey appeared

on the table. The coffeemaker burbled comfortingly. Ellie didn't speak until she'd gotten Jake busy with eating and drinking.

When they'd both finished, Ellie fired up Jake's laptop computer. Her own was on the fritz, which was why she'd come over here in the first place, she'd already confided. "Mind if I use your email?"

Jake waved assent.

Moments later: "Who's Nemesis?" Ellie asked. "You've got an email from . . ."

Jake turned from the sink. Having a housekeeper who was also your live-in stepmother was a sure way to begin cultivating tidy habits.

"No idea. Open it, please." She rinsed the last cup, sprayed the sink, and wiped everything thoroughly. When Bella did this, it produced sparkling results.

But when Jake did, it didn't. Perhaps she hadn't practiced enough to make it perfect. "Um, Jake?" Ellie said.

On the screen, the email from "Nemesis" contained three words: BEWARE THE FOURTH. Ellie turned. "Is this some kind of a joke?"

"I'm not sure." Jake yanked all the kitchen windows' shades down. "Ellie, have you seen a strange guy riding around town on a bike this morning?"

Silly question. In July, prime Maine tourist season, it seemed half the population of the world was riding a bike around Eastport. Still:

"Big ears, red-and-white-striped shirt?" Ellie asked.

"That's him." Jake described the visit, and his threatening rant. "And by 'the fourth,' he must mean the Fourth of July."

Which was two days from now. Jake went to the back parlor, where Wade stored records of his harbor-piloting trips in a big green logbook: the ship's name, her owners, the cargo, captain's name, and notes on unusual incidents.

A Post-it note was stuck to his computer screen as a reminder: military F-18s would be flying over Eastport on the holiday, and he wanted to be sure to see them, or hear them if they arrived after dark. Jake pulled the curtains closed, casting the bright room into gloom.

Back in the kitchen, they peered again at the laptop screen. "A Web-based email address," Ellie noted. "He could have signed up for that address just this morning." To harass Jake with, she meant. She shut the laptop. "But you know what? I think we should just forget about it."

"Really?" Jake eyed her doubtfully.

Ellie spread her hands. "Really. I mean, you don't know who he is. For all you know, he bothers everyone he sees. And even if he really is mad at you for some reason, or thinks he is, that still doesn't mean he'll do anything."

"I suppose." Had she *really* thought he seemed familiar? "And the email . . ."

"You don't know it's from him," Ellie replied. "It could be some joke thing from one of Sam's friends, for instance."

True; home from college for the summer, Sam commandeered all electronic gadgets on sight, and her laptop was no exception.

"And if he *was* going to do something bad, why warn me about it, right?" she asked slowly, trying to convince herself.

"Right," agreed Ellie decisively. "So come on, let's check out the Fourth of July preparations."

Her own daughter, little Lee, was at a children's party with her cousins. So Ellie was at liberty for a few hours.

"We'll get ice-cream cones," she added persuasively.

"Well . . ." She could take another whack at the porch later. And what harm could some guy on a bike do her, anyway?

"All right, let's go then," Jake gave in, throwing a sweater over her shoulders as they went out into the bright day.

But even as she turned her face gratefully to the sunshine and smelled the sweet, salt-tinctured fragrance of a Maine island in summer, one phrase kept repeating in her head over and over:

Beware the Fourth.

At age twenty-three, Steven Garner was on the first serious mission of his life, and so far it was going pretty well.

He'd set out on the bike just to get a look at her house, for instance, but instead he'd gotten to confront her, too. He'd already set up other things meant to unnerve her, which should be delivered soon if they hadn't already been.

Later, he meant to provoke all her fears, drive her right up to and over the edge of terror. But scaring her face-to-face, in advance of the main event, was a bonus.

He smiled, still not quite believing that he was actually in Eastport, where he'd fantasized being—where he'd imagined acting on his plans, finally—for so long.

But now here he was. Ahead, Passamaquoddy Bay spread blue and calm, puffy white clouds and seagulls floating above it like features in a child's watercolor. He braked the bike to a halt.

To his left, the old red-brick public library was having a sale on its lawn, used books and strawberry shortcakes. Across the street, a pub had set up a barbecue grill on its deck.

People in shorts and T-shirts wandered around munching hot dogs from the pub. Some got beers from the keg; others headed to the library for dessert, and a book to read while they ate it.

Steven considered what to do next. The street was blocked off by sawhorses and tape with the words Do Not Cross on it. But the tape was to prohibit cars, not people, so he edged his bike past the barriers and continued toward the harbor. Might as well get the local geography straight in his head.

The guidebook he'd studied on the bus ride that had brought him here said Eastport was on Moose Island, a chunk of granite two miles wide and seven long. Now he walked the bike along the town's single downtown street, facing the bay and appropriately enough called Water Street.

Opposite the harbor, two- and three-story brick or wood frame buildings housed shops on their first floor, apartments—mostly unoccupied, he decided, from their bare windows—on their second and third. The shops offered hardware, pizza, T-shirts, and local art. There was a tattoo shop and an attorney's office. Beyond that, a florist displayed red, white, and blue chrysanthemums.

No McDonald's or Pizza Hut, though. Steven wondered how he would find anything to eat in this town. He was not going to put any strange burgers or sausages in his mouth, that was for sure.

He paused outside a secondhand shop to get his bearings. The street was full of booths selling trinkets and more strange foods—fried dough and smoked salmon, cups of fruit ice and big paper cones brim-full of onion rings.

Across from a huge statue of a fisherman, a wide wooden pier stuck out into the bay. Beside it hulked a pair of tugboats, one red and the other blue. On the pier's other side, a schooner floated; near it, a scrawled sign advertised whale-watching and sunset cruises.

Yeah, he thought skeptically, imagining the boat's bowsprit sticking straight up for an instant before the whole craft sank. The very idea of getting on a strange boat with strange people—

But never mind, he concluded. They'd probably think what he was up to was pretty strange, too, if they knew.

Displayed behind the glass of the store window, cups and saucers in the Golden Wheat pattern reminded him of his mother. So did a tin percolator, a china planter shaped like a panther, and a fake fur coat. Behind them in the shop, a lady in a turquoise velour pantsuit sat at a card table.

At the sight of her, a sharp pang of homesickness struck him and he turned away, moving on to a craft store whose offerings he found even more upsetting: crocheted pot holders and macramé plant hangers, paint-by-number landscapes and stitchery portraits.

All were things that might have been his mother's, that she might have displayed back when she was alive. Which now she wasn't; many items just like these were in her house right this minute, waiting to be thrown away.

But they might wait forever, because there was no one else to do it, and he wasn't going to. Now that she was gone and he was out from under her thumb, he had better things to accomplish.

Better, and more important . . . The thought summoned up all the preparations he'd made and the items he'd brought with him, sharp ones and shiny ones. . . . Oh, the things he would do. And soon; the Fourth of July was nearly here.

But for now, his first impulse had been correct. He would learn the territory, the hiding places and points of usefulness; while looking so much like the other tourists, he was as good as invisible.

Wandering on past the big granite post office building, he came to the Quonset hut from which he'd rented the bike. Here he paid to keep it for a few days more, then continued out the wide concrete breakwater.

On it stood a wooden hut called Rosie's, with people lined up in front. It was a hot dog stand, and despite his earlier resolve, the aromas enticed him mightily.

But he resisted, because as his mother always said, you never knew what people might have done with restaurant food before you got it. That was why it was best to eat at home, where you were sure your meal was clean; next best was a fast-food place where you could see into the kitchen.

Failing that, you could go to a grocery store and buy things in factory-sealed packages. Not the stuff that got wrapped in the delicatessen, gooey egg sandwiches or rolls full of mystery meat, but brand names that were machine-sealed were okay. So his mother had said on the few occasions when he couldn't be home for the good, nourishing meals she put on the table for him.

Nutrition, in fact, had been a significant problem since she had died. She'd known how to make the things he liked: meat loaf, mashed potatoes with butter, and vegetables—green beans or peas.

Always canned vegetables, because processing destroyed the germs and other contaminants. And they at least were easy to get. But here in Eastport, he had nowhere to cook even the few meals he had learned to prepare.

He'd bought packaged food, but even that was all stashed at the place where he was staying. And he didn't want to go near it again until later this evening, when it was dark.

Somebody might see him. And that could jeopardize his plan. Which mustn't be allowed; since his mother died, he'd thought of little else but getting vengeance for his father.

His father's death. His father's murder. And now . . .

He stood on the breakwater, holding the bike up, staring at the waves. His stomach growled but he ignored it, because—

. . . now it was time.

Chapter 2

Save and label leftover paint for later touch-ups.
—Tiptree's Tips

In Eastport, the Fourth of July was like Christmas, New Year's, and everyone's birthday all rolled into one. And this year it came on a Sunday, so the celebration would last all weekend.

"Yikes," said Ellie as firecrackers popped nearby.

"No kidding," said Jake as they headed down Key

Street past the old Shead mansion, once a grand, prosperous dwelling but now sadly dilapidated.

There were several dozen more old houses just like the Shead mansion in Eastport, once a family's home but now too expensive to maintain and heat. So they stood temptingly empty. . . . But one old money pit to take care of was plenty, Jake thought as she hurried on.

At the foot of the hill, burnt gunpowder floated on the air, and bagpipes played "Amazing Grace" somewhere.

"Look, there he is," said Jake, spotting the bike guy past the costume contest now happening straight ahead.

Local ladies in ball gowns rubbed elbows with ones in cavewomen outfits. Men in pirate garb, Tarzan outfits, moose suits, and superhero costumes guffawed at another fellow dressed as a pear.

"Where?" asked Ellie, squinting into the crowd.

Pointing, Jake eyed her unpleasant visitor again. He was half a block ahead of them, pushing the bike.

"I thought you were going to forget about him," said Ellie.

"I would have," Jake lied, "but he's right in front of me."

They lingered by the hardware store to let him get farther along. But that put them across from a booth selling fruit-syrup-doused slush cones in colors suggesting exotic poisons.

No one was dropping dead, though, so Jake decided to get one. "I just wish I knew if I *should* forget him," she told Ellie as the boy in the booth shot crimson liquid onto her treat.

"Or tell Bob Arnold about him," she added, wishing the words in her head (*bewarebeware*) would stop clattering like the rattle of a snare drum.

Or a snake. Across the street at the end of the fish pier stood Eastport police chief Bob Arnold himself, pink and plump and arrayed in full cop regalia: uniform, duty belt, and weapon, plus nightstick, radio, handcuffs, and black leather boots.

Ellie shook her head. "Come on, Jake, what are you going to tell him? That there's a stranger in town?" She waved at the mobbed street. "There's hundreds of strangers in town. Thousands, even."

"I guess," said Jake. By now the guy had blended into the crowd, past the audience of proud parents gathered near the fish pier's parking lot for the children's talent show.

A boom box blared the opening notes of Herb Alpert's "Taste of Honey" while a tutu'd four-year-old stepped uncertainly onto the makeshift stage, twirling a baton.

Was he down there somewhere? Jake wondered distractedly.

Maybe he'd doubled back. Maybe he was *behind* her. Nervously she glanced over her shoulder, then up and down the street again.

No one; she let out her breath. And Ellie was right: she was being silly. She turned back just as the child tossed the baton up hard, spun around, and caught it behind her back.

A tiny miracle; even she looked completely astonished. *And that,* Jake thought, obscurely comforted, *is what the Fourth of July is all about in Eastport, Maine.*

Kids ran by with cans of Silly String. The stuff made a mess but was never prohibited; the drunks would be out tonight, too, as rowdy as ever. But both were also part of the holiday. Bob Arnold always said that if nobody drowned, crashed a car, or got shot, it was a successful Fourth.

And somehow, no one ever did. "Fireworks tomorrow night," said Jake, feeling herself relax.

Ellie smiled. "And grilled fish tonight, if they catch any."

Another holiday tradition. Ellie's husband, George Valentine, was fishing with Wade and Sam, for brook trout.

"Oh, they'll catch some. They always do. And we'll cook them like always."

"Like always," Ellie echoed. Tossing their spent cones in a nearby trash can, they wandered on. Nearby, more firecrackers exploded; this time it was Jake who jumped a foot at the sounds, so like gunshots, but her alarm didn't last.

After all, she was here in Eastport, and in Eastport on the Fourth of July, nothing bad could happen.

Or so it seemed.

As it turned out, he didn't have to wait until dark to get into the abandoned house he'd chosen to squat in. Instead, at about two in the afternoon a parade of monsters—dragons, giant squid, the abominable snowman—galloped past the old dwelling.

It was a children's parade, he realized. Banging drums, tooting horns, and howling the sounds they imagined were made by real monsters, the kids drew a crowd in their wake; soon the area around Steven's hideout was deserted.

He eased the bike into the unkempt yard. He'd taken a lot of time when he'd arrived in town the day before, picking a place. It had to be empty, of course, with a door he could use without being observed. The yard had to be screened by trees, bushes, or a fence, and a high vantage point for a lookout was desirable.

He hid the bike among overgrown bushes, then stepped through a rotted archway that in the old days had held up lattice. With a last fast glance around, he hustled up the back steps onto an old wooden porch. From here, he could see what had been the garden, full of overgrown lilacs. At the yard's center, the old peonies' shaggy heads were the same pink as his mother's housecoat.

By the end there, she'd neither bathed nor dressed, so he'd gotten used to that housecoat. Cringing at the memory, he let himself in through a door that was nearly falling off its hinges.

Inside, light filtered through filthy windowpanes and between the slats of yellowed venetian blinds. A leak somewhere above had released all the plaster from the walls and most of the ceiling. An old-fashioned porcelain sink remained, as did a hideous old gas range.

That was all, and the power was off. But he

wouldn't have dared use appliances or lights anyway. Things like that could get him caught.

In the ruined room with the dust motes swirling slowly in the air he'd disturbed, he crouched by the backpack he'd left leaning against a half-collapsed wall. From it he took a box of crackers, a can of green peas, and a can of Campbell's tomato soup. Placing these on a paper napkin, he sat on the plastic drop cloth he'd spread earlier over the linoleum least affected by the roof leak.

There was a hole in the wall from a woodstove's vent pipe, and he also tried to get as far as possible from that. You never could tell what might scurry in and out of such a thing.

Unseen things, gleefully creeping . . . *No.* Grimly, he focused on the good, clean food items before him: Wrapped. Sealed.

You are what you eat, his mother used to tell him. And *Don't put that dirty stuff in your mouth.*

Sometimes it was only a street vendor's hot dog that he'd bought on a class field trip, trying to be like the rest of the kids, that aroused her wrath. Sometimes it was worse.

But he didn't want to think about any of that anymore. It had taken him a long time to understand how right she was, how a boy had to be careful, sometimes excruciatingly so.

Because people would try corrupting him. They would succeed, even, sometimes. And what a fellow had to do then was . . .

Stop. There was no point to any of those thoughts,

either. And anyway, he would never have to do any of those things again.

Because now . . . Now he was doing *this* thing, and not only would it avenge his father's death—his *murder,* his mind made sure to correct him viciously—it would also go a long way toward redeeming Steven himself, wouldn't it?

Not that he hadn't already begun taking care of his own problems. And ironically, in the end the help he'd needed in that area had come from the same source as the problems themselves: being a mama's boy. He knew she had made him . . . strange. Clean food, meticulously cared-for clothing . . . These, he had been given forcefully to understand by the other youngsters in his school, were not the concerns of a normal young American male.

And girls or women were of course out of the question. Having one; being . . . intimate. The thought made him shiver with revulsion and something else that he did not want to identify.

But fortunately, being his mother's son had also given him plenty of time to pursue indoor interests: reading, fiddling with computers—he smiled, thinking about how useful this talent had become lately—and watching TV.

By chance, one of his TV shows had featured a detective's obsessive-compulsive symptoms. Portrayed negatively, but for Steven they had turned out instead to be immensely useful.

He couldn't figure out why people wanted to get rid of these symptoms. Didn't their sufferers understand that without them, they might not be able to function at all?

The minute he'd seen the TV detective engaged in a bout of handwashing, then wiping down a chair with an antiseptic towelette, Steven had known that as far as his everyday anxieties went, his troubles were over.

Well, maybe not *over* over. But at least now he had a way of tuning them out, sometimes long enough to get a few things done. Things like obtaining an eye for an eye and a tooth for a tooth. A drop of blood or a . . .

Stop. No sense going on about that, either. He was here, on the brink of a great deed, so he had to keep his strength up.

With his hands trembling from hunger, he opened the soup, the vegetables, and the crackers. Slowly, not letting himself hurry—

Without warning, a flashbulb of memory went off: his mother's face twisted in a grimace, her wild, furious voice—

Greedy boy!

—but with the ease of long practice he brushed it aside, went on preparing his meal.

Crackers here. Open soup can here. Peas, counted carefully, lined up like soldiers.

He began to eat, dipping the crackers in the soup, following them with peas one by one: dip, chew, pea.

There had to be an even number of peas and an odd number of crackers, and the cracker with soup on it counted as two things. It took concentration to keep it all straight.

By the time he had finished, light from the windows slanted in darker gold rays than before, and he still had to clean up.

Pea can inside the soup can. Soup can in the cracker box and the box out the door, he decided. Hurled as hard as he could.

Risky, but there was no help for it; leaving trash inside bred vermin. Rats, mice, fleas, flies . . .

He opened the back door, peering out. The garden looked onto an alley and beyond that to the rear of a huge, white-clapboarded old church. There were no windows in the rear of the church. No view from the houses next door, either, through the lilacs.

He threw the cracker box out into the ruined yard, where it was swallowed up by rank weeds between the trunk of a gnarled apple tree and a massive hydrangea, each blue bloom as big as a human head.

Blue head. Blue face . . . Another memory flash, more hideous than the earlier one, took him by surprise, sending him reeling back blindly so that he nearly stepped off the rotten porch. He grabbed the decrepit porch rail; it held . . . barely.

Gasping, he hurled himself back into the house and put his shoulder to the door until it shut with a groan. Staggering to his pack, he dug frantically in it for the pump bottle of hand sanitizer.

He squirted the chemical-smelling stuff into his hands, then rubbed madly, scrubbing it onto his arms and slapping it on his face, where it stung his eyes and its taste nearly made him gag.

But gradually he relaxed, his panicked breath slowing. The relief would not hold; he would have to do it again many times before the day was through.

Still, now he could think again, *exist* again. If only, he thought as he tucked the germ killer into his pack once more—

There was another bottle in there, too, and a third one just in case.

If only he could drink the stuff.

By the time Jake and Ellie got back to the Key Street house, it was mid-afternoon and four more email messages had arrived.

WATCHING YOU, said the first. THINKING OF YOU, declared the second. MISS ME? asked the third.

And finally: YOU CAN'T ESCAPE, said the last one.

Earlier, Jake had been using the computer to learn how much paint she'd need, to put two coats of exterior latex onto thirty-two hundred square feet of siding. But now she felt like pitching the thing through a window.

Ellie appeared from the kitchen, where she'd been making tea, and saw the look on Jake's face. "You know, maybe we should just call up Bob Arnold and tell him—"

"What? That I want him to stop some anonymous pen pal from sending me mean messages?"

With its elaborately tiled fireplace mantel, chair rails and wainscoting, and the original wavery-glassed windows hung with heavy green silk draperies, the dining room looked much as it had nearly two hundred years earlier. Ordinarily, Jake found it all immensely tranquilizing.

Just not now. "I don't think Bob's got time in his holiday schedule for a wild-goose chase," she added. "Besides, even if it is the bike guy, he can't possibly really do anything to me. I'm surrounded here by my family and friends."

As if to emphasize this, Prill the Doberman stalked in with neck hairs raised and ears pricked. Not that she would really do anything, either; since her days as a rescue, Prill had mellowed so that now she only looked like a furry killing machine.

Jake smoothed the dog's hackles. "Don't worry, girl. I'm just annoyed."

And really, calling Bob truly was out of the question. With the town so full of visitors they were practically spilling into the bay, he was already way overworked.

On top of which, computer crime was hardly his specialty. If this even was a prosecutable crime . . .

So Prill let herself be persuaded that nobody needed biting, and lay down. Changing her mind about tea, Ellie started the percolator; she preferred it to the Mr. Coffee.

And Jake returned to the porch, where she collected tools: scrapers, sander, extension cord, gloves, safety glasses. . . .

With her arms loaded with stuff, she staggered forward. One more trip with a broom and dustpan and she was done for now.

Good old belt sander, she thought, then stopped as

an odd feeling prickled between her shoulder blades; a targeted feeling.

Ridiculous, she told herself. It was only her imagination, all roiled up by the stranger on the bike and those weird emails.

But when she went into the house, she made sure to hook the screen door. She closed the inside door and locked it, too.

Just in case.

Downtown at the corner of Water and Dana Streets, the new Pickled Herring restaurant offered fresh grilled vegetables and delicately sauced entrées, a level of cuisine Eastport diners had once had to travel to Portland to enjoy.

Standing in the backyard examining Wade's freshly cleaned catch, Jake thought eating out was sounding better and better.

But: "Brook trout," Wade said stubbornly. "Grilled ones."

He was tall and solidly built, with blond brush-cut hair, eyes that were blue or green depending upon the weather, and the kind of square-jawed good looks that she'd thought occurred only on the covers of romance novels until she met him.

"I've had my mouth set for those fish since this morning," said Wade, resting his chin gently on the top of her head.

"Mm-hmm," said Jake, who with his arms around her and his heart beating close to her cheek would've agreed to anything.

But the fish were tiny. "No one would have to cook. Or," she added, "wash dishes."

This being, she knew, a persuasive argument, just not quite persuasive enough. Then inspiration hit her.

"Maybe we could get the chef at the Pickled Herring to cook your catch," she suggested.

Because grilled fish was indeed a tradition for them on the Fourth. But starving wasn't, and although the boys had brought home a dozen fish, the edible portion of each was smaller than her hand.

"Done up quick with that mustardy dill sauce you like," she went on temptingly. "For hors d'oeuvres."

Which was how a few hours later they all sat at the Pickled Herring's largest table, next to the big front window, devouring these crispy delicacies while drinking appletinis.

"Elegant," pronounced Jake's stepmother and housekeeper, Bella Diamond, taking her first sip from the frosty glass.

Rawboned and henna-haired, with big green eyes and a jaw full of mismatched teeth, Bella had work-worn hands that could have belonged to an auto mechanic, and in the lace-trimmed blue shirtwaist she had on, she was way overdressed.

But she had the best heart in the world and would have stepped in front of a locomotive for the family she'd acquired by marrying Jake's dad, Jacob Tiptree.

Also, Bella was adventurous when it came to mixed drinks. "Watch out for those things," Jacob cautioned his wife.

Lean and hawk-faced, with stringy gray hair tied back in a leather thong, wearing bib overalls and a flannel shirt over work boots so battered they resembled Civil War relics, he was an unusual-looking person, too.

To put it mildly. "I think the word appletini might be code for dynamite juice," he added to Bella.

"Watch out yourself, old man," Bella retorted. "Who had to help who upstairs the last time we tried a new beverage?" But her voice was warmly affectionate.

"Tell Wade about your pen pal," prompted Ellie. In a sparkly little black dress whose hem fringe hit her knee, a silvery-gray crocheted shawl light as a spiderweb, and heeled sandals, Ellie appeared as usual to have floated down from some idiosyncratic fashion heaven.

"Nasty emails," she added, at Wade's inquiring glance. "But we don't know who sent them. So . . . more like a secret pal."

Jake glanced uneasily through the restaurant's front window to the street as a chill went through her. Great, now she was feeling superstitious about the bike guy; speak of the devil, etc.

She opened her mouth to change the subject, but Sam got in ahead of her. "Yeah, I saw those."

He reached out and speared another hot grilled brook trout with mustard sauce. Crispy, smoky, and melt-in-your-mouth tender, the things were addictive.

"They were weird," Sam added. "I borrowed your laptop when I got in," he added, to explain how he'd seen the emails.

Nearly as tall as Wade, with dark, curly hair and

matinee-idol good looks, Sam bit the trout in half, washed it down with a swallow of root beer.

He didn't drink alcohol, after a time of drinking a lot of it. Jake hoped his abstinence would continue, but with Sam you never knew; it was the dark side to his otherwise sunny character. She and the rest would've gladly drunk root beer along with him, but he insisted people enjoy their favorite beverages.

The world would always have alcohol in it, he said; it was his job not to drink it. "I could try tracing them down for you," he offered. "The emails."

Meanwhile, Wade shot her a pointed *Why didn't you tell me about this?* look. "No ideas who sent them?" he asked.

Drat, she thought. This weekend was supposed to be a stress-free holiday for him: no freighters to bring into the harbor, no antique firearms waiting to be worked on.

"Well," she began slowly, but just then the waiter brought platters out.

Baked haddock for Ellie and Bella, a T-bone for Sam, duck in orange sauce for Wade, for Jake's dad, and for George Valentine, plus pizza for Jake: specifically, artisan pizza with barbecued chicken, caramelized onion, and enough blue cheese to sink a barge.

Ellie's husband, George Valentine, ate a bite of duck breast and sighed happily. Compactly built, with the jutting jaw and milk-white skin that ran in many of the old families in downeast Maine, he had the banty-rooster bearing of a fellow who talked with his fists.

Which he often did. Besides being the man you

called for a bat in your attic, skunks in your trash cans, or a massive old tree limb balanced atop your roof beam after a storm, George had been known to throw a first punch just to get the fight started, so he could get it over with.

Now, though, a guitar duo played jazz standards at one end of the room, a grill man tossed pizza at the other, and in the middle, George ate duck à l'orange and liked it.

But then Wade started in on the nasty emails again, and this time the food didn't keep him from wanting an answer, pronto. So Jake supplied one as best she could:

"Youngish guy. Clean-cut, riding a bike."

There was no point in mentioning how familiar he'd looked and sounded. She still didn't know why, or even if the sense she had that she knew her visitor from somewhere was accurate.

She glanced uneasily out the window once more and spied no one looking in. But the street was still jammed with people, and among that many faces, who could be sure of picking out just one?

"He seemed to have a grievance against me," she went on. "I got the feeling that taunting me was why he was here."

Her dad's bushy eyebrows knit with concern. "And then the emails started?"

"Yes. But there's no way of knowing if they're connected."

The jazz guitar duo reached the final notes of "Take the 'A' Train" and began playing "Stardust." Jake's father patted Bella's left hand as with her right she finished her appletini.

George winked at Ellie. Wade got his wallet out. Sam filched the last slice of pizza from Jake's plate and devoured it. I am, Jake thought with sudden clarity, the luckiest woman in the world.

"The guy on the bike and those emails coming right after, it could've all just been a—"

"Coinky-dink," Sam supplied, taking a swig of root beer, and the rest nodded in agreement.

But none of them really believed it; she knew from the looks on their faces.

And unfortunately, neither did she.

Once it got dark, Steven felt safer about leaving the vacant house. One more stranger in a town that was full of them at night on a holiday weekend . . . Who would notice?

But just to be sure, he propped a hand mirror on one of the sagging shelves in the ancient pantry. Switching on his battery lantern, he got to work with a tube of surgical glue.

His nose wrinkled, partly from the pungent glue smell but mostly at the sight of himself in the cheap little mirror. Those big ears of his belonged on a cartoon character, the way they stuck nearly straight out from his head.

But now a firm squeeze of the glue tube here, a dab and a push there, and one ear was firmly secured flat to his head. Next he did the same on the other side, and presto: perfectly normal.

On the outside, anyway. He frowned, wondering if the ears might've given Jacobia Tiptree a clue to his identity earlier. Probably not, though. The one time she'd seen him before, he'd been only a kid and his father had been her focus.

His father, and what she'd refused to do for him. Such a small thing, really, that she could have done so easily. And if she had helped, everything would have been different.

But no sense crying over spilled milk, as his mother used to say, although she'd never said it when Steven spilled it. Then, somehow there'd been plenty of sense in making him cry.

But done was done, and what he needed to think about now was what he meant to do. Soon . . .

Now, in fact, because all this was part of it, his mission already well under way. Tease her, torment her . . . these thoughts calmed his nerves, slowed his angrily pounding heartbeat. He left the mirror on the dusty shelf and returned to the old kitchen.

The smell here was of wood rotting and rodents multiplying. Stealthy flapping sounds from somewhere upstairs said that bats made their homes here, as well. His flesh crawled at the idea of the creatures swarming over him if he should fall asleep.

But that wasn't likely, or at any rate not soon, for he had things to do, didn't he? And his eagerness would keep him awake.

He shut off the lantern. But he would need it when he came back to the house later. Climbing onto a shaky chair, he began pulling shades made of big black trash bags down over the kitchen windows.

He'd taped them together earlier that day, and thumbtacked them to the tops of the window frames back when it was still daylight. Once the bags were lowered and secured with more tape, he turned the lantern on again, then crept outside to check his work.

From the yard, not a gleam of light showed from inside the house. And during the day, all anyone would be able to see were sagging, yellowed venetian blinds, like always.

Satisfied, he went back inside, pulling the broken door shut behind him as quietly as possible, though the music and laughter of the holiday revels going on a few blocks away likely covered any sound.

Spread out on the tarp-covered floor were more of his equipment: plastic handcuffs, the gag and blindfold. Scissors, adhesive tape, his laptop, and a digital camera, too, of course.

Steven turned his attention to the laptop. Luckily, there were lots of unencrypted Wi-Fi networks around, so he could get onto the Internet without trouble.

The laptop itself ran on special batteries. Buying enough of those had been the greatest expense of the project. The weight of them in his pack had been a pain, too.

But there was no help for it; he couldn't be sure he'd have a chance to recharge any of them secretly. And secrecy was key.

Powering the laptop up, he accessed the account he'd set up weeks earlier with the anonymous mail-drop service. The service, which allowed him to send messages with no fear of being tracked down and identified, was expensive.

But the cost had been worth it, as had the work of setting the messages up to be sent out automatically. More opportunity for confusion, for misdirection . . .

Bottom line, more chance for the kind of fear he meant to inspire before he really got down to business.

Accessing his mail-drop account, he saw the check mark beside each message he'd uploaded before beginning this trip. The marks said the messages had been delivered. Excellent . . .

Next he visited the local public library's website, found from the information on it that as he'd expected, he could indeed use their printer for a small fee.

Also, he could upload files to the printer, either on-site or remotely, the printout itself to be collected later. As he'd also hoped, it was a color printer. . . .

Fabulous. Everything was as he'd planned. So a walk downtown to where the celebration was going on was a reward he deserved.

And perhaps, if he felt daring, even farther than downtown. After all, he too was celebrating independence. Free from grief, from guilt . . .

Free at last from his obligation to do something, someday, about his father's real killer, Jacobia Tiptree. Because maybe he was a mama's boy, spoiled and petted. Bullied, too; her prisoner, right up until the end.

To the last gasp. But at the heart of the matter . . .

Down deep, he was his own man. And now . . .

Now it was time to prove it.

Time for her, too, he thought. To understand, to regret. To apologize, even.

Yes, he decided, giving his glued-back ears a last satisfied pat. Among other things, he would most certainly extract from her that most useless of declarations: the heartfelt apology.

Chapter 3

To hold a small nail straight,
grip it with needle-nose pliers.
—Tiptree's Tips

Late that night, upstairs in bed, Jake looked over at Wade and found him asleep with his book on his chest.

"The Muzzle-Loader's Handbook." She read the title softly aloud. The dogs looked up alertly.

"Not that kind of muzzle," she told them.

They looked disappointed; muzzle-loading was their favorite activity, if the load was kibble. Plucking the book from Wade's hands, she switched off his lamp.

At least somebody was getting some shut-eye around here. But she could already tell that for her, it wasn't in the cards.

Careful not to step on any squeaky floorboards—even the most dedicated old-house repairer couldn't fix them all—she padded downstairs.

Under a tin ceiling whose ornately molded surface had begun shedding flakes of antique paint—wire brush, stepladder, tack cloth, Rust-Oleum, she thought—the dogs pranced with her to the kitchen.

After dispensing a biscuit to each of them, she made tea. She carried it to the front parlor, where the Victorian-era furniture, heavy velvet hangings, and Oriental rugs made a cozy refuge.

Turning a lamp on low, she drew the silk quilt from where it draped over one corner of the settee. She would curl up, she decided, and in the dim lamplight manage to doze, or at any rate to rest.

But in the next instant a shadow moved swiftly across the front window shade. The dogs leapt up, stiffened, Prill wuffing warningly, and even Monday growling deep in her chest.

Holding her breath, Jake moved the shade aside a scant half-inch. Outside, the night was still and clear; the newly risen full moon hung balloon-like in an indigo sky, turning the narrow patch of the bay she could see from here into a sheet of silver.

Nothing moved. All the neighboring houses were

silent. The Doberman stood beside her briefly, then strode from the room, the measured click of the dog's toenails sounding distantly from the rest of the house as she made her inspection.

Finally she returned, teeth bared in a dog grin. All clear, the big animal's face and body communicated plainly.

"Everything okay?"

The voice from the hall startled her. But it was only her father, in striped pajamas and a nightcap like a character out of a Dickens novel.

Jake waved at the window, feeling foolish. "I thought I saw something."

Yawning hugely, Prill lay down again as Jacob Tiptree came into the room. Jake let herself lie down, too, pulling the silk quilt up. Silly, she thought.

"I could go out looking," he offered. "Or call Bob Arnold."

She smiled at the thought of her father in his nightcap, chasing a prowler. "No, thanks."

A leaf, a plastic bag blowing by the window . . . anything might have made that shadow. "I guess I'm still spooked from this morning."

"Been to the cellar?" To the weapons lockbox, he meant.

"No. Not yet. I guess maybe I don't quite want to admit how nervous the guy is making me."

There'd been no more emails. "And anyway, I don't haul out a gun for just anything," she added. "You know that."

Her father, on the other hand, was the kind of fellow who, if he heard a strange sound in the house at night, came down with a pistol loaded and ready or he didn't come down at all.

Now the shape of the weapon showed in the robe pocket. It was a .380 ACP semi-auto, she happened to know: tiny, effective.

"I'm not even certain the emails were from him," she said.

Amusement crinkled the skin around her dad's eyes. Of course they were, his look seemed to say gently. Only a fool would think anything else, under the circumstances.

"So you've got an enemy," he said, ignoring her attempt to evade this truth. "Maybe you should think about why."

She nodded reluctantly. Her present life, spent fixing up an old house, wasn't malice-worthy. Her few civic duties—serving as ballot clerk, cooking for Meals on Wheels now and then, attending town meetings—weren't likely to make her a target, either.

Once upon a time, though, after she'd fled Manhattan, some of the biggest crooks in the city had been out for her blood. She'd known their secrets, and if she ever revealed them, they'd be deprived of a lot of money and personal freedom.

But: "It's been a long time since any guys from the old days were interested in me," she said. "Those fences are mended."

Besides, the statute of limitations had passed. "He did have a New York accent. But he was too young, mid-twenties, maybe. He couldn't have been anyone from way back then."

Her dad nodded silently.

"Sam looked at the computer when we got home," she went on. "He says whoever sent those emails knew just how to do it."

Routed them, Sam had said, through anonymous mail servers so he or she couldn't be traced back and identified. Or not with the skills Sam had, anyway.

Her dad got up. "Better get some rest," he said as he headed upstairs, and when he'd gone she found the weapon he'd had in his pocket on the table by the settee.

And although she was not usually a fan of guns lying around the parlor, this time she didn't mind. With it in hand, she took one last tour around the silent house.

Quiet in the dining room, the back parlor, and the laundry. By the glow of the night-light, the kitchen appliances gleamed and the floor shone with Bella's final mopping, which she'd done very cheerfully under the influence of those appletinis.

"You know the drill, right?" Jake asked Prill, patting the dog's smooth neck.

"Mmph," said Prill darkly, lying down by the back door. Her powerful body made a solid thump when it landed, and there was a purposeful gleam in the dog's eye, too, Jake thought.

It made her feel better, and so did the silence outside when she peered again out the front window. Downtown on Water Street it was most likely a much livelier matter even at this late hour, but here there was only the hoot of a distant foghorn.

Then nothing. Nothing else, and no one at all.

She hoped.

•   •   •

Running away from her house in the dark, he couldn't believe what he'd done. Stupid . . .

He could have been caught. But he hadn't been able to resist the temptation to creep right up to her window and . . .

God, she'd been right there. One solid punch to that flimsy window screen and he could've—

He hadn't thought of the streetlight behind him, or how it would cast a shadow to betray him. It worried him that after all his planning, his enthusiasm had still gotten the better of him.

But the exhilaration was worth it. At the corner he slowed, trying hard to look like just another Eastport holiday reveler.

Water Street on a holiday night was like something out of his dreams. People wandered around with smiles on their faces as if nothing could hurt them. Music from boom boxes and children's rides, shouts of roving teenagers, and pungent food smells came from all directions.

At the tempting aromas, his stomach growled ferociously, and suddenly another rebellious impulse seized him: Why shouldn't he eat? Why did he have to follow his mother's rules, even now when she was dead?

Before he could stop himself, he'd walked right up to one of the tents and bought himself a bratwurst on a roll, and a can of soda. The sausage, freshly grilled and still spitting hot juices from the fire, sent up a spicy perfume that made him tremble.

Angrily he shoved the food into his mouth, unable

to resist his hunger. He finished it quickly even though it was hot, then moved on to a table full of handmade chocolates.

He bought a large box of assorted ones and forced himself to resist tearing it open before he'd paid for it. Then, ripping at the transparent wrapping paper and fumbling at the cardboard, he grabbed a handful of sweet chunks and devoured them, and quickly felt the sugar hit his bloodstream.

Instantly a rush of shame hit him. What in God's name had he been thinking? That stuff could make him sick; it was filthy; who knew who or what might've been touching it, contaminating it in unspeakable ways. . . .

Shut up, shut UP, he shrieked silently at the voice in his head. Her voice, her never-ending harping and criticizing . . .

People moved innocently on the street around him. He wanted to kill them all. How dare they be so happy, so *free?*

But in the nick of time he caught himself. He wasn't here to express old resentments. He was on a mission.

An important one. A sudden revulsion for the remaining candy struck him; he dropped the rest of the box in a nearby trash can. The bratwurst hadn't been the best idea, either, he realized.

But it was not a disaster, he told himself firmly, even as his hands began making those uncontrollable washing movements again. He would do better next time, and clean himself thoroughly once he got back to the vacant house.

He was here to pursue his plan, and no minor

lapse—a hot burp from the spicy sausage soured his throat, making him grimace—could be allowed to stop him.

And eventually, under this onslaught of calming self-talk, he felt his disgust subside, his nausea ease. Enough, anyway, to try going on with what he'd been doing.

As far ahead as he could see, more attractions beckoned, some mere card tables with awnings, others elaborate commercial affairs with trailers and flashing lights. He strolled toward the blare of canned music from a Guess Your Weight and Age tent.

A Native American man gripping a carved wooden walking stick sat on a chair in front of the tent. An aging German shepherd lazed at the man's side while a couple of small boys up way past their bedtimes crouched by the animal.

The old man looked up. His eyes were the same dark color as the chocolate taste still in Steven's mouth. The man sat still. Only his gnarled hand tightened around the carved walking stick as his gaze met Steven's.

Sensing its master's alertness, the dog rose, sending the little boys scurrying back. The man spoke a few muttered words to the animal in a language Steven didn't know.

In response the dog sat, fixing Steven with its flat stare as he went by. He felt its eyes on his back. Its attention gave him a creepy feeling, as if it were seeing *into* him. But:

Forget them. They're not what you're here for.

And what could they do to him, anyway? Nothing.

He moved on, resisting the urge to hurry. He had no need to be afraid.

He was the one who should be giving people a creepy feeling. *If they only knew* . . .

He pressed past a cluster of teenage boys in baggy shorts and faded T-shirts, then some older, less innocent-looking young men dressed in black denim jackets, black jeans, and scuffed boots.

Eastport's wild bunch, he thought as they sullenly shifted to let him pass. One made a remark he couldn't hear; the others laughed meanly at it. A bottle crashed by his feet.

He kept his head up. But they'd seen the momentary hunching of his shoulders, as if in anticipation of a blow.

They'd frightened him on purpose, tormented him because they could. And for that, one of them had to die.

The thought flew into his mind unbidden, but the instant it took shape he knew it was true. It was the real reason he'd come out here tonight, when it would've been much safer and simpler to stay in, and now he allowed himself to admit it.

Once his dad had died—*murdered, my father was murdered*—he'd never been allowed to attend festivals, street fairs, or any celebratory event where the common people gathered.

"Germs," his mother would pronounce in a disgusted voice. "They're dripping with ger-r-rms."

Listening, he'd practically been able to see the organisms, slimy and putrid, that might infest him at a public event. Then he would look around at his own safe, surgically clean home, filled with his own good clean toys and books and the many other solitary amusements his mother bought for him, and he'd decide on his own that he didn't want to go.

"Oh, that's all right, Mother," he would flute in his good-little-boy voice. "I'd rather stay here with you."

Which of course had been her real plan all along. But his presence here wasn't to make up for it. No, he was here to—

Another bottle crashed near his shoes; beer foam splashed his slacks. "Hey, faggot."

Fury made his face hot. That was always it, the worst they could think of. What they were most frightened of themselves.

And they should be frightened, though not of that. He stopped. "What?" he said into the air that was suddenly sparking with possibilities.

Nearby, an impromptu dance party had begun, musicians and a small amplifier providing music from a makeshift stage.

Once he would have fled. But with his mother's death, it was as if a clear glass jar had been lifted, freeing him.

"What?" he repeated softly as the youths circled.

Two on one side, two on the other. Swiftly he assessed them and identified the leader.

Tall and ginger-haired, the gang's front man squinted at Steven through clear gray eyes that gleamed a surprising amount of malignant self-awareness. Caution, too; just not enough.

"What're you, some kind of freaking freak?" Under

his black jacket, he wore a work shirt with the name *Jerry* on the pocket.

"Answer me, you freak," taunted ginger-haired Jerry.

The others grinned, nudging one another. Steven wondered if he was about to get a beating.

Jerry put his grimy hand on Steven's chest and pushed. "You think you're better'n us?"

Steven wondered how guys like Jerry always knew that. It was as if they had radar for normal IQ or above.

And hated it. "No," he lied evenly. "I don't think so."

The guy shoved him again, harder. Steven's foot crunched onto the broken bottle. Jerry's pals snickered appreciatively.

"That's a real pretty shirt you got on, lemme see," slurred the one with the worst acne, snatching at it with dirty fingers.

Just not being drunk gave Steven such a huge advantage, he thought it was hardly fair. Stepping back, he knew he shouldn't push his luck. But he couldn't resist.

"No," he said mildly again, then blew a loud, wet raspberry at the kid.

The youths glanced astonishedly at one another. "Oh, man," breathed the blocky one in the Iron Maiden T-shirt. The quartet closed menacingly around Steven.

But just as the first big fist came at Steven's face, a hand reached out over his attackers' shoulders and everything stopped.

"All right, all right," a tired male voice uttered.

Another hand, pink and plump, joined the first, then each hand clamped firmly onto a black-clad shoulder and pulled.

The phalanx of hostile bodies parted. Between them stepped a cop. Or at least he was wearing a cop's uniform.

"Boys, I'm gonna tell you this once. And you especially, Jerry," the cop added to the ginger-haired youth. "I want you all to leave this fellow alone. I get a report he's had any problems? You're gonna have problems with *me*. Okay?"

Shaking off the cop's grip, Steven's adversaries all nodded sullenly. "Yeah, yeah," they muttered.

"I mean it," the cop pressed. "I ain't a bit scared of any of you. You all know that from our past history together, right?"

The hooligans were too stubborn and dumb to back away, which let the cop make his point from a distance of about three inches.

"Right?" he repeated insistently. He had little red rosebud lips, a fluff of pale blond hair swept over the top of his head, and an air of simple unflappable confidence that said he was way more effective at law enforcement than he looked.

"Or maybe you'd hear me better if you were in the backseat of my squad car? Maybe I'll find out you've got some more of the M-80s you've been setting off all over town?"

"No," the gang's leader muttered, and seemed ready to say something more. But then he thought better of it.

"Come on, let's go find candy," he told his pals, and that puzzled Steven. He'd have expected these guys to be beer hounds, not chocolate fiends.

But he forgot about it as they all skulked off and the cop turned to Steven. "As for you, you look like a nice guy, and this is a nice town. Believe it or not," he said.

"But stay out of that crew's way. I might not always be here to pull your butt out of a sling, you get me?"

You don't understand, Steven wanted to say. From down the street the gang's leader shot Steven a look so full of threat, it was all Steven could do not to laugh out loud.

That guy, he wanted tell the cop. *It's his butt you saved.*

Jerry's. Because of course Steven couldn't kill him now. If the red-haired guy turned up dead, the cop would remember Steven.

And as delightful as it would be to watch those mean little gray eyes widen in fear, then bulge with the onset of asphyxia, it just wouldn't be worth it.

"Yes, sir," he answered politely. "I appreciate your help."

In a way, he really was grateful. He wouldn't have liked taking the beating those guys had been about to deliver, even if it did give him an excuse.

"Thank you." His voice shook with the adrenaline that had flooded him, facing the four hoodlums. Still, something in it must've betrayed the fact that he was not as frightened as he appeared.

The cop narrowed his eyes. "Yeah," he said, "I'll bet your gratitude knows no bounds."

But just then a barrage of firecracker explosions and a loud scream for help from somewhere nearby got Steven off the hook.

"Hang on, I'm coming!" the cop shouted, grabbing the radio on his belt as he ran. Turning, Steven walked toward a lantern-lit beer garden, scanning the throngs for his attackers.

But ginger-haired Jerry was gone, along with his black-clad pals. *Too bad*, Steven thought. A few inexpert punches, a bruise here and there . . . he'd have had to absorb that much from them.

But Steven felt sure he could have taken it easily, whatever they'd dished out. And then . . .

Then he'd have surprised them. Because it was all falling together now. He could feel it: the time, the place, his pent-up fury.

The taste of the too-rich food in his mouth. He let his gaze wander to the shadows past the streetlights, under the trees. At this hour, fatigue and alcohol sent groups and a few solitary revelers staggering unsteadily from the festivities.

Some got into their cars and drove away; he wished them more luck than they deserved. Others with weaving steps traced a zigzag pattern into the darkness alone.

One in particular caught his eye, a blonde girl in a tank top and shorts. Around her neck hung a thin gold chain that gleamed when passing car headlights hit it.

Steven eased alongside her, glanced over at her to see what the chain's pendant spelled out in gold script.

And couldn't believe his luck. *Candy*, it read.

Veering away, the girl stumbled a little; he caught her arm, steadying her. With a curse, she jerked from his grasp.

"Get away from me." She'd been crying; he could hear it in her voice. And she was drunk.

"Beat it," she told him angrily.

He stopped, letting her get ahead of him as she moved into the darkness away from the streetlights, until the sound of her uncertain footsteps had faded into the gloom.

When she had gone, he waited a little longer, in case someone else caught up. But no one did, so he followed her.

I want to go home. . . . She didn't think it was murder, didn't fear she'd burn in hellfire for what she now had planned.

She didn't even really believe, yet, that it was real. So why, every time she thought about it, did she feel like her heart was being gouged out of her with a rusty ice cream scoop?

For an unguarded moment she let herself think what it might look like: red hair, for sure. And brown eyes like her own . . .

But thinking that way would only break her heart even more.

Home . . . She strode on, weeping again, the gold signature medallion Jerry had given to her back when they'd first started dating bouncing on its gold chain.

Past the Motel East parking lot, she turned down the alley linking Water and Sea streets. It was dark and rutted, but she'd lived in Eastport all her life, She could've done this blindfolded.

On Sea Street, she turned unhesitatingly into the darkness. At least here she could cry freely, without anyone coming up to her and asking her what was wrong.

Probably the medallion was stolen. That'd be just like Jerry; why buy what you can get free? And now . . .

Probably he'd never even loved her. She took a shuddering breath as, to her left, the dark bulk of the old tin can factory loomed. To her right, a patch of waste ground sprouted burdock, Saint-John's-wort, and a few ragged softwood trees.

And straight ahead stretched Sea Street itself, dark and mysterious-looking. But now her own home was less than a mile distant; minutes from now, she'd be in her own bed.

So she pressed on, past the ruined wharf running alongside Passamaquoddy Bay. It was low tide, pale stones and the stumps of old wooden pilings littering the beach.

Sniffling, she felt the clean, salt air clearing her head. After all, it wasn't as if Jerry's meanness was big news. She should've known what he would say, and besides, it was crazy, the whole idea of him being a father.

Still, she hadn't been prepared for his look of scathing hatred, as if he might just reach out with both hands right there and—

"Get rid of it," he'd snarled. "I ain't havin'

no damned kid. I mean it, Candy, you'd better do it, or . . ."

Not I'll help pay for it or even I'll go with you. Just Do it or else.

With a sneer of disgust, he'd spun away from her. "C'mon," he'd told his pals, who had been standing just out of earshot.

Then he'd left her with her mouth hanging open in shock and the first burst of fear invading her heart. Alone . . .

Now, trying not to cry again, she rushed on; in just a short while she would be in her own room with the door closed, avoiding her mother's anxiously well-meaning questions. Already in her bag was the clinic number, which she'd saved because in her heart she had known all along that she'd probably have to use it.

Tomorrow she would make the call. After that, it would just be a matter of waiting until it was—

Over. But then . . . *Wait a minute,* she thought. *I don't* have *to do it. Do I?*

Experimentally, at first. The sudden lifting of what felt like a heavy stone from her heart, though, couldn't be ignored.

As if she'd known all along what she really wanted to do. *Could* do, if only . . .

If only she just did nothing at all. *I don't want to,* she thought again. *And I'm not going to.*

Without conscious volition, she drew the card with the clinic number on it from her bag, ripped it into pieces. They fluttered from her hand out over the beach to the water, and into it.

Gone . . . A sound halted her; she turned, puzzled. Silence, now. But the sound had been there, a noise like maybe a rock falling. Or a stone being pushed aside by a careless foot . . .

Suddenly the night felt less familiar. But when nothing more happened, she hurried on again.

Silly. Still, it *was* dark down here, and there were a lot of strangers in town. That guy who'd accidentally-on-purpose bumped into her, for instance; she paused again, recalling him.

But he wouldn't have followed her this far . . . would he? She quickened her step. Soon she passed the lobster traps stacked row on row behind the fish mart and reached the part of the street that was only a bare track running along the ledge.

Now she was almost running, but when the sound came again, nearer, it was too late to get off Sea Street: cliffs jutting up on one side, a high, sharp drop to the water on the other.

Without slowing, she glanced over her shoulder. "Hello?"

No answer. The footsteps drew nearer.

"Jerry," she quavered, "is that you? Come on, now, don't . . ."

Scare me. "Who is it?" she demanded, but again there came no reply, and she began running for real.

Run. The lights of Middle Street appeared, mist halos around them. As she reached them a car went by.

Thank God . . . But when the car's lights vanished, she was all alone again and the footsteps sounded implacably once more.

Swiftly she turned right, away from the dark road

home, up a short hill and back to Water Street. There, houses stood packed close together. Once she'd reached downtown, she might be able to catch a ride home. She quick-stepped another block. . . .

And her heart sank, for ahead under the next street-light a man stood. Waiting, hands at his sides.

Watching. Far enough away so she couldn't tell who it was. *And how did he get there?* her mind inquired unpleasantly. *How'd he get out in front of you like that?*

He took a step toward her. Whirling, she ran onto the porch of the nearest house and pounded on the door.

"Hello? Help . . . help me, someone?"

But no one answered. *All downtown at the party—*

She tried the door—locked. She didn't have a cellphone. Scurrying off the porch, dashing across the silent street, she managed to put some distance between herself and the approaching figure. But there was no way to avoid him completely.

Not unless she turned back into the darkness. And she wasn't going to do that.

Hurrying along, she tried to figure a route that would get her downtown safely, then suddenly recalled she had a half-empty beer bottle in her purse.

From earlier, when she'd thought she wasn't going to be a mother, so she could drink. Reaching into her bag, she grasped the bottle by its neck, just as a street sign loomed up out of the darkness and her heart leapt with hope. *Eagle Street . . .*

It was only a short, dead-end alley leading to the

edge of the cliffs overlooking Sea Street and the bay. But there were at least half a dozen houses on it.

Maybe one of them would have someone home. And even if not, there were lots of places to hide in the yards and sheds of the old dwellings.

Gasping with fright, she scanned the street once more. Her unwanted companion was about half a block away now, not moving.

It was the way he stood so patiently that scared her worst of all. As if he knew that, sooner or later, he would get what he wanted. Turning, she dashed into the refuge of Eagle Street.

After a moment, the dark man-shape followed.

Just before dawn, Steven slipped through the fog back to the old house he was camped in, feeling transformed.

A few hours ago he'd been scared by his own recklessness and furious with himself for giving in to it. But now he was starting to think he might be able to get away with anything.

On the streets nothing moved, not even the squad car he'd spied a few times earlier. Everyone had gone home, the food tents and trinket tables on Water Street zip-fronted and tarp-covered.

He crept into the musty-smelling wreck of the old kitchen and stripped off his clothes. He removed the flakes of dried glue from behind his ears and scrubbed all over with more of the wet towelettes from his pack.

A car went by outside; a foghorn hooted. Someone downtown turned on a boom box tinnily playing "The Star-Spangled Banner."

Gunshots rang out.

Towelette clutched in hand, he froze in mid-scrub, his heart nearly leaping out of his chest. But then . . .

More gunshots, a measured barrage of them. Down at the foot of the street near the breakwater, he realized, relieved.

Of course; it was a sunrise Fourth of July ceremony, with an artillery salute. He'd seen notices of it posted on telephone poles. He'd been lucky to get inside before it began.

He spied his laptop on the floor and thought about hunting around the neighborhood for an outdoor electrical outlet, to recharge its batteries. That way, he could save the new ones he'd bought.

But it wasn't worth the risk. Most of his computer work was done now, his messages and images all uploaded and scheduled for sending. They'd already begun reaching her, and the next one was due to arrive soon.

He did have one last prank to play before the main action of his plan began, but between his own gear and the local library's facilities, he was already well equipped for it.

Rinsing his mouth with one of the juices from his pack, he spat the liquid into the old sink, then jumped as, behind the wall, something moved with a faint scratching of tiny claws.

Rat, he thought, and glanced around for something to hit it with, should it emerge. There—

On the floor lay a chunk of firewood left over from when there'd been a woodstove in here. He snatched it up and hefted it: just right for clubbing with.

He washed some crackers down with the rest of the juice, noting with surprise that somehow, the last few hours had erased his need to be compulsive about counting the bites.

I'm a new man, he thought with a shock of wonder. Everything is different.

After dressing in fresh clothes from the pack, he put the soiled ones on the floor, well away from his little campsite laid out on the tarp he'd spread.

Not far from the clothes heap, one of the kitchen's doors led to what had once been a cellar stairway. Now it opened onto a pitch-dark drop, the steps fallen away long ago and the darkness breathing out a rank smell of ancient dampness.

Never mind, though; he wouldn't have to be here for very much longer. Outside, it was growing lighter. More cars moved in the street, and soon what lay motionless on the path by the cove would be found.

It was a good time, he thought, to try getting some sleep. Glancing around a final time, he saw that all was in readiness for the events to come.

An unbroken chair that he'd found in an upstairs bedroom, check.

Electrical cord, check. Blindfold, handcuffs, duct tape, scissors, check.

And a digital camera with a card reader, double check. With luck he would fill its memory card many times, uploading it to the laptop whenever it reached capacity. Later, the laptop would serve as a scrapbook he could revisit anytime he liked.

Satisfied, he settled to sleep. But soon a sound woke him. The rat from the wall had emerged, creeping boldly onto the tarp.

It was probably smelling the crackers in his pack, Steven thought. Slowly, not taking his gaze off the animal, he let his hand move until his fingers found the thick chunk of firewood.

And closed upon it.

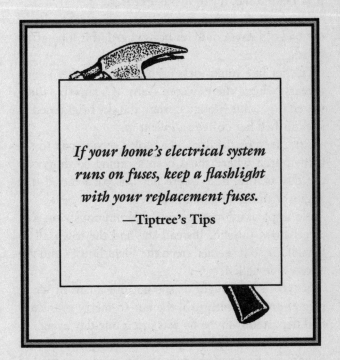

Chapter 4

*If your home's electrical system
runs on fuses, keep a flashlight
with your replacement fuses.*

—Tiptree's Tips

After a night of little sleep, Jake expected
to feel lousy the next morning. But instead she woke
bright-eyed, long before anyone else in the house was
up and about.

Coffee in hand, she took the dogs out into the backyard. With a hot-pink sun just rising through the fog

that still hung on the horizon and the sky deep blue overhead, she breathed in the cool air gratefully.

New day, she thought. Another chance to put the past behind me, try to make up for it.

Or try to do better. Funny how a faint reminder of the bad old days could hit her so hard, this long afterward.

Put her in a funk, mess up her sleep, get her seeing threats where there weren't any. Or maybe there weren't. . . . But enough of that; the sky brightened as she finished her coffee and went in.

After feeding the dogs, she took a second cup to the front porch where she'd been scraping so diligently the day before, and where her unsettled mood had begun with the ring of a bike bell.

No unpleasant stranger pedaled ominously on Key Street now, though. Instead she had the town all to herself, or so it seemed from the silent houses and the empty sidewalks.

Maybe, she thought as she got out a can of white primer and a paintbrush, the not-so-merry prankster had departed. Maybe he was just a one-day event.

Gone, she thought hopefully, crossing her mental fingers as she pried the top off the paint can, poured white, soup-thick liquid into a painting tray, and dipped the brush.

Two coats of primer followed by two of paint was the way to be sure an outdoor structure stayed painted here in Maine. On an island, especially, salt air began attacking paint finishes almost before they went on, corroding new ones even as the old ones got covered over.

And—pessimism flooded her suddenly—her old house was enormous. Hundreds of square feet of antique clapboards needed scraping, sanding, setting-in of the old nails so they wouldn't rust, and even caulking in some of the more disreputable spots.

Just the porch alone, with its elaborately turned wooden rails, posts, and pilasters that all required careful brushing and re-brushing, was a gargantuan project. Abruptly her earlier vision of a pristine white entryway complete with big clay pots of red geraniums seemed overambitious.

To put it mildly. But she did already have the paint can open and the brush wet. Also, it was unlikely that she would be interrupted for at least a couple of hours.

And finally, she'd already bought those big clay geranium pots, each of which cost the earth even though that was pretty much all they were made of. So, starting at the left-hand corner of the deck near the screen door, she began brushing primer into every nook, cranny, nail hole, and crevice, inch by patient inch.

Whereupon all at once the whole job suddenly seemed possible again. As did everything else: the centuries-old house, the remaking of her whole life.

This, she thought, watching the white-paint expanse widen. This is why I do it. Before she knew it, she'd covered a few more decking planks, then more still, and a whole rail-and-post unit.

By the time the sun rose high enough to flood the streets with golden light, joggers and dog walkers were out. Even a few bicyclists pedaled by, their faces bright with the pleasure of the sweet, fresh air and the absence of car traffic.

None of them paid her any attention or looked the least bit familiar, and soon she stopped bothering to look up each time she heard a derailleur's whir. When the creak in her back and a cramp in her brush hand—as well as the need for more coffee—got her off her knees, to her own surprise she had nearly emptied the paint can, and a fresh coat of white primer covered the whole porch.

And the second coat couldn't go on until the first dried, so it was break time. After finding and brushing smooth the drips of excess paint on the vertical surfaces of the job, she scraped the brush on the rim of the open can.

Next she wrapped the brush in layers of plastic wrap to preserve it for the few hours it would take the primer to dry. Finally she tapped the paint can's top back on with little raps of the brush handle and set the can on some sheets of newspaper.

Inside, she expected to find the coffee stewed to black syrup and the house still hushed. But instead Bella was up, already busy damp-mopping the floors.

The smell of kitchen cleanser floated in the air along with the aroma of fresh coffee. The windows stood open wide, the white lace curtains fluttering in puffs of cool, salt-freshened air.

"Is Sam up, too?" Jake asked. The coffee was delicious, much better than the dregs she'd left cooking in the pot. Across the back lawn an army of robins marched, cocking their bright eyes skyward while breakfasting on worms.

"Up and gone," said Bella. The muscles in her long,

ropy arms flexed visibly as she rubbed the mop over a stubborn patch of imaginary dirt.

"Wade, too, and your father. Slipped out the back way; they didn't want to interrupt you while you had a good head of steam up."

All three men were on the fireworks committee, charged with handling everything but the explosives themselves. Later that day a professional team from the suppliers would board a barge and get towed out onto the water, where they—the fireworks, not the men—would be detonated in about—Jake checked the kitchen clock—twelve hours from now.

"And Ellie stopped by," said Bella.

The dogs danced around; Jake gave each one a biscuit. Prill wolfed hers and looked up eagerly for another; Monday nibbled delicately but finished it.

"Good pup," Jake told the old Labrador, whose clouded eyes seemed to brighten minutely at the sound.

"She says do you want to meet her for breakfast?" said Bella as she ran hot water over her mop. "Ellie, I mean."

Jake watched Monday walk slowly to her bed and sink into it. "Oh?" she said distractedly. "She say why?"

All the restaurants downtown would be jammed, what with the crowds in town. And anyway, Ellie would have already eaten her breakfast with George, hours earlier.

Wringing the mop out, Bella shook her head, her big green eyes scanning the kitchen alertly for further grit, grime, or corruption. "Just said she had news."

Jake would've tried to keep Bella from spending her every waking minute housecleaning, but attacking dirt banished whatever demons the stiff-necked, ungainly woman needed to keep at bay.

Or it seemed that way, anyway, so Jake had shut up about it, and since then they had gotten along just fine. "News? But we saw her just last night."

Still sipping her coffee, she wandered into the dining room and powered up her laptop in case Ellie had sent an email about it. Outside the wavery, antique panes of the old windows, shafts of sunlight drew gauzy puffs of evaporation from the damp grass.

No reply from Bella. Probably she was already on to a new task: scalding out the wastebaskets with boiling water, maybe, or sterilizing the stove knobs.

Jake clicked on "Mail," then waited as what appeared to be a rather large file began downloading into her mailbox.

Just for you! read the item's header. Impatiently she waited with her finger poised over the delete button; emails with titles like that were usually spam.

By the time it occurred to her that it might be another nasty message like yesterday's, a photograph had begun appearing scroll-wise on the screen, unreeling from top to bottom.

A color photograph . . .

At the halfway point, she pulled a chair out from the dining table. When it finished, she sat down hard in it.

The photograph was of someone sitting in a chair, too, taken from behind. But the person in the picture was tied to the chair with what appeared to be clothesline.

Harsh flash illumination whitened some parts of the scene and blackened other parts. The figure's head slumped forward, so that at first glance it seemed not to be there at all.

But it was. Sort of. "Bella," she whispered to her stepmother but got no answer. Monday came stiffly into the dining room, shoved her grizzled old head into Jake's lap, and whined.

"It's okay, girl," said Jake, smoothing the dog's ears as the last section of the photograph appeared on the screen.

The last, worst part. "Everything's fine," she murmured, and felt the sweet old animal relax against her.

But it wasn't fine, was it? She stared at the photograph.

Not at all. Not even a little bit. Because she recognized it.

Remembered it, rather. From the bad old days . . .

Closing the laptop so Bella wouldn't come in and get a glimpse of the screen accidentally, she pressed the print button on the computer, checked the wireless icon to make sure the file was transmitting to the printer in Wade's office, and went upstairs to get dressed.

Correction: ran up the stairs. As if the hounds of hell were behind her.

Which, in a way, they were.

•　　•　　•

Twenty minutes later, Jake met Ellie White downtown at a table in the Blue Iris, a small combination
café and gift shop overlooking the water.

On the table between them, a manila folder shielded
the printed-out photo from casual eyes. If anyone else
in the restaurant had spied it, it would've ruined their
breakfasts and their sleep that night, too.

Probably for many nights.

"Good heavens," Ellie said faintly as she peered at
it, then gestured at Jake to close the folder. "And
you're telling me you know who this is?"

Jake nodded grimly. "A long time ago, a fellow I
knew very slightly got in gambling-debt trouble,
big-time. This—"

She gestured at the folder. "This was the result. The
photo got sent around; not to me, but somebody I
knew got one."

Because after all, what good was making an example of Steven Garner if no one knew about it? She
shuddered, remembering.

"But why . . . ?" Ellie began.

"I'm not sure," Jake replied, although she was,
now. And she knew who the bike guy must be, too.

She just didn't want to confront it yet, or at any rate
not out loud.

"And your news is?" she asked Ellie, not expecting
it to be good.

Because things like this didn't happen all by themselves, did they? They came in groups, like invading
armies or the clouds of germs Bella always thought
were descending on everything.

The restaurant's window table overlooked the

half-submerged old pilings of what had long ago been a steamboat wharf. From it, travelers had embarked upon journeys that might end in Boston or the West Indies, or even the Far East.

Now waves sparkled between the pilings. "The news is, they found a body this morning," Ellie answered. "Some tourists taking an early stroll found it."

Her red hair glinted in the sun. "Down there on Sea Street." She gestured past the rotted wood pilings to where an unpaved track curved along the steep bank of a tidal inlet.

"I didn't tell Bella because I didn't want to upset her," Ellie added.

With a sheer drop to the water on one side and a granite cliff rising on the other, Sea Street was a busy, scenic walking path in the daytime. But only locals traveled the dark, out-of-the-way route at night.

"Do they know who?" Jake asked. "Or how? And how'd you find out about it, anyway?"

"George got beeped." Which made sense; besides being on call to repair nearly anything municipal that got broken—a valve at the sewer plant, a leak at the city buildings, a fuel pump on a squad car—George was also a volunteer emergency medical technician.

"He didn't want to talk about it," Ellie added. "But I heard him and Bob Arnold down in the kitchen, afterwards."

In the past, the Fourth had always passed without fatalities despite the raucousness of the celebration. But not this year, apparently. "I guess someone must've fallen," Ellie said softly.

The cliff over the path was forty feet high, with

nothing to grab on to on the way down. "Landed on solid rock, got a broken neck. And bounced a few times, I gather, from what I overheard."

Ellie shivered a little, then turned once more to the folder on the table between them. "The message said what, again?"

"That it was just for me," Jake replied as their breakfasts came: a bowl of oatmeal for Ellie, an omelet for Jake. But neither had much appetite.

"So you're thinking . . ."

"Yes. I'm pretty sure the guy on the bike sent it."

Jake ate a bite of egg she didn't want. She had no specific reason to think that the body on Sea Street was part of it all, too.

But she couldn't shake the notion, and five minutes later, leaving their breakfasts unfinished, they crossed the street to Bob Arnold's office in the Frontier Bank building.

A red-brick and granite confection from the early 1800s, the bank with its ornate moldings and widow's walk resembled a wedding cake. But inside, everything was clean and utilitarian feeling; the bulletin boards where interest rates and Christmas club info had once been tacked were now plastered with public-service placards and wanted posters.

Bob Arnold sat at a gray metal desk behind what had been the bank's customer service counter. "I don't care," he said flatly into the phone, and listened for a moment.

Then, "I don't care," he said again, and stood up.

"You just get me five deputies. I've got thousands of people here, more tonight, and we've had a fatality already. You send them, or I'll deputize my own, whether I'm empowered to or not."

He put a wry twist on the word *empowered*. Way out here in Eastport, Bob's law-enforcement mandate was to keep things from going to hell in a hand-basket; how was his own lookout.

"We're going to have a bigger police presence here," he finished, "and if you want those extra officers answering to you instead of me, you'll send them."

He slammed the phone down and glared at Jake and Ellie. "Now, what do you two want?"

In the small offices at the back, Eastport's pair of part-time cops were on their phones, also.

"No," said Joe Dahm, a tall, salt-and-pepper-haired black man whose voice carried a Jamaican lilt. "I don't know any more. No, we don't have a confirmed . . ."

". . . identity," Wad Hardesty said into the other phone. "We were hoping to maybe show you some personal items that you might be able to . . ."

Jake tossed the manila folder with the photograph in it over the counter, onto Bob's desk. Scowling, he opened it, and then a change came over his face.

Not a pleasant change. "Jesus H. Key-rist," he breathed, and opened the gateway to the area behind the counter.

"Siddown, both of you." He pointed at the straight chairs facing his desk.

They sat. Outside, another day of holiday activities had begun; just now the pet parade was passing, with much barking and meowing plus a few ba-a-as, oinks, and whinnies.

There was even a moo; Jake and Ellie looked star-tledly at each other. But Bob wasn't interested in the menagerie being led past his office. "Where the hell did that come from?"

The photograph, he meant. Behind him, one of the officers was trying to calm someone who'd just caught on to the reason for his call.

"No, ma'am," he said. "We're not sure she . . . It's just there are some items to . . ."

Bob sighed. "Yeah," he said quietly. "Items like a driver's license, a movie-rental ID card, a Social Security card . . ."

"It came by email this morning," answered Jake, gesturing at the horrid photo.

"I think I know who sent it," she went on, and Ellie glanced at her in surprise. Swiftly, Jake summarized her history with the doomed gambling debtor, Steven Garner Sr.

Ancient history. But . . .

"But there was a guy hanging around my house yesterday, and I got some bad emails."

Bob frowned. "So you think he sent 'em? The guy's son?"

She nodded reluctantly. Bob was an old-fashioned, nuts-and-bolts, don't-waste-my-time kind of a small-town police chief, and right now he was busy as hell.

Holiday weekend, a town full of people, an acci-dental death—or she still hoped it was, anyway. And now this . . .

"He has," she told Bob, "an identifying feature." Feeling obscurely foolish, she described Steven Gar-ner Jr.'s protruding ears.

"The guy from yesterday has them, too," she said. "I'd have probably recognized him just from that, if—"

If she'd had even the slightest idea that anything from the old days would come back to bite her this long afterwards.

"Okay," Bob exhaled when she'd finished. The cops in the rear offices had put down their phones and were leaning back, drained. "Leave this with me. Anything else happens, you call."

He hoisted his body from the chair. "One thing's for sure, whoever sent you that picture went to some trouble to do it."

She looked quizzically at him. "You ever try to track down somebody's email address, you don't know it already?" he asked.

"Oh. Right."

But someone had learned hers. "Do you want me to bring the laptop down here?" she asked.

He stared out the old bank building's big glass front door. On the heels of the menagerie, the Little Miss Eastport pageant had begun, frilly-dressed four- and five-year-olds scurrying by.

"Yeah," he said. "This place is going to be crazy soon. Even crazier than it is now. Crime lab van, state major crimes guys, who knows who all."

To investigate the death on Sea Street, he meant, because it probably had been an accident. But it wasn't officially one until the medical examiner said it was one.

"Guess I'll have to close my plant room," he added. The bank vault was what he used for an evidence

lockup. But in Eastport there was so little call for se-
cure evidence storage that nowadays he had a grow
light in there, with African violets blooming under it.

"Portland's got a fancy new division for computer
crime; we can ask them for help."

The little girls outside wore white nylon anklets
with lacy ruffles, and shiny patent leather shoes. She
wondered suddenly whether the Sea Street victim had
been in the pageant, once.

"What was her name?" She looked up at Bob's
grim face. "On the paperwork, I mean, that the Sea
Street victim had."

"I don't want to say yet, Jake." News like that, he
didn't want the next of kin finding it out from someone else.

Not that hearing it out of a cop's mouth made it
any better. "But I can tell you this much. We're not
going to confirm an ID by asking the relatives to view
the body."

Brr, Jake thought, understanding what he must
have meant. "And I don't want anyone seeing her
who doesn't have to," he added.

Ellie turned. "Why not? Isn't that usually the way
they—"

He shook his head. "Not this time. They'll know
her clothes and personal items, probably. Some jewelry, pretty much makes the case for who she is, seems
to me."

He sighed sorrowfully. "But that forty-foot drop
broke every bone in her face and a whole lot of them
in the rest of her body, too."

He gazed out at the bright day. "If she hadn't left a

purse and a half-drunk bottle of beer at the top of the cliff, I wouldn't be thinking now that she either fell or jumped off it."

Outside, some kids chased one another with cans of Silly String. A red, white, and blue Model T juddered by, lurching and backfiring.

"Bashed up the way she was," Bob finished somberly, "I'd be thinking someone must've beaten her to death."

Bella was at the dining room table with the laptop open when Jake and Ellie returned from seeing Bob Arnold. The awful picture was on the screen; she turned haggardly to them.

"Oh," Jake said, realizing in horror what must've happened. "Bella, I'm so sorry, I should have warned you not to—"

Although it was Jake's machine, as she'd been reminded only the night before, everyone in the house used it.

"I was hunting up a fish chowder recipe," Bella whispered. "A while ago, I'd deleted the email that it came in, and—"

And when she'd opened the mail program to look in the trash folder for it, the photograph appeared. Jake put her arms around the older woman's bony shoulders.

"You poor thing, to have that pop up at you."

Bella was rugged, but no one was tough enough to see that without being affected. "Come on," Jake said. "We'll go out to the kitchen and I'll make you a nice cup of—"

Tea, she was about to finish, but before she could, Prill the Doberman came flying out from where she'd been lying half asleep under the dining room table. With a volley of ferocious barking, the big dog charged to the back hall.

By the time Jake caught up to her, with Ellie right behind, the back door was closing. A blur sped away from the back porch.

A familiar blur . . . "After him!" shouted Bella, and dashed out herself, across the back porch and down the steps into the street before Jake could do anything about it.

"Bella!" She grabbed at Prill's stubby tail as the dog shot out, too, missed it, and watched the animal gallop after Bella and their unwelcome visitor, speeding away on his bike.

"Stop! Bella! Prill!" Jake shouted, but neither of them heard her. Bella was making way too much noise herself, squawking out a series of threats in language that Jake had never before heard from the bony old woman.

Meanwhile, Prill's angry barking covered Bella's use of curse words—loud, varied, and surprisingly creative—in a way that Bella would probably find pretty convenient later, in the you-must've-misheard-me, I-never-said-that department.

The bike rider reached the corner and vanished around it, the bell still brring!-ing tauntingly. Prill and Bella followed, but moments later they returned, winded.

"Oh, if I could've got my hands on him," Bella panted out, her big, work-reddened hands making wringing motions that for once had nothing to do with dishcloths.

Whining, the big red Doberman scrambled up the back porch and wriggled into Jake's arms. "Okay, girl," Jake whispered with her face buried in the dog's smooth neck. She was so glad to see them both back unharmed, she had no energy for scolding.

Because if they'd caught him, she didn't know what he might do. And nothing would be worth losing either one of them. . . .

"Everything's okay now." But it wasn't, for just inside the back door lay a small box.

A cracker box, taped shut . . . Lifting it cautiously, Jake felt a small, soft weight shift inside.

I'll bet that's not anything good, she thought clearly.

It wasn't.

Long ago in Manhattan, Jake had learned a few things from her crooked clients, including what message a package with a dead rat in it was meant to convey: that you were a rat, too.

And that you were as good as dead.

"Okay, let me get this straight," said Wade. "First, some strange guy rides by the house on a bike, saying hostile things to you."

He and the other men had finished prepping the barge and the support boats for the professional team that would be detonating the fireworks tonight. Now he was driving her around town in his pickup truck, trying to calm her down.

"Yes, but Wade, they weren't just any hostile things."

On the sidewalk, little kids waved flags. Ahead, a flatbed truck sported a dozen folding chairs and a sign reading *Welcome class of 1972!!!*

"He was saying I'd done something, that murder will out. And now I know what that means."

Wade waited for the flatbed to pull through the intersection onto Washington Street. As it began its sharp uphill course past the post office building, all the chairs fell over.

"Okay. So who is he?" Wade asked as they passed the white clapboard Baptist church building, now home to the Arts Center. Along the sidewalk on both sides of the street, people already had set blankets and lawn chairs out for the parade later.

"Someone from back in Manhattan," she admitted reluctantly. "Because . . . listen, you know I was no angel back then, right?"

Wade steered the truck along Deep Cove Road. "Jake, whatever happened, the important thing is that it was back then. And this is now. And," he added reassuringly, "I do know the difference."

Relief flooded her. "And try to relax, will you?" he went on. "Because right now, at least, I'd say you're fairly safe."

For emphasis, he angled his head at the shotgun racked in the rear window. The ammo boxed under the seat was only birdshot, but an assailant would find it persuasive enough.

Wade himself, squarely built and with the kind of blocky fists that could double as wrecking balls, was pretty persuasive-looking, too. She let her head rest against his shoulder.

"Thanks." Swiftly she summarized Steven Garner Jr.'s grievance against her, that he believed she was responsible for the death of his father.

There was, she decided, no need to go into the gory details. Or that she was convinced the dead girl down on Sea Street was somehow involved.

Because that really was just speculation. . . . "What I don't get, though, is why he's decided to come after me now, after all this time. And . . . how'd he find me?" she asked Wade. "How did he get my email address?"

The truck sailed down a long hill and through an S curve. "That's easy," he replied. "The new town address book."

"Oh," she breathed. The Eastport Improvement Society had made a project out of collecting the email addresses of everyone in town.

"Of course. That must be it." A town email directory would improve interpersonal networking, the Society group had said. But the net they had created was likely the one she'd been caught in.

Out Deep Cove Road, the water spread sapphire-blue and sparkling. A heron stalked the shallows, deliberately lifting first one long, sticklike leg and then the other.

Wade turned the truck into Shackford Head State Park. In the lot overlooking the cove, they got out into a silence broken only by the breeze in the old trees.

Wade slung his arm around her. "Come on, let's stretch our legs. No one can find you out here, I guarantee it."

They climbed a narrow path, crossed a plank boardwalk over a shallow bog teeming with life, and emerged into a forest where massive tree trunks held up an arching roof of evergreen boughs.

Shafts of sunlight slanted down, as solid appearing as gold bars. "So the big ears are the identifying feature," Wade said.

She understood: he was talking about how to recognize Steven Garner Jr., so he could do something to him.

Nothing too terrible. Just enough to make him cut it out, which ordinarily Jake could've endorsed, no problem. But she had a bad feeling that this time Wade's approach might backfire.

"If he gets beaten up, he might get madder at me."

Wade himself wouldn't even have to do the deed. A longtime downeast Maine native, her husband had friends and relatives all over the county, many of them as solidly put together and battle ready as he was, at least in the fisticuffs department. All Wade would have to do was pass the word, and Steven Jr. was toast. But:

"Jake, you know me. I won't hurt the guy."

Ha, she thought, because she did know him. And what he meant was he wouldn't hurt him much.

"But," he went on reasonably, "it's going to take a

while to get any action out of the Portland police, don't you think?"

Of course it would. Meanwhile, Garner was here now.

"And," he added, "this business has captured my attention."

Which was what he always said when he was provoked past all reason but didn't want to alarm her. Because in Eastport, it was very well known that if you captured Wade Sorenson's attention, he might react by capturing you.

And then your attention would get captured. "But, Wade," she began again.

"All right, all right," he gave in easily. "No clobbering. Word of honor. But don't worry, we'll figure a way to fix this."

They emerged from among the evergreens onto a trail leading slantwise across a steep granite slope. Patches of scrubby grass and pale, greenish-gray lichens grew in the thin soil.

High over the water, the trail's end was like the prow of a great ship. Jake stretched, letting the wind blow through her.

Wade stood beside her. "I won't do anything," he told her again, which reassured her so much that she forgot to make him promise also not to tell anyone else about Garner's antics.

Such as, for instance, those friends and relatives all over the county.

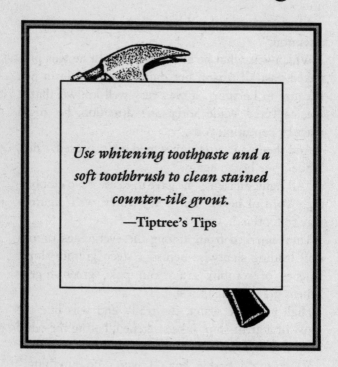

Chapter 5

*Use whitening toothpaste and a
soft toothbrush to clean stained
counter-tile grout.*

—Tiptree's Tips

"**The early Romans used to make concrete,**
did you know that?" said Ellie later that morning.
They were out in the backyard of Jake's house on Key
Street, mixing concrete.

Jake attached the hose to the outdoor spigot. They

could have used premixed concrete and saved themselves some trouble.

But she had some bags of sand to get rid of, left
over from other projects, and opportunities to use
fifty-pound bags of sand didn't just happen along
every day. Thank goodness.

"Nope," she said. The morning had bloomed into a
day of sparkling sunshine. The warmed air was fruity
with the perfume of blooming beach roses.

But a fog bank hung on the horizon. "I wish the
early Romans were doing it right now, though, instead of me," she added.

While Ellie gathered more tools and equipment,
Jake slammed the last nail into the last of the four
plywood boxes she was building.

Forms, they were called. Sam wanted some anchors
for a few rowboats he'd fixed up and was planning to
sell, out at the Boat School, and there were still
enough tacky patches on the porch primer to keep her
from working any more on that project today.

So, since she wasn't too busy with *that* to do *this,*
and she *did* know how to put a batch of concrete together ... Besides, she couldn't refuse Sam such a
simple favor when he'd worked so hard refurbishing
those rowboats.

Or it would've been simple if the Romans had been
doing it, she decided as Ellie hauled the garden cart
across the lawn.

"Limestone, calcium, iron, aluminum," Ellie recited. "Those are concrete's main ingredients." She
was just brimming with interesting facts this morning.

"Did you know that?" The boxes to pour the concrete into now stood ready and waiting.

"No," Jake replied, glancing nervously at the forsythia and bayberry bushes edging the yard. No strange faces peeped through the shrubbery at her.

But she still felt . . . observed, somehow. "No, I didn't know that, either." Watched, as if . . .

With an effort she turned back to Ellie, who was trying hard to cheer her up. "But then the recipe got lost," Ellie said.

Which got Jake's attention, finally. "Really? For concrete? Do you mean they just . . ."

"Uh-huh." Ellie nodded emphatically, which caused even more of her pale red hair to fall from the loose chignon she'd pinned it into.

"Yep. Just forgot how to make it," she went on. "I guess what with their empire shrinking and so many of their far-flung colonies rebelling against them and all, they got preoccupied."

"Huh," Jake said, distracted again as she dug in the pocket of her canvas work apron. She laid a level on two corners of a wooden form, then set a carpenter's square into one corner to ensure the final product would be rectangular and not some other, more exotic geometrical shape, as Ellie continued:

"And can you imagine what a drag that must have been? Last year, you could build a terrace or a bunch of massive foundation blocks or a spillway for your canal. . . ."

"No kidding." Jake paused in the act of shifting a forty-pound sack of cement to the other side of the lawn cart.

"But this year . . ."

It was a law of nature, apparently, that forty-pound sacks were always on the wrong side of the lawn cart.

". . . this year, it's back to mud, sticks, and stones," Ellie finished.

And that by the time you discovered that the forty-pound bag was on the wrong side, the cart's wheels were always stuck.

"But how did it get lost? The recipe, I mean."

Because that was the difference between concrete and cement: what you added, and the proportions you added it in. Sand, stone, and water; how much of each you used was the key to the result.

"Rome fell. Attila the Hun and so on," Ellie explained. "So I guess with barbarians sacking and vandalizing from the outside, and then all the plotting and poisoning that was going on on the inside, well, a lot of things must've gotten misplaced."

With the tip of a penknife, Jake tried loosening the string that tied the top of the cement bag shut. As usual, the bag tore before the string loosened; yet another of the laws of nature.

Concrete-mixing nature, anyway; a small gray cloud of cement dust puffed out of the bag.

"And nobody found it again until the sixteenth century," said Ellie, meanwhile filling big plastic buckets with the hose. They'd also set a wheelbarrow full of construction sand nearby.

Or rather, Ellie's husband, George Valentine, had set it there for them; filled with sand, that wheelbarrow was heavy, and he was the helpful type.

"Which is when a British guy finally figured it out again," Ellie went on with the story.

Jake looked around at the sand, the cement, the forms, and the buckets of water. Also at the concrete-mixing tray, made of heavy-duty black plastic and the size of a child's wading pool.

In fact, until they pressed it into service for this job, it had been used as a wading pool. But little Lee was with her dad for the afternoon, and they planned to have it cleaned up by the time she got home.

So: water, forms, ingredients, tools . . . "You know what?" Jake remarked in surprise. "I think we're ready."

To mix, she meant. She stood up straight, her back creaking warningly at the movement even without having hauled any sand.

Simple or not, the job was not for the faint of spine. But around her on the grass lay the four plywood forms, shimmed beneath with shingle scraps so their tops were level. Near them lay four galvanized eye-bolts with brackets.

Concrete blocks, after all, made lousy anchors unless you could tie something to them. She turned to the cement bag.

But just then from the open kitchen window wafted the aroma of frying linguica, a kind of Portuguese pork sausage with onions, garlic, and paprika mixed in. With it Bella was making kale soup, the fragrance an invisible ribbon of tantalizing promise.

The ribbon seized Jake's nose. Her stomach made sympathetic growling sounds. And mixing and pouring the concrete would surely take another hour at least, whereas if they stopped now . . .

"Tools," Ellie said helpfully; she'd smelled the linguica, too. And somehow, Ellie always required huge amounts of nutrition to maintain her sylphlike form.

"We should go in and make a list, to be sure we've got the right ones," she added.

This, of course, was merely an excuse for going in; the required tools—trowels, shovels, smaller buckets for doling out water from the bigger ones—were already there with the rest of the equipment.

But once they got inside, Bella would urge lunch on them, which was Ellie's real plan; not only was she hungry herself, but she took her friend-care responsibilities seriously.

Jake smiled. "Okay," she agreed, putting down her shovel. But just then Wade drove into the driveway.

He didn't look happy. A needle of alarm pierced her. "What's the matter?" she asked anxiously.

"Nothing." He crossed the yard and put an arm around her. "I heard from a few people, that's all."

She followed him to the back porch. "Wade, you told, didn't you? You put the word out about Steven Garner, and—"

"Hey, it never hurts to have your folks know you might need them to watch your back."

"So? Did somebody find out something . . . ?"

Bad, her mind finished grimly. Wade paused at the door. "No. Well, not exactly. But I called a few guys and they called a few guys."

When Wade called his buddies, it was like casting a fishnet. It always caught something.

Not always something good. "Gave them a description of your pal."

Jake nodded eagerly. "And?"

"And nobody's seen hide nor hair of him. Well," he amended, "downtown last night, one guy said he might've seen somebody like that nearly getting pounded by a few hooligans. But he didn't see him up close, and Bob Arnold broke it up before it could turn into anything. And after that—nothing."

He held the door open for her. Inside, the kale soup aroma was warmly comforting. "The state cops are here, by the way," he added. "They still think the girl on Sea Street was accidental."

A sound from the street cut him off, one bright, sharp brring! A bike bell . . . the too-familiar sound revived her earlier feeling of being watched; turning to the door, she scanned up and down the sunlight-flooded street.

On it, though, there was no sign of any bike or rider; if it had been him, Steven Garner Jr. was gone.

But in her heart, she knew now that he would be back.

She didn't want to talk about it. But she had no choice. A blast from the past was here, and she could either warn them about it or not.

"Listen up, everyone," she said when she had gotten them all gathered around the dining room table.

Bella served the soup, accompanied by hot, crusty sourdough rolls and glasses of sparkling apple juice made from the windfalls she and Jake had collected the previous autumn. Then she sat, too.

"What's happened?" she asked, clasping her large, bony hands anxiously together.

"I'll tell you," said Jake reluctantly. "Right now I'm going to tell you all about it."

Wade knew her history, of course, and her dad did, too. But the others didn't; she'd never wanted them to.

"Eat some of your soup first," Ellie said kindly. So she did, hoping it would give her strength. Then she began:

"Back in the city, I was a complete jerk."

Bella's bony face took on a rebellious look. "No," Jake told her stepmother, "let me finish."

She looked around at the others. Sam, especially, was not going to like this.

"See, I was a money manager. Freelance. An advisor to the rich and loathsome," she added with a crooked smile.

She'd also been (1) married to a brain surgeon who thought that fidelity was only the name of a large investment firm, and (2) the mother of a boy who at age twelve was so worldly-wise, he already had his very own stash box, stocked with his own marijuana and rolling papers.

But never mind that now. "Sam and his father and I lived in a co-op building so exclusive, even the pets had trust funds."

She paused, took another spoonful of soup. Her neighbors in the city had regarded the smell of cash as aromatherapy, and she'd been no different.

At first. "So on the plus side, we had plenty of money," she said. "But on the minus side, some of it was dirty, because some of my clients were so crooked, their limos should've been fitted with machine-gun turrets."

And though she'd tried to ignore this fact about them, in the end, she couldn't. After a while it had gotten so bad that she couldn't buy a Ferrari, a new pair of Jimmy Choos, or a baby grand piano for the apartment where no one ever played so much as "Chopsticks," without seeing a body in a car trunk or a forehead with an icepick in it, through the lens of her mind's eye.

"So eventually I gave it all up." Not soon enough, she added mentally as around the table, they all listened with interest.

Again she was tempted to mention a certain philandering brain surgeon, so chronically unfaithful to her that his nickname around the hospital was Vlad the Impaler.

But that was no excuse. Besides, it would be unkind to Sam. "Just before I did, though, I got a visit from a fellow I knew."

Once, Steven Garner Sr. had been a regular client of the loan sharks in a certain New York crime family, one whose cohorts included guys with colorful nicknames like Sticksy and Bones.

Not to mention Jerry "Da Bomb" Baumann. But by the time Garner came to her office, he was out of favor with his preferred lenders, on account of being too fond of dogs and horses.

"Specifically, ones he could bet on," she continued.

"He owed so much money and repaid so little of it, he'd put his pals in an impossible position.

"If they killed him, as they were threatening to do, they'd never get their money back. But if they didn't, they would never get any back from anyone else, because no one would be scared of them anymore."

"Wow," said Sam. He'd never heard any of this before. "So then what'd they do?"

She smiled at him. You poor kid, it's no wonder you got so messed up.

She replied, "They decided to cut their losses. If he didn't have fifty grand by the next day, he was guaranteed a spot in the nearest landfill."

So his pitch to her had been simple. No promises, no guarantee of a payback. She went on with her story. "A guy like that, you had to admire him. Just 'Lend me the money, or they'll kill me.'"

"And they were your clients?" Ellie asked. "The men who were threatening to kill him?"

She was trying to sound nonjudgmental, but Jake could tell she was a little shocked. Who wouldn't be?

"No, not those guys." Fellows with names like Sticksy and Bones had never darkened her door; even Da Bomb had found it only by following Garner, probably.

"But their bosses were, some of them." The higher-up men in politics, banking, and law . . . the power, in other words, behind the cashmere-coated thugs everyone else thought headed organized crime in the city back then.

To them, Jake's unlucky visitor was just so much

machine-gun fodder. They'd have him killed in the afternoon and eat dinner heartily with their families that night as usual, because when you were in their line of work, sooner or later you had to make an example of someone.

Still, she wasn't a fool, and she wasn't about to hand over fifty grand on the strength of a sob story. "So I refused." She finished the tale, looking around at the faces staring wide-eyed at her over their soup bowls.

"Wow," breathed Sam again. "I never knew you'd worked with such serious . . ."

Criminals. The kinds of guys who would kill you as soon as look at you. Not that she'd seen it that way at the time.

But back then, she hadn't really looked at it very much at all, had she? She'd kept her own eyes conveniently averted from what she'd done, whom she'd done it for . . .

"Yeah, well," she said inadequately. "It's not something I'm proud of. When your dad died . . ."

In a cruel irony, Sam's father, Victor, had succumbed to the kind of brain tumor he'd spent his life saving other people from getting demolished by.

". . . I did an accounting of all our money," she went on. "His and mine, and whatever came from crooks, as best I could figure, I donated to a victims' rights organization."

Which had hurt more than the fifty grand would have, not that it had set things right. It didn't even begin to wipe out all the harm she'd done. And it didn't make her feel any better now, either.

What she had been back then was the dark place in her soul, and she would never really be able to make up for it. Even now, she still had nightmares about it. And in one of them, a guy with big ears and a really bad gambling habit asked her for money.

Worse, he'd brought his son along, probably hoping that the sight of the kid might persuade her. A little kid with ears just like his dad's . . .

"So then what happened?" Ellie asked. "After you didn't give him the money he wanted?"

Jake tried to reply and couldn't, as more of the awful memory poured in. The kid, looking over his shoulder so reproachfully at her. But that wasn't all she had seen in his eyes—not by a long shot.

She just hadn't let herself know it back then. She took a deep breath, let it out.

"I don't know for sure. I never heard from him again, I know that much. He wasn't the kind of guy whose death would make the papers. Especially if—"

She stopped. She'd thought enough time had passed so she could stop glancing over her own shoulder.

Wrong. She cleared her throat. "Especially if no one ever found the body," she finished. "But there was a photograph that got sent around not much later, of a guy tied to a chair."

She'd never seen it, not back then. The story was, though, that the postmortem photograph of Garner had even been sent to his wife.

Her husband, murdered and tied to a chair . . . Just to make sure, according to the story, that other late borrowers got the message: Pay up, or your family will suffer, also.

"And then we moved here," said Sam. Her son was looking at her with an expression of horrified sympathy in his eyes, worse even than if he blamed her.

Bella, too, and Ellie. I don't deserve any of you, Jake thought as the silence at the table lengthened, everyone trying unsuccessfully to think of something to say to her that might make her feel better. Then:

"Look," said Wade, spreading his hands on the table. "First of all, the guy's debt wasn't your fault. Fifty thousand? You'd have to have been nuts. And second, maybe this guy just wants to scare you, harass you, you know. As a kind of punishment."

"No." Everyone turned as Jake's dad finally spoke.

With his long gray hair tied back in a leather thong and his faded bib overalls pulled up over a red, many-times-laundered flannel shirt, Jacob resembled a living relic from the peace-and-love sixties.

But instead of patchouli oil and flower power, his Summer of Love had featured revolutionary manifestos cranked out on a mimeograph machine in a Greenwich Village basement, plus plenty of black powder and fuse cord. For a while, whenever a protest got capped off by a spectacular but harmless explosion, he was who the cops had started looking for.

Then Jake's mother had been murdered and he'd had to go on the run for real, and Jake hadn't seen him for thirty years.

"This fellow means it," he said now. "He's not kidding."

"How do you know?" It was the last thing she wanted to hear. Yet his saying it was oddly comfort-

ing because it echoed what she already knew somehow.

He looked levelly at her. He hadn't murdered her
mother, but she hadn't known that for thirty years,
either.

"One"—he held up a finger—"he came all this way
after all this time."

He had a point. "And two, that rat?" he went on.
"That came in the cracker box?" He'd taken charge
of disposing of the hideous thing. "It had this in its
throat."

It was a small, rolled-up piece of paper. When he
unrolled it, she saw that it had writing on it: DeAd-
DEaDdeADdEaD.

"Oh," Jake said weakly. The note didn't mean anything, it didn't even make sense, she told herself. But
the message was clear.

"You know what? He's scaring me now. He's really
scaring me."

"Yeah. Because how many people can you think of
who would do this?" her dad said. He put the rolled
paper back in his pocket. "About time we started taking this guy a little more seriously."

"I'll take him serious," Bella muttered darkly. Her
scowl warmed Jake's heart.

"So you think he really wants to hurt me, or . . ."

Worse, she didn't quite add out loud, but everyone
heard it. Her dad didn't mince words.

"Yes, I do. And I think it was the motive last night,
the girl on Sea Street."

"Oh, no—" Bella began sorrowfully, but Jacob cut
her off.

"I think he did it, even if the cops don't. To put fear in your heart the way he thinks you put it in his old man's. And . . ."

"But isn't that taking an awfully big risk?" Wade objected. "Kill someone? Just to scare somebody else?"

He looked around at the others for agreement. "I mean," he said, "in addition to the whole huge thing of just being able to kill someone at all. Human-being-wise."

"On top of which," Ellie agreed, "that would make Jake more cautious, wouldn't it? So it'd be counterproductive if his plan was really to do something to her."

But Jake's dad just shook his head again. "Doesn't matter. Point is, getting her nerves jangled, raising her suspicions—it makes it all more fun, increases the challenge for him."

He spoke sympathetically, but he wasn't about to sugarcoat it. "That's what he wants. I knew guys back in the city. . . ."

He poured black coffee, the pot's syrupy dregs, and drank some, over Bella's protests.

"Some of them were flat-out nuts. They'd get an idea, then things took on a life of their own. And then, of course, there's what Wade said, the whole idea of murder."

He looked at Jake, his eyes steady. "Because if he's never done it before, and he's set on doing it to you . . ."

She got it, chillingly. "A rehearsal."

"Good heavens," gasped Ellie. But when she met

Jake's glance, it was in her eyes that she felt it also: that it could be true.

Crazy, maybe. Utterly beyond the realm of normal behavior or thinking. But on a gut level . . .

Down deep, it made sense: crime and punishment. Her crimes, which she'd foolishly thought she could leave behind and forget . . .

Now, after all this time, someone had finally shown up to say otherwise. Wade rose from the table.

"It still seems like a stretch. But if it is all connected and some scumbag's got Jake in his sights . . ."

He grabbed his jacket from where he'd hung it on the back of his chair, ready to go out right now and end the threat to her.

"I'm coming, too," said Sam, getting up as well.

"No." The word hung in the air; surprised, they all looked at her. "You won't find him."

Sam and Wade looked mutinous, the rest confused. Bella spoke up. "But he has to be in town here somewhere. So why can't they just hunt for him until they—"

"Because there's one thing you don't know about him," said Jake. "One specific thing. But I do."

She went to the window. "Like I said, his dad wasn't a mob guy himself, but he knew them," she said.

"And more important, they knew him. His habits, his talents, and so on. And once in a while, they'd hire him to do a specific job for them."

She looked around the room. "Hideouts. He knew how to pick one, use its strengths, minimize its weaknesses."

Wade nodded silently, beginning to understand, as she continued. "He could figure out how to get in and out of almost anywhere without being noticed, what to bring along so a man wouldn't have to leave for a while if he didn't want to."

"You think your guy picked up tips from his father?" Wade wanted to know. "And . . . Jake, you're really sure it's him? From what you've said, he was just a young kid when you last saw him."

Regretfully, she shook her head. "I'd have known him sooner if I hadn't been trying to bury the memory all this time."

Sam sat again. "As for his dad's skills," Jake went on, "even on a holiday weekend with everyone in town, I don't think anyone could hide out for very long in Eastport without them. Wade, you said yourself your pals had their eyes peeled for him earlier."

He conceded her point with a nod.

"He might be gone by now," Bella suggested. But a downturn at the corners of her big green eyes said she knew that was an unlikely hope, too.

"His dad once hid a fugitive from justice for six months," said Jake, "right under the noses of the federal marshals and the guy's own crew, who wanted to kill him before the marshals could get him and persuade him to betray them."

"Really?" said Sam, fascinated. "Then what happened?"

"Nothing you need to know," Jake replied. Bloody outcomes, unfortunately, were the norm when it came to those guys and their stories.

"Aw, Mom," Sam protested. But like the others, he understood now that the danger was real.

And that she'd brought it upon them all. "Okay, then," Ellie said briskly, breaking the spell as she got up and began clearing the table with quick, sharp movements.

"You need to go find Bob Arnold again," she told Jake. "Give him that paper and tell him what you told us. I know, it all sounds nuts." She clattered soup bowls into the sink. "But I guess it's not. Bob needs to know."

About Steven Garner, his son, and what she'd done all those years ago. Or not done.

"Okay," Jake said reluctantly, hating the thought. "But after that," she added, "I'm coming back here, and all of you are going to help come up with a plan to trap this guy."

Grabbing a sweater, for the sky had begun thickening with a thin afternoon fog, she waited while Sam went upstairs to get his own jacket.

Meanwhile, Bella wiped the kitchen counters, even though they were already so clean brain surgery could've been done on them, while Wade and her dad went off to talk it all over between themselves.

Ellie put her dishcloth down. "Jake, are you going to be all right? George will be fine with Lee for the afternoon, so if you wanted me to stay, I could. . . ."

Jake managed a smile. "Thanks. But you go on home now. I'll need you later."

To help put the plan together, she didn't finish, and talk the rest of them into it, too. Because they loved her, and wanted her safe.

But trapping Steven Garner was the only way to guarantee her safety or theirs, now.

And traps . . . well, traps needed bait.

At just after noon, Steven Garner pedaled out County Road on the rental bike. Despite little sleep and having consumed only a few crackers, canned peas, and some juice recently—he didn't count the junky stuff he'd eaten as actual food—he felt great.

Terrific, actually. With ears carefully re-glued, a ball cap on his head, and sunglasses on his face, he had no fear of being recognized; amid the throngs crowding the island this weekend, he looked like any other average Joe out for a ride.

And the dead rat in the box, not to mention the message in it, had been a stroke of genius, with another ride past her house ringing the bike bell only hammering the message home:

That he was in charge. That he could do anything he wanted and get away with it.

He grinned, turning his face to the sun. His plan, more than a dozen years in the making, was about to come to fruition, and with it, his old life to an end. . . .

What he might do next, he hadn't decided. But he'd done a bit of online research into the Philippines, which he thought he might enjoy. They were crazy about computers and gambling there; with his electronic expertise and knowledge of sports wagering, he felt confident he'd find a niche for himself.

Imagining this, he coasted down a long hill leading back into the center of Eastport, between rows of neat, white wooden houses with crisply mowed green lawns and black-mulched flower beds brilliant with summer blooms.

Cars lined both sides of each street now, and from every direction couples and little groups streamed toward the downtown festivities. Slowing, he hid among them, sometimes walking the bike and sometimes riding, just another tourist on a Maine island with nothing in mind but to watch a parade, see some fireworks tonight.

When he reached the abandoned house on Washington Street, he slid the bicycle among some overgrown bushes, just as before, and waited until the coast was clear before slipping through the yard to the broken back door.

Inside, dusty light slanted through gaps in the trash-bag window shades he'd fashioned. As he'd expected, once the sun was past its zenith he spied all the spots that needed patching, tiny untaped areas and flaws in the bags' plastic.

A feeling of urgency seized him at the sight, because it was crucial that no gleam manage to betray him tonight. Pulling the roll of duct tape from his pack, he moved methodically from window to window, bag to black plastic bag, sticking bits of tape onto the bright places until each tiny light leak was abolished and the room stood in darkness.

Next, now that the windows were shrouded, he turned to the lighting scheme he'd planned for the inside of the house, since once he had her here, he would need to be able to see her.

In his mind's eye, he envisioned it now: Her body,

secured to the old wooden chair with the same tape he'd used to patch the trash bags at the windows.

Her mouth, tightly covered over, too. And her eyes, taped shut only for as long as he wished to remain unseen by her. Until at last—

This part he'd imagined a thousand times. . . .

At last, he would reveal himself by the light of the many candles he was distributing around the room now, a hundred fires he would ignite so the shadows danced as the flames flickered—

Two on a counter, three on the floor, everywhere more of the tall, white tapers until the room itself was like a candelabra bristling with waxy stalks, their sweet scent floating in the still, warm air.

He tested the lighter he'd brought with him; it hissed once and ignited. Good. He placed it in the wrecked sink, where he would be able to find it even in the dark.

The candles would be atmospheric; gaslights, he thought, would be even better, and from the small, round holes in what still remained of the plaster, he knew there had once been some here.

Even the threaded ends of the copper piping still protruded from a few of them, and there was a tank in the yard whose gauge he'd examined, discovering that it was even now partially full.

A home owner or tenant had put it there years ago, no doubt, and by some oversight no one had ever removed it.

Experimentally he turned the knob on the wretched old stove. A hiss and the reek of rotten eggs said that the flammable stuff still flowed. But he doubted the gas fittings in the walls were still connected, and anyway, there weren't any gas lamps in the house.

Too bad; they'd have been an interesting touch. He turned off the stove knob, noting by his wristwatch that it was already nearly one o'clock. That meant Jacobia Tiptree's last morning on this earth had drawn to a close; now it was afternoon, and in only about seven hours night would fall.

Then it would be dark in here.

That is, until he lit the candles, and by their flickering, elemental glow he would do what he'd come to do. Afterwards he would live in triumph, having avenged all. And then . . .

Well, then he'd need something else to occupy himself. But there was a whole world full of people to wreak vengeance upon, wasn't there?

So maybe he wouldn't go to the Philippines right away. Once Jacobia Tiptree was gone, he felt certain he'd be able to think of someone else who needed attention in the getting-what-they-deserved department.

And he—cold, perfectly unfeeling, and experienced in these matters—

He'd be the man for the job.

Chapter 6

> *Try repairing a noisy refrigerator*
> *by tightening the bolt that secures*
> *the condensation tray (often*
> *located at the lower rear of the*
> *appliance).*
> —Tiptree's Tips

Talking to Eastport's Chief of Police, Bob Arnold, was easy. But convincing him wasn't.

"You think he's on a vendetta," Bob said flatly, leaning back in the chair behind his desk in the police station.

"Exactly," said Jake.

It was one thirty in the afternoon. The state cops and the medical examiner were already on their way back to their armory in Machias and laboratories in Augusta, respectively.

The bruised and bloodied dead girl on Sea Street, they'd decided, was an accident victim; for one thing, it was simpler and easier on the family than calling her death a suicide, which was the other option. No evidence of anything else, they'd said.

"For vengeance," Bob said. "Thinks you as good as killed his old man. So now he's come here to do the same to you."

"Precisely," she responded, encouraged that he understood so well. "You've got it completely right."

"You know this because he emailed you a picture that could have been faked."

"And a dead rat," she added. "Don't forget that."

"And a dead rat," he agreed drily. "Don't worry, I'm not forgetting it."

Bob was a good friend, one who'd pulled Jake's feet out of a few fires over the years, when her nosiness and stubbornness had gotten her and Ellie into . . . situations.

Deadly ones, some of them, punctuated by screaming, gunfire, or (to Jake) intensely nerve-racking combinations of the two.

And she'd very much like to prevent that kind of thing from happening again; to rule it out completely, that is, instead of trusting what was turning out to be a rather thin patch of luck at the moment. But her story was too weak, the evidence too thin. . . .

"And you think," Bob said, "that just for starters

I'm going to get the medical examiner and the state boys to change their determination on the girl's cause of death, based on your story."

"Um, well . . ."

"A dozen people saw her staggering drunk last night. A dozen more saw her wandering away. Alone," he emphasized.

"It's dark back there," she pointed out. "Someone else could have showed up. And anyway, I'm not asking you to—"

"You heard me requesting five officers for today. You stood right there and listened to me doing it. Well, I got them."

"Great! Then you might have a little time to—"

But there she stopped, because the truth was, she didn't know what she wanted him to do. She hadn't even come in here to ask him to do anything; it was Bob who'd assumed she had.

"Look, all I'm saying is—"

Ignoring her, Bob motioned as if he was talking on the phone, which for a wonder did not happen to be ringing for once.

"Why, yes, Mr. State Cop Murder Investigator. I've got a lady here, she says that your earlier conclusions were all wrong. Yep, she says a weird guy on a bike did it, and she knows 'cause she used to be money manager to the mob."

"Not only to the mob," she replied, stung. "I had my share of perfectly legitimate clients."

By some definitions, anyway. But Bob looked unmoved. "Okay, okay," she said, giving in. "I just wanted you to hear it from me, what happened at my house. And my thinking on it."

"Great," Bob said tiredly. "Now I know your thinking." But then his tone changed.

"Jake. I'm listening, okay? But what you're telling me, it might be annoying. Scary, even. And I get that, I really do. But none of what you could actually swear to—what you know, not just what you surmise—rises much above the level of mischief."

"Except the computer stuff." Her laptop sat on his desk; a call was already in to the Portland computer crimes division.

"Correct." He'd written down all the other incidents she'd told him about, too: the harassment on the front porch, the rat, the bike-bell tauntings.

And he was right, when you listed them all like that on paper, they didn't look like much. "So what am I going to do," he asked, "start a house-to-house for the guy?"

"No," she replied, softening. "No, I guess not."

Bob always did what he could.

"It's just that if anything else happens, I don't want you to say later that I didn't . . ." she continued.

His rosebud lips pursed. "Yeah. Like that's ever helped me before, knowing in advance what you're up to. But believe me, Jake, I really wil—"

Then his phone did ring; waving her away, he answered. On her way out she heard him talking to the Bangor *News* stringer, supplying the details about the "accident on Sea Street."

He really was a good guy, though, she thought as she went out the big glass door of the old bank building, and as she reached the sidewalk she realized that after talking to him, she actually felt better.

Just not a lot better. The only way to achieve that was to find Steven Garner . . . and stop him. Fortunately, though, Bob was not only a good guy; he also had good ideas, even if he himself didn't always see their brilliance right off the bat.

On the way back up Key Street, sniffing the delicious smells of backyard barbecues getting under way and hearing the slightly hysterical laughter of children galloping through games of tag, she counted in her head the number of vacant houses in town.

After dwindling for years, Eastport had been undergoing some repopulation recently, mostly by retirees with plenty of cash and a long-cherished dream of living year-round, or at least all summer, in a place like this. Thus many of the architecturally lovely, structurally tragic old dwellings had owners now, people who paid the taxes and had the lights turned on and the water connected.

That is, if they weren't being torn down to make way for new, easier-to-maintain homes; the latest in demolition methods some newcomers were trying was to cut all the big beams in an old house, leaving it standing on the strength of the equivalent of a couple of toothpicks. Then they'd hit the place with a bulldozer.

Which was not a method she endorsed; for one thing, it was dangerous as hell, since you couldn't guarantee a house standing on toothpicks would even wait for the bulldozer before it fell.

A few of the town's worst old structures, though,

weren't even getting that unorthodox shock treatment. Instead they still had bats in their belfries, not to mention squirrels in the eaves and rats in the cellars. The squirrels were the worst, old-house-maintenance-wise. . . .

But never mind; the point was there were a finite number of untenanted old places in Eastport, especially now when the fair-weather visitors were so numerous that permanent residents called them "summer complaint."

And that meant a finite number of possible hiding places for Steven Garner Jr., ones that could be identified, located, and inspected, she thought optimistically as she climbed the back steps of her own old house.

Too optimistically, as it turned out. Like, by orders of magnitude. But just then, all she thought was that maybe this all could be cleared up before the fireworks began tonight.

And then she'd really have something to celebrate. "Hey, everybody," she called as she went in.

They were all in the kitchen, even the dogs. Prill ran up to her, stubby tail wagging; Monday smiled from her dog bed.

"Bob Arnold said something very interesting just now," Jake announced. House to house . . .

"And it gave me an idea. . . . All of you, listen to this!"

It wasn't so much that they were stupid, Steven thought as he watched people streaming purposefully out of Jake Tiptree's house, but that they were so un-imaginative. Didn't they realize he'd have figured out that they might start looking for him? And now here they came, right on schedule. . . .

He'd climbed to the ancient tree house high in the maple, in the overgrown backyard of the vacant old house on Washington Street. From here, he could see half the town.

More to the point, he could see her house. But she couldn't see him; no one could. The maple leaves hid him.

Climbing up here at all had been worrisome, first because while he was doing it, people could see. While he'd been hand-over-handing it up the rickety plank rungs, he'd been terrified, just waiting for someone down on the ground to yell out suddenly at him.

And then, as his father used to say—his dead father, his murdered one—the jig would be up. But no one had yelled, and soon he'd begun to understand that nobody was going to.

So he was safe. No one was at home in the houses bordering the yard where the maple stood. He could see right into all of their windows from where he perched, and it was obvious: nothing moving any-where inside.

On this beautiful early July day, they were out en-joying the weather and the celebration. Music drifted up from Water Street, along with the occasional ran-dom toot of a trumpet or rattle of a snare drum. The parade was about to begin, he gathered from the ex-pectant tone in the voices of people now lining both sides of Washington Street.

Which was perfect: they were all out front, while he was out here keeping an eye on things. On her.

Ms. Tiptree, he thought, mentally giving the honorific an unpleasant twist. She thought she was so smart. But if she had been, she'd have realized he was already a step ahead of her.

At least a step. All those people charging out of her place, six of them, including her . . . What could they all be doing, looking so determined, besides setting out on a search for him?

A child could've predicted it. And the tragedy was, it all could have been prevented. First by her giving the money to his father all those years ago . . .

Thinking this made his gut knot, his lips twisting back in a snarl of mingled pain and fury and his fingers tightening on the maple's rough bark. If she had . . .

But she hadn't; that part was over and done with. He broke off his thought to watch one of her helpers. The son, it looked like, walked up to an empty house a few doors from her own.

Steven pulled his digital camera from his jacket pocket and aimed it. The zoom lens was powerful; he'd purchased the camera with just such a capability in mind, not just close-up but truly telescopic. After firing off a few shots—he needed it only to be recognizable, not perfect, to serve the purpose he had planned for it—he tucked the camera away again, chuckling.

He settled more comfortably on the tree-house platform, then snapped to attention. There she was, coming out of the house after all the rest had gone on ahead.

His eyes felt suddenly like the ray guns from the comic books his father used to buy and sneak into the house for him so his mother wouldn't see. Eyes shooting death rays . . . If he could have frizzled her to a smoking wisp where she stood, he would've.

But he couldn't, of course, and the memory of his mother's outraged shriek when she'd found the comics didn't help his state of mind, either. Shakily he started down the tree.

Then halfway to the ground, it hit him how dirty it was. Insects, birds, spiders . . . Who knew whether they or the invisible vermin infesting them carried disgusting diseases?

Probably they did. Touching the ground at last, he ran to the house, grateful for the screen of shrubbery and feeling all at once as if he must surely be crawling with filth.

For a while there, he'd thought the events of last night had freed him. But no . . . probably he'd be counting the peas he ate again tonight, too.

At the moment, though, the nastiness cloaking him left no room in his head for that. Inside, in the silent gloom of the old kitchen, he scrubbed himself: arms, legs, hands, feet. . . .

Everywhere. Finished, he rinsed his mouth thoroughly with a thin mixture of water and the ancient, pearlescent green dish soap in the plastic bottle on the sink.

Bar soap would've been better. More traditional, he thought with a pained smile, for even now he was not completely without a sense of humor about his own situation.

Bar soap was what his mother had used on him, inside and out. But in the end the taste of the dish soap was so nauseating, he figured it must have gotten the job done at least as well as she could have.

After all, he recited to himself once his stomach settled enough so he could think again, it's the thought that counts.

And now it was past two o'clock. Time to get a move on; luckily, he was already undressed. Also fortunate was the fact that there were hardly any raw, bloody places on his skin, though he stung all over as if he'd been dipped in acid.

The wipes, he'd gathered from the writing on the container of them, were intended for counters and stovetops, not humans. But hey, he told himself, feeling lighthearted after the rub-a-dub session, we do what we can with what we have.

Thinking this, he began putting on the garments he'd brought along for the next phase of the operation:

His mother's second-best dress, the deep purple one with the long sleeves and plain, not-quite-straight skirt. He'd chosen it because he could walk in the shoes that went with it, dyed, low-heeled purple pumps in soft, flexible Italian leather.

Fortunately, his mother's feet had been quite large. Like her hands. The better to swat you with, you little . . .

He shut off the thought—it was always a lot easier

to do that after a good scrubbing, he'd found—then returned to the task of costume assembly.

Under the dress, he'd put on an old undershirt of his own, the cotton thinned and softened by frequent washings until it was like silk. It didn't show through the bodice of the outfit, and the skirt was lined so he needn't bother about that, either.

Stockings, though. He'd bought a pair of panty-hose in the supermarket at home, tossing them casually into his cart as if he bought them all the time, when in reality his heart had pounded.

What if somebody notices? he'd thought as he waited in line. A man buying pantyhose . . . maybe he wanted them for a disguise. Or so the cashier might think, and she might mention it to a friend.

Or the friend of a friend, and one of them might be a cop. A suspicious cop, who might even have followed Steven all the way here to Eastport, and right now . . .

Shut up, shut up, he ordered himself fiercely as he yanked and tugged at the pantyhose. He was sweating now, and it was hard to get these things on, the mesh pulling the hairs on his legs the wrong way and the pants part seeming to stop mid-thigh. He didn't need some crazy person in his head providing a running commentary.

A paranoid running commentary, because no one knew he was here. No one but her—and her few friends and relations, none of whom were any match for him—and that only made it better.

More rewarding, because the knowledge frightened her. But it didn't help her. Nothing could, now.

Nothing at all. Working the stretchy fabric inch by inch, he got the stockings' waistband up around his middle at last, and by tugging repeatedly at the foot and leg parts got them arranged so that it might actually stay there.

Finally he bent to his pack to retrieve the one item that made the rest of the disguise work. No need to glue his ears back this time. And not much makeup needed, either; his beard was so skimpy, he could go for days without shaving.

Carefully he lifted the thing, pulled the tissue paper from inside it. The sharp scent of mothballs mingled with a whiff of Shalimar made his eyes water and his gut clench suddenly.

Her scent . . . as if summoned by an evil spell, his mother rose before him. Boy! Answer me! What are you doing in there? Are you getting into my things?

Then came the clipped, sharp rap of her steps in the hall, a sound he'd learned to dread; just thinking of it now brought the taste of a bar of Lifebuoy back into his mouth, gaggingly.

Oh, you'd better not be. She'd grate it out at him, drink in hand. The ice would tinkle as she marched toward him.

You bad, bad, boy.

"Shut up," he whispered, dropping the thing he'd held.

Or had it squirmed from his hands? The nearly overwhelming impulse to begin washing again flooded him, to scrub and scrub until . . .

"Just shut up, now. Or . . . I'll tell Dad."

The vicious monologue cut off abruptly. Her

ghostly presence shrank to a wink and vanished. Threatening to tell his father had always worked back when she was alive, too.

And when his father was alive. Afterwards, though . . .

Swallowing a sob, he straightened himself in the dress and stockings, picked up the purse that went with the outfit. He had not imagined that of all the tasks in his plan, this was the one that would be so . . .

Hard. But he was fine, he told himself; ordered himself to be, really. He could work with this, walk in the shoes, manage to keep the pantyhose from sliding off his middle, somehow.

So that the only thing left now for him to put on was . . .

Try it, boy. Just try it, and see what happens. You little loser, you little worm—

All snarled at him in a drunken slur. But for now, the spell was broken.

"Shut up, Ma." He lifted the thing he'd dropped.

She couldn't stop him. Couldn't do anything to him. He moved the thing toward his face, breathed again the old, mingled smells of mothballs and Shalimar.

He couldn't decide which fragrance he found more evocative, the sweet or the deathlike. Could not in fact decide with any real precision which was which. With trembling hands, he placed the thing he held very carefully onto his own head.

It was a gray, professionally styled wig, made from his mother's own hair, which she'd cut for the first time in her life on the day the men came to tell her that Steven's father was dead.

After they'd departed, she'd gone straight to the utility drawer in the kitchen and gotten out the sharp scissors. Steven recalled feeling relieved even through his grief when he saw what she was doing.

Half relieved, anyway, he thought as, placing a small hat atop the wig and pinning it there with a hat pin, then tucking the camera into the purse he carried, he stepped out of the abandoned house on Washington Street. That mass of his mother's long, wavy gray hair falling to the floor, her wild, incoherent weeping as she'd hacked at it . . .

Still, at least she hadn't been going for the scissors to use on him. His childish relief hadn't lasted very long, though. Because with his dad dead, young Steven had been alone with her, no one around to intervene. And then the real horror had begun. . . .

Squelching the thought, he stopped at the door. What was he forgetting? Then he remembered; quickly he drew out the camera again, popped the card from its slot and then into his laptop's card reader. After uploading the photograph he'd taken from his perch in the backyard tree house to his computer, he revisited the local library's website once more.

With just a couple of taps on the keyboard, he emailed the photograph to the library, specifying by marking a check box that he would visit the library to print it out himself, so prying eyes would be less likely to view it.

Amazing, what you could do with technology nowadays . . . He grinned, thinking this. Now, though, he must hurry. This part was a bit tricky, and the timing was tight.

But he loved it, he absolutely . . . Outside, the sunlight was bright even through the thin fog covering the island. Wincing, he put his sunglasses back on.

Touching the wig to make sure it was straight, he began walking in the general direction he'd seen Jacobia Tiptree headed. The pantyhose chafed uncomfortably and the shoes pinched his feet like torture devices; still, he smiled as he proceeded, barely able to hide his euphoric glee.

She wanted to find something. He was about to make sure that she would. And when she did, he wanted to be there.

Watching, until his waiting was over at last.

"Hey." Jake stopped dead in the middle of the sidewalk. She had remembered something, and now she couldn't unremember it.

"That concrete we said we'd mix." Overhead, the sky grew steadily milkier; to the south, a cloud bank lay on the horizon.

Motionless, or so it seemed from here. But out on the chilly ocean, things were lively indeed, she knew: warm air rolling east off the sun-heated land, an offshore summer breeze in full force skimming the cold wave tops.

When that happened, the air cooled. The water vapor quickly condensed. The result:

"Fog," said Ellie, following Jake's gesture. "Oh, darn," she added. "I hope it doesn't . . ."

"Rain," Jake finished grimly. "If it doesn't hold off, it'll drown out the fireworks tonight. But from the look of it . . ."

As they watched, the cloud bank seemed to thicken and grow taller, like a muscle bulking up. Right now, it was still far out over what Sam liked to call the briny deep.

But it wouldn't be for much longer, and they'd left all the cement, sand, tools, and the mixing trough, too, uncovered in the backyard; annoyed with herself, Jake pointed this out.

"Drat," said Ellie, looking reluctant. There was no help for it, though; that cement mix couldn't be allowed to get wet, and a tarp over the whole project wouldn't help matters at all.

"Double drat," Jake agreed as they turned back toward the house. "How inconvenient is this?"

Rain or even just a thick fog wouldn't only ruin the cement bag they'd opened; in addition, it would turn the remaining bags to solid, utterly unusable objects that were also so heavy, it would take a block and tackle—or several large men, none of whom they'd wanted to enlist any further in the project—to move the ruined bags to the bed of the pickup truck.

And thereafter, to the dump. "Oh, let's just mix the stuff," said Ellie resignedly when they reached the yard. Which did make some sense; even the hose was still turned on, not even leaking.

Which was the saving grace of the whole operation, thought Jake. But just then a tiny fountain began spurting near the hose nozzle, its spray creating a tiny rainbow.

She stifled a curse. "All right," she allowed grouchily. "I should have my amateur home-repair license taken away, you know that? What was I thinking of, leaving all this—"

Because the absolute first rule of home fix-up was Finish What You Start, and the second rule was Put Stuff Away.

Behind the fountain, a wisp of breeze caught the corner of the open bag, sending a gray-white puff swirling up. The hose leak's spray caught it and spattered the result onto the grass.

"I guess we'd better just do it," she went on, "before the weather decides to mix this stuff up for us and then the rain comes and slops it all over the tarp."

At least the firs and the low, red-fruited barberry bushes around the edges of the yard lent privacy. But as she shoveled sand from the garden cart into the mixing trough, Jake glanced uneasily up at the pointed trees.

"Oh, come on," said Ellie, understanding Jake's unease. "You don't really think . . ."

"That he's up there? No." Jake ran water into the trough. This was the tricky part, adding enough water but not too much.

"Not in the trees, anyway. But I still feel . . . watched."

Using a trowel, she stirred the water, sand, and cement mix experimentally in the trough, then added a little more water.

"Nerves," Ellie diagnosed. "You know he's around here, and not knowing exactly where makes you feel he could be anywhere."

"Or everywhere," Jake agreed, looking up once more. The only things in the trees were a couple of accidentally released small balloons and a flock of enthusiastically cheeping purple finches.

From downtown came a blare of patriotic music played through a loudspeaker, followed by the revving of engines that signaled the imminent start of the parade. Jake stirred harder.

"Maybe one of the others will find Steven Garner while we're doing this," Ellie said hopefully. But then, "Um. Jake?"

Never a good sign. "What?" Jake snapped a little more tartly than she'd intended; her mood was deteriorating rapidly.

"Well," Ellie responded mildly, "not to be nitpicky. The thing is, though, we're mixing concrete here. But the forms"—she pointed at the wooden boxes that the concrete was to be poured into—"are over there."

Oh, blast and damnation.

"And we can't just pick the forms up and move them," Ellie went on, her forehead furrowing as she worked it out in her head, "because . . ."

Because the forms had to be level. Otherwise, as Jake had figured out and carefully allowed for earlier by placing a level on them, the blocks that came out of them wouldn't be square.

And now . . . now the concrete had been mixed and was already beginning to set. Much longer and it would be too thick to pour.

Or in this case, shovel; the trough was too heavy to

lift. So it was too late to move the forms now. Or . . . was it?

"Okay, just wait here a minute," said Jake, crossing the yard hastily.

Grabbing up the forms, the shingle pieces they'd used for shims beneath them, the eyebolts she meant to set into the concrete, and the bolt brackets that held the eyebolts, she stalked back to the mixing trough and dropped them all.

Then, while Ellie waited bemusedly, she sprinted across the lawn to the corner where the compost heap loomed behind a screen of forsythia. There in the cool gloom, she took deep breaths, clenched her fists, and uttered the very same swear words that Bella had used a little earlier, one after the other.

Finally she strode back to the mixing area, refreshed— and freshly unnerved. Because while she'd stood by the pile of coffee grounds, lawn clippings, and eggshells, relying on the power of bad language to flush fury from her system, she'd seen . . . what?

"A flash," she told Ellie as she set up the concrete forms again, working fast so they could actually fill the forms without the concrete turning to hardened lumps on the shovels.

She hoped. "Like . . . from binoculars," she added unhappily as she replaced the shims.

"Really. From where?"

Jake laid the level across one corner of the first form and then across the opposite corner. "The top floor of the old meetinghouse," she replied. "Where you would go, if . . ."

If you wanted to spy down into the backyard of my place, she didn't finish. But Ellie understood.

The meetinghouse, a massive old white clapboard structure, was attached to an even larger old house much like Jake's own.

Unlike hers, though, it was uninhabited. And there were no curtains at the windows.

Bending to finish shimming the form boxes level again, Jake peeked sideways; no new flash came from the attic window. Meanwhile, the sky went on thickening, pale wisps of humidity sailing across it like ghostly streamers.

With an effort, she restrained herself from looking again at that bare window; half of her wanted badly to concentrate on the concrete and ignore everything else.

But the other half felt as if a target had been painted around her.

"Okay," she said grimly as the last of the concrete went into the first plywood form box.

Swiftly she set the stainless-steel bracket and bolt into the wet mixture. "Okay, if there's someone up there, let's just think about what that means."

That he'd been watching, that he knew where she was right now . . .

Ellie shoveled sand into the now-empty mixing trough, then cement mix. A cloud formed overhead, and one fat raindrop fell from it, forming a crater in the dry, powdery stuff.

"Hurry," she said as Jake picked up the hose. And then: "He wanted you to see him, before, didn't he? To know he was around."

"So maybe he does now, too," Jake agreed. Soon the second form was mixed, poured, and fitted with a bolt.

More raindrops fell. "D'you have another tarp?" Ellie asked.

Despite a forecast promising the first rain- and fog-free Fourth of July in years, Moose Island was not much more than a hunk of rock halfway to the North Atlantic. So forecasts always had an air of fingers crossed behind the back.

Like now, for instance. "Yeah," Jake said, and dropped the shovel just long enough to retrieve another plastic sheet from the yard shed.

Which posed a further chore: finding enough rocks, bricks, and other heavy objects lying around the yard to hold the tarp down over the newly filled forms.

"Jake," Ellie said thoughtfully, holding the hose up.

"What?" Jake dropped the tarp and grabbed the mixing trowel again as Ellie ran water into the trough. If you didn't want any rocks, there would be dozens of them lying all over the—

"Why d'you suppose he's watching? If he is," Ellie added as Jake stirred the fourth and thank-God-last concrete batch.

"Well . . ." She thought for a moment, trying on alternatives. Then: "I don't know," she admitted at last. "Unless he's got a high-powered rifle, he can't do anything from that distance. Can he?" she added nervously.

And if he did have one, all of this taunting he'd been doing would be beside the point. Straightening, she felt body parts protesting; mixing concrete was a lot like lifting it, only you did it while bending over.

"What I do know is, he doesn't know we know he's there."

"Because?" Ellie shot the hose stream over the shovels, the trowel, the mixing trough, and her own hands.

"Because I just peeked again, and the binoculars are flashing again." That, or he didn't care if they saw him; the thought deepened her anxiety.

Naturally, as they spread the tarp over the concrete forms, the rain quit spitting; in the yard, vapor wisps dissolved.

On the horizon, though, that fog bank still squatted. "Yes, I just saw the flash, too," Ellie confirmed. "So what'll we do?"

Jake dropped rocks scavenged from the dahlia bed's edging onto the tarp's corners. "I don't know that, either."

Rain or shine, by tomorrow that concrete would be set up, and the tarp wouldn't be needed anymore. So for now the job was done; together they heaved the rest of the last bag of cement into the cart and hauled it across the yard to the shed.

"The bottom line is," she went on, "there's no way to be sure what he's up to. But there are twenty-four vacant houses on the island, including the meeting-house."

And he was in the meetinghouse right now. Or somebody who was likely spying on them was in there, anyway.

They pushed the cart into the shed and closed the

doors on it. "I left the houses that are way out on the outskirts of town off the list. . . ." she said.

Right now Wade and Sam, her dad and Bella, and Ellie's husband, George, were entering and inspecting the houses, except for six near Jake's own place. Those, she and Ellie meant to examine.

". . . Because I doubt he'd pick somewhere far away to hide out in," she continued. "But why would he let the lens glare give him away? It's not rocket science that it might," Jake added.

They went inside. From the kitchen, there was no direct view to the meetinghouse's top floor.

Or vice versa, thankfully. Ellie scrubbed more cement dust off her hands, then splashed her face at the sink. "Unless he . . ."

"Wants us to know he's watching?" Jake finished for her.

"Because he's luring us into a trap," Ellie agreed. "You know, I'll just bet that's it, the little sneak."

Jake wandered thoughtfully to the back door. She looked out into the bright street, just as a gray-haired woman in a purple dress walked by, heading downtown.

The woman looked like her feet hurt, Jake thought, in those heels. "Maybe," she told Ellie. "Or maybe he just wants . . ."

The woman smiled shyly, catching Jake's eye and fluttering her fingers in a shy wave, then limped on.

"I don't know," Jake repeated impatiently, turning from the door. "And you know, I'm already tired of wondering about it. We were going to look in the meetinghouse anyway, weren't we?"

"Yes," Ellie replied doubtfully. "But—"

"But nothing." She plucked a leather leash from the hook by the back door, then a dog collar. Hearing the jingle, the big red Doberman trotted from the parlor inquisitively.

"Come on, Prill," Jake said. Eagerly the big red Doberman allowed herself to be hitched up to her leash once more.

Then Jake stepped outside with the dog and Ellie followed. On the porch, the faint mingled smells of mothballs and Shalimar perfume hung in the warm air.

"Let's just get those houses checked—the old meetinghouse first, of course—and get this over with," Jake said.

Thinking even as she spoke that it probably wasn't going to be that easy.

And naturally, it wasn't.

Chapter 7

> *Repair a dented wood floor by
> placing a clean, damp cloth
> over the dent and touching it
> repeatedly with a steam iron
> until the wood swells, removing
> the dent.*
>
> —Tiptree's Tips

The vast white bulk of the old nondenominational meetinghouse loomed so tall that from close up, it appeared to be toppling forward. Around it on either side of a cinder-paved circle driveway, the grass had been mowed by someone using a hand scythe; the long cut swathes dried greenish-gold in the afternoon sun.

On the front steps, two massive clay pots of red geraniums bloomed exuberantly; it was where Jake had gotten the idea for her own front porch.

If I ever get back to it, she thought. The front door of the meetinghouse stood open a few dark inches.

"He wanted us to know he was here," she told Ellie. "He's been tricky so far, and that makes me think the binoculars glare was no accident."

Up and down the streets around the meetinghouse, tourists and locals strolled. On the breeze, the greasy smell of grilling hamburgers floated.

"And that suggests maybe there's something here he wants us to see," she added, holding Prill's leash securely.

But do we want to see it? she wondered silently, and gave the open door a push. "Hello?"

No answer from inside. Prill stiffened, though, sniffing something. "Easy, girl."

The dog settled, padding obediently forward. "Look," Ellie said unhappily.

The main room was a small chapel, with seats and a podium plus smaller tables on which printed matter was arranged: flyers, music sheets, posters for the summer lecture series.

A vase of garden flowers had been knocked off the podium and broken, the water still running between the front pews.

"Oh, what a shame!" Ellie knelt to rescue the scattered blooms while Jake and Prill went on past the podium to the rooms behind: a small kitchen, a lavatory, two parlor rooms, and what had once been a library.

Over the years, the non-chapel area had sometimes been used as living quarters, and intermittent attempts to clean these rooms had been made. But the result was that each parlor still held stacks of things nobody wanted, but no one wanted to take responsibility for throwing them out, either.

A wicker birdcage, for instance, complete with stuffed bird (a parrot, Jake thought) stood on a tall stack of old *National Geographic*s in one parlor, while a jumbled collection of skis, ice skates, and snowshoes stuck every which way from behind an old steamer trunk in the other.

A winding stair led to the second floor. "No one down here," Ellie reported, dusting her hands after disposing of the vase pieces.

Jake looked up the stairs. "Mmm. Someone was, though. Unless you think that vase hopped off the podium by itself."

"No," Ellie agreed unhappily. "And that front door didn't end up standing open by itself, either."

Jake dropped the dog's leash and made an after-you gesture, Ellie returned it theatrically, and while they were standing there debating the question of who went first, Prill started up, her muscular legs making quick work of the stairs.

But at the top the dog let out a low growl, and Jake hurried up after her into the smells of long-abandoned clothing, long-unused bedding, and mouse droppings.

"What is it?" called Ellie from below.

Jake stared, reaching down to calm the suspicious

animal with a pat on the flank. "I'm not sure. Maybe nothing."

Prill tended to growl first and ask questions later. "Be careful," Ellie warned as Prill advanced along the hallway to an open door, toenails clicking.

"I will," Jake said, taking a step forward onto the hall's old linoleum. Its pattern, tan lattice entwined in cabbage roses, was one she recognized from her broom closet at home.

"I'm just going to—" she began, and then too late realized she'd hit a trip wire of some kind, Prill's lower profile having passed without triggering it.

A swishing sound came through the air, and so did a paint can. The can flew at her, missing her head by inches as she ducked fast.

Then it sailed on by, hitting the wall beyond with a hollow-sounding clank. White primer splashed out over the wallpaper, a faded lavender scenery print of milkmaids lugging milk cans.

"Jake?" Ellie sounded alarmed. Jake stared at the paint trickling down as if running into the wall-paper's milk cans.

Then she found her voice. "I'm fine," she called. Prill came out of the first bedroom and stalked into the second one, ears pricked and neck hairs bristling.

Ellie reached the landing, took in the situation. "Wow," she breathed. "Someone set up a—"

"Booby trap," Jake agreed. The trip wire was a thread stretched waist-high between the top railing post and the wall, where a hook had once held some-thing: a baby gate, maybe.

Something long gone. Like her jokester/assailant was now.

"You okay?" Ellie's face was full of concern.

"Yeah." Still, her heart thumped against her ribs. "Surprised me, is all." She sat down on the top step, unwilling to admit how much it had unnerved her to see the shape flying out of the hall's gloom.

But Ellie knew. She stepped past Jake, to give her a chance to compose herself. "Prill?" she called.

The dog came obediently out of the second bedroom. Ellie turned to the door to the third-floor stairs.

"We're going up," Ellie told Jake. "Whatever this is, we might as well get it over with."

With that, she opened the door and went through it; Prill followed as Jake got to her feet and hurried to catch up.

"Hey, you two . . ." The stairs were narrow and steep.

At the top, Ellie passed through another door, with the big animal close behind. Again Jake followed, emerging into a light, airy chamber, framed and plastered but with no further ornament.

Even the doorframes, unlike the elaborately carved and varnished woodwork of the lower floors, were plain, flat planks, two simple uprights capped by another untrimmed board.

"Wow," she said inadequately, almost whispering it.

Windows on all sides let the sky into the empty room, its raw plank floors bleached by sunlight over the decades. Nothing had been stored here; too many stairs, she supposed. "This is . . ."

Beautiful. The walls, the floors . . . all bare, and

someone had whitewashed the plaster a long time ago, so that now it was the color of old bone. That and the room's emptiness made it feel almost weightless, as if it might sail off the top of the house.

"Look," said Ellie, turning from the bare window.

Crossing to it, Jake peered out. Even without binoculars, she could see the concrete-mixing trough leaned up against the cellar doors, the hose coiled by the spigot.

She could see the corner of the front porch, too, where earlier she had set the near-empty gallon can of white primer.

Now it was gone. "He used it," she said, staring out at her house. Her own home, where her family lived . . .

"He walked right up onto that porch and took the paint can, probably while we were around back mixing concrete, and brought it here."

She turned from the window. "This is all my fault. I could have prevented all this."

But Ellie replied indignantly, "Jake, it is not. Anybody who thinks anybody should just hand them—"

Fifty grand. A lot of money. But for her, it really hadn't been, not back then.

"Still, he thinks it was. An eye for an eye, I guess, is what he's here for."

"Yes, well, I'll eye-for-an-eye him."

Below, the island spread out green and lovely, the gardens pristine and houses festooned with flags. Snippets of patriotic tunes drifted up even through the attic's closed windows, and the bay's silvery glitter made everything seem to shimmer.

Ellie let an impatient breath out. "I swear, Jake, sometimes I wonder what happened to all those smarts you had in Manhattan."

Jake turned. "What do you mean?"

"Well," Ellie said reasonably, "if you'd given him the money, what would've happened? Anything different from what had happened before, anytime he'd had any?"

"Probably not," she admitted. One last all-or-nothing fling at the racetrack—how would Garner have been able to resist?

"All right, then," said Ellie, satisfied, and then, "Look."

Through the high attic window, they watched the parade begin snaking at last out of its staging grounds, out on County Road between the firehouse and the Youth Center. A man with a bullhorn waved his arms; from here, he was the size of an ant.

"No sane person would have done what he asked," Jake said. "And even if I had, it wouldn't have—"

You don't know that, her mind contradicted her cruelly. You might've saved his life, if only you'd . . .

The fog bank still lay like a line scrawled with gray crayon on the southern horizon. "—it wouldn't have made a difference."

She turned toward the stairs. "And we've found what he meant us to, so let's go."

They descended two flights and made their way between the old pews toward the exit. Here in the chapel area, the place wasn't so bad. Spare and serene feeling, the room was lined with tall bare windows still paned with early-nineteenth-century glass.

"I hope those F-18s Wade's so excited about don't end up breaking all the old windows in town," Jake said, gazing around distractedly.

The flowers that Ellie had rescued and put into a coffee can on the long wooden table by the stacks of literature didn't hurt, either. The other rooms, though, full of boxes of old letters and books with their spines broken, unlabeled film cans, and more . . .

Much more. On her way through, she'd glimpsed ancient bank statements, receipts tumbling out of their manila envelopes, old membership lists. Other boxes held a moldy variety of old clothes and jumbled kitchen implements.

"Someone should really clean this place out." She stepped into the sunshine with a sense of relief. "A Dumpster and a few days of filling it with all that crap could be some benevolent person's gift to this place," she said.

The gutters could use replacing, too, and a couple of the windowpanes on the second floor needed . . .

"Right, it's the rest of it that's such a problem," Ellie agreed, still lingering inside. "Meanwhile, I'm glad it was just a paint can that jumped out at us."

Jake went on assessing the old structure, unable to help seeing all that it needed. At least the entry had been remodeled, with a ramp and a set of wide steps built of pressure-treated lumber, so people wouldn't break their legs going in and out.

"Yes," she said, "I guess he must've just wanted me to know he'd gotten close enough to my house to . . ."

"Um. Jake?" Ellie's tone alerted her. Reluctantly

she went back inside, where Ellie was at one of the literature tables.

From among the profusion of tracts and sign-up sheets—a spiritualist lecturer, a community organizer's talk on motivating volunteerism—she'd plucked an item unlike the rest of the long table's offerings.

It was a photograph, an eight-by-ten, full-color photo that, judging by the blurriness of everything but the central subject, had been taken with a zoom lens.

"It was at the end, there. Just in with the other pamphlets and so on."

Suddenly dry-mouthed, Jake took the photograph from Ellie's hands. "Sam," she whispered.

It was from today, she could tell by the clothes he wore: a view of him leaving the house. Prill's head showed faintly behind him, framed in the lower part of the screen door.

A ball cap sat on his dark curls, and his whole long, rangy body looked relaxed and carefree, lips pursed so you could almost hear the tune he was whistling.

He'd been on his way out with the others to inspect the vacant houses in town, in case Steven Garner might be hiding in one of them. On the photograph, there was a clumsy but effective bull's-eye target crudely drawn in black Magic Marker around his head.

"I'm sorry," Ellie whispered. "I almost wish I hadn't—"

"Don't be. We needed to know."

Blocks away, snare drums rang out a rhythmic anthem. A flute trilled "Yankee Doodle."

A car backfired. Even at this distance, Jake flinched.

Sam. With a target drawn on him.

Around his . . .

"Let's go," she urged grimly. "We've got more empty houses to check."

. . . around his head.

In Eastport, that holiday weekend was not a good time to be a big-eared but otherwise ordinary-looking young guy, if nobody knew you.

Matt Stottlemeir, though, was not aware of that fact. All he knew was that his pretty, blonde wife, Maria, and their two-year-old twins were already here somewhere.

They were down from Fredericton, visiting the American side of the family. They'd been here a week, and now he was here to spend the weekend with them; once he found them, he intended to watch the parade, have a barbecue with Maria's American cousins—nice people who made great potato salad and served an abundance of excellent Maine-brewed beer—and see the fireworks tonight.

If there were any fireworks. Locking the car and leaving it on a side street, Matt cast a doubtful eye at the sky. Hazy now, it had thickened considerably since he'd come through the customs and immigration station at the border in Calais.

A farmer who cultivated over four hundred acres of potatoes, broccoli, and corn, Matt decided it looked like rain. Odds were, there weren't even going to be any fireworks tonight, and he had an enormous amount of work to do back at home.

But Maria had been insistent, and besides, how else was she going to get back with the kids? For a farm family nowadays, if you couldn't hitch a machine to it, there was no sense owning it.

Still, he told himself as he strolled toward the sounds of music, sirens, and other parade-related cacophony across town, the beer would be good. And maybe if he got a few bottles of it into Maria, she'd be good to him tonight, too.

Seeing as he'd come all this way for her. The cousins' guest room, he remembered with a reminiscent grin, was quite a distance from the rest of the house. Meanwhile, Eastport was a pretty town with nice old homes and a spectacular waterfront looking out onto Passamaquoddy Bay; not bad duty in any case, he reflected.

Now, where would Maria and the kids be sitting? The parade, he recalled as he reached the corner of Water Street where the library lawn sported a War of 1812 cannon, usually came right by here.

The cannon did give him pause. My people, he couldn't help thinking, got shot up by your people.

But that was a long time ago. Nowadays, just about everyone on this side of the border was cousins with someone over there. Maria and her folks, for instance. Scanning the crowd lining the street and not seeing his wife and kids, he turned uphill, away from the downtown congestion.

Probably they were on the other side of town, near Maria's cousins' place. It was faster to cut across on a side street, he knew from previous visits, and before long he'd reached a narrow lane where he was alone until an old pickup truck appeared from around the corner, muffler dragging and carburetor wheezing.

And three guys piling purposefully out of the cab. "Hey! You with the ears!" one of them shouted.

Taken aback, Matt pointed to himself. "Who, me?"

The men advanced on him. All three of them had the kind of swaggering, no-kidding walk he associated with bar fights.

Also, they were large. Still, he couldn't believe it. "Uh, fellas, I think you might be—"

Making a mistake, he'd meant to finish, but just then one of the guys stepped up and seized him by the collar.

"This is a message from Wade Sorenson. Better quit hasslin' his wife," the guy said.

"Who?" Matt managed to gasp through the grip of the guy's fist at his throat.

The guy shook him hard. "Don't try to pretend you don't know what I'm talking about. Beat it. Get out of town."

The guy let go, shoving Matt hard. He landed on his butt; no real harm done, he knew right away. But it made him mad, and in the next moment he was on his feet again, fists windmilling and his boots doing a creditable job of butt-kicking.

In the end, though, it was three against one, so they just grabbed him and held him, none of them even needing to throw a punch. And he still couldn't figure out why they'd picked him.

"Don't forget." The guy who'd accosted him first aimed a nicotine-stained finger at him. "Next time it'll be worse. We got a pal, cuts fish bait for a living. You don't want to meet him."

They strode away, leaving Matt standing there in the street catching his breath.

Sorenson, he thought as the old truck wheezed and clanked to life, then squealed in reverse back to the corner and roared off.

Wade Sorenson.

Back on Washington Street, Eastport's Fourth of July parade was about to begin. Returned from his errands—the paint can had been an inspired touch, he thought proudly—Steven found a spot on the curb uphill from the post office and sat down to wait.

Beside him sat an elderly man with a long white beard, dressed in a yellow slicker and sou'wester and carrying a homemade trident. Steven tried not to gawk, but the man didn't seem to mind being stared at.

"Hello, young lady!" the old man shouted. "Great day for a parade!"

"Mmm, yeah," Steven muttered, taken aback. The trident was made of a broomstick and some wadded-together aluminum foil. This guy, Steven thought, is even more of a nutcase than me.

The idea was alarming, suggesting as it did that quirks other than his own might be in play today, maybe even affecting his plans. And sure enough, just then a clown from the parade ran over, outsized rubber shoes flapping.

The clown honked the bright red rubber bulb-horn that was his nose, then pressed a green plastic toy pistol into Steven's hands. "Here ya go, madam! Have a blast!"

Steven took the toy gun, aimed it at the clown, and pulled the trigger. A bunch of paper flowers burst from the barrel.

The clown looked narrowly at Steven from behind his makeup. Something in Steven's face seemed to have alerted him that this was not your average lady parade-goer.

But then he whirled away, his jumbo, white-gloved hands suddenly brimming over with candy, which he kept flinging to the curbs and sidewalks, where the children scrambled for it.

"Hellooo!" shouted the old guy sitting beside Steven as a float titled The Class of '65 rolled into view. Struggling to his feet, he hustled gimpily alongside until he was hauled onto it by the class members.

His father, Steven realized, would have been about their age now. He wondered if his dad would've needed glasses, and if he'd have lost his hair. He wondered if by now some sort of emotional connection to the man might've arisen in his own heart.

His father was his protector, his savior from Mother's wild mood swings and crazy regime. That alone was reason enough to miss him—that if he'd lived, things would've been different.

But would Steven have been different, too? Would he have the things, the sensations or whatever they were, that everyone else called feelings? Those mysterious urges to be close to other people, and somehow to understand—or share, or whatever it was—their feelings?

Steven didn't know. He suspected not, actually. At least with regard to other people, the only such sensations he'd ever experienced were unpleasant.

But maybe he'd have had the opportunity to find out, if his father were alive. Which he wasn't. *And we know whose fault that is, don't we?*

Indeed, and Steven was in the process right now of taking care of that little matter.

The matter of vengeance. He shifted uncomfortably inside the dress he wore, unsettlingly loose in some places and too tight in others. On his head, the gray wig was heavy and hot, and squidgy feeling from sweat where it touched his scalp.

It exuded a perfume smell so strong, it was like having a scented candle in his mouth. On his swollen, bruised feet, the shoes, too, were hideously painful, with their stacked heels and the cutaway places where his toes poked through.

As for the pantyhose, he thought anyone who willingly wore such a garment deserved what they got. The waistband felt like a dull razor was being run around his middle, the crotch hung in a way that felt horribly insecure, and the stockings' mesh plucked out the hairs from his legs one stinging strand at a time.

On the other hand, the disguise itself seemed to be working well. His mother had been a tall woman, about his own size, and, of course, he'd picked the right crowd to hide out in, too.

The guy with the trident had rolled away on the float with his class, but now here came another weirdo, this one dressed up like a Native American. . . .

Wait a minute, that guy really was a Native American, and so were the others with him, Steven realized suddenly. Their float, pulled by a pickup truck, was decorated to resemble a birch-bark canoe plying waves, cardboard porpoises sporting in its wake.

In the canoe, men in costumes and headdresses tapped skin drums and chanted in a language Steven didn't understand. A big German shepherd lay at their feet, head up and ears pricked.

Not until the animal's gaze met his, and one of the men's did, too, did Steven recognize them from the Guess Your Weight and Age booth the night before. The dog, his eyes like dark stones, made as if to get up until without missing a beat on the drum the man stopped the animal with a small gesture.

The dog's gaze seemed to bore right through Steven, and all at once he felt that everyone, not just the man and dog, could see through the ridiculous getup he wore, right through to his sweating scalp and rubbed-raw waist, and to his heart, black and stony as the big dog's eyes.

Still chanting, the man took in Steven's made-up face and his unlikely costume expressionlessly. Panic pierced Steven; was his disguise really so transparent? Was everyone here just being polite, trying not to look at him the way he'd avoided gawking at the old man with the trident, trying not to laugh?

He nearly bolted, but with his last shred of willpower he stayed seated on the curb. To his left where the old man had been, a little boy in a sailor suit bounced happily, waving a flag.

Younger than I was when . . .

Everything led back to that, didn't it? But he silenced the thought. No time for reminiscing now; this was serious, with no room for sloppy, emotional mistakes.

And anyway, he'd worn this whole costume a dozen times, alone and in public. He'd ridden the subway in it, walked the sidewalks of Manhattan, gone to stores, concerts, and even church services, soldiering on despite agonies of chafing and toe-pinching.

He'd gotten his share of funny looks in it then, too, but that was all. No one had ever confronted him. So why would here be any different?

Because here's where it counts, an inner voice whispered to him slyly. Here's where you can fail. . . .

Shut up, shut UP, he told himself furiously. On his right, a plump, sunburned woman dressed in a red, white, and blue tracksuit sat licking an ice-cream cone. Steven, intent on showing that damned inner voice of his a thing or two, mustered his courage.

I can do this. . . . "Good ice cream?" he inquired pleasantly. Fortunately, his own speaking voice was high enough to belong to a deepish-voiced woman.

A smile spread across his neighbor's broad face. She had one of those perfectly smooth complexions very fair-haired people sometimes got, poreless and pale except where the sun had turned it pink.

A pan of milk, his mother would have called it scornfully as she brushed back her own mane of wavy hair. She'd been beautiful once, too. . . .

Firmly he slammed a mental door on her image, which at the end was not so beautiful.

"Excellent ice cream," affirmed the tracksuited

woman, and he felt his confidence return somewhat. But then, "Are you from here?" she added. "I don't recognize you at all."

"Uh . . ." He searched his mind frantically. He'd had a story all worked up about where he'd come from, how he happened to be here. But there'd been so many things to do and think about in the past twenty-four hours. . . .

He'd forgotten it. Panic stabbed him; he felt his mouth work uselessly. But just as quickly as she'd terrified him nearly into incoherence, the plump lady now rescued him.

"From away, huh?" She popped the tip of the cone between her lips and crunched it.

She's laughing at me, she knows, she's . . .

But she wasn't, and she didn't. Instead, she reached over with her ice-cream-sticky hand and actually patted him on the shoulder.

"That's okay, honey. We're happy you're here anyway."

Then she spotted another parade float—this one decorated to resemble a spaceship, and occupied by the local high school band—and recognized someone on it.

"Hoo, Wesley!" She jumped up and waved the napkin that had been wrapped around the ice-cream cone. "Hoo! Good on ya! Woo-boy!"

With an embarrassed grin, the gangly high-schooler on the float waved back, then returned to playing . . . a flute, was it? Or maybe a piccolo.

The woman sat. "My nephew," she confided. "My brother's oldest boy. His dad's in Afghanistan now."

Steven nodded. Mine's in a grave somewhere. A shallow one, maybe a landfill. Or a barrel in the East River.

"My other brother got killed in Iraq," she said. "Roadside bomb."

Steven made what he hoped were sympathetic noises as the band float went by; up next marched a contingent of old men in military uniforms. Vietnam veterans, according to their posters and banners; he squinted between them at the old house he'd been squatting in, just across the street, and wished he were inside it.

But he'd had no choice; he'd had to leave it long enough for Jacobia Tiptree—or one of her friends— to search it. Which of course he'd known would happen; Tiptree was evil, not stupid.

Blending in here in Eastport meant having somewhere to go at night, not wandering the streets, where the cops would take notice of you and remember you later.

And anyway, the things he had to do needed to be done in secret, behind walls and under a roof. Just which walls and roof would be an easy assumption, too: the ones no one else was using, of course.

So while they looked for him in the town's vacant houses, he was out here, dressed and made up so that neither Tiptree nor any of her pals would recognize him. Still . . .

Another trickle of sweat tickled his scalp under the wig; if he couldn't shed it soon, he might scream. The dress clung to his back damply as the July sun beat down on him. The shoes tortured his feet.

And he might have to go on like this for hours, maybe even all day. Not until he saw her or one of her friends enter the old house across the street, then emerge, having found nothing, would he be able to reenter it safely himself. Until then, he'd just have to tough it out. . . .

The ice cream woman got up. "Tomorrow night, though?" she said, brightening. "There's going to be a Navy flyover. A pair of F-18s coming home from Greenland, on their way to their base."

He nodded politely as she went on. "To honor our boys here," she told him. "When you hear them, you remember my brother, okay?"

"Uh, you bet," he replied, realizing too late as she moved away that it was not the kind of thing a woman would say. Then before he could make anything of this worry, a new one arose: the quartet of rowdy young men who'd harassed him the night before were here, striding belligerently toward him.

Still in all black, they shoved rudely among the parade watchers, and because he hadn't looked away quickly enough, one of them spotted him.

And—he felt something like an electrical shock go through him—recognized him. Or recognized something, anyway—his fear, his vulnerability.

It drew them like a beacon; in the same black Iron Maiden T-shirt he'd been wearing last night, the short, blocky one nudged the others and said something.

Steven held his breath, but it was no use; they all looked over at him, grinning and sniggering. The

ginger-haired boy in his black pegged jeans and
leather jacket narrowed his eyes, as if calculating the
distance between them.

He had on a thick spiked leather wristlet, and wore
a bike chain wrapped around his waist like a belt.
With his mean little eyes fixed on Steven, he took a
step.

A purposeful step . . . But just then another parade
float went by, quickly followed by a contingent of
marching baton twirlers. Through the confusion
Steven tried keeping his eyes on the black-shirted
hoodlums.

One moment, they were still there. But in the next,
they weren't. Where . . . ?

He looked around wildly—no sign of them. Clumsy
in heels, he got to his feet, still scanning the crowd.

Gone. They hadn't had enough time to get far,
though, and he knew he hadn't mistaken their interest.

He turned too fast, nearly twisting his ankle. Maybe
they'd split up and were even now circling around
behind him. . . .

"Hey." With a sinking feeling, he recognized the
voice at his elbow. Somehow the ginger-haired guy
had gotten across the street and right up alongside.

His companions, too. Steven could feel them back
there, all grinning and shifting while they waited for
their leader to tell them what to do.

"You look sweet in that dress," the ginger-haired
hoodlum said, and the other three whinnied with
amusement.

Glancing over his shoulder, Steven saw them elbowing one another. He'd have wondered how they knew, but he didn't have to; all his life he'd attracted guys like this: dull, brutal.

When he was around, they were like predators smelling meat. "Yeah," fluted the short, blocky one mockingly. "Real sweet. Hey, gimme a kiss."

Steven glanced around for help. But none was forthcoming; in the crowd, no one seemed to notice a malignant foursome menacing a gray-haired lady in a purple dress.

Or maybe they were scared. Either way, the lover boys seemed to know how far they could go, getting right up in his space but not touching him. So even if a cop appeared, what could he say? That they were standing too near? Laughing where he could hear them?

And anyway, police notice was the last thing he wanted, yet another inconvenient fact they seemed to have picked up on. Guys like this, Steven thought, were like wolves culling the flock.

As a contingent of official cars including a sheriff's squad rolled by, one of them shoved Steven. He staggered on the heeled shoes and nearly fell in front of the nearest cop vehicle.

Would have fallen, in fact, if not for the wiry grip on his forearm, pulling him back. "Steady, there, sweetie." The voice, low in his ear, came on a gust of beer breath. The tight grip released, though not before giving his forearm a hard pinch. "Wouldn't want you getting hurt."

Steven gasped, tears of pain prickling in his eyes,

and pressed his lips together to keep from crying out. The cop in the last squad car smiled and waved at the parade onlookers. When the car had gone by, the other two roughnecks moved in.

One had a narrow face like a ferret's; wispy hairs sprouted from his thin upper lip, which was pulled back into a snarl over brownish teeth.

The other, baby-faced and with a wandering left eye, wore a look of anticipation as he glanced back and forth at his buddies, eager to learn what new outrage they might decide to perpetrate.

"In fact, just to make sure nobody hurts you, seems like you oughta come with us," said the ginger-haired one.

Then all four boys formed a sort of escort around Steven, forcing him away from the parade audience and onto the empty lawn behind. With the crowd still watching the passing entertainment, it was as if Steven were alone with the bullies.

Alone . . . And if he called for help, it would quickly come out that he wasn't who he seemed to be, wouldn't it? That he was a man in a dress and wig, and why was that?

It would be the first thing the police would want to know, but not the last. And he would have no good answers for them. His mission would be over, all because of . . .

Rage rose up in him, hot and poisonous. All he'd worked and planned for . . . all of it would be finished. And then—

No, he thought calmly, surprising himself. I won't let them.

Casually he opened the purse he carried; in its flap was a small mirror, so a lady could check her makeup. Now the glass showed his cheeks streaked with tears.

But it showed his wig, too, and the small purple straw hat with the pink rose perched atop it, secured with a pearl-tipped hat pin.

I look like my mother, he thought, and the notion gave him a shudder. He reached up as if to straighten the hat.

"Come on," snarled Ferret Boy. "Never mind that. You come with us. We'll have ourselves a party."

Stepping forward obediently—

Lamb to the slaughter, he thought. Just not this time.

—Steven reached up and slid the hat pin smoothly out of the hat. Out on the street now, a brass band slam-banged deafeningly along, horns shrieking.

"Okay," he said. Then with the pin in his fist and his thumb on the pearl, he swung his arm around four times fast.

On each swing, the pin's tip sent a thin, crunchy feeling up into his hand, and suddenly all four of the young thugs fell away from him, screeching.

Dropping, they rolled on the grass, howling wonderfully, each one clutching a different part of his anatomy. Hands at his sides, Steven stood watching them curiously. Fascinating . . .

A few parade watchers looked over, too, long enough to see who was adding this strange counterpoint to the passing din. But when they saw who it was, they looked away again; the welfare of the black-clad boys, it seemed, was low on their priority list.

Ha, thought Steven, stunned at the success of his maneuver. But then he realized: he needed a follow-up. Needed one badly, in fact, because those guys weren't going to lie there forever.

Well, three of them weren't. The ginger-haired guy winced, spotted Steven, and bared his teeth reflexively. But a look of puzzled fear was in his eyes, too, increasing as Steven crouched by him.

"I know what you did last night."

"What?" The guy grimaced, confused. But then his gray eyes widened in understanding.

"Bull," he snarled. As the truth dawned on him, though, a look of thwarted animal rage distorted his features.

Steven had hurt him badly, and he still didn't know how. But now he seemed to realize that his opponent could do worse, much worse. With a groan, he rolled over and began crawling away.

Young Ferret Face had begun climbing to his feet. But as soon as he was upright, his eyes rolled back into his head and he fell again. This time he stayed there.

Steven looked down at the hat pin gripped still in his fist. Then he released it down a nearby storm drain. Slowly and with as much dignity as he could muster, he crossed the street between a parade float depicting Washington at the Delaware and one that carried a real, live brown-and-white cow.

Eastport's on the Moo-oo-ve! read the float's banner. His heart thudding with excitement, he spared a moment of sympathy for the bunting-draped farm animal, then eased between it and the final float of the parade, a giant sardine on wheels.

Excitement and relief, because while he had been getting recognized, and victimized, and nearly kidnapped with a view to being cannibalized—

—or so he'd feared; who knew what they'd had in mind—

—he'd missed what was going on at his hideout. Now, though, two people were exiting the house. Steven recognized Jacobia Tiptree's son, Sam, and the older woman, bony and henna-haired, who he thought must be the maid or something.

From their faces he could tell they'd found nothing and no one. Just as he'd planned, he reflected, as behind him a flurry of activity began around the fallen young men; an accusing hand went up, pointing the way he'd gone.

But the sardine float blocked their view of him. Slowly he backed into the overgrown yard of the old house, toward the lattice screening the back lawn. Glancing quickly right and left, he assured himself that still, no one saw him.

Then, swiftly, he stepped up onto the rotted wooden porch and leaned against the ancient, frame-sprung door, shoving until it opened just enough to let him slip into the darkness inside.

The welcoming darkness, a place where he could wash, eat, and rest.

And get ready for his next move.

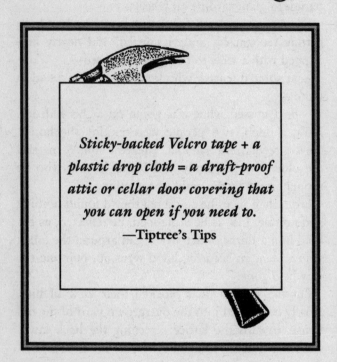

Chapter 8

Sticky-backed Velcro tape + a plastic drop cloth = a draft-proof attic or cellar door covering that you can open if you need to.
—Tiptree's Tips

I'm telling you, Jake," said Eastport Police Chief Bob Arnold later that day. "It might not've been the dumbest stunt you've ever pulled. But . . ."

Bob stood on the front walk, scolding her while she bent to the porch steps. The second coat of porch primer went on a lot faster than the first, partly because it was easier to paint on than raw wood, whose grain caught the brush bristles.

But partly it was because listening to Bob made her hand move so much faster; her frustration had to go somewhere. And it couldn't go to him; the police chief was just trying to do his job.

"You and Wade are both lucky the guy doesn't want to press charges," he continued. "Menacing, harassment . . . guy who pushed him, he could be looking at battery, maybe even assault."

She kept the paintbrush moving. "So why isn't he? Pressing them, I mean?"

Bob shook his head. "Come all the way down here from Canada, spend money on a lawyer, it's not worth it to him." He took a breath. "Besides, truth is that all they really did was scare him, and no guy wants to admit that."

But then his face grew stern again. "Great big ears, the guy has. The one who got menaced, I mean. And he says the ones who did it told him Wade sent them. Now, why d'you suppose that might be?"

"I have no idea," she managed through clenched teeth. "Why d'you think I'd know anything about it?"

But that was the wrong question, because Bob had an answer for it, and watching him give it was like watching a teakettle blow.

His pudgy fingers stroked his pink, plump chin in pretended thought. "Jake, first some stranger starts harassing you. Sensibly, you come to me for help, but you don't get very much satisfaction out of that, because . . ."

He let his voice trail off suggestively; she finished his sentence for him.

"Garner didn't do anything illegal, or not anything you can arrest him for right this minute. Also there's been an accidental death you've had to take care of, and it's the holiday, so you're right out straight, even without my troubles."

"Key-rect," he responded briskly. "Absolutely correct on all counts. Which is not to say I haven't been trying," he added. "I told all my guys about your stalker or whatever he is, made sure they know to pick him up, they have the slightest reason."

"I know." Of course he was trying. But Garner was like the fog, here one minute and dissolving away the next.

"Why couldn't you just hunker down and wait while we get the computer crime division involved, people who *can* help?" Bob sucked in a breath. "But no, right away you've got to go all proactive about it. You talk to Wade, and *his* next move—"

She cut Bob off briskly. "Wade did not assault anyone. Or ask anyone to."

The second coat of primer was on the porch already, as if by magic; she couldn't have done it any faster with a spray painter.

Anger, the other home-repair tool, she thought. "You want to ask him about that," she continued, getting up, "he's upstairs in his workshop."

She dragged the brush bristles hard against the paint can's rim. "And even if he did tell somebody what's been going on—" she began, because she hadn't specifically asked him not to, had she?

Bob rolled his eyes. "Oh, here we go now," he groaned.

She tapped the lid onto the paint can with a tack hammer. "If he did," she insisted, "it's because he's trying to help me."

Once they'd left the chapel, it hadn't taken her and Ellie long to check the remaining vacant Eastport houses on their list. But they'd come up empty, as had the other searchers. Afterwards she'd thrown herself into the painting project again, just so she wouldn't feel later that she'd wasted the whole day.

Bob's squad car idled at the curb. The paint-stirring stick lay on the grass. She plucked it up, wiped both sides of it with a bit of rag, and laid it on the paint can.

"Just some poor guy, a case of mistaken identity," said Bob, "he gets hassled because of your—"

"Hey, I said I was sorry." She was, too, about the mistaken identity part.

"Listen, though," she added, relenting. "Would it help if I went over to where this guy's staying and apologized? Because it is . . ."

My fault. She'd told Bob so. "I mean there's really no getting around it that if it weren't for me . . ."

Bob took off his uniform hat, gazed downhill at the water as he slicked his few sweat-damp strands of blond hair back, put the hat back on. "Nah," he said finally. "Let's just leave well enough alone for now. Guy calms down, no reason to chance riling him up again."

Which made sense; Jake nodded in agreement, closing the subject. So now the way was cleared for what she really wanted to talk to him about.

"Hey, Bob," she said mildly. "Look over there on that lawn chair, will you? Under the brick."

Sighing impatiently, he plucked the photo from the chair and squinted at it. "What's this?"

"It's a snapshot of Sam, taken by Steven Garner. He left it in the meetinghouse for me and Ellie to find earlier today after he lured us there by making me think he was spying on me from an upstairs window."

She took a breath. "Which he also was doing."

Bob looked up from the photo. "You sure about this? I mean, you can . . ."

"Prove it? No, of course not. No more than I can prove any of the rest of it."

"Still think he was involved with the thing on Sea Street?"

The girl's death, he meant. "Yeah. Yeah, I do."

From downtown, random blats and bleats of the high school band's instruments sounded at irregular intervals. A firecracker went off, and then another.

Jake regarded the porch she'd just painted. "And Bob, here's the other thing I think about it."

Paint dripped off one of the risers. She swiped at it with the brush and made it worse, then smacked the brush down hard.

"He believes I killed his dad. Or that I was responsible for him getting murdered, anyway. And he's been thinking about that and mulling it and obsessing over it since he was ten years old, and now he's here to do something about it."

"You don't know that," Bob protested, spreading his hands. But this time she wasn't having any.

"I may not be able to prove it. But I do know."

Inside, Bella was running the vacuum cleaner. Wade was up in his workshop, as she'd said; together with Jake's dad he was busy sharpening all the small tools he used on gun-stock repairs.

And Sam was in his room trying to trace the scary emails she'd gotten, still without success. "Tell me, Bob, does the idea of a dry run sound reasonable to you?" She took the photograph from him. "Or do you really think a local girl got a few beers too many in her and proceeded to walk off a thirty-foot cliff that she's known about all her life?"

Bob looked uncomfortable. "Yeah, well . . ."

He really did mean well. And he was a friend. She sat down on the lawn chair.

"Bob, that picture was a message to let me know it's not just me he's after. He'd hurt Sam to get at me, I'm certain of it."

"You think maybe he killed the girl for practice. And . . . he's making you feel guilty a little, too?" Bob asked perceptively. He was a very good cop.

"Yeah." She looked up at him. Creating order from disorder by way of the old house wasn't having the desired effect lately—not on her conscience or on the rest of her life, either.

And it certainly wasn't helping put the past in perspective where Steven Garner Sr. was concerned. "I mean, I'm still pretty sure that if I'd given his dad what he wanted, the exact same thing would've happened. Only first he'd have gambled it all away, and *then* they'd've killed him."

But not *absolutely* sure. And almost as much as anything else, it was still the notion that she could've prevented all this that was driving her nuts.

Regret for the past is a waste of spirit, they told Sam at his AA meetings. What they didn't say, though, was how to stop regretting it.

"Anyway," she said. "We did look in all the empty houses we could think of, in case he was in one. But no dice."

A static burst from his radio distracted Bob; he went over to the squad car to listen. When he returned:

"I gotta go now," he told her. "But, Jake, I wish you'd talk to Wade, before he . . ."

Gets anyone else beat up. Bob didn't finish. But it was what he meant. "Why don't you tell him yourself?" she asked mildly.

Bob gave her a look. "Because if I do, he'll say something and then I'll say something. And you know how that might end up."

She did.

"But *you* could. If anyone can," he added.

Without answering, she put the paint can and bag of wadded-up papers against the house, on the lee side where a breeze wouldn't scatter them; the sky was gray now, with little gusts rustling.

"Because bottom line, it's called conspiracy to commit a felony," Bob continued. "Now, I'm not threatening," he added hastily as she turned, outraged.

"Bob, if a man can't try to defend his wife, I don't know what—"

He held his hands up, palms out. "I'm not saying he can't, Jake, I'm not saying that at all. I'm just pointing out the possible downside if it happens again. Already I've got to track down that first bunch and give them a talking-to."

The ones who'd menaced the unfortunate Canadian, he meant. "But hey, do whatever you think is right. I've got to go."

He strode toward the squad car; she followed, knees creaky from the hard porch steps. "What's going on?" Hope pierced her suddenly. "They haven't picked my guy up, have they? That's not what the call was?"

Littering, jaywalking . . . anything to get him off the street. But of course that would have been too easy; Bob got behind the wheel.

"No. It was from the hospital up in Calais. Some local boys got their butts kicked a little while ago on Washington Street."

While they'd been talking, the squad car's engine had died; the chief made a face at the key hanging in the ignition. "You prob'ly know 'em, that bunch that's been running wild downtown the last few months."

In Eastport, knuckleheads were as common as anywhere else, but hardened delinquency was rare. Hanging out and drinking beer, maybe a little pot smoking in the wildest cases . . .

Mostly that was as bad as it ever got. But the bunch

that Bob meant was an exception. "With the black jackets?"

"Yeah," he replied, settling uncomfortably in the squad car's butt-sprung driver's seat while waiting for the engine to quit racing. At 110,000 miles, the only part of the vehicle still in decent condition was the sunrise stencil on the door panel.

"Same ones I caught trying to blow up the hot dog stand on the breakwater a few weeks ago," Bob said.

With, of all things, wired-together bundles of M-80s plus remote triggering devices that they'd found on the Internet and ordered with their parents' credit cards. It seemed that even the dumbest clucks—and in the most remote places, too, like Eastport—could get hold of sophisticated stuff to do mischief with now.

"Funny thing, though," Bob said as the car stalled. With a sigh, he started it again. "Well, not ha-ha funny," he amended as the Crown Vic's big engine roared to life. "That call I got?" He touched the accelerator cautiously to steady the idle. "Call was to say one of 'em just died. Weird part is, all of 'em got stabbed by someone at the parade, and they won't say who. Like they're scared of whoever it was."

"No kidding." The ghost of a chill went through her.

But that was ridiculous. Garner's gripe was with her alone, so why would he pick a street fight?

Unless maybe they'd picked one with him. . . .

"Stabbed with what?" she asked distractedly.

The police chief shrugged. "Something long and

thin, the docs said, from the tiny holes it made. Like a shish kebab skewer, maybe, or . . ."

But even as he spoke, a mental picture rose in her head, of a woman on Key Street a few hours earlier.

She was an older woman, gray-haired and wearing a purple dress and hat . . . an old-fashioned hat, the kind women once secured to their hair with a—

"Hat pin," she said. "I'll just bet that it was a—"

But just then the old Vic's engine settled at last and he drove off without hearing her.

Shuddering, Steven pulled the soft gray wig from his head and stuffed it into his bag, his nose wrinkling with distaste at the damp, perfumed smell coming from it.

He stripped off the clothes he'd been wearing, the dress and stockings and the hideous undergarments. Naked in the gloom of the ramshackle old kitchen, he pulled wet towelettes from a fresh packet and wiped his face with them, wrinkling his nose at their sharp reek.

As he did so, a vivid mental snapshot rose up, of his mother at her dressing table, fussing with her face. Dabbing and patting at it while he watched from her doorway, enthralled.

She'd been beautiful before all the bad things began happening. Fun, too, sometimes, spending all afternoon working on puzzles with him, or watching old monster movies, the two of them shrieking together as the big, fake-looking lizard rose up out of the waves to stomp Japan.

Even then, though, she'd shown signs of what was to come. Rages, weeping, cursing his father and sometimes Steven, too.

Afterwards she was sorry, begging them to forgive her, buying Steven special treats and demanding to know he still loved her.

Now he drew a fresh towelette over his eyelids, then drew his mascara-caked lashes through it as he'd seen her do, so long ago. After that, with his own clothes pulled on again, it was time to return the room to its previous state, as well.

First, the windows: he stood on the chair he'd found to pull the tacked-on trash bags from the holes he'd stuffed them into, in the broken plaster above the window frames.

The plastic tarp on the floor and the items he'd spread out on it had been harder to hide. Luckily, though, he'd had the wit to make sure the tarp had grommets, metal-reinforced holes at the tarp's edges, through which a rope could be run.

So he'd done that, turning the tarp into a huge blue plastic bag with a drawstring made of clothesline around the top. All his stuff *in* the tarp, drawstring pulled tight, and presto, the bag went down the stairway hole with the things inside.

He'd tied the line's loose ends in a knot he'd learned long ago, when he'd been in Cub Scouts. That is, before his mother had decided that Cub Scouts was too dangerous an activity for her son.

Once out of her frantic sight, he might be snatched by a filthy pervert, catch a ghastly disease from a bus seat, or eat and be fatally sickened by the refreshments at the scout meeting. Once his dad was gone, there seemed no end to the dangers a boy might fall prey to; by the end, even talking on the phone with a school classmate was . . . but never mind.

That was all over now. A sad smile curved his lips as he hauled the blue tarp bag up out of the cellar by way of the old door, which now opened onto a pitch-dark drop. Beyond it the stairs had been and, like his mother, were no more.

Next: the hook that had once held broom and dust-pan was invisible unless you looked for it. Lifting the clothesline from it, he slid the line from the grommets and coiled it neatly, for he intended to use it again soon.

Finally, with the room once more sunk in gloom and his equipment ready at hand, he allowed himself to recall the rest of what he'd accomplished.

The look in that guy's eyes when he realized what had just happened . . .

Anger, of course. But mostly fear. And . . . respect. As Steven moved away from the ginger-haired fellow still prostrate on the ground, he'd heard sirens approaching, seen the guy already calculating what to say to the cops about his injury, and those of his friends.

The ferret-faced boy, lying there near death . . .

Or so Steven hoped. Don't mess with me, he'd telegraphed with his brief final glance at Mr. Ginger Hair. And in response, the guy had looked away in surrender.

Because he knew Steven had something on him, something big, that he didn't want Steven to tell anyone about. So now Steven was safe from Mr. Ginger

Hair and his pals. He could concentrate on readying the ruined kitchen for the next part of his mission, the capture and confinement of Jacobia Tiptree.

On gathering and arranging all the needed equipment, for instance: the clothesline, of course, and the chair, both placed now at the tarp's center.

Next he carefully removed gold-framed photographs of his mother and father from his pack and placed them on the wrecked kitchen counter. The photographs were both studio portraits, his mother against a stock matte-brown backdrop, wearing a green suit with a mink collar, smiling with blood-red lips and already, in Steven's opinion, a little wild-eyed.

Though at the time, she'd probably been thought of as merely vivacious. Steven's father, dark-haired and with his own enormous ears sticking out like the handles on an urn, gazed gravely from his photo, which he'd sat for only at his wife's insistence.

Steven recalled the quarrel: *What if something happens to you? And me without even a picture of you?*

She'd ranted about it for weeks, until Steven's dad gave in. Now his eyes seemed to watch Steven, but without any opinion or expression in them that Steven could discern.

It made Steven uneasy; both pictures did. But he wasn't here for his own comfort, was he? "Good," he whispered into the room's silence. Now for his preparations to be complete, there were just two more tasks left to do, the trickiest of all. But tasks involving other people always were, he knew, so he was already resigned to this.

Also, it would be expensive; he pulled his wallet from his pocket and checked it. As he'd expected—

—*but you can never be too careful,* his mother's voice intruded briefly until he banished it—

—the ten crisp, new hundred-dollar bills he'd placed in it before leaving home were still there. He hadn't even known back then exactly what he'd end up spending them on, only that a good amount of cash on hand never hurt anything.

Outside, the parade had gone by long ago. The curbs and sidewalks were empty. As late afternoon came on, the action had shifted downtown, where the food tents, trinket tables, and other holiday venues were in full swing.

Later, when darkness fell, there would be the fireworks. Absently, Steven put a few broken crackers in his mouth and washed them down with a swig of juice, noticing as he did that his supplies were running low.

But no matter. By tonight, food would be the last of his concerns. He'd have found the ginger-haired guy again and given him his task, and explained carefully to him why he'd be wise to complete it properly.

And he'd have one thing more; that's where the cash came in. Something besides food to occupy him, something to do in a place where no one expected him to be.

Something *better.*

The idea sprang up full-blown, and the minute it occurred to her she knew she was going to have to try it. The trouble was, it would take some cooperation from the rest of them.

And getting that would be the real challenge; determinedly, Jake climbed the stairs to Wade's gun-repair workshop.

"He's going to try to get me, you know. Or Sam. I don't care what Bob Arnold says, if we don't stop Garner, he's going to—"

The workshop smelled sweetly of black powder, turpentine, a variety of stains and varnishes, sawdust, and a whiff of gun oil. To Jake, the mingled scents meant normalcy and security.

Only not right now. Unhappily, she crossed the rough plank floor to where Wade stood under the hanging work-lamps.

Ordinarily she loved this space. But now the brightly lit shop with its familiar long tables, drawers full of gun parts, and shelves packed with reference books, its specialized tools neatly hung on hooks and pegboards, all seemed to exist beyond a pane of invisible glass, one she couldn't break through.

A glass made of fear . . . Looking up from his workbench, Wade ran a big hand distractedly over his brush-cut hair.

Clearly she'd interrupted him. "I'm sorry, I thought you were done—"

Working. But in reply he merely closed the repair manual he was poring over and smiled, gesturing at a stool by the table.

"I am. Just mooching around now."

He enjoyed being in the shop, where his harbor-piloting work too seldom allowed him to spend time. "But what do you mean, stop him? We couldn't even find him."

His blue-gray eyes crinkled ruefully. "And I guess Bob's put a stop to my unofficial efforts."

He'd already called his pals off their assignment to locate the big-eared stranger, not that many of them were worried about Bob Arnold, or an assault charge, either.

Rough and ready was a mild term for what most of Wade's pals were. But one case of mistaken identity was plenty, he'd said, and besides, on the holiday they should be with their families.

"What I mean is, if he's going to grab me—or try to do whatever he's got in mind—he's got to see me. Alone, without anyone else to back me up."

Wade's craggy face creased in a frown. "Maybe so, Jake, but you're not going anywhere without plenty of reinforcement until I know he's out of the picture. Sam, either," he finished.

Which surprised her; Wade rarely issued ultimatums. He was not that kind of guy. And anyway, she wouldn't have listened.

But from his tone she could tell that this time, she'd have to do some fast talking to convince him . . . starting by agreeing with him.

"Right. And I don't want to be without it, either. Because Steven Garner Jr. . . ."

She paused, feeling again the drowning sensation that had swept over her at the sight of Sam's picture with a target drawn on it. "He's just flat-out scary," she finished.

Wade's face said he was glad she realized that. "But, Wade, what if I had a really ridiculous amount of backup?" she added. "I mean, so much of it that no one could possibly harm me?"

Fast talking, indeed; in fact, it was nearly embarrassing. But there was such a thing as exaggeration for effect, and from the flicker of interest in Wade's eyes as she spoke, she thought she might have achieved it.

Or begun on it. "See, he wants to hurt me. Punish me. That's what the picture of Sam was all about."

Not that Garner wouldn't hurt Sam if he could, she knew. But once the shock of the marked-up photo had eased, she realized, too, that for Garner, Sam wouldn't be enough.

That punishment by proxy wouldn't do it for him. "He wanted to scare me, and he's done that. But what he wants, what's really going to float his boat, is—"

"You." Wade said it flatly. She could see the stubborn resistance in his eyes, his two big hands loosely clenched on the worktable, and the squared-off set of his broad shoulders—

But he was listening, and that was something.

"So what if I put myself out there," she persisted, "but you all were watching from somewhere nearby? Tonight, say, on Water Street. I'm on the sidewalk, you're all . . ."

He nodded, reluctantly. "Waiting. You lure him out, let him try something so Bob Arnold has a decent reason to grab him up?"

"You all could be right upstairs in the windows that look down onto the street. While I . . ."

Wade looked thoughtful—not convinced, but considering it. "I get it. I don't like it, but I get it. And it could work. . . ."

If he had his way, he'd still just knock the guy's block off and be done with it. But first they had to find the block. . . .

She pounced before he could reconsider. "That's it, then. You find my dad and tell him. I'll let Sam and Bella know what we're doing, and Bella can call Ellie and George."

She headed for the stairs.

"Wait a minute," Wade said, stopping her, "how come you're not going to call Ellie yourself?"

Generally, whatever Jake knew, Ellie knew about it no more than five or so seconds later, and Jake was the one who told her.

But not this time. "I need to, uh, get ready," she improvised, and ignored his frown at the evasiveness of her reply.

Because persuading him of the safety of the plan she'd made was one thing; actually making it safe, though, was another.

Entirely another.

From an upstairs window, Harold Finnegan watched his ginger-haired son, Jerry, slink into the house. Why'd the kid always have to look so sneaky? he wondered. As if it was in his bones, looking like he was up to something.

Shaking his head, Harold turned from the window

as the front door closed quietly. Not slammed, for once.

And that's the kind of small favor we're grateful for around here nowadays, Harold thought. If the kid comes home without the cops chasing him, shuts a door without breaking every window in the house, we're good.

Twenty years earlier, he'd thought his heart might explode with happiness at the birth of his son. Now, after what felt like a lifetime of defiance and delinquency, he couldn't wait for the kid to get out of the house.

"That you, son?" Harold returned to the desk in his upstairs study, and the papers piled on it. People didn't realize how much work it was chairing the Fourth of July committee.

"Yeah." Footsteps up the stairs. Harold could tell from the energy in his son's step that he was going to ask for something.

Jerry always ditched the sullen act when he wanted a favor. "Hey, Dad?"

Harold looked up. In the doorway, Jerry leaned casually, all six feet of him. Skinny and pale, those squinty gray eyes of his glancing around Harold's study calculatingly.

Looking for something to steal, Harold thought. Rotten of him, he supposed, but he couldn't help it.

He knew Jerry, knew him too well. "What's up?"

The boy sighed. Not a boy anymore. He was a man now, God help him. And soon, despite everything Harold had tried to do—it hadn't been easy, raising the kid without a mother, but he'd tried—soon he'd find out what that was like.

"Listen, I need a little help."

Harold blinked in surprise; that was a new one. Not money, the car, or—please, God, not again—a lawyer.

Harold swiveled his desk chair to face his son. "Yeah? With what?" he asked, but he never could have expected the answer he got.

"I want another job." Jerry squinted as if just saying the words hurt him. "I mean . . . the thing is, I've been thinking."

Another surprise. Jerry had quit the job at the gas station after a week. Harold tried to cover his astonishment by nodding ponderously. "A new job, huh? Well, son . . ."

Jerry broke in. "Yeah. It hit me, like, what a waste I've been. Like, doing nothing. Being a parasite."

Harold blinked; where the heck was this coming from? But then enlightenment dawned. That girlfriend the boy had, Candy, her name was, Harold thought; love was at last civilizing the kid.

Harold's own mood brightened. His last hope for his boy had been that romance might do what he himself had been unable to.

"You don't say," he responded. "Well, that's good news. I'm proud of you."

Jerry grimaced, writhing. With the unaccustomed praise, Harold thought, and felt a twinge of shame: I didn't praise him enough. Not that there'd been much to praise for, but . . .

"Tell you what, next week you and I can sit down with the paper, have a look at the—" Want ads, he'd been about to say.

But Jerry was already shaking his head impatiently. "No, you don't get it. I need a job now."

Harold's heart sank. That was always the kicker, wasn't it? All his life, what Jerry wanted to have, do, or be, he always wanted it now.

And never mind what anyone else wanted. Still, a job would be a good thing for him. Let's not take the bloom off the rose.

He spoke carefully. "So what did you have in mind?"

Still leaning in the doorway, Jerry relaxed slightly. "Well. I mean, just to get me started, you know? Like, ease into it."

Backpedaling on the now part, softening it. Oh, the kid was slick, you had to give that much to him.

Jerry's throat moved as he swallowed. "So I was thinking it should be just, you know, plain old work. Lifting things, moving things."

His eyes met Harold's. "Like that truck on the breakwater now. Unloading it. Maybe they need help doing that," he said.

Which was when Harold's bullshit detector went off, so loud they could probably hear it across the bay on Campobello.

At the same time, the little burst of hope he'd been feeling fizzled and died. "Yeah, huh?"

Thinking Kid wants a job like I want a hernia. All he wants is to get close to that truck.

Him and his pals. To do something to it, maybe.

Or . . . no. To steal something from it. But they wouldn't be able to, because . . .

Because it was the fireworks truck, sent by the company, and a guy from the company was watching it 24/7.

A big, burly guy. As head of the holiday committee, Harold had been made aware of the company's security arrangements.

Recalling this, he felt a slow smile spreading across his face and his head begin nodding as if he were just now realizing the goodness of Jerry's idea. The smartness of it.

"Yeah," he said again, watching contempt flicker briefly in his son's gray eyes. *He thinks I'm buying it.*

Thinks I'm stupid. But whatever Jerry had in mind, it would not get far—the fireworks themselves were nailed into wooden crates, untamperable—and neither would Jerry and his buddies, once they'd tried it.

Then we'll see who's stupid, he thought. "Sure," he said, turning to pick up the phone on his desk.

As it happened, they were a man short on the unloading team. Wade Sorenson had volunteered for the job, but he'd had to drop out.

"Jerry," Harold said, thinking again of the fireworks truck's big driver and of the guy riding shotgun with him, even bigger.

"Jerry, you're in luck. I think we can get you the job you want, right away. I'll do it right this minute."

"Thanks," Jerry said, but he didn't sound very grateful.

Not that Harold had expected him to.

. . .

As a handgun meant primarily for self-defense, the Smith & Wesson .342 Titanium Special had one big advantage: no hammer spur. This meant nothing stuck out from the top of the gun, so it didn't get caught on a pocket thread or on some other part of the user's clothing just when speed was critical.

Jake pulled the lockbox out from behind the loose brick in the cellar wall, slipped the key into the lock, and opened it. Inside lay the handgun and boxes of bullets.

She didn't like needing them, but she'd already given back the little popgun her dad had left with her the previous night. And if there'd ever been a time when a backup plan was a good idea, this was it.

"Mom?" Sam called down the cellar stairs.

"Just a sec. I'll be right with you." She relocked the box, stuck it back into its hiding place, and stuck the brick back in, then slipped the weapon and ammo box into her sweater pocket.

With luck, she'd never need them; by late tonight she could come back down here and tuck them away again. The operative word being *luck* . . .

"What're you doing?" Sam called.

"Nothing." She tried to sound matter-of-fact. But it wasn't easy when you were loading yourself up with enough firepower to stun a moose.

Well, maybe not a moose—at least not on the first shot. But the handgun still had plenty of stopping power, and it was light and easy to fire, even with the powerful ammunition she'd chosen for it.

Fairly light, anyway; at nearly two-thirds of a

pound, it made her pocket sag, especially with the ammo in there with it. She put the box in the other pocket so at least she was balanced.

Then with a sigh she climbed the stairs; other than on the shooting range, being armed at all still made her feel as if she were carrying a rocket launcher around.

At least the gun had an internal locking system, which she hadn't yet unlocked; not being a habitual deadly weapon carrier, she felt a lot safer with the trigger-blocking key in the "no-fire" position.

For now. Later would be a different story; then she might end up wanting a rocket launcher.

Or two. But there was no sense in anyone else knowing how nervous she was about all this, and especially not Wade. He was already plenty iffy about a plan that made her into the bait.

Which she would be; to be any more vulnerable, she'd have to be wiggling around on a fishhook.

But as it turned out, she needn't have worried, or at least not about that. "Bad news," Sam said when she reached the kitchen, where he'd been waiting for her.

Bella was busy scrubbing the wooden knobs on the beadboard cabinet doors. If she rubbed them any harder, Jake thought, they might burst into flames.

Her dad sat at the kitchen table, his long gray ponytail tied back today with a rubber band; he kept the leather thong for dressier occasions.

He didn't look happy, either. Less happy, even, than when she'd told him and Bella about her plan.

"What?" Jake asked, and in answer he angled his head at the kitchen windows, where the fading sky made blackish cutouts of the pointed firs at the edge of it.

"Oh, no," she breathed. The fog bank that had been sitting low and motionless to the south all day now stood halfway up the sky, like some dark giant peering over the horizon line. But that didn't mean it was getting taller.

Instead, it was getting nearer. And the fireworks scheduled for tonight wouldn't begin until dusk, which in Eastport in early July meant eight or a little after.

By then, visibility would be about five feet. It might even be raining. Bad weather for fireworks, and that meant—

"It's starting to look like everything is off for tonight," said Bella. "I heard it just now from one of the committee men."

Each year, the Fourth of July committee put the celebration together and ran it with the kind of precision usually reserved for moon landings, and what they said about it was what happened.

"They haven't quite canceled," said Jake's dad. Turning, he looked out to where the clouds loomed like a big gray hand, ready to flatten the fun.

Not to mention her trap-springing plans. "But the weather's starting to look pretty foul, and if they want to do it tomorrow night, they've got to start making arrangements now, figuring out where to store the fireworks, and putting 'em there," he added.

Which meant canceling tonight for her, too. Jake sank into a chair across from him. She wasn't sure if she felt more relieved or disappointed.

Even-steven, really, she thought. "I understand."

Because fireworks were temperamental items. Once a certain humidity level was reached, you couldn't light them, and even if you could, no one would be able to see them.

There'd just be a damp fizzle . . . also like her plan.

"Yeah," said Sam. "Sorry about that, Mom. But you know," he added, brightening, "tomorrow night's better for me, anyway."

Sam was, of course, part of the contingent of on-lookers she'd been counting on. To be fair, though, she hadn't exactly made a point of letting him know just how serious this all was.

Partly, she knew, she was simply in the habit of sheltering him. But it was also because she disliked so much reminding him of those days, back when this mess began.

Or recalling them herself.

He spread his hands placatingly now. "I mean, if you were still doing it tonight, I would totally be there. But since you're not . . ."

He looked embarrassed. "There's this girl I met. Staying at the Motel East, with her folks."

His late father's adventurousness with women had not been a part of Sam's inheritance—the opposite, in fact. So when he met a girl, it was an event.

"She's really nice. You'd like her," he said earnestly.

Jake rolled her eyes at her son; since when was that the point?

"Well, I like her," he amended with a shy laugh. "I could go see her tonight, too, if there's nothing else going on. See, she and her parents are leaving first thing in the morning," he added in sudden appeal, "and—"

"Okay," she gave in, not that he really needed her blessing. "It doesn't matter, anyway. With no fireworks, which means no crowds, there's no reason for any of us to go, is there?"

Garner wouldn't try grabbing her or Sam, or doing whatever other bad deed he had planned, on an empty street. He'd need crowds for cover. And Sam was a grown man after all, even though she still thought of him as a kid. At her assent, he brightened eagerly.

"Hey, I knew you'd understand. Tomorrow we'll do it, though, right?"

He was already pulling on his jacket and plopping his ball cap on his head. "Uh, don't wait up for me," he added.

"I thought you said her parents were with her," Bella said, turning from the cabinets, where she'd left off cleaning knobs and was now polishing the doors themselves to an incandescent glow.

"Well, yeah," he replied, a little grin spreading across his face. "They are. But, you know, not in the same room."

He hurried out before Bella could think of any more details to question him about. Jake's dad got up as well.

"Well, old girl," he said to Bella. "Time for us to mosey."

"You're abandoning me, too?" Jake protested as Bella put on her sweater and found her purse.

"I'm out of bleach," she replied, "and oil soap and Brillo pads." She generally bought the economy-sized versions of these in the nearest market town, thirty miles distant. "And as long as I'm going, your father thought we'd . . ."

Since their marriage, the two hadn't had much time alone together; living with Jake and Wade in the house on Key Street was pleasant and convenient for all concerned, but not very private. And the St. Andrews Hotel, in the Canadian bayside town of the same name, was luxurious, and right across the border.

So it had become a favorite with them; besides, they knew Jake and Wade didn't get a lot of time alone together, either. "We'll be back home tomorrow afternoon," her father told Jake reassuringly. "If you still had plans, of course we wouldn't go, but . . ."

But now she didn't. "Of course," she told them firmly, shooing them out.

Which was when Wade finally came down from his workshop with a look on his face. Not a terrible look, not even a very serious one.

But a look nonetheless. "What?" Jake demanded. "Don't tell me you have to go somewhere now, too?"

Because one thing about everyone else leaving the house was that it left her and Wade alone. And apparently the same thought had occurred to him; he wrapped his arms around her. What he said next, though, dashed her hopes.

"Listen, is there any chance that you could go and stay with Ellie and George tonight?"

While everyone else had been abandoning ship, she'd heard the phone ring. But he'd answered it from upstairs.

She wiggled from his embrace. "Wade. What's happened?"

It couldn't be a ship coming into the terminal, needing a harbor pilot. None were scheduled, not on the Fourth.

Or there hadn't been until now. "Turns out a crew member on a boat bound for Canada has a diplomatic problem," he said.

She blinked. "What do you mean? That he can't get into the country?"

Wade nodded. "So they have to come here. Some immigration problem the guy has. Strictly a paperwork problem, but . . ."

He shrugged helplessly. "But they're being hard cases about it at Canadian immigration. They wanted to know could I help out, but I already told them no, I had a situation here of my own. So forget it."

She let out the breath she'd been holding. Not that she'd have had any problem staying alone; the dogs would be here, and there was no likelihood of anyone getting past Prill.

But her next emotion was guilt, mingled with the knowledge that George and Ellie had a spare room no one was using. And her own plan was postponed, anyway, so . . .

Her look said as much: that really, there was no reason he couldn't go.

"Yeah," he replied, "I figured when I looked out the window that we're off for tonight. But that doesn't matter; as long as your pal's around, I'm a constant presence around here."

He gave her shoulder a squeeze. "So get used to it."

No problem, she thought, already planning ahead for dinner; when Bella wasn't cooking, they often ordered out. Since tonight it was only the two of them, though . . .

"They're just going to have to sit there in international water until someone can get out to them," Wade added, meaning the Canadian boat with a non-entry-eligible crew member on it.

"It does mean I'll be here for the flyover tomorrow night. Poor guys on the boat, though," he added. "I bet that's costing them a hefty bundle."

For a freight carrier, time spent sitting idle anywhere was cash down the drain; that was why if he took the job, especially on a holiday with so little notice like this, the bonus would be substantial.

A windfall, actually. But with Steven Garner Jr. lurking nearby, she knew better than to urge him; even her staying at George and Ellie's wouldn't make him feel any better about going, after he began thinking about it.

She started to ask if he felt like grilling steaks, maybe opening a bottle of wine. But before she could say anything, the phone rang again.

"Jake?" Bob Arnold said as soon as she answered. "Good news, you can relax."

"Who is it?" Wade wanted to know from over her shoulder.

"We've got the little bastard in custody," Bob told Jake.

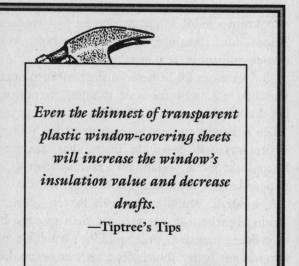

Chapter 9

Even the thinnest of transparent plastic window-covering sheets will increase the window's insulation value and decrease drafts.
—Tiptree's Tips

Y̶ou're sure?" Wade asked again three hours later.

"Completely," she replied, thinking ahead to a whole lovely evening of solitude.

That hadn't been her plan, but time alone was rare enough that she would take it when she could get it.

And now with Steven Garner Jr. already on his way to the lockup thirty miles south in the county seat of Machias, she could enjoy it.

Right now it was five in the afternoon, late enough for a wine cooler but still light outside even though the fog loomed ominously, a thick gray curtain halfway out on the bay.

"Really, I'll be fine." She sipped a cool mouthful, let it roll luxuriously around before swallowing.

Wade hiked his duffel bag higher up onto his shoulder. The tugboat was scheduled to leave the fish pier in fifteen minutes.

"All right, then." He said it reluctantly. He wasn't blind to the possible pleasures of home, either. But duty called, and so did that hefty bonus.

"I'll be back in two days." The ship he was assigned to idled hundreds of miles due east, burning up fuel and man-hours in international waters on the far side of Nova Scotia.

Not allowed to enter Canada with the iffy crew member on board, it was also at the moment not welcome stateside. But the paperwork was in process so it would be by the time he got there.

"Great," she said, still giddy with relief at the news that her stalker had been grabbed. Or rather, had turned himself in, for reasons she couldn't fathom.

"Bob Arnold says Garner just walked into the cop shop, slapped his ID on the counter, and said he'd been hassling me and did they want to arrest him," she repeated wonderingly.

So Bob had, mostly to get the guy out of Bob's hair—and Jake's, too—for a couple of days. Later,

Bob had told her, they could work on proving or dis-proving Jake's still-active suspicion that Garner had already committed one murder here in Eastport.

But for now they had trespassing, terrorizing, and telephone harassment: the three T's, according to Bob's account of all the paperwork he'd filled out so as to speed the guy on his way.

"We get his prints, a cheek swab, coupla more things, maybe, we'll know if he had contact with the Sea Street victim," Bob had said confidently.

Not that he knew for sure Garner would give per-mission for those. He didn't know why Garner had surrendered himself, either, and once he'd done so, Garner himself had zipped his lip and was refusing to talk to anyone but a lawyer.

Which, because he had no money and it was a holi-day weekend, would take time to arrange. But it would happen, Bob promised.

Jake sighed deeply, feeling the day's tension lift. "You be careful out there," she told Wade.

He ruffled her hair, then drew her in and kissed her. "Yeah. You too. See you soon."

Then he was gone, and the old house felt suddenly huge and empty around her. But none of that, she scolded herself briskly, and turned to the dogs, who cared nothing for who was at home and who wasn't as long as someone was in charge of kibble.

Prill danced around the kitchen while Monday sat patiently, a doggy smile on her sweet old face. "There," Jake said, pouring the food out for them, and when they had finished she leashed them up for a walk.

But she'd barely gotten around the block with them when the fog finished descending, turning the night damp and chilly. And Monday didn't like going too far on those old legs, especially after sundown, when her cataract-clouded eyes couldn't see far in the darkness. So they turned for home, and once inside, Jake went around switching lights on and making sure doors were locked.

You dope, she scolded herself again as she did so. What, are you going to be afraid of the dark now, too?

But the answer was no, especially once she'd started on a second wine cooler, this one considerably less diluted with fruit juice than the first. Still, even under its influence she didn't feel nearly as good as she'd hoped, partly because the fog had brought true darkness on so much sooner than she'd expected.

And partly because Steven Garner's grudge against her still loomed in her thoughts, even though he was safely behind bars. Through the kitchen windows, she watched the lights in the other houses dwindle to tiny sparks, then get snuffed out as billows of fog rolled in over the island.

Soon her own house felt like an outpost, nothing visible outside but the drifting mist coalescing now and then to drizzle. On the plus side, by now Bella and her dad would be settling into their room at the hotel in St. Andrews, while Sam was ensconced cozily somewhere with his new girlfriend, too, no doubt.

So no one would be driving. And Wade's tugboat wasn't even a minor worry, equipped as it was with the latest in navigation gear and able to find its way through anything short of hardened concrete, especially with Wade himself at the helm.

Which he surely was; it was a harbor-pilotish quirk of his that if he was on a boat, he was steering it. Reassured on the topic of everyone else's safety and now confident of her own, she pulled the window shades, snapped on another kitchen light, and put on the radio, tuning it to the Eastport high school station.

A reggae tune lilted into the room, not one she knew; it was one of her favorite things about Tiger Radio, as it was called, that she heard things on it that were (a) music she'd never heard before while also being (b) music she wanted to hear again.

Soon her favorite I'm-all-alone meal was ready: deviled ham and hot baked beans on toast, with a whole steamed artichoke for the vegetable. A real glass of wine, no fruit juice included, accompanied it, and by the time she'd finished it she felt much better, indeed.

Just because somebody said you did something, that doesn't mean you're guilty, Ellie had insisted to her that afternoon, and now with the food and wine in her, the admonition sounded halfway convincing.

But it had never been about what Garner thought, anyway, had it? Instead it was her own memory niggling at her, and always had been. She ran hot water on her plate, rinsed the few pieces of silverware she'd used, and wrung out the dishcloth. When she had finished and hung up the dish towel, in the lamplight the kitchen looked nearly as whistle-clean as Bella would've gotten it.

Nearly. She stood indecisively a moment. Then with

a sigh she dampened the dishcloth again and began wiping countertops.

By seven, she'd polished all the appliances, including the metal pans underneath the stove burners, mopped the floor, and cleaned out the refrigerator. The kitchen smelled sweetly of Ajax, fresh coffee, and newly laundered throw rugs.

"You know," she told the dogs, who sat listening politely as they always did to humans who were in the throes of losing their marbles, "Bella's right. This cleaning business is very calming."

Like old house repair. Which reminded her, there was a loose wire in the light switch of the chandelier in the front parlor, and just barely enough evening light still coming in through the hall windows so she could probably fix it.

"Wait here," she told the canines, and went to the cellar to fetch the stepladder. She'd already been down there once to put the handgun and the ammo back in the lockbox; Ellie could pop in anytime, and she might have Lee with her.

And it was just good practice. After she hauled the ladder upstairs, she remembered that if she was going to work on a light switch, it would be a good idea to turn off the power to it first, so she went back downstairs again and did that. The dogs' heads were swiveling back and forth as if they were watching a tennis match, and her legs were tired from all the stair climbing.

But never mind; she was on a mission, so from the

toolbox she took a pair of screwdrivers—a big one for the switch cover and a tiny one for the set screws holding the wires inside—and got to work, first removing the switch cover, then loosening both strands of the electrical wire itself.

By now it was getting really dark out; she hadn't banked on those extra trips to the cellar. So it was harder than she'd planned, seeing which wire was which: the copper one versus the silver one. And it made a big difference how you attached them.

Copper wire to copper screw, silver to silver; she wasn't entirely certain what the problem would be if you did it backwards, only that it was sure to make your house burn down in the middle of the night.

And, of course, with the power to this part of the house off, she couldn't turn on a light. . . . With a mild oath, she turned and promptly bumped painfully into the stepladder, which she'd brought not to work on the wires but to replace two burnt-out bulbs in the chandelier.

Rubbing her bruised elbow and uttering another oath, this one much less mild, she proceeded to Wade's workshop for a small flashlight; this she mounted to one of Sam's ball caps with duct tape before putting the cap on.

By now the two dogs were practically rolling on their sides with helpless laughter, which they diplomatically disguised as yawning and pacing around the back door impatiently. It was, Jake realized with a prickle of anxiety, already past eight.

The dark gray sky outside the front hall windows would soon be pitch black, and on top of that it was nearly time for the animals' final evening walk. Also, somehow she'd already lost one of the screws from the switch-cover plate.

There was, she thought—not, alas, for the first time—a fine line between the kind of home repair that tranquilized you and the kind that drove you shrieking out into the night. But she had to go out anyway—the dogs had quit pacing and were leaning against the back door with their legs crossed, pleadingly.

So: Collars. Leashes. "Out," she told them, and they pranced happily ahead of her, even Monday, who lately had to sometimes be helped down the porch steps, her arthritis had gotten so bad.

Out on the sidewalk, after a disoriented moment of wondering where that bright glow was coming from, she took off the cap and pried the flashlight from the duct tape, then switched it off and stuck it in her pocket. On a night like this, so foggy that the light's beam just bounced back from the water particles hanging in the air, visibility was actually better without it.

After that, despite the murk, it was lovely outside. Pale yellow coronas radiated from the streetlights, and from windows in the houses all around, white-gold squares fell onto the dark lawns. Turning back, she saw her own big old white house looming in the mist like some huge ship afloat on a sea of night.

"Wuff," said Prill, stopping short. The dog's ears pricked alertly and her stubby tail stood up as she stared ahead.

Monday gazed blindly, but there was nothing

wrong with her nose. "Umph," she muttered, not liking whatever it was, either.

Getting a good grip on both leashes, Jake peered into the mist. As usual, Prill made a fine early-warning system, but she was as likely to warn about a bit of litter blowing in the street as she was about a potential assailant.

And Jake could hardly see at all. The fog was now billowing so thickly, it didn't even look real—more like special effects.

"Prill," Jake said, "let's go."

There were no potential assailants out here. The dog glanced back at her, then returned to staring holes in the mist, and took a stiff-legged step forward. Then she froze once more.

Monday whined as Jake half turned. "Okay, let's just go—"

Meeyowrowowyowowl! Something small, black, and very fast came out of the dark yard to her right, straight at her. At the very last instant, it changed course, scrambled up Prill's back, and leapt from her head high into the air.

Prill spun around and snapped where the thing had been, missing it by a hair. A cat hair, Jake realized, but knowing it didn't help matters as now the feline dashed the other way.

Monday charged, yanking on her leash; Prill hauled in the opposite direction. Then they reversed, and suddenly both leashes were wrapped around Jake's legs. She sat down hard while the dogs tried pulling her arms out of their sockets; when that failed, they tried crushing her to death by sitting on her.

Sorrysorrysorry, their heaving sides, lapping tongues, and panting breaths seemed to say very urgently in the darkness. But it was a cat! they emphasized. A cat!cat!cat! It was a—

The animal that had caused all the commotion, of course, was long gone. Probably it was back in the bushes there somewhere, laughing its head off, she thought sourly.

And painfully, Jake moved her arms and legs around, checking for fractures. None were obvious; the palms of her hands and one knee felt hot and sticky, though.

Like the skin had been removed from them, and half of it probably had. Also, her butt felt like somebody had just smacked it with a two-by-four.

"Yes, I know what it was," she said grouchily, clambering up. And then, "Yowtch."

Brushing her hands on the sides of her pants made embedded pebbles fall out of the wounded flesh. Also, straightening her right leg out was no barrel of laughs.

"I swear, from now on both you dogs are going to wear—"

Choke collars, she was about to finish, although she would never really have done any such thing to them. Then she noticed Monday hiding behind her leg. Prill stood at military attention.

"Uh, hello?" she said, exasperated, to the animals. "You want to let me in on what it is this time? That you're going to drag me to my death about? Or should I just lie down and bang my head on the sidewalk here, and save you the trouble of—"

A shape stepped out of the fog. At the sight her voice froze in her throat.

A man, his features blurred by mist and darkness, stood motionless, maybe half a block from her.

The night seemed suddenly very still, the houses so far away she couldn't have reached any of them in time to—

She opened her mouth to shout. A croak came out. Prill's low growl was barely audible.

"Hello?" she whispered. Stupid, stupid, why had she not just taken the dogs out to the backyard?

Eastport was so safe at most times of the year, it was a shock when the holiday filled it with strangers. Unpredictable ones, who might . . .

The shape was gone. She blinked—no one, and both dogs were now sniffing around unconcernedly.

And now that whoever it was had gone, she too felt relief wash over her. And a bit of embarrassment . . .

Dark and foggy, yes. But, that's what it was on an Eastport night in midsummer. No big surprise there . . .

Or anything to get spleeny about, either, she told herself, spleeny being what Eastport natives said when they meant nervous without any good reason.

"Come on," she commanded, doing an about-face on the sidewalk. A stroll in the other direction, toward the streetlight at the far corner and the much-more-brightly lit houses around it, suddenly seemed vastly preferable to the wet gloom ahead.

Fifteen minutes later they were back inside, all the doggy chores completed and the porch light switched off. And as it turned out, the break had refreshed her;

once she got started again, it took only a few more minutes to finish rewiring the hall switch, and after that, replacing the chandelier bulbs was easy.

Though getting up and down the stepladder wasn't; her leg twinged, and she'd never been much of a heights specialist. Done at last, she emitted a sigh even deeper than the one she'd let out when the mysterious fog-figure stepped back into the mist.

If he'd even been there at all. Maybe he hadn't. Nerves from the long, worrisome day, the empty house, and then those glasses of wine . . .

It was, Jake thought, just as likely that a combination of darkness and fog had produced the shape, a breeze had dissolved it, and the dogs had merely been staring after that dratted cat.

Now both animals padded upstairs, Prill big and ungainly but as athletic as a racehorse, her muscles moving powerfully under her glossy coat, and Monday climbing stubbornly, determined to go up, too, despite her age.

As Jake stowed away the stepladder and slotted the tools back into the toolbox on the hall shelf, the low hoot of foghorns drifted through the locked screen door.

The inside door was open because it was summer, but the screen door was locked because she wasn't a complete fool. . . . The pleasures of solitude, she was beginning to think, were a tad overrated.

Finally she closed the inside door and locked it, too, and made a cup of chamomile tea to bring with her up to bed. Prill had Wade's side of the mattress already staked out for herself, lying the long way on it, while Monday stretched across the foot.

But in the bedroom doorway, she paused. It was ten o'clock; plenty of time yet, really, to do at least one more chore. The float in the toilet tank needed replacing, for instance, as did the bottom square of carpet on the stairs up to the third floor, where her father and Bella lived in their own cozy apartment.

The top hinge on the closet door needed tightening, too, and the bottom one needed shimming, to square the door so its bottom edge no longer scraped the old hardwood floor.

Or, she thought wryly as she got into bed—or as far in as the dogs would let her get, anyway—I could just cut a quarter-inch of wood off the door's bottom, the way everyone else does.

Either way, it wouldn't take long, and neither would any of the other small tasks that needed doing in an old house: window weatherstripping (in Maine, July was not too soon to begin on winter chores), radiator repainting (likewise), or sanding the old floor in the guest room (not a winter task, but likely to become one if she didn't get to it soon).

And that was just the start of her chores list. But instead of doing any of them, she decided to relax against the pillows and have a sip of tea, and then rest her eyes only for a moment.

The dogs snored: Prill daintily, Monday adenoidally. Leaning back, feeling how tired she was, she thought she should probably get them both off the bed.

If Wade were here, he would do it. She wondered if

he'd gotten to the container ship yet, out on the water. She wondered if Bella and her father were having a good time in St. Andrews, and whether they would come home tomorrow or stay another day.

She thought it was probably a good thing that Sam might've found a girlfriend, even if she did live somewhere else; he was lonely, she knew, though he tried putting a good face on it.

She hoped the girl didn't drink, and thought she would ask Sam about it when the opportunity presented itself. If it did.

And that was the last thing she thought until sometime later, when the crash of breaking glass woke her.

She jerked straight up in bed, in the dark. At some time she must have shut off the light and shooed the dogs onto the floor. Now Prill's big toenails were already clicking out into the hall, her steps hurrying downstairs.

Jake snapped the light on, her legs swinging out of bed even as she tried blinking away the clammy remnants of a bad dream. Now there was only silence except for Prill's anxious patrolling from room to room.

But a moment ago . . . no, she definitely hadn't dreamed it. She went to the bedroom window, put her face up to the screen, and listened, at the same time trying to remember the exact quality of the sound that had woken her.

Window breaking? Auto glass? Real vandalism was

as rare in Eastport as other serious crime, the black-jacketed boys who were a thorn in Bob Arnold's side lately being the exception.

In the darkness of the hallway, she crept to the small front-of-the-house guest room whose floor she'd been thinking of sanding earlier. From its window, she could see down the street to the water.

Under the mist-shrouded yellow streetlights, the white fog still drifted in billows. But nothing else moved and the lights in the nearby houses were out. Then . . .

Another crash, followed by the tinkle of glass shards, came from down there somewhere. But this time it was a familiar sound: a bottle breaking.

She tried to remember when she'd heard exactly that sound before, realized it was a memory connected with Sam, and chose not to pursue it. But there was no doubt now what it was. Or that it came from the other end of her house, the driveway side.

Slipping downstairs, she tiptoed through the kitchen with Prill by her side. Silent as a ninja, the dog padded toward the kitchen door leading to Wade's shop, then through it.

Outside, another bottle smashed. "Go lie down," Jake told the Doberman, who swerved smoothly at the command and headed back to her bed in the kitchen.

Then Jake went on, thanking her stars that when the chips were down, the dog was so obedient. If Garner were out there, of course it would be a different story. But this was just some beer-bombed neighborhood offspring, probably, whose parents would not be happy if their kid limped home with bite wounds. And she could always call Prill if she needed her.

"Good dog," Jake called over her shoulder. Prill's low answering grumble meant she didn't like it a bit, but she stayed put.

Only then did Jake open the back door and peer out. Sheets of mist swept like ghosts between the maples and the long, thin arms of espaliered fruit trees against the new lattice put in by her father.

The cool, damp air smelled like an ocean wave, saline- and iodine-tinctured. High overhead, the fog thinned swiftly and rags of moonlight trailed through, making the sky dramatic.

Tasting salt on her lips, Jake felt the hairs on her arms prickling sharply as tiny, cold droplets beaded on them. "Who's out there?"

No answer. She wished she hadn't put the gun away, and turned to go back inside just as a small shape sailed out of the gloom in a long arc, crashing down onto Wade's pickup truck. The bottle—a small fruit juice bottle—bounced off the hood.

Probably it had made a dent. "All right, that's it."

No creepy prowler was out there. A thrown bottle, that was drunk-and-rowdy material just as she'd thought, the kind of thing some dumb bunny might do after a few too many.

She stomped down the steps onto the driveway gravel. "I've called the cops."

Which she hadn't, of course, and now she was glad of it, and that the gun wasn't in her hand, too. Just what she didn't need, she thought, annoyed, a false alarm so that afterwards Bob Arnold would take her legitimate worries with even more grains of salt.

She strode down the driveway. "So you'd better scram," she said clearly into the darkness.

Not shouting, though—no sense waking the neighborhood. "I mean it."

As if it wasn't enough for some jerk to come suddenly out of the past like some late-night movie monster, lurching up out of a swamp. It wasn't enough that he'd hassled her in her own yard and sent terrorizing emails, thrown a dead rat into her house and scared her wits out with a target-scrawled photograph of Sam.

No, on top of *that*—

"I'd better hear you beating it down that street right *now*," she growled into the gloom.

—on top of *that*, here was some *other* little jerk who had to use the holiday for an excuse to raise hell.

Oh, but she was burned up over it now that she was completely awake. And Wade wouldn't be happy about that dent, either.

"I mean it," she finished from the end of the driveway. And that was as far as she'd gotten when the door—her *own* door, the one into her *house*—slammed behind her with a loud bang.

And then the porch light went out.

For an instant, she just stood there with her mouth hanging open. *Son of a*—

The next thing she thought was that she should go next door, or down the street, to any house that she knew definitely had people in it, and pound on the door. Ask them to call Bob, stay there in their house and wait for him—

Anything but go back into her own house, alone, and confront an unknown intruder. But the upstairs window of Wade's workshop, full of wood and volatile wood-finishing liquids, not to mention boxes of shotgun shells—

—and a phone, the nearest phone is in it—

That window looked out from a rich cornucopia of burnables, accelerants, and explosives.

And right now orange flames were flickering in it.

The guy had come up to Tim Sawtelle on Water Street. Tim had never seen the guy before in his life. Quickly the guy struck up a conversation, saying he'd noticed that he and Tim looked quite a bit alike.

Which was true. Not a lot alike, but there was a general resemblance. Once Tim agreed that this was so, the guy made him an offer: five hundred bucks if Tim would turn himself in to the cops, using the ID the guy gave him.

The name on the ID was Steven Garner Jr. The photo on it looked like Tim, too; even a little more so, maybe, just on account of it being a lousy photo. The guy said all he needed was for Tim to spend a couple of nights in jail; when he got out, which the guy swore a few nights was all it would be since after all he wasn't really Steven Garner, there'd be another five hundred for him.

And to Tim Sawtelle, who (as even he would admit)

was not the sharpest pin in the cushion, a thousand dollars was a whole lot of money. So now he sat in the darkness of the backseat of the aging squad car as the deputy Eastport cop drove very fast down Route 1 toward the next town south, which was Machias.

The county jail was there, and the courthouse, too. In the morning, Tim would be arraigned on a charge of trespassing, that being what they'd wanted Steven Garner for, as it turned out.

Not much of a crime, especially on a holiday weekend in Eastport. But the cop he talked to had been very interested, for reasons Tim didn't understand.

And to tell the truth he didn't much care about them. He'd come from Bangor to join the fun, not realizing the weather would put a damper on everything and not having anything else to occupy him: no job, no girlfriend.

He'd figured he might as well just see what was up in the easternmost city, as people around here called it. And boy, had he ever.

In the squad car the plastic perp window between him and the cop was closed, probably because the cop didn't want to have any conversation, which was fine with Tim. The way the cop drove on the rough, curving road with its bumpy, potholed surface little more than a track where no trees grew, threw him from side to side so hard that if he tried talking, he'd probably just bite his tongue anyway.

At least the cop hadn't cuffed him behind his back. No reason to—Tim had walked into the police station of his own accord, to surrender. That he'd done

it with a false ID was something the cop hadn't figured out yet, and Tim was starting to think he might
be in some trouble over that.

But whatever. He was no angel, he'd been in jail
before. There wasn't much in one that could scare
him.

He was tougher than he looked. And it was five
hundred in cash, nice new bills. At the jail, he would
be obligated to hand the money over, but he'd get it
back.

He settled into the cop car's fraying bench seat.
Outside, the night rushed by, dark and foggy and
smelling of evergreens and sea salt where it came in
the front driver's-side window. Tim shivered a little
in his denim jacket, wishing he had worn more.

Probably he would have to give that up, too, and
put on the cotton jail scrubs. Ones with short sleeves,
and the blankets in jail were always as thin as a bail
bondsman's smile.

This being the holiday, it could take a couple of
days for them to run his prints and cross-check the
identity on the Social Security card he'd showed them
in the police station.

When they did, they'd find out he wasn't Steven
Garner, and the charade would be over.

He didn't know what he'd be charged with then;
some kind of fraud, maybe. The stranger hadn't explained that part, only that Tim wouldn't have done
any damage or violence.

So he wouldn't be in *that* much trouble. A lot of
rigmarole, probably, jail food and stern-faced judges

at the hearings and a court-appointed defender, if it all even went that far.

He might have to pretend he was nuts, or maybe he'd just say he'd been drunk. *But hey, easy money,* Tim thought as the squad car turned in at a red-brick building whose dimly lit sign read WASHINGTON COUNTY JAIL.

The car slowed, came to a stop at a door marked intake. Getting out, the cop pressed a buzzer on the door.

Easy money.

Inside the house, with the fire crackling upstairs in Wade's shop, the first thing Jake heard was both dogs pacing back and forth anxiously on the other side of the closed door between the workshop and the rest of the house.

The door that had been open a few minutes earlier . . . but the animals were safe for the moment, anyway, she realized in relief. And right upstairs in the shop hung a fire extinguisher, a brand-new, fully loaded one; she'd put it there herself.

Those two facts were the upside of the situation. But (1) when she tried it, the door with the dogs on the other side of it wouldn't open, so she couldn't get into that part of the house, and (2) the house itself was on fire, for Pete's sake.

Or a significant portion of it was. Stumbling up the stairs through the acrid smoke that was thickening fast, she grabbed for the fire extinguisher. Maybe she could still—

Gone. Where the extinguisher had hung on the wall halfway up the stairwell, now just an empty hook mocked her through the smoke while a few feet away, bright fire crackled.

Smother the flames with something, she thought desperately. A mental picture of a pile of horse blankets, salvaged by Wade from the selling-off of a nearby tack shop's old inventory, rose in her mind. They were in the far corner below the shotgun-shell-reloading station. . . .

Coughing and wiping tears from her eyes, she reached the top of the stairs, peered through a dense smoke curtain. Except for the fire itself, the shop was pitch dark. Her frantic fumbles at the light switch were ineffective.

And why is that? her mind screamed frantically at her, but she had no time for the question now.

Flashlight, I should've brought a . . .

The dogs were still on the other side of that jammed door—whimpering now, their pacing heightened to scratching at the doorframe. Was the intruder there, too, somehow not getting bitten?

But that wouldn't have been so difficult. The intruder might've fed the animals; even Prill was a sucker for snacks, and Monday's friendship could be had for the price of a biscuit.

Meanwhile, with each moment that passed, the fire caught more furiously, first nibbling, then loudly munching whatever debris it had gotten started in: a small pile of something, apparently, because the flames weren't spreading yet. So if she could find the blankets by feel, spread them atop that rising glow . . .

An arm came out of the choking smoke, caught her around the waist suddenly, and flung her to the floor, hard. A bright light came straight into her eyes, blinding her, then shifted so she could see. . . .

"Hello, Jacobia." That voice . . .

It was him, she knew. But the face was wrong . . . a shudder of horror went through her at the sight, the features all elongated and flattened. She started up, but he put a foot on her chest and shoved.

It was a woman's nylon stocking pulled over his head, the old-fashioned kind; that, or he'd cut the leg out of a pair of pantyhose. Eyes like holes, and the mouth . . .

"I could kill you now." The voice was hollow, as if shouted from the bottom of a deep hole.

"Or I could just tie you up and leave you here. To burn," he added with lip-smackingly ghastly enjoyment. "Burn to a crisp."

She tried to roll sideways; he leaned down, touching a cool something to her throat.

Knife, she realized with a fresh burst of fright. It moved against her skin.

"That's right," he whispered as flames crackled higher and brighter.

"So many options. And I'll admit it, I've wanted to kill you for so long, it feels strange not to do it."

He chuckled hideously. "Now that I've got the chance."

In the kitchen, Prill howled pitifully; it was Monday whose bark now sounded fierce, a deep, warning utterance Jake had heard only a few times before from the animal. It was the sound of a dog pushed past its limits in the civilized-behavior department, and Jake would have done a lot to see Monday charging up the shop stairs now.

Maybe she was old, but the black Lab still had a few good teeth in her head, and now she sounded as if she wanted to get some use out of them. Her assailant heard, too.

"Superglue," he confided cryptically with a repulsive smile as he straightened, holding the very same flashlight that she'd neglected to grab off the hall shelf as she'd gone out.

The stocking over his face turned his every expression into a fright mask. "A little dab'll do ya," he sang quaveringly.

Not that his appearance had been any great shakes without a sock over it . . . Another hard shiver went through her as she recalled first seeing him only a day ago: smirkingly pleased by his own creepiness.

As he was now. But the knife, at least, was no longer at her throat. "If you want a door to stay shut," he went on in a whisper, "superglue it."

"Great tip," she managed. His foot was on her throat now. "What the freak do you want, Garner?"

Only she didn't say "freak." He grinned but didn't reply.

With his foot still firmly planted on her, he glanced back at the fire, now about the size of a blaze in a small fireplace. It still wasn't spreading, because he'd piled the flammables in a metal dishpan Wade used sometimes for soaking wood strips to make them pliable.

But sooner or later it would spread, and then it would get to the shelf where Wade stored wood stains, lacquers, and varnishes for restoring old gun stocks on the antique weapons he repaired.

Above that, their shapes clearly outlined in the orange-and-yellow glow from the fire, were more of the liquids he used in gun work: paint thinner and acetone, mason jars half full of the amber fluids, a whole collection of ruined paintbrushes soaking with their bristles aimed down.

Because as he said, the old natural-bristle brushes were better than anything he could buy new. He just had to recondition them. But now . . .

A furious sob stuck in Jake's throat: Wade would likely never see anything in here again. Including me . . .

Mechanized shrieks from somewhere nearby stabbed her ears; they'd been going on for a long time, she realized distantly, only she hadn't noticed.

A knife at your throat will do that to you. . . . It was the smoke alarm, piercingly loud, audible not just here in the shop but out in the street, too. . . .

And that pulsing white light at the shop window wasn't the fire. It was the fire alarm's LED lamp, and something else.

Something outside. Headlights, turning into the driveway . . .

He saw it, too, and under the stocking his awful grin changed abruptly to something much worse: ugly, deeply malicious, and not the least bit sane.

"Bitch," he grated at her. His face was distorted

with rage. But at the same time he looked confused, and distracted just enough so that she might . . .

She kicked at him, felt her foot connect. Crumpling with a groan, he hurled the fire extinguisher at her, then staggered and half fell down the stairs, stumbling at the bottom.

On the other side of the door, both dogs went wild; a little longer and Prill might chew right through it. Groaning, he made it to his feet, as pounding began on the door leading outside.

Through the stocking she glimpsed fright on his face as he realized he might be trapped. But then he saw the laundry room door, and through it the window.

"Jake!" It was Bob Arnold outside.

"Bob, he's—" But her attacker had already hurled himself at the old window glass; it shattered outwards as he went through it. By the time she reached the shop door and flung it open, his footsteps were thudding away on the other side of the house.

"Bob," she gasped, unable to get her breath suddenly.

He seized her shoulder with one hand, peering anxiously into her face. The alarm still howled rhythmically upstairs.

"Are you all right?" he demanded, already thumbing his radio with his other hand. She shook him off, pointed.

"That way . . . I think it was—"

The fire upstairs crackled. Her legs suddenly buckled out from under her as he summoned help.

He dragged her out, away from the house. Already in the distance, sirens began howling. "Bob . . ."

He ran for his car, which he'd left running, and reversed out of the driveway in a spray of gravel.

Garner, she thought. But he was supposed to be . . .

Clambering up, she staggered inside. The dogs hurled their bodies against the still-closed door leading to the kitchen.

But on this side of the door stood a bucket full of water tinctured generously with lemon juice. Bella kept it there for mops that needed emergency sweetening; she hated a sour mop.

Seizing the bucket, Jake ran upstairs. The fire still burned merrily, happy for the moment with its meal of swept-up sawdust, wood shavings, and the bigger sticks and chunks of old scrap wood now beginning to burn in earnest.

But the smoke had found its way to the open screen window a few feet away. So she could breathe now. . . .

Resisting the temptation to toss the water onto the blaze, Jake forced herself to approach it calmly. Careful, careful . . . Tipping the heavy bucket, she let the water stream onto the fire.

Hot sizzles of steam erupted, startling her. Too much water and the sparks would fly. Careful . . .

She tipped it more, flooding the remaining embers. Now a wet, sodden mess covered the floor under the window.

A hissing stink boiled up. She put the bucket down, scanned around in the harsh glow of the fire alarm's battery-powered LED.

No flicker of flame showed from anywhere, and no smoke wisps rose. The air was thick with haze, but it was mostly steam from the water on the burning wood scraps. Through the window came the howl of a fire truck's siren approaching.

Gazing around once more, she cursed loudly and creatively at the smoke-smelling disarray that just minutes ago had been Wade's workshop. Then she grabbed a crowbar from the hook where he kept it, went back downstairs—cursing some more at the broken window in the laundry room—and applied the crowbar to the glued-shut door to the kitchen.

The dogs leapt gratefully at her as sirens screamed out front, red whirling beacons strobing the night. Hastily she shoved both dogs into the back parlor and shut the door on them.

Then, imagining with dismay the dirty boot marks, smudgy handprints, and the many other grimy evidences that Bella would no doubt find to exclaim over when she got home, she went to let a crew of excited firemen into the house.

Hustling as fast as he could through the dark streets of Eastport, Steven Garner could barely keep from laughing out loud even through his pain. It had all worked so well. . . .

He hadn't known she'd be alone, of course, until nearly the last minute. But when he'd watched her husband leave the house with his duffel over his shoulder, then followed him downtown to the dock and waited while he got onto a tugboat, Steven had realized: he was even more home free than he'd expected.

It just went to show that luck really did favor the prepared mind. He hadn't known how, exactly, he would terrify her, let her know that he could get at her anytime he wanted. . . .

But he'd known he would, and now simply by taking advantage of the opportunities that had presented themselves, he'd made her understand that he was in charge.

Congratulating himself, he sidled into the dark, overgrown yard of the abandoned house on Washington Street. Pulling the stocking off his head, he wiped at the cold sweat in his hair, the chill fog cooling him after the heat of his exertions.

Probably at the jail the poor sap he'd paid to say he was Steven Garner—complete with a halfway decent resemblance and all the required ID to make such a claim believable—was having a bad night.

But it was what he'd promised to do in return for the money, so he could hardly complain. Of course, there might be a little more to it than he'd expected. . . .

Half on agreement, half later . . . Steven felt a smile curl his lips as he patted the other five hundred still in his pocket. Fat chance the guy would ever collect it; by the time he got free and came looking for it, Steven would be long gone.

He shoved his way past the broken door into the old house. Inside, the air smelled of mice and damp.

He pushed the door shut and leaned against it. The sirens in the distance had stopped, but the quiet out there was deceptive; by now they knew he wasn't in custody, that he was still at large and pursuing his plans. . . .

That's me, he thought, unable to supress a chuckle at the memory of how he'd escaped the plump cop simply by doubling back and waiting until the cop had gone. At large and in charge.

Now that they knew, though, he was going to have to be even more careful. Because first they would search the empty houses again, and all the campgrounds and tenting areas on the island, in case he was in any of them.

They'd be visiting fields, beaches, and wooded areas, too, just in case. Now that he'd invaded her home and put his hands on her, anywhere he might be hiding would get a thorough inspection.

But he had anticipated this stage of the operation long ago when he was planning it, so he was ready.

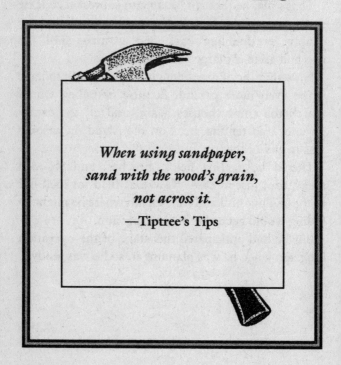

Chapter 10

*When using sandpaper,
sand with the wood's grain,
not across it.*

—Tiptree's Tips

Morning dawned cool and clear, the fog drawing back like a thick blanket they all crawled out from under, blinking in the sunshine.

"Mom, are you sure you want to do this?" Sam leaned against the front porch rail, coffee cup in hand. The fireworks had been postponed for twenty-four hours. She thought about what would happen after that: no more festivities, no more crowds of strangers thronging the sidewalks.

Which meant Garner would come after her tonight. Or perhaps sooner.

"Absolutely. I should've gotten out in front of this when I first realized who he was."

She knelt on the porch deck, wiping pools of the overnight's puddled drizzle with a towel. "Hand me that hair dryer, please."

She'd plugged it into an extension cord so she could get it all the way out here and down to the bottom step. Sam bent and handed it to her. "Okay, but make sure you—"

"Yes, yes, don't stand in a wet spot, I know." Actually, the running of any indoor electrical appliance while outdoors was not exactly a recommended procedure.

But she was too wired up herself to care. Also ticked off, frazzled, bone-tired, and flat-out mad as hell. "Don't worry, I'm not going to be holding it at all, most of the time."

The hair dryer was the pistol-grip kind, with a flat base that you could set the handle into so the dryer would stand up by itself. She arranged this, then aimed the nozzle at the largest wet spot—the steps' surfaces were cupped with age, so water collected in them—and turned it on.

"I don't see why wiping's not enough," Sam said over its whine. "Seems to me you're going overboard on the prep work."

He wasn't talking about the fire; no one was.

They were all so shocked to the bone by it, they didn't want to.

Or didn't dare to, as if fright over what Steven Garner might do next was the cat that had got all their tongues.

She began toweling the next step. Gently, though; the fresh primer she'd brushed on the day before was set firmly enough to wipe, but not to scrub at.

"The whole definition of doing enough prep work is going overboard on it," she added, this being one of the first and the most difficult lessons she'd learned working on the old house.

"Take paint scraping, for instance," she went on, angling her head sideways at the old dwelling's white clapboards. "To scrape correctly, first you take off everything that's loose."

Knowing where this was going, Sam made as if to back up into the house. "No, no," she told him, "stay where you are."

"Mom, I've already got a job, you know. At the Boat School."

She wiped the next step. "Then, after you get all the loose stuff off, you do what's not loose. Say, maybe ten percent more of the old paint."

Which was the hard part. Because first of all, as this very porch had demonstrated, even what looked loose really wasn't. Paint chips that appeared ready to fall off by themselves clung on like barnacles if you waved a paint scraper near them.

"Sam, you could save me a lot of money."

If she hired him to help scrape the part of the house that she still intended to paint sometime this summer (if I survive tonight, her mind insisted on adding snarkily), she would pay him a fair rate, of course.

But it wouldn't cost what she'd end up paying professional painters in Eastport in the summer, when demand for them would be so high that they could charge the really premium prices.

And that, as she'd also learned from experience, was another part of fixing up an old house in Maine: buying stuff when no one else wanted it, whenever possible.

"And maybe it would be . . . Well . . . Maybe I would enjoy working with you on something," she added.

Before you finally leave home for good, she didn't say, in part because she didn't like thinking about it. But Sam would go off to live on his own sooner or later; his long adolescence was nearly done.

No drugs, no booze, not for a long time now, and he'd put on weight through the chest and shoulders. He still had the long eyelashes, lantern jaw, and fast grin, plus the quick, agile body that made him a natural on boats.

But he was a man, and in a thousand small ways he had begun acting like one. Like now, for instance: "Yeah. Maybe, huh?"

He eyed the hair dryer's progress, crouched and moved it to the next wet spot. "Okay," he agreed. "You're right, that might be fun."

He straightened. "Let me know when you want to start."

And just like that, it was decided. Jake stopped wiping at the porch and looked around at the fresh, clear morning, with the sunshine's warmth drawing gauzy puffs of condensation up off the wet street.

Out on the green lawn, a couple of robins each tugged at the ends of a single earthworm. A black-and-white cat crept toward them, her stealth spoiled at the last minute by having to stop and shake her paw in disgust at the wet grass.

But then: "I wish you wouldn't do this thing to-night," Sam said.

From the porch steps, she could see all the way to the bay. Far out on the watery horizon, the fog bank lay diminishing like a thin, dark gray pencil line.

"I'll be fine." She picked up the towel again. "You know why the hair dryer's not too much prep work, right?"

He shot her a look. "Yes, Mom," he replied patiently. "It's because if it's even a little bit wet, the paint won't stick to it. I've worked on enough wet boats to know. And don't change the subject," he added.

She shrugged. "I'm not. There's nothing to discuss. This guy isn't going to give up, he'll just keep after us and after us, and I don't think the cops will find him, either."

Using teams of local volunteers, they were already combing the parks and beaches, and checking on every visitor in every motel, bed-and-breakfast, and boardinghouse for miles around.

"Or not in time, anyway," she added.

"You still think he's killed people?" Sam crouched on his haunches, coffee cup in both hands.

She hesitated. Worrying him hadn't been part of her plan.

But maybe he should be worried. "They both died, I know that much. The girl who's supposed to have fallen, down on Sea Street. And the guy with the stab wound . . ."

"Billy Wadman," Sam supplied the name; she hadn't known it before.

"He was kind of a schmuck," Sam said. "But he wasn't such a bad kid. He just hung around with the wrong . . ." Sam looked up, getting it suddenly. "Really? You think that your guy was the one who—"

"Killed him, yes. Bob Arnold said there was some kind of a scuffle among the boys just before it all happened. No one says they saw Steven Garner there. But . . ."

Suddenly the sheer fright of the night before hit her again. She turned away so Sam wouldn't see it in her eyes, the horror of being surprised in her own home. And then the fire . . .

She hadn't faced it yet, but soon she meant to go back into Wade's workshop and clean it all up. It would be good to have a job to do when she went up there again.

It was good having one now. "But last night, Garner had a stocking pulled over his face," she finished.

Sam didn't reply, just crouched there listening with both hands wrapped around his cup. She took a breath and went on.

"For a disguise, I mean." Though it hadn't been very much of one. Partly she imagined it was so that, worst case, she wouldn't be able to testify with true certainty that it had been him.

But mostly, she knew, it had been for the shock value. To up the whole fear-factor portion of his program.

And it had worked. "So I'm thinking, if he used a disguise once, then maybe . . ."

"Yeah. Why not, huh? Maybe he was disguised when he stabbed Billy Wadman, too, and that's why nobody remembers seeing him."

Sam stood up. "Makes me like your plan even less, though. I don't see why you have to be the one who . . ."

Lures him. Stands out there like a goat tethered to a post, waiting for the predator.

"Because I'm the one he wants." She laid the towel aside. Now just a few hours of dry morning air and the porch would be ready for the first coat of paint.

"You are, huh?" He pulled a folded sheet of paper from his back jeans pocket, opened it.

It was the photograph of him, with the target on it. "How'd you find . . . ?"

She'd stuck it under the phone books, to hide it from him.

"I was trying to look up the phone number of the Motel East, so I could find that girl I met and break our date for tonight."

A smile of complicity made him look for an instant just like his father at that age. "Plans with my mom," he explained.

She faced him. "I don't get it. I thought you'd be spending all day trying to talk me out of it."

Sam laughed, shaking his curly head. "I am," he admitted ruefully. "But I know better than to think it'll do any good."

Then his face changed. "And listen, there's one other thing I wanted to say. Two, actually."

His hands moved awkwardly on the cup. "I'm, uh, really glad the guy didn't hurt you."

She felt ridiculously touched. "Thanks, Sam."

Tears brimmed her eyes, but if she let them spill over, he might never say such a thing again, so she didn't.

"That's very nice to hear. And what was the other thing?"

"The other thing is, you don't have to do it. I mean"—Sam's face wrinkled with unaccustomed emotion—"you don't have to do it for me."

He sipped from his cold cup, grimaced, and flung the rest of the liquid onto the grass. "Because the thing is this. I know you think . . ."

He broke off, began again. "I know you think you were a not-so-good mother. Back then."

She waited. It was exactly what she thought. But she hadn't realized he knew it.

"You probably think it's why I started using and drinking," he continued. "Like, when I was so young. Because of things you did. Or didn't do. You and Dad, but mostly you, probably."

No kidding, she thought. "Sam," she said, "if I'd had your life back then, I'd have tried to find some kind of painkiller for it, too."

He raised an eyebrow at her. "Yeah, well, you could

also say I had three squares and a pretty fancy roof over my head."

His look now was startlingly adult. "Which I get is not your point. I mean, especially the whole Dad thing and all," Sam added.

The whole Dad thing . . . She had to laugh. He did, too; they had reconciled, both of them, with Sam's dad before he died.

"He was a piece of work, though, wasn't he?" she said.

Sam nodded emphatically. "Hey, maybe it's *his* fault I turned into a drunk."

He went on, "But see, the thing is, nobody knows. What they might have done if some things were different and which things it would have to be."

He took a breath. "So don't feel bad about it, is what I'm trying to say here."

A tear escaped; she brushed hastily at it. "Yeah, well. If you're okay now, then I'm happy."

"But I still think this thing tonight is crazy," Sam emphasized. "Unless . . ."

She seized on the word. "Unless what?"

"I want to be in on it." She'd already said no way, that his role tonight was to stay with Bella and handle the phone, in case calls that were crucial came in from her or anyone else.

She'd also told him what an important job it was, being the information manager on such a dicey project. That staying up-to-the-moment and keeping everyone else that way, too, could be the make-or-break on the whole thing.

But he wasn't buying it. "I'm coming along, I'm sticking by your side," he declared now. "And—"

Here it came. He knew about the gun box in the cellar, had known for a long time. So no real surprise that he would want . . .

"I want a gun," Sam said. "With me, loaded and ready. Or I'm not going, and if I'm not, you're not, either."

She waited for him to say something more that she could spin some other direction so she wouldn't have to refuse him.

But he didn't. "Sam, you downtown in a crowd with a—"

Concealed weapon. Yeah, Bob Arnold would really be able to get behind that, she thought sarcastically. The only thing he'd want more was maybe everybody carrying plague-germ vials.

"I can get one," Sam said quietly, "on my own."

Of course he could. He had plenty of young male friends in Eastport, and plenty of *them* had weapons. For hunting, mostly.

"Look," Jake backpedaled, "maybe we're going just a little overboard on all this."

Although Sam with a weapon might not actually be such a bad idea. Thinking about the face in the stocking mask, she thought rocket launchers in the windows would be about right, too.

Plus maybe a moat. With piranhas in it. And alligators, to supplement the man-eating fish.

"I mean," she went on, "we don't really know for sure. . . ."

That Garner has actually killed anyone, she was

about to finish. Just then, though, Bob Arnold drove up in the squad car and knocked that idea into a cocked hat.

"It's worth my job if this gets out," Bob explained. He'd asked her to ride with him around the island in the squad car instead of him going inside to talk with everyone.

"The Fourth's a big deal," he added, as if she didn't know. He pulled the car away from the curb outside her house. "And what I've got could ruin it. But it's not official, so mum's the word."

He drove out Key Street past the Dead River oil company, the ball field, and the old train yard, now a vacant, grassy expanse behind the IGA parking lot.

"I don't understand. Has one of the boys from yesterday said something?"

The ones who'd been stabbed at the parade, she meant. Bob turned left onto County Road, past the wood-frame youth center building with its paved lot and basketball hoop.

"Nope. Guy who turned himself in last night won't say boo, either."

They drove past the abandoned schoolhouse with the two huge maples nearly blocking its twin front doors—one for boys, one for girls—and then the low concrete bunker-like buildings of the water-treatment plant.

"A cop at the jail in Machias knew him, though, from when he used to work in Bangor. That's how his act fell apart so quick."

Jake grimaced. "So let me get this straight. The fellow last night identified himself as Garner. And showed ID to prove it."

Bob nodded. In the fields around them, vast green swathes of cinnamon fern spread between mountain ash trees, their clusters of berries just now turning orange, and wine-red clumps of sumac.

"And he's not saying why he pretended to be someone else?" she asked.

At the southernmost tip of the island, they crossed the long, freshly paved road leading out to the freighter terminal. "Nope. But you've got to figure, Garner must've paid him to do it."

Jake nodded bleakly. "Yup. You don't steal ID and then use it to turn yourself in with, usually."

From here, the view down the bay was unobstructed: first the blue, glittering water, next a scattering of green, rocky mounds with names like Burial Island and Treat's Folly, and finally the bridge linking the town of Lubec with its tall white steeples to the Canadian island of Campobello.

"So I'd think Garner was out of the picture," Jake said.

Bob nodded again, grimly. "We all did. So Wade went to work, your dad and Bella were off playing tourist—"

"And Garner could visit me." She turned suddenly from the spectacular expanse of water and the sailboats tacking prettily in it. "But . . . why did you show up?"

They drove slowly uphill past four massive old elm skeletons whose dead gray trunks were as big around as Volkswagens; the trees had died long ago of Dutch elm disease but had never been cut down.

So now here they still stood, slowly decaying, occasionally dropping wood chunks the size of chest freezers into what once had been a house and was now just a cellar hole.

"That's what I want to talk to you about," said Bob. He steered around the sharp curve onto High Street, and back toward town. "See, I told the state cops what you said about that dead girl down on Sea Street."

"Really." She felt like shaking him. But she couldn't, since for one thing he was driving, and for another he would get to it, whatever he meant to say, when he was ready.

He always did. "About how she knew the local geography, and how a girl from here, even drunk, wouldn't likely fall."

She began feeling alarmed. What was it that was so bad, he didn't want to tell her?

"So to make a long story short . . ."

Thank God. "Hey, Bob? I'm getting old, here."

He nodded reluctantly. "I know. I just . . . well."

He took the turn onto Pleasant Street, past the community gardens with their high, mulched rows and their electric fences strung up against the deer that herded on the island in summer.

"Girl's purse was there," he said. "State guys took it, turned out there were prints on it. Not hers."

"That was fast," she observed, and didn't add unlike your storytelling style.

"Yeah. It was fast, because the thing is, see, there

was a regional alert already up for the Garner fellow."

The New England region, he meant, and the different state police departments communicating with one another in it.

"Garner did something else before he got here," Bob added. "Back in New York. So they were already all geared up; they had fingerprints on him, sent out with the bulletin."

So if someone picked up a suspect, they'd be able to tell in short order whether or not it was Garner. . . .

"And the ones on the purse matched?" She put it all together finally. "They were his prints?"

Bob sighed. "Yeah. So, long story short, a whole bunch of New York cops are on their way up here right now, to find him and grab him. They'll be here by late tonight."

"So you're not supposed to let word get out 'cause they don't want you to spook him."

"Got it in one. I guess the safety of a whole townful of people, not to mention all the visitors we have this weekend, doesn't signify compared to—"

In Maine, the only town cops who investigated murders were the Portland and Bangor departments. Otherwise, it was the state police all the way—or the out-of-staters with warrants—and the townies were supposed to keep right out of it.

She sank back in the car seat. "Just tell me, Bob, okay? Why the New York cops are so hot to capture some little mutt from the Bronx, or wherever."

"Staten Island," he said, still stalling. But then he gave in all of a sudden.

"Okay, look. He's been living with his mom all his life, but last week a neighbor went in, made a complaint to the cops there. Says the place isn't kept up anymore, no one coming or going, the lights go on and off but it's like they're on a timer."

Jake didn't like the sound of that one bit. "And?"

Across the bay, Campobello Island lay like a long green bar between the blue water and blue sky. "And the neighbor wanted the house checked," Bob said. "So they did. And inside . . ."

A cat streaked across the road; Bob braked hard, hurling her against the seat belt.

"What about inside, Bob?" Jake asked as the Crown Vic's big engine died, mustering the last tattered shreds of her patience to keep herself from shrieking.

Bob looked at his hands on the steering wheel. "Inside, they found his mom. Air-conditioning on high, place was like a freezer in there, they said."

He turned the key; nothing. "Inside, there's a lady wrapped up in a blanket with only her face showing, sitting in a chair."

"And what did she say about it?"

The air-conditioning wasn't unusual; after all, it was the middle of summer. And that Steven Garner's mother might be just as much of a nut job as he was came as no great surprise, either.

He'd had to get it from somewhere. She looked inquiringly at Bob.

"Nothing. She didn't say anything."

Uh-oh. "Because she was deceased," he continued as the Vic's engine finally caught. "And according to the cops down there, it looked like she'd had a little help getting to be deceased."

"Oh," she breathed, feeling suddenly funny all over.

Not ha-ha funny, either, because six hours ago Steven Garner had had his hands on her, hands he'd apparently also used to—

His own mother. "Pull over."

Bob obeyed. She opened the car door, sat sucking in gulps of salty air. A hundred yards distant, white seagulls rose and fell as if bobbed up and down by invisible filaments in the breeze.

She wished the air could scour her clean, starting on the inside and working its way out. "So Garner killed the Sea Street girl."

"Probably he did. I don't know how else his fingerprints would've gotten onto her purse."

Bob waited. When she was sure she wasn't about to lose her breakfast, she swung her legs back into the car.

She slammed the door; he drove on.

On Battery Street, looking across the cove to Sea Street and the place at the foot of the cliff where the girl's body had been found, Bob turned right, up Middle Street toward home. "As for the stabbed kid, the other boys who were there when that happened still aren't talking about it." Bob sighed. "State guys are on that now, too, of course."

Now that someone besides me says Garner's in on it all, she thought with a burst of bitterness. But Bob knew that, too.

He glanced at her. "Look, Jake, I couldn't just—"

"Yeah, yeah. Forget it, I know you did what you could."

After all, if it hadn't been for him pressuring the state cops to fingerprint the purse, the New York cops wouldn't be riding to the rescue right this minute, would they?

Not that she had any great confidence that they'd be any help. "If he did stab the Wadman kid, too," Bob said.

"Oh, of course he did! Who else would? You think we've got two killers running around Eastport this Fourth of July?"

"Jeez, I hope not." He pulled the car over to the curb in front of her house, the big, old white structure with its fat red-brick chimneys and oversized porches looking solid as a fort to her.

Or it had until last night. "But if he did it, I just don't know why the other boys won't say so," Bob finished.

She bit her lip, remembering her terror in Wade's workshop. "I do."

That face, those eyes . . . "He scared them," she said. "He may look like a twerp, but believe me, he's capable of it."

And of a lot of other things; the unpleasant mental picture of the dead woman sitting in a chair with the air conditioner on high rose in her mind unbidden.

"And if those New York cops are right about what Garner did to his mom, the boys are right to be scared of him," she added.

Besides, their saying who'd stabbed them wasn't

going to help find Garner now, was it? Or maybe there was another reason they'd decided not to cross him. . . .

But then a new thought hit her. "Why'd you tell me all this if I'm not supposed to let anyone else know?"

"Because I know you, Jake. You've got some kind of a plan to do something about him already, and—"

"Plan? Me have a plan?" She tried lightening her tone, but just then Sam appeared on the front porch. Even from here, she could see the pistol grip sticking out of his jeans pocket.

He must've heard the car drive up, maybe thought it was some friend of his own, not realizing that instead it was her and Bob.

And now it was too late; Sam had qualified at the shooting range, even had a carry permit for a weapon. But that didn't keep a look of deep disapproval off Bob's face.

"Yes," he pronounced drily, his gaze following Sam. "A plan. Like you always do."

He leaned intently toward her, raising a pudgy index finger that looked to her as if it could do damage, should he decide to start poking with it.

"Jake, you tell that kid that if I find him with a weapon on him tonight . . ."

"Okay, okay." But there was something else in Bob's face, too, something he hadn't said yet.

"Bob," she said, "let's just pretend I'm a grown-up for a minute, okay? What is it you're not telling me?"

He looked even more reluctant.

"It's about him, isn't it? Or . . . about the mother," she guessed, and saw Bob's expression change.

"That's it," she said. "All right, lay it on me, or I'll go right out this minute and tell everyone I run into about the New York cops who are coming here, and why."

Which she wouldn't in a million years, and he knew it. But he'd been getting ready to tell her the rest of it anyway; he'd just been nerving himself up to do it, she realized. And after what she'd heard so far, what could be so bad that . . . ?

"Okay," he gave in. "First, the situation they were in. From what the city cops said, it was, um, unconventional."

But that couldn't be all. She flexed her fingers in a "give it" gesture. Grudgingly he complied.

"The house was . . . sterile. Everything with plastic covers on it. Furniture, lampshades. And the place stank of bleach. There were ultraviolet lights installed in the bathroom and over the kitchen sink, an ozone machine in the bedroom he was using. All anti-germ stuff. And there was a lot of merchandise, all home-shopping products stored everywhere. Still in packaging, mostly."

"And?" That Steven Garner and his mom weren't great examples of perfect sanity wasn't a surprise.

It wasn't enough to put that look of disgust on Bob's plump features, either. Eastport in summer was like paradise, but he'd seen plenty here, in all four seasons.

"And the other thing is . . . well. Like I said, they found her sitting in a chair. Clear plastic sheeting over her, of course. But what I didn't say was, she'd been dead for a while."

He straightened in the driver's seat, frowning out through the squad car's front windshield as if the sparkling view could take this next part out of his mind.

"And he'd been living in there with her. With her sitting there. For months."

"Oh," she breathed, understanding now why Bob hadn't wanted to talk about it, or even think about it.

She didn't want to, either. But he wasn't finished. "That's not the worst of it, though. The cops said she'd been there so long, and the air was so cold and dry from the air-conditioning, that she'd turned into . . . well, a mummy, sort of."

He took a deep breath, spat out the rest. "And I don't want you fooling around with this guy, Jacobia," he finished. "Because the body in that house, the one that used to be our pal's mom?"

He turned to her. "It had a meat cleaver in its forehead."

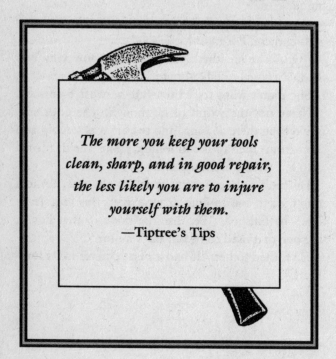

Chapter 11

*The more you keep your tools
clean, sharp, and in good repair,
the less likely you are to injure
yourself with them.*

—Tiptree's Tips

*R*ub-a-dub-dub. **No tub, but he was used to** that. Back home, a real bath or a shower was something he got only at the YMCA's locker room, anyway; the facilities at his own house were still full of his mother's collectibles.

Stuffed animals, commemorative coins, Ginsu

knives, salad spinners . . . For a while there, while the phone was still hooked up and the TV worked, she'd spent all day watching the shopping channels, clutching the remote with one hand and the phone with the other.

By the time he'd put a stop to it, finally, the house was crammed to the ceilings and the checking account she still had access to was nearly depleted. If he hadn't managed to trick her into signing a power-of-attorney form, she'd have spent all they had. Which was what that final quarrel had been about . . .

But no, he refused to think about that. Instead, by the glow of the tiny flashlight he aimed around the dilapidated kitchen in the vacant house, he checked yet again to make sure all evidence of his presence there had been removed.

Even the black plastic trash bags that he'd tacked over the windows were rolled up and pushed in behind the chunks of broken plaster above the window frames, unnoticeable. Later he would be able to pull them down again.

Later, in the dark . . . Anticipation quickened his pulse, made his fingertips prickle with the urgent desire to be at work.

Patience, he counseled himself.

It would be only a few hours now, he knew. Only a few hours until the reward for all his planning and preparation would finally come. Finished with the towelettes, he stuffed them into his jacket pocket for later disposal.

Hurry . . . Because by now they'd be hunting for him again, searching all the places they'd looked in before, and even more of them. An event like last night's wouldn't go unpunished.

Or at least they would try. And sure enough, even as he thought this a car pulled up in the street outside. Hurrying to the front room, he peeked out and saw the plump cop he'd encountered the first night he was here, who'd gotten between him and the black-coat crew.

Steven smiled reminiscently as the cop got out of his car and stood eyeing the house. With a hand on his sidearm, he started up the cracked front walk.

Naturally the cop would come here first; it was right across from where the stabbing incident had happened. And the cop wasn't a fool.

Not a complete fool, anyway . . . Steven rushed to the kitchen again, hesitated at the cellar door that opened blackly onto a rectangle of nothing. Only darkness, and a drop . . .

He jumped. Landing with a thud that knocked the breath out of him on the moldy mattress he'd placed here to break his fall—

The cellar, he'd discovered upon closer inspection, was not empty after all—quite the reverse. People had been tossing items they didn't want anymore down here for quite some time.

—he writhed inwardly at the stinking dust that rose up from the squalid bedding, imagining the dust mites in it. Then, as the sound of the cop's feet on the broken back steps sounded hollowly and the unhinged door scraped heavily across the floor above, Steven shone the penlight around again.

Reassuring himself that yes, the ladder was still

down here, so he could get back up again. Of course it was; where would it go? Everything is fine, he recited to himself silently, only his nerves making him doubt.

But just as the cop entered the house, he realized: The mattress. Lying there so conveniently under the door opening, its presence would suggest something to the cop if he looked down.

Steven jumped off the thing as if it were radioactive, then gripped the ropelike handles fastened to its sides. Above, the cop crossed the kitchen, his weight making the floor creak.

As each step sounded, Steven dragged the heavy mattress across the cellar's rough dirt floor a little more, away from the doorway overhead. Finally the cop paused.

Holding his breath, Steven flattened himself against the grimy cellar wall. His stomach roiled with the filthy contact.

Cobwebs, insects, mouse droppings . . . A flashlight beam stabbed down at an angle where the cellar steps had been. Now they were nothing but a jumbled pile of lumber; he had shoved them away so he could spread the mattress he'd found.

The flashlight snapped off. The cop moved toward the front of the house, then up the stairs to the second floor, where the ruined rooms had once been bedrooms.

There was a thud, and a low, scraping sound as the cop moved some heavy object. Crouched in silence, resisting the strong urge to squirm with the grit and filth silently sifting down from the disturbed floor-boards, Steven began to sweat.

He hadn't thought the cop would show up so soon. But this would pass. It would, he insisted to himself.

Unable to resist, he aimed his penlight up, to make certain again that nothing horrible hunkered on the thick beam just over his head, that no many-legged insect was about to drop onto him, or worse.

Then: Huh, he thought. That didn't look good. . . . The beam stretched the length of the cellar, ancient and huge, ten inches thick at least. Papery strips of bark still clung to it, and the gouged marks of hand tools showed on its rough sides.

But it was also cracked. And although Steven's experience with anything house-maintenance-related was limited to lightbulb changing and, in a pinch, snow shoveling, even he could see that the fracture was more than a cosmetic defect.

Way more. . . . He frowned as, two floors above, another thud was followed by a muttered curse. It sounded as if the cop had fallen over something.

Or into something. Steven smiled distractedly for a moment at the thought of the cop going through a rotted floorboard, crashing back down into that ruined kitchen, and ruining himself in the process.

But then his gaze was drawn back to that broken beam again. He let his eye follow its sagging line to . . . there:

A deep notch, running almost all the way through. Originally it had been cut to make room for the big pipe that ran beneath.

And he was no expert—the opposite, in fact—but to him it looked as if the cut had weakened the beam.

Ruined it, even. The crack went through the thinned part of the wood, and the rest of the beam bowed downward. Substantially downward, he thought, making it easy to imagine that at the slightest excuse, the whole floor above him could come crashing suddenly down. . . .

The whole house, even. Suddenly all he wanted in this world was to get the ladder; lean it in the doorway, whose gray glimmer in the darkness looked like salvation to him all of a sudden; and scamper up to safety. Because that wasn't safe, couldn't be . . .

Footsteps stomped across the kitchen floor again, startling him. He'd been so focused on that precarious beam, he'd forgotten to listen. But now there the cop was again, inches from his head.

The footsteps stopped. The cop was listening. Steven snapped the penlight off, closed his eyes, and held his breath, just as he had when he was a little boy, right after his father died.

Right after his mother started getting really . . .

Crazy. She was loony tunes, wackola, and so are you. Bad, dirty, and . . .

No, I'm not! he nearly screamed, so near to weeping suddenly that his nose stuffed up and his throat thickened with tears.

But no. He wasn't, and he wouldn't. He was fine, he was . . .

His fingernails dug so painfully into the palms of his hands that he felt certain they must be bleeding. Then the cop started walking again overhead.

Creak . . . creak . . . Steven let his breath out cautiously as the footsteps moved away, crossing to the window by the old sink and scuffing through the grit on the floor.

He'd been smart not to sweep it, though the dirt on it was a torment to him. The old trash he'd left littering the floor and the mouse droppings were even more revolting. But everything here had to be just as they expected, even the filth.

Now the rough cellar wall dug into his back as he waited to learn: despite all Steven's care, had the cop still figured out something?

Or . . . smelled something? The moist towelettes, Steven thought with a burst of fright; their antiseptic scent would clue the cop in, if he caught a whiff of them.

He closed his eyes again, the slow moments passing one by one as he waited. But then his lids snapped painfully open at a new sound, even more startling because it was unfamiliar: snap-popple-snap-hissss!

Then came tinny voices: the cop's radio, Steven realized in a wash of relief, and now the cop was talking into it as he moved around in the house.

"Yeah, I'm over here on Washington Street, went through the old Diamond place. It is a mess, yeah. It's a damned shame about these old buildings."

Steven couldn't see much in the pitch darkness of the cellar, but he could still feel the notched-out beam overhead, poised to crush him.

"It's about ready to fall down any minute, from the looks of it," the cop said.

You don't know how ready, Steven thought. It was

no wonder that the kitchen floor sagged so badly, that the plaster had . . .

In the midst of this thought, it hit him, what he would do if he were the cop. Too late . . .

The footsteps were moving again, across the floor as the cop went on talking. "When I get done here—"

The footsteps approached the cellar door. The cop's voice got louder, then louder still. . . .

Steven scrambled under the old mattress still lying on the dirt floor, still too near the door opening.

"—I'll check a few more," the cop said as he stuck his big flashlight through.

". . . gotta be somewhere," said the cop. His flashlight beam stabbed the gloom, picking out rusty tools, the broken staircase pieces, the hulking remains of an ancient furnace.

Go away, Steven thought as the flashlight beam found some busted-up lawn chairs leaning against the disintegrating carcass of a moldy recliner. Go away, go—

The footsteps receded. The hiss-and-pop static of the cop's radio shut off abruptly. The broken back door let out an agonized creak, then a thud as the cop shoved it shut.

But . . . It could be a trick. Not until he heard footsteps going away down the front walk, then the squad car as it roared roughly to life, nearly died, and finally caught again before pulling away did Steven crawl out from under the mattress.

Shuddering, he bit back a moan of horror. The smell was bad enough, mold and damp mingling sourly with some other stink that he didn't even want to try to identify.

Worse, though, were the soft crumbly bits of its stuffing clinging to him from head to toe. He brushed frantically at them with both hands, praying that they weren't really moving, oh God they're really . . .

But they weren't. When he snapped the penlight on again, he saw that they really were only stuffing bits, just little crumbs of soft yellowish foam rubber, nothing more.

Nothing worse . . . So just take it easy, he told himself as he aimed the light around the dank cellar. The ladder he'd spotted earlier was the only thing here that wasn't old and ruined beyond repair.

A stepladder—perfect. He aimed the light back at the broken beam again, confirming that it was cracked all the way through, one half sagging a good inch or more lower than the other.

But that didn't matter anymore; he was hiding, not buying the place. With the cop gone, his heart rate was settling, too. . . .

Because he wouldn't be here for long. He aimed the penlight carelessly at the next beam over . . . and froze, a slow, delighted smile spreading over his face even with those bits of mattress fluff still clinging to it.

Because what the penlight found were hooks. Great big rusty iron ones, a whole row of them, with square-headed spikes driven through eyeholes in their shafts, fastening them to the beam.

Lined up there in the gloom, the hooks looked like the props from some ultra-low-budget horror movie, the kind that featured college kids, a maniac, and a chain saw all trapped in a cabin.

One, two, three . . . four hooks, he counted, each

rustier and uglier than the last, in the basement of an abandoned, falling-down old house that the cops had already checked—

He couldn't help it; he laughed out loud. Because it didn't get any better than this, did it? The police chief had been here; he said there wasn't anyone in here.

So they wouldn't be back. They'd be looking elsewhere, while he—oh, it was perfect.

It was just too perfect. In the cellar's far corner, under a pile of musty old curtains, he'd stashed all his stuff, his pack and floor tarp and the bag with his few remaining groceries in it. He'd planned to hoist them up the stepladder once the search of this house was done, back into the ruins of the kitchen.

There, with the windows covered and the hunt for the missing woman going on everywhere but here, where she actually was—

Because maybe he hadn't had time to learn much, but he had absorbed one rule about hideouts from his old man: the best ones were the ones that had already been ruled out twice.

—he'd execute the final activities of his mission.

And of her life. Now, hoisting the stepladder, he placed it under the cellar door. It didn't go quite all the way up, but it would do; he was a young man, and agile enough.

He could make it from the top of the stepladder to the door and through it. As for Jacobia Tiptree, well . . .

She wouldn't be going up again, anyway, would she? The minute he'd seen the hooks, he'd known that hauling all his stuff back up the ladder was going to be unnecessary, as well.

Because down here was better. Rummaging in the pack, he brought out a coil of clothesline. With his jackknife he cut off three lengths of it, made a noose at one end of each—that Cub Scout experience, again—then tied slipknots at the other ends and hung them one apiece on the iron hooks he'd found, tugging on them to tighten them.

By the time he was finished, his eyes had adjusted to the darkness of the cellar, but he realized he would have to cover up the grimy cellar windows, too, before night fell. If enough light came in now for him to see by, then it could leak out. And—

Candles, he would have to bring all the candles down here. Dozens of them, but that was all right. He had time; that broken beam had held up this long.

It would last for another night. Meanwhile, between now and nightfall he could wash again, eat up the rest of the peas and crackers he'd brought with him, even have a short rest. But for now . . .

Now he examined his handiwork. Three ropes, each with a loop at its end, hung from the iron hooks.

Two cuffs and a collar. Perfect, he thought, beginning his climb up the ladder.

Absolutely perfect.

"Wade's not going to like it," declared Ellie as Jake hauled the first of two cast-iron porch railings across the back lawn.

They needed painting, to go with the newly painted porch. And the only sensible way to do it was with a spray can. . . .

But in Jake's experience, a can of black spray paint near a white clapboard house was certain disaster. So she'd set up some wire tomato-plant cages to lean the railings against, far enough from the house so that even she couldn't have an accident with the spray paint.

Well, probably she couldn't. And anyway, Wade wasn't here. "And don't you try to talk me out of it, either," she told Ellie determinedly.

Tomato-plant cages, when you lined up enough of them, were surprisingly strong, and it didn't matter if they got black paint accidentally sprayed on them.

But that wasn't what she meant. "I've already told the rest of them, and they're all on board."

Sam, her father, Bella . . . Surprisingly, Bella was the most enthusiastic of the three. Or maybe it wasn't; the mess in Wade's workshop had struck at the heart of all Bella held dear: order, cleanliness, and Jake's own safety.

Not in that order. But right now, Bella was up there wiping off all Wade's tools one by one with a soft cloth; she'd already done the windows and the floor.

"All I need now is for you and George to help, too," said Jake.

"Your dad's even going along with this?" Ellie hauled the second cast-iron porch railing across the lawn to the tomato cages, then checked to be sure that the fastener screws for both railings were still safely in her pocket.

"He wasn't at first," Jake admitted, surveying the rest of the equipment. Big sheet of cardboard, check; big box of latex gloves, check. She glanced at the house, whose white clapboard back wall was so tall, it appeared to lean down at her.

"But when he heard what went on here last night, he was all for getting one of Wade's shotguns and going out after the guy himself."

Both ridiculously early risers, Bella and Jake's father had come home from St. Andrews that morning just after Bob Arnold had departed.

"What about Sam?" Ellie asked. "Because the very idea of you wandering around downtown alone, just waiting for some nutcase to grab you—"

"He didn't like it, either. But the whole point is that I won't be alone," said Jake, shaking a spray can of Rust-Oleum hard so the metal ball inside bounced, to mix the paint.

"Step back," she warned, because Ellie's dungarees were old and faded, but over them she wore a white cotton peasant blouse with red embroidery on it, an obvious black-paint magnet.

Next she pulled on a pair of the latex gloves, held the sheet of cardboard behind the first porch railing with one hand, and pressed the sprayer button with the other.

"I won't be alone," she went on as black aerosol hissed from the can, "because you'll all be strategically stationed."

Paint blackened the cardboard she'd positioned behind the porch railing, and the glove on the hand she was using to position the cardboard with, too. And as if by an afterthought, some paint did manage to reach the railing itself.

Which was the difficulty with spray paint. "I will be

lollygagging," said Jake, stopping to shake the paint can again, but not for too long; if she did, the nozzle would clog up.

"Strategically lollygagging," she emphasized. Then: "Remind me again why I'm not using a brush?"

A globby blob of black paint spat out of the nozzle and began dripping down the railing—the other difficulty.

"Because I am," said Ellie, stepping forward briskly to dab at the drip with one. "Anyway, I assume you're going to do all this tonight when everyone's downtown, waiting for the fireworks?"

"Correctamundo," said Sam, coming out the door and across the lawn to inspect their progress.

Ellie looked disapproving. "I'm amazed you'd let your mother go down there unprotected," she told Sam, "knowing how . . ."

Jake shot Sam a warning glance. If Ellie—or, God forbid, Bob Arnold—found out she was planning to let Sam carry a weapon no matter what Bob had said, the resulting sucking noise would be the sound of her plan going down the drain.

Not that there'd be any reason for him to fire it, she told herself. With as many people as were expected in town tonight, to fire a weapon anywhere near them would be a disaster.

But he could aim it, and Steven Garner Jr. would be able to see him aiming it. And that was the important part. Jake put the emptied spray can down on the grass, picked up the full one.

"He's only doing what I've asked him to. He'll be watching me every minute, from one of the upstairs windows overlooking Water Street," she finished, aiming the fresh can with a flourish.

She pressed the spray button. Nothing happened. "And if one of you is stationed in each one of those buildings, I don't see how he can get near me without someone noticing."

She quit pressing the button, shook the can hard again. "So if you see him, you'll call all the others' cellphones."

Which of course they'd be carrying. "And," she added, still shaking the can, "I'll have one, too."

"Uh-huh." Ellie still looked doubtful. But she was starting to come around. "And then what?"

"Well, the next part's a little tricky," Jake admitted. "You wait until he does something. Grab me, probably. Or try."

She pressed the button again; nothing. The very idea of Mr. Crazypants getting near her made her cringe. But the only way to catch him was to lure him out into the open, it seemed.

And tonight was the night. "How do you know he'll do that, though?" Ellie asked. "Try something, I mean. For that matter, how do you know he'll even be there, or do anything at all?"

"Because this is his last chance. Tomorrow everyone leaves. Eastport won't be crammed to the gills with strangers anymore; he won't be able to blend in."

She scowled at the spray can, which still wasn't working. "Bob says the guy's got some prior offenses," she added. No sense going into more detail. "So once we get hold of him, the cops will take him into custody and that will be that," she finished.

Ellie looked suspicious. "If Wade were here . . ." she began. He wouldn't approve, she'd have finished.

"But he's not." Wouldn't approve was a mild phrase for what Wade's reaction would be if he heard about this.

Which he wouldn't, until afterwards. Ellie still didn't like it, either. She was going for it only because at the end of it Jake's problem would be over, and that was really all she cared about—Jake's dad and Bella, too.

Jake gave the spray-paint can a final, ferocious shake. On any other day, she'd have already gone to Wadsworth's hardware store on Water Street for another.

But the truth was, with Garner still on the loose, she was afraid to. The rest of them didn't quite get it yet, not even Bob Arnold, and not even after last night.

But she'd seen it in Garner's eyes, heard it in his voice, and felt it in his murderous grip: that now, he was just toying with her. But what he wanted to do was kill her.

Vengeance: in his own time, and on his own terms. In the place of his choosing, too. She hoped that the next time she saw Garner, she wasn't in it.

Thinking this, she pressed the button on the paint can once more. To her surprise, it worked perfectly.

Too bad the nozzle had somehow gotten turned around, aimed straight at her. A black splotch bloomed on her sweatshirt front.

Like a bull's-eye . . . and that spooked her, somehow. In the next moment, she'd have opened her mouth to tell Sam there'd been a change of plan, that not only was he officially disarmed but he wasn't going downtown with them tonight, either.

That they'd have to come up with some other way for him to be useful. He'd have raised a fuss, of course. But she could've thought of something to placate him.

Perhaps having spied something in her expression that he didn't like, though, he was already walking away from her across the summer-green grass of the front lawn.

Worse, though, was who else she saw when she looked up from the spray can: her husband, Wade, crossing the lawn toward Sam.

And worst of all was what he saw: that damned pistol, still sticking up out of Sam's pocket.

"So you were going to do all this without me." In his workshop, Wade sat on the antiseptically clean maple stool pulled up to his similarly clean workbench.

A surgeon could've transplanted kidneys on that bench, it was so spotless. But even through the fragrance of Bella's Pine-Sol, the air up here still stank of smoke.

The burnt washtub pretty much gave it away, too, and if she'd gotten rid of it, he'd have asked about it.

He scowled. "You were going to go downtown alone tonight and dangle yourself in front of that lunatic?"

Not were, she thought. I am going to. Just not

alone. "Wade, it'll work. Wherever Garner shows up, there'll be at least two people to rush down and . . ."

He shook his head in disgust. "You couldn't have held off? I said I'd only be gone for—"

"Right, two days." As it turned out, the ship's crew member had resolved his security difficulties, so the vessel didn't need to come into Eastport after all, eliminating the need for a harbor pilot.

"But if our situations had been reversed, would you have held off?" she asked, and when he hesitated, she went on.

"He's been in our house twice." Well, the time with the rat, he'd only thrown something in, but that was close enough.

"He's harassed me, he's taunted me, he's terrified me, and he's attacked me. He's nearly burned the place down."

She met his gaze. "He killed a girl on Sea Street, or I'm pretty sure he did. It's a good bet that he stabbed a kid over on Washington Street, too."

Swiftly she filled Wade in on the rest of the details, including that the New York cops were on their way here this very minute, and why.

"But they won't be in time, Wade. He's planning something. I can feel it, he's just gearing himself up for . . ."

Downstairs in the kitchen, Bella was taking all the knobs off the cabinets again, this time scrubbing them with her special toothbrush, the one with the wire bristles.

"You'd have done the same," Jake repeated. "If

you were here and I was away, you'd have tried to do something, too."

Surprisingly, Wade hadn't objected at all to seeing Sam with a weapon, which was the part she'd felt most doubtful about. That she'd meant to carry out the plan alone, though . . .

Exhaustion hit her—that, and her ongoing feeling that this was all her fault. "I should have just given his dad that money."

Because if she had, who knew what would have happened? But whatever it was, a disgruntled offspring wouldn't be blaming her now. Blaming her, and trying to get revenge . . .

But to this Wade reacted sharply. "Oh, come on. Is that how you want to live your life? Doing things a certain way, or not doing them, just because someone else threatens to make you feel bad?"

He had a point. But in the mood she was in now, she couldn't resist turning it around.

"So when someone else threatens to make me feel bad, I should resist. But not when you do about this, is that it? Now I should be reasonable and let you tell me the right thing to do."

Wade pursed his lips, narrowed his eyes. "It's not the same" was all he could think of to say. "It's not the same thing at all."

Which was when her temper threatened to get the better of her; she got up from her own stool at the workbench opposite him, averting her eyes from the charred floorboards under the window.

"Listen," she said, "I can see you feel strongly

about this, and I do, too. But I don't want to argue. We can talk about it again later. Okay?"

"Yeah." His voice and his face were stony. But Wade was no more up for an extended argument than she was.

"Yeah, okay," he repeated, and as she went down the shop stairs she heard him moving around, checking to see that all his tools and so on had been put back where he wanted them. Then:

"Jake. Be careful, all right? For the rest of the day . . ."

A retort rose to her lips, something along the lines of her not needing a babysitter. But Wade wasn't like that; he was just worried, and after all that had happened, he had a right to be.

She was worried, too. She reached the downstairs door, put her hand on the knob, and paused.

She was very glad he was home. "I'll be careful," she called back upstairs to him on her way out.

But she was still thoroughly annoyed.

It took a few hours for Steven to get all his things rearranged down in the cellar again, the tarp spread, and himself cleaned up again and fed. By then it was a little after two in the afternoon, and he still had the rest of the day to endure.

He couldn't very well ride the bicycle past her house again; he'd upped the ante too much for that. But he couldn't just sit down here all day, either.

For one thing, it was filthy. Now that he'd used a whole pack of the antiseptic towelettes just getting to feel halfway normal again, he didn't want to have to do it a second time.

And for another, he was too excited. Just being alive, his own heartbeat thumping and his breath moving in and out of him, felt thrilling, like a roller-coaster ride that didn't end.

But mostly he just didn't like that big broken beam hanging over his head. Sure, there were other beams holding the house up.

It gave him the creeps, though, every time he shone the penlight up there.

All that weight, a whole house sitting on something he could see was cracked through. And not shining the light up there was worse, because then he couldn't see whether or not the crack had gotten any bigger.

Although it hadn't. He told himself it certainly hadn't. Those things took forever to happen, buildings shifting on their foundations and so on. This house must've been here a hundred or more years; maybe the beam had been cracked nearly all that time. If old buildings could just collapse, you'd hear about it happening. It would be on TV, in the news. Nevertheless, he felt better when once again he mounted the wooden stepladder he'd positioned below the cellar door's opening.

There hadn't been any sound from up there since the cop had gone away. Cautiously, Steven reached the ladder's top, put his hands up onto the doorframe, and stuck his head through.

A startled rodent squeaked, inches from his face. Rearing back, he nearly toppled off the ladder, but recovered in time to see the animal scuttle to a hole in the baseboard and vanish into it.

Rat. He felt his gorge rise. Bad enough up here, but later he'd be down in the cellar again, and . . .

But he wouldn't be alone then, would he? The thought cheered him immensely. Maybe he could even introduce her to the little beasties. . . . A grin stretched his cheek muscles, so wide it nearly hurt. It just went to show there was always a bright side to even the darkest situations.

Bright for him, anyway . . . He hauled himself up through the doorway, careful not to kick the ladder over as he went; now that he'd hauled the mattress out of sight, he had no other way to get down.

And that reminded him: the rope. He'd slung what remained of the clothesline around his neck before climbing the ladder; now he cut another, longer length from the coil. In the afternoon light streaming in through the filthy old kitchen windows, he fashioned another noose, larger than the ones he'd made before.

Big enough to go all the way around a person's waist, with their arms tight at their sides. Because otherwise, that person could untie the knot, couldn't they?

And that wouldn't do. But now they—she—couldn't. He tossed the noose on the counter under the window, beside the old sink that was such a horror, he could barely glance into it.

Never mind, though. The fright of the rat's appearance had receded, and he felt happy again. He was on the right track, he was heading for his final triumph. . . .

Soon all this would be nothing more than a bad dream. He crossed the sagging kitchen floor to the broken door, shoved it open, and stepped outside.

Squinting in the bright afternoon light, he touched his ears to make certain the fresh application of glue had worked. Then he popped the baseball cap from his duffel onto his head, and a pair of sunglasses onto his face.

A Red Sox T-shirt, navy shorts, and white sneakers completed his costume. In real life, he would never have worn any of these items, which was, of course, the whole idea.

He looked like . . . someone else. Anyone else; just not Steven Garner, the guy the cops were looking for. And in Eastport on the Fourth of July, there were about a million guys he did look like.

So he was safe. Casually he strolled down the broken front walk of the old house, to the street. From there he continued on downtown between the food tents and trinket tables. Good smells assailed him: hot dogs, cotton candy, fried dough.

But now he wasn't even tempted. Partly it was that what he'd already eaten today had been satisfying enough.

Mostly, though, he just felt stronger. Much stronger; able to eat or not eat whatever he liked with no repercussions. The scrubbing thing was easier, too; normal cleanliness didn't have to involve scraping off skin, apparently.

He supposed it was all on account of the other things he'd been doing. Things he'd only dreamed of . . . and with his ultimate goal now in view, he was practically invincible, the blood of one enemy on his hands and another soon to come.

Ducking suddenly to his right, up an alley behind the row of old Water Street buildings whose front windows looked down onto the festivities, he located again a low shed he had glimpsed the day before, just a shell of an old hut with no door in its entry opening, and a ragged hole where a window used to be.

From it, he could see all the way down the alley to where it opened onto the street, and all the people passing by. Which they would also be doing tonight, visible through the alley's opening.

And as he'd hoped, placards in every window downtown said the holiday fireworks had been re-scheduled for tonight, so that hours from now—

She would come, he was certain of it. After all he'd done to her in the past forty-eight hours, she would have some plan in mind, maybe even in cooperation with the police, to trap him.

His heart swelled in anticipation. When she came, he would be here, waiting. And then . . .

Then he would swoop down upon her, snatch her away, and the best part, the very best part, was—

She would never even see him coming.

Chapter 12

*A load-bearing wooden beam
(that is, a beam that holds the
house up) is only as strong as
its weakest spot. So don't cut
notches into them.*

—Tiptree's Tips

Pulling into the long, curving dirt road to Shackford Head State Park, Jake saw at once that there were plenty of cars in the parking lot. Probably the trail would be crowded as well with hikers, families, and even a dog or two.

None were in sight now, though, giving her the illusion of solitude without any of the anxiety-provoking reality. Perfect, she thought as she got out of the car; she needed to cool off, get some exercise, take deep breaths of the sweet, fresh air.

For peace of mind, having other people well within shouting distance was a safety requirement at the moment, whether or not she resented it. But luckily, here she could have it both ways.

She slammed the car door, crossed the field overlooking Deep Cove. Out here on the grassy bluff, looking back across the water, things fell into their proper perspective.

She was fine, unharmed, and so was her family. Tonight she would do nothing more daring than she did every Fourth of July: walk downtown, see the fireworks. She wouldn't even carry a gun.

Having one in the crowd tonight would be even riskier than going unarmed, she'd decided, and anyway, Wade would no doubt be carrying one. All she had to do was be there, then wait for other people to pounce on Steven Garner when he showed himself.

Thinking this, she started uphill past the large wooden sign at the trailhead. NO GUNS, NO FIRES, NO UNLEASHED DOGS, the sign instructed in big white letters; few enough restrictions, she thought, in exchange for the illusion of solitude, the unspoiled wilderness available here in the park.

Not that she was really alone. With all those cars in the lot, no doubt the next person or group was no more than a hundred yards off, easily within hearing distance if they made any noise at all.

But at the moment nobody was, the forest more

inspiring of whispers than shouts. On either side of
the first, sharply uphill part of the trail, young hard-
woods sprouted, but after that the park was mostly
old spruce and pine, a blanket of tan evergreen needles spread between their massive trunks.

She climbed steadily until the path emerged into a
field of tall grass, then crossed the swamp on the narrow boardwalk. At its far end the real forest began,
wild and ungroomed.

Black, fallen carcasses of ancient blowdowns angled this way and that, like twisted girders of a fallen
skyscraper. Rising up through them, new growth
spread an evergreen canopy overhead.

Here, too, lay silence, other hikers no doubt also
hushed by the once-great trees now lying motionless
and mute. She went on uphill, stepping over exposed
tree roots as big as her forearm; soon the air cooled,
only a few flickering slants of sunlight penetrating the
green shade.

But the dampness was refreshing, and the smell of
pine mixed with salt air felt cleansing on the inside,
too. A few hundred yards farther up the trail, she sat
down to rest on a bench made of a split tree trunk.

But as soon as she'd stopped moving, the questions
she'd been avoiding popped into her head: What if
Garner never went downtown tonight at all? What
if he didn't mean to use the fireworks as a diversion,
to perpetrate something dastardly?

And even if he did, the whole notion of watchers
from the windows above Water Street, strategically
stationed so wherever Garner was spotted they could
rush down to move in on him like pincers . . .

Way too optimistic, she concurred with Wade's opinion now that she didn't have to admit it to him. Just one small deviation on Garner's part from anything she expected, and—

A faint sound from behind her interrupted her thought; she froze, listening. Scanning the trail in both directions, she saw no one either way, and suddenly it struck her that all those people she had expected to meet weren't materializing.

Maybe they'd taken side trails, down onto the beaches or out to Ship's Point, the high, rocky tip of the promontory the park was perched on. But for whatever reason, they weren't here. . . .

She got up, began walking back down toward the parking lot. The sound came again, a crisp rustling that stopped whenever she did, whereupon all at once the trail seemed isolated, indeed, and she regretted her certainty of having companions on it.

Around her the dark green pine boughs looked nearly black in the shade of the treetops. Cadaverous old spruces, with grayish limbs hung with moss, loomed threateningly. Suddenly she felt like running, but before she could, a hand on her arm stopped her.

Reflexively she hurled both arms up, kicked back hard with her right foot. A sharp exhalation of surprise said she'd nearly connected.

"Hey," said a familiar voice, "easy does it. It's me—"

She spun around. "Wade! You scared the—"

The amusement in his blue eyes changed instantly to contrition. "I'm sorry. Honestly." He spread his hands in apology. "I followed you out here to say I'm sorry. I didn't think . . ."

He wrapped his arms around her, and after a moment she let him. "It's okay. I thought it was him."

She stepped away. "Wade, don't you see? It's like being in prison, this feeling. And while he's free and walking around, I'll always feel this way."

A party of tourists came around a bend in the trail. A small brown dog romped beside them. Jake had time to notice the shorts and T-shirts they all wore, and to think about all the mosquitoes they would encounter up ahead where the trees gave way to insect-infested meadows.

Then they were gone, glancing curiously as they passed; and the dog's happy yapping faded, too. Jake looked at Wade.

"You were saying? About an apology?"

Wade stared purse-lipped at his shoes. "Well. The thing is, you were right that I wouldn't have waited for you. That I'd have gone ahead and done something on my own. And—"

And that you had a life before I knew you, in which you did worse things. Scarier, too.

Although perhaps not so blatantly dangerous. In the bad old days, she'd pretended what she did was normal: creating financial strategies for guys so habitually criminal, any dollar bill they owned should've borne an engraving of Captain Kidd.

Now, though, the illusion she'd created for herself back then was gone. Now the reality showed through: That all of those guys had been psychopaths, pure and simple. That she was lucky none of them had taken a sudden notion to kill her.

That all along, it had been only a matter of time, and now the past had reared its ugly head to bite her at last.

All of which showed on Wade's face: that it was here, and had to be dealt with one way or another. They turned and walked together back down the trail, forest sounds rising around them: chipmunks chittering, a swoosh of wind in the tops of the pines, a boat engine muttering on the far side of the tree line, where the rocky cliffs dropped straight down.

She took his arm, matching his gait with her own. "I guess in a way I'm just getting what I deserve. Delayed justice."

Wade stopped short, turning to her. "Please don't say that. Everyone makes mistakes, Jake. But to say you deserve something bad to happen to you on account of it . . ." He shook his head. "That's a trap. You aren't the person you were back then. And for all you know, if you'd done what he asked, something even worse might've happened."

They began walking again, down the last steep path section. "And either way," she said, "the fact remains that—"

"That he's got to be caught," Wade finished. "And those New York cops aren't going to be here in time to do it."

She glanced at him in surprise. "Bob Arnold stopped by just after you left," he explained as they came out into the parking lot. "He's pretty ticked, having to sit on his hands and wait for the city boys, as he calls them."

By now the sunlight was the color of honey pouring slantwise onto the water. "Maine has state cops, too," Jake pointed out. "And the girl on Sea Street, that's their problem, not New York's. Why aren't they taking the lead?"

Wade shrugged. "They would be. But it's a combined task force now, according to Bob, and not only does New York have way more evidence on Garner than Maine does, but their crime happened first, so they want first crack at him."

Which meant their making the arrest. "Yeah, right," she said, unconvinced. "More likely, some New York district attorney wants to make a career move, thinks a big, gory murder case with plenty of juicy publicity will help."

He tipped his head. "Could be that, also. Some politics in the mix, and some time just to get things organized, too."

She made a face as he went on: "But for whatever reason, Bob says he was told to sit tight. And you have to admit, a bunch of squad cars speeding in here with their lights flashing and their sirens howling wouldn't exactly help us, anyway."

"True." It was a nice fantasy, big-city cops riding to the rescue. But once they got here, why would they be able to find Garner any faster, or even at all?

They didn't know Eastport, its hiding places or its people. They wouldn't be able to sort out the locals from the visitors. And he'd already shown himself to be clever not only at hiding but also at disguising himself when he wanted to.

No, the way to catch him wasn't by looking for him. It was by luring him in. And not only that—

"Once they do get here, they'll probably just spook him," she said. "He'll take off, wait around somewhere else until the authorities give up on Eastport."

"That's what I'd do," Wade agreed. "Which I guess deep-sixes my other suggestion."

She glanced at him. "Wait ourselves? Sit in the house with all the lights on, take turns sitting up at night, stay on alert until he's apprehended?"

Wade's truck was parked near the trailhead. "That was what I was thinking," he admitted. "But—"

"But I believe we've just established that he might not be apprehended, not for weeks, maybe. Or months." Or until after he gets his revenge on me, she didn't add. After I'm dead.

But Wade understood. "Get in," he said. "Sam can come and get your car."

He held the door and she climbed up gratefully, ready to go home. But that, it turned out, wasn't where they were headed.

"Tonight could be our last chance," he said. "Once all the crowds leave, Garner might change his tactics."

To better ones, he meant, ones that could succeed before they managed to get up to speed on his new strategy.

"But if I'm going to be in on this harebrained scheme of yours," Wade added as he drove back down Washington Street toward downtown, "some reconnoitering is in order."

On Water Street, he slowed to examine the store-fronts and the windows of the vacant rooms above them.

"I wonder why the owners don't sell tickets on the Fourth," said Jake, "so people can watch fireworks from indoors."

As the sun sank, a perceptible chill was already gathering; summer nights in Eastport could be balmy, but more often they were good excuses for electric blankets.

Wade shook his head. "Someone would fall through one of the old floors, owner'd get sued."

They drove on. "I don't like the alleys," he said, frowning at the narrow openings between the old buildings.

The police had opened the street to traffic long enough to get the food and beer trucks down to re-supply the restaurants. Wade slowed the pickup, still eyeing the alleys and old structures on the wasteland behind the buildings.

"See the shed back there? I'd want someone on the roof of that." He pointed at the low, rickety wooden structure. "And at the top of all those other little alleys, too," he added. "Guy won't necessarily just come strolling at you down the sidewalk, Jake. I give him more credit than that, don't you?"

"He won't necessarily come at all," she said, not knowing whether she hoped he would or not.

Up ahead, a pair of Bob Arnold's deputies were putting the yellow sawhorses back out so no more vehicle traffic could enter. Wade raised a companion-able hand as he threaded the truck around them.

Down on the breakwater, the last of the fireworks were being loaded onto the barge, under the big dock lights. Wade frowned at the sight. "Hope those guys know what they're doing."

She turned in surprise. "They might not?"

He shrugged. "New team. Old fellow from the company retired last year, whole new crew took over. They've got all the proper licenses and all, but . . ."

But in the blowing-things-up department, no license could compare with years of experience, his frown said. "Worse case, they can just scuttle the barge and jump overboard, I guess," he added, not very reassuringly.

They turned onto Washington Street, uphill past the post office building, then between the big old houses, some vacant and others occupied, toward Key Street and home.

"Anyway, I could be wrong," she said as they pulled into the driveway, "but I think Garner's going to show up."

The porch light was on, and inside, the delicious mingled fragrances of fish hash, garden green beans freshly picked and snipped, and biscuit dough just now lightly browning floated in the back hall.

Bella turned from the stove with a spatula in her hand and an apron around her middle, her air the calm, commanding one of a general readying for battle.

"It's all under control for tonight," she announced before Jake could ask. "Sam's got the keys labeled and on chains."

So people could get into the rooms above the downtown stores to watch over her on the street, Bella meant. "Your father is out borrowing a few more cellphones," she added.

Because George and Ellie didn't own them; Ellie said if she wanted to be reachable by telephone 24/7, she'd just sit by the one at home.

And George . . . well, he had a beeper for his emergency duties, but otherwise if it were up to him the mail would still be traveling by pony express.

Bella dumped the green beans into boiling water and went on: "Also, Bob Arnold says his guys have checked all the empty houses and everywhere else they could think of. But no luck."

With a deft motion of her wrist, she turned the skillet-sized pancake made of fish hash, which on the cooked side was already a rich, tasty-looking brown. "He said he wanted me to be sure to tell you they're doing their best."

Jake nodded; she believed it, and not only for her own sake. Bob and his guys would be eager to show the New York cops that at least they'd been trying to find Steven Garner.

Or "the subject," as they'd be sure to start calling him as soon as those other cops actually arrived. Right now, with a few thousand extra people in town for the fireworks, what they were calling him wasn't printable.

"And George Valentine stopped by, too. He left that." Bella waved the spatula at the table. On it lay a small, dark electronic gadget.

An unfamiliar electronic gadget, at least to Jake. But at the sight of it, Wade's eyes brightened.

"Gotcha," he said.

"It's a kid tracker," said Sam later in the parlor, turning the item in his hands. "See, it's even got a panic button."

"But how does it work?" Jake peered at the thing Wade and Sam seemed to think was the answer to their problems. "I mean, where do you watch whoever you're tracking?"

"On your computer screen," Sam replied. Her laptop was open on the coffee table. "See, you log in to the company's website."

He tapped keys; moments later a map of Eastport appeared on the screen. The map was remarkably detailed, even showing the small alleys between the downtown buildings.

"It's really sweet, Mom. If you push the panic button, it sends a message anywhere you want. I'm going to set it up so it emails to right here, and Bella can—"

"Oh, no." Jake glanced toward the kitchen where Bella worked intently, scrubbing the pots and pans.

Jake lowered her voice. "Sam, I adore Bella, you know I do. But if there's any chance I'm going to be sending panic messages, I want someone on the other end who's not going to panic, reading them."

Sam looked up warily, knowing Bella was not inclined to do any such thing. "Yeah, well, don't get any ideas about me. I'm going to be—"

"No, you're not." Wade came into the parlor behind them. "I told you already I don't like the idea of you in a crowd with a loaded weapon. Besides, I want somebody with a little springiness in his nervous system to sit at that computer. You're elected."

Sam's face darkened mutinously. "But—"

He'd stowed the gun in his room after Bella objected to his sitting at the dinner table with it. Now Jake felt a moment of sympathy for him; going out armed to protect his mom was the kind of task a young man could get excited over.

By comparison, watching a computer screen wasn't, however necessary it might be. "Sam, please. I really need you to do it." Outside, the light was fading fast and the streetlamps were on. Only an hour or so and it would be completely dark. It was nearly time to go. "Sam?"

He sighed heavily. "All right. I don't know why I'm always the one who—"

"Think of it as payback for all those times you used to lock yourself in your room and refuse to come out," Jake told him.

Sometimes for days, back in that other life, the one she was trying now to put an end to at last. He had the good grace to look embarrassed.

"Yeah, yeah," he gave in grudgingly. "Guess I'm lucky nobody from back then is after me, huh? The way I behaved."

He turned back to the screen, tapped a few more keys. "Okay. Put the tracking module in your pocket."

She did, and he pressed the computer's refresh button. When the grid on the screen had vanished and then redisplayed itself, a small red icon showed, with a label: Key Street.

"So it works." She felt her heart flutter nervously.

By now George and Ellie would already be downtown, waiting. With any luck, Steven Garner would be down there, too.

Jake got up, hoping it turned out to be good luck, and not the other kind. Outside the parlor windows, the last of the day's light drained from the sky.

"It's showtime," she said.

Cars lined both sides of Key Street, parked everywhere they could squeeze in. Lawn chairs stood three deep in the yards where a view of the harbor sky was possible, and the sweet smoke from a hundred barbecue grills all over town made the cool air pungent.

Parents carried infants and led trudging toddlers down the hill toward the waterfront. Older kids waved plastic light swords, tossed foil bomb-bags and stomped them, setting off loud reports. Rowdy teenagers ran and shoved one another, while aging couples, stepping carefully in the gloom, clutched one another's arms and leaned together.

"You're sure you're up for this?" Jake's dad asked quietly as they walked along together.

"Yes. And anyway, I don't think I have much choice."

In the end they'd stationed Bella at home with Sam, in case he needed to send her somewhere to do something based on what he saw on the computer screen. Jake felt a sudden strong pang of wanting to be there, too, but banished it with an effort.

"Garner's not going to quit," she said. "He's got it in his mind that I killed his dad. If he isn't stopped, sooner or later he's going to . . ."

But what Garner might do didn't bear thinking of, especially when she recalled what he'd already done. She squeezed her dad's arm and released it. "Look, there goes the boat."

A broad, beamy fishing boat fitted with dragging tackle for urchin and scallop fishing moved away from the breakwater. On it were the men from the fire department, charged with responding if any emergency developed.

Which it had never occurred to her that any might, until Wade made his comment about the new team. Behind the boat moved the barge with the actual explosives loaded onto it, while out on the dark water floated the lights of dozens of other small- and medium-sized vessels.

Some people apparently wanted cold salt spray to go along with their light show. Wade frowned at them.

"Someday something flaming's going to fall on one of them," he said. Which he said every year, and nothing bad ever happened.

It occurred to her that in the public-safety department, he was a bit of a worrywart. They reached the downtown buildings overlooking the harbor.

"You up there," Jake told her dad, pointing at the windows over the front door of Wadsworth's hardware store.

He took the key she handed him and vanished

through the side door leading to the stairway up. Moments later his face showed briefly in the window above, and he flashed the high sign.

Then George and Ellie hurried over for their keys. "You be careful," Ellie urged, giving Jake a quick hug.

"I will." The whole street was practically solid with people milling around, waiting.

Ellie took the key for the big apartment over the gift shop just past Furniture Avenue, overlooking the first of the alleys Wade was worried about, and went in.

George strode away up the alley itself, to perch atop the old shed back there and keep watch on whoever went by the alley's opening onto the street. "That leaves me," Wade said.

They made their way together between the shouting middle-schoolers and their harried parents, a gang of teen girls madly texting even as they tottered on their stack-heeled sandals, and a quartet of pleasantly sozzled, Uncle Sam–costumed men singing patriotic songs as they weaved along arm in arm.

Wade stopped in front of the old Berman building, once a row of department stores and now transformed into gift shops, an antiques store, and a soda fountain. Turning, he gazed sternly at Jake.

"You'll stay between us," he ordered. "At all times, where one of us can see you, right?"

It gave her a little more than two blocks of street to cover as she tried to lure Steven Garner Jr. into their trap. "And you'll keep that tracking gadget. . . ." Wade went on.

"In my pocket," she agreed. "You've all got your cellphones, and the minute I spot him, I'll press the panic button."

That would send a message to Sam at home, who would at once ring all the cellphones, to alert the watchers in case they had not seen Garner already.

"And you'll put this on," Wade said, pulling a hat out of his sweatshirt pocket.

It was a ball cap with a tiny blinking LED light clipped to the bill; he put it on her head and settled it there, then held her face in both his hands for an instant. "So I can . . ."

Relief washed over her. Thinking up the plan from the safety of home was one thing; going through with it was quite another, she realized suddenly, especially at night and in a crowd.

The streetlights shone yellow, casting a warm glow on the assembled revelers. She'd thought it would be plenty to see by, but now it only seemed to make their faces blur anonymously.

Still, Wade couldn't lose track of her. "Thank you." She smiled up at him. "Now go on, before he sees you."

With a nod, he was gone, hustling in through the glass door between the soda fountain and the antiques store.

Its big glass front window held old Eastport artifacts, wooden lobster traps and handmade herring seines and fingerless mitts, their woolen fabric stiffened with ancient salt and sweat into the shape of some long-dead fisherman's hand.

And all at once she was alone, feeling as if that cold hand were around her heart. Alone in a crowd, she thought, slowly making her way back down the sidewalk to the hardware store.

Because that was the plan: back and forth, until either the bad guy showed up or the evening ended. Like dragging a piece of bait through the water, hoping that a fish would—

"Excuse me." A young man in a hurry pushed past, bumping her as he went by; for a heart-stunned instant she thought it was him, but it wasn't. She relaxed again.

As much as she could. Across the street in the darkness behind the law office, firecrackers erupted in a fury of light and gunshot-sounding reports; she jumped again.

But it, too, was a false alarm, and by now she was almost back to Furniture Avenue, its gloomy mouth opening like a narrow maw. Crossing the alley, she refrained from glancing up it toward the shed where she knew George Valentine sat.

But she was happy to know his guardian gaze was upon her as she crossed the alley and continued on toward the hardware store. A little girl sat on the bench out front, crying while her mother tried to comfort her by telling her the fireworks would surely be starting any minute.

"But I want them now!" the girl sobbed, and Jake knew just how the child felt. Come on, come on, she thought. If he's going to try to grab me, let him get going.

But he didn't, so she went on walking back and forth among the children and the adults, the tourists and the local people, all waiting for the action to begin, too.

Before long, night finally fell completely and the waiting audience members began settling into the places they'd chosen for watching the show. I should have worn better shoes, she thought as she finished another circuit to the antiques store, then back. She had on sandals, and it was getting cold; around her, people pulled on jackets and sweatshirts.

And . . . hats. Lots of hats, many of them ball caps, and most of those with—she couldn't believe it. But there they were:

Blinking LED lights. Drat, she thought, spotting the trinket booth selling caps printed with the logos of sports teams, each cap with a light unit clipped to its brim.

Just like her own. The light clips were sold separately, as well, not just with the hats. And they were everywhere: blinking from babies' bonnets, ladies' scarves, teens' jackets . . . They were everywhere.

Blinking and winking, a bright-dotted sea of them. How would Wade or anyone else pick her out in all those . . . ?

But then another, much bigger light drew her gaze abruptly, a sudden brilliance out on the water. It was a flare shooting up, but not the standard kind.

An "ooh" rose from the crowd as the flare flew a hundred or so feet into the air, dragging a flame tail, then exploded with a dull pop into a stunted pinwheel of red and gold.

She knew what had happened: a fireworks shell had misfired. In previous years, Wade had been on the fireboat, so she'd heard how much the guys hated duds.

Uneasily, Jake put a hand in her jacket pocket, touched the tracking device, and located the panic button with her fingers. Out on the water, red and white boat lights bobbed; a small plane few overhead, then circled out toward the island of Campobello.

But nothing else happened. "Maybe that was just to get our attention," said someone nearby.

Jake turned sharply, thinking she knew the voice. But in the crush of people, she couldn't pick out whose it was. Meanwhile, by now the temperature had dropped to that of an autumn evening, and the crowd's constant murmur took on an impatient undertone.

"I hope they hurry up," complained someone. "I'm freezing."

Me, too, thought Jake, turning again in front of a display of antique tin-can labels, mostly for sardines, which at one time had been the small bayside city's foremost industry. Scanning the throngs, she searched for a pair of big ears, for a face that she had last seen under a stocking mask, and most of all for a pair of eyes whose malevolence she hoped to forget, someday.

But not tonight. Maybe he won't come. But . . . how could he resist? It was the perfect chance for him to grab her.

Or so he would believe. Come on, she thought. "Come on," said someone, aiming the remark out at the water where the barge still floated.

But there was no answer, and nothing else happened.

So they waited, and then they waited some more.

From where he sat atop the battered old shed at the top of the alley, George Valentine could see all the way down to Water Street and beyond, out the wooden fish pier and on to the water.

All in all, he thought it was a good place to be. Back in the old days, before everything got regulated all to hell and gone, he'd been among the men out on the barge, handling those high explosives like he had some idea what he was doing.

But those days were over, too. Now that he was a family man, his days of setting bombs off—even these beautiful, celebratory ones for tonight—were behind him.

Not that this fool's errand he was on right now was much better. But Jake had her mind made up, and his wife, Ellie, was Jake's best friend, and her mind was made up, too.

And George knew his own mind and its contents were not even faintly relevant, once those two got their heads together. Jake was as independent as a hog on ice, and Ellie was no better.

Which was why he sat cross-legged on the shed's just-barely-slanted wooden roof. His long johns kept him warm, the tread on his boots stuck to the rough plank roof so his butt didn't slide, and he wore a warm hat, unlike the tourists who seemed to think a ball cap would keep their ears nice and cozy.

Also, with a cellphone in his pocket and his own good head on his shoulders, he felt entirely able to handle whatever might happen next, mostly because he had always done so.

Then came the shell misfire, a thump-and-sputter he recalled from his own times on the barge. "Jeez," he muttered, wincing at the memory of the sparks falling, sizzling metals and chemicals that if they landed on you would burn you to the bone.

After that, silence. No yelling, so that was good. On the barge the guys would be readying another shell. He wrapped his arms around his knees and waited.

Not too many people were passing by the alleyway's opening now; they'd all found their spots and planted themselves to watch the show. Only Jacobia kept trudging by every few minutes, first one way and then the other.

And then . . . and then just about the time he expected her to show up again, she didn't. George frowned in the chilly darkness atop the shed. Had he gotten distracted waiting for the fireworks to begin in earnest, and lost track of the time?

He didn't think so. He thought about calling one of the other cellphones to find out if any of the watchers in the buildings' front windows could see her.

But then he hesitated, because meanwhile, one of them might be trying to call him, maybe even with an urgent message. No, better to look for himself, he decided, and if he saw her, then he'd just scramble right back here.

So he did, hopping down from the shed roof to land on the old asphalt alley paving, then scampering in darkness between the brick buildings almost down to the sidewalk. There he paused, peering to the left and right . . . and spotted her.

She'd stopped to gaze out at the dark water where all the boats' running lights mingled to form a swathe of bobbing red and white gleams. Everyone else seemed to be looking out there, too.

He squinted that way himself. It did seem like a long time since that misfire had gone off. He thought the results of it might be giving the guys some trouble somehow, keeping them from getting the next one set up.

He hoped that was all it was. And if it was, he understood their caution; having several hundred pounds of unfamiliar bombs on a boat with you in the dark did tend to get on the nerves of even the most experienced Fourth of July fireworks handlers.

Which these guys weren't, from what he understood. Jake, though—she was okay. George turned, not stopping to try to catch her eye. The idea was just to check on her, and besides, if the guy really was here, George didn't want to tip his hand.

The key word being *if*. But his was not to reason why, George told himself as he hoisted up onto the shed. He'd volunteered to help—well, his wife, Ellie, had volunteered him, actually, but it came to the same thing—so that's what he'd do.

He resettled himself on the slanting planks just as Jake crossed the alley again, her head turning sharply away from him toward the water as she went by, as if she was watching something very interesting happening out there.

Hunkered down inside the shed behind the Water Street buildings, Steven felt and heard the man climb back onto the roof overhead. It had been at least five minutes now since that odd-sounding thump had come from the water, and Steven had almost decided he'd better go down to the street, too, and find out what was going on.

Instead, the man had come back, his gait and posture showing that he was unconcerned, and resumed his perch. Steven resigned himself to a continued endurance of the funky stink in here, then congratulated himself on this decision as moments later, Jacobia Tiptree appeared at the end of the alley again.

Luck, he thought, rubbing his hands together. He'd been here since late afternoon, ever since leaving the old house. It hadn't been in his plan, but once he got downtown he realized his chance to hide anywhere around here might vanish at any time.

So when he'd reached the shed and the excellent concealment it offered, he'd decided not to let its advantages slip away. A small, confined space, an unappetizing appearance, a great line of sight all the way to the street . . .

He couldn't have found a more fortunate location if he'd put it here himself. Not that it was *all* good, filled as it was with old clay plant-pot shards, moldy straw, and various other objects so disgustingly deteriorated, he couldn't even identify them.

Now, with his back aching from the long confinement and low headroom, the stink of ancient potting soil long left to nourish colonies of bacteria, viruses, and maybe amoebas—God, he hated the very word amoeba—invaded his nose and throat. Everything he touched felt gritty, slimy, or a combination of the two.

What this place needed was Lysol. Or better yet, a match and gasoline. But there was no help for it, or for this squalid hut he was squatting in, either. Once he was finished here, he would find a hotel with a chlorinated pool somewhere and check into it, he promised himself, and soak to his heart's content. . . .

Boots scraping the shed roof dragged him from his thoughts. A fine rain of grit filtered down onto him where he crouched; he leaned forward to peer through the low door and see what was up. But then he realized the man up there was simply shifting position.

And then . . . there she was again, in the gap between buildings at the end of the alley. She looked annoyed, as if she, too, was getting impatient for the right moment to arrive.

Soon, he promised her, his hand going to his pocket for the knife just as she turned and looked straight up the alley. Right at him . . .

But no, that couldn't be true. She didn't know he was here. Then with a jolt of realization he understood: she was looking at the man sitting above him, up on the shed roof.

Oh, you clever dickens. Guards—she must have helpers posted around here, watching. That's who the man above was. . . . And wasn't that an interesting new bit of strategic information?

New and crucial . . . Lucky, lucky. He grinned in the fetid gloom of the horrid little shelter as she turned once more, squared her shoulders again, and took another step.

What a bust. **Despite** the brisk exercise she was getting, the chill in the evening air made Jake shiver. Back and forth . . .

Halfway up Water Street again, she met a family headed away from the waterfront, two harried-looking young parents trying to get a pair of disappointed five- or six-year-olds into their car seats before the tantrums started.

"I guess they're not going to have fireworks tonight," said the dad, gripping one child's hand and shooing the other ahead.

"But why?" demanded the kid in the death grip. He was clearly the powerhouse of the two youngsters; his brother just looked woebegone.

"We don't know why," began the mom, possibly on the verge of losing it herself. Obviously it had been a long day. "But, honey, I'm sure that when they do decide to have them, they'll—"

Jake didn't hear what the frazzled mother was trying to put over on her child, but she felt a spark of sympathy for the task of getting a kid to walk away from any long-promised treat. With Sam, she'd practically had to throw a net over him.

Until he'd gotten too big to throw a net over, and

another set of problems had begun. She turned from the departing family just as a flash from the water caught her eye, the bright, fierce glare shimmering on her retina even after it subsided.

The sound, an instant later, was like a heavy wooden mallet on wet sand. Not dramatic or even very loud; heads turned toward it here and there, but not in alarm.

The next explosion, though, did cause alarm.

And the ones after that.

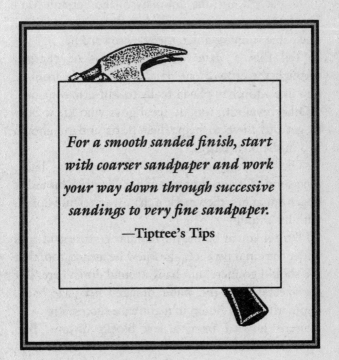

Chapter 13

For a smooth sanded finish, start with coarser sandpaper and work your way down through successive sandings to very fine sandpaper.

—Tiptree's Tips

Fireballs erupted into the sky over the water, and suddenly everyone around her was running. The sound came from everywhere, loud, reverberating explosions one after another.

It was obvious what was happening out there: the fireworks. Something had gone wrong. Jake hesitated, not knowing what to do or which way she should be going, then recalled the cellphone in her pocket along with the GPS locating gadget.

She backed into the doorway of the Berman Mall but didn't know who to call. Just then George Valentine came running down the alley toward her.

"Tell Ellie I went!" he shouted as he charged through the crowd, one hand thrust out in front of him like a football player ready to stiff-arm someone.

Other men ran, too, all local guys who knew how to get out there to help, their skiffs and runabouts tied in the boat basin.

"Okay!" she yelled to George's departing back, then spotted Wade sprinting at her. He stuck his index finger out at her, then made a thataway gesture uphill, with his thumb.

I'll meet you at home, the familiar gesture said, and under the circumstances she knew he meant, too, that she should go there, not hang around down here. But the spectacle on the water dragged her gaze back, boom after fiery boom in nightmare succession.

Sirens howled from a few blocks distant. Bob Arnold shouted into a bullhorn, trying to direct spectators to clear the way for police and emergency vehicles. Somewhere, someone was weeping loudly.

Another volley of what sounded like cannon fire boomed out, golden streamers rising like a fountain of fire from the water. The running lights of the spectator boats moved away, sensibly, except for a couple of larger vessels whose work lights had come on, washing their decks in white.

The air smelled like burning gunpowder mingled

with chemical stink. Little bits of grit began raining down; they stung her skin. She drew her hands into her sleeves, hunched her shoulders to get her neck down inside her collar, and began to walk quickly up Water Street toward Wadsworth's hardware store.

There was nothing she could do here, and as Bob's voice on the bullhorn kept saying, staying meant being in the way. And if her dad hadn't already started for home on his own, he'd probably be at Wadsworth's.

Either way, her own project was done for tonight, and most likely it was done for good. She'd just have to let the police try to catch Garner, she realized grimly.

If they could. And if that meant living like a fugitive till they succeeded . . . well, she'd just have to.

But as she reached the alley George had come barreling out of and began crossing it, a hand shot out. Yanking her back by her hair before a squeak could escape her mouth, it shook her hard, then shoved her roughly against the nearest wall.

Her head smacked the brick so hard, she felt her jaw nearly dislocate. Her knees went watery as the hand seized her collar, then slapped tape over her mouth.

It all happened so fast. . . . She fell, the side of her face scraping the brick wall on her way down. Through one eye already beginning to swell shut, she saw people, just a few feet away.

But she was back here in the shadows, and they were looking toward the lights, so they didn't see her. More tape went tightly around her wrists, binding them.

A knee in her back urged her up as a hand went roughly into her pocket, found her GPS locator.

"I knew you'd try something like this." Hot breath gusted at her. He gave the gadget a low, underhanded toss so it slid on the alley's pavement, downhill until it stopped on the sidewalk.

A passerby bent and picked it up, peered curiously at it for an instant, and went on walking, dropping it into his pocket.

Desperately she moaned through the tape.

Don't take it! Please, just leave it where you found it, or my son will think that—

That she was still here, watching the fireworks accident's aftermath or even helping somehow. Because whenever something bad like this happened, someone always called Wade, and if not, then they'd have been trying to find George.

So Sam would know quickly about the mishap on the barge. And given her propensity for sticking her nose into things, he would not think it was strange that the GPS device, supposedly still in her pocket, was now on its way up Water Street.

After a little while, he would catch on that something had gone wrong, that his screen was showing locations she wouldn't be in. But by then it would be too late.

Distantly she understood that the explosions had stopped and that the dull *boom boom boom* she now heard came from inside her.

That it was her own heartbeat. Through a nearly overpowering wave of dizziness, she wondered how long she would go on hearing it.

On the other hand, she was still alive right now. So maybe she could still think of something.

"Walk," said the man who had seized her, very near. Which ordinarily would have been a big cue in the think-of-something department.

Something like jerking her head back, breaking his nose with it. Or kicking him; who said that had to be done frontwards?

But a sharp little tickle of something just under her left ear suggested a more cautious strategy, one that wouldn't put the tip of whatever he was pressing there right through her jugular.

Or whatever. Some big, highly pressurized blood vessel. Her legs went weak again.

"Stand up straight," he hissed at her. "Walk. That way."

Past the shed, the alley curved around toward Washington Street. But nobody ever came this way anymore; when the alley was built, Model T's might've used it. But there wasn't enough width to get a modern car through here comfortably, and as for any pedestrians, it was too dark.

Really dark. On the other hand, apparently somebody liked it that way. . . .

A figure materialized in the gloom. The pinch at her throat kept her still as it approached. A flashlight beam hit her in the face, blinding her, then shifted minutely sideways to light up her captor's. Then it went out.

"I want my money," said a voice out of the darkness as the figure stepped forward.

Garner ripped the tape from her face, cut her wrists' bonds with a swift, businesslike flick of something she didn't want to think about at all, then pressed whatever it was into her neck.

He didn't have to tell her to keep quiet. She knew.

"And I want it," the figure added, "right the freak now."

They'd kicked him the minute they found out he wasn't who they were looking for. Mad about it, too. They took away the jail scrubs, the hygiene kit with the comb, toothpaste, and the little wrapped bar of motel soap in it, even the tray with the paper cup of watery coffee and the jailhouse breakfast on it, powdered eggs and blackened toast.

Not that any of those things were any great loss. It was what they'd given him in return that burned him up so badly: a freaking court date.

In the gloom of the little alley behind the buildings, he took another irritated step toward the little jerk who'd gotten him into this mess. Freakin' little liar, he was.

"So hand it over. The other five hundred."

Because that had been the agreement, and he'd lived up to his side of it. Spend a night in jail, big deal, he'd thought.

And now look. "I mean it," he said, sticking his hand out.

For the first time, he noticed the little jerk's ears, big and sticking out like his own. But it didn't make him feel the least bit sympathetic.

It made him feel like ripping them off, maybe threading them onto a chain or a leather thong and wearing them like a necklace; oh, but he was ticked off now. The little jerk had a woman with him, one hand tight on her arm, other arm around her shoulders. She didn't look too happy about it.

But the hell with her, too. He had his own problems. "You didn't tell me it was a felony, what you wanted me to do."

Because this Garner guy, there was a warrant out for him, and getting in the way of it at all, that was a big deal. Cops'd had him in a room all damned day, asking him questions.

And they'd kept his five hundred bucks. Evidence, they said. He'd get it back, they'd promised him. Eventually.

Yeah, right, he thought. Sure he would. The only reason in the world that he wasn't still in jail right now was that he'd done his best to tell them what they wanted to know.

The woman looked hopeful. Scared, too, like maybe she wanted him to do something about her situation. Help her out, maybe get her away from this weird dude. Play the knight in shining armor.

Not freakin' likely. He got his money, he was going straight back to the cops, drop a freakin' dime on this yo-yo here.

Maybe if he did that, he'd get a head start on a way out of his troubles, which he wouldn't be in if it weren't for—

The guy took his hand off the woman's arm. Kept his other arm around her shoulder, though, his hand right up there in her hair.

"So they gave you a lot of trouble, huh? Down there at the jail?"

Which was his opening, maybe get a little more

than the five hundred. His eyes began adjusting to the dark back here, a little bit.

That buoyed his confidence, too. "Yeah," he told the guy. "I didn't know you were—"

A wanted man, he'd been about to say. But wait. Don't tell him that. It was already too late, though.

The guy's eyes narrowed. "Didn't know I was what?" he asked mildly.

The woman's eyes darted back and forth. She looked like she was about to say something. The guy jerked his arm sharply as if to remind her of something.

She sucked a breath in but kept silent, and what was up with that? he wondered suddenly.

But never mind, it was none of his business. Just get out of here, he thought. Just get the money and . . .

"Nothing," he said, hearing the sullenness in his own voice. He stuck his hand out, palm up.

"Hey, man, I've got no problem with you, okay? Whatever you and the lady got goin' on here, I just want my—"

The guy's right hand flashed out fast and then back again, gripping her ruthlessly.

"Hey!" Pain flared in his hand. He looked down; something was stuck in it. Through it, actually.

All the way through it. Reflexively he grabbed the thing and pulled. "Hey, man, what the freak did you . . . ?"

With another sharp flash of pain, the thing came out. It was long and very thin . . . a hat pin. His grandma used to use them.

"Why'd you do that to me, man?" he demanded,

still not quite believing it. But as he spoke the guy's hand came at him again.

He backed away, but not quickly enough. And this time it was not a hat pin, he saw as the hand moved right up under his chin.

This time, it was a knife.

One-handed, the other still with the sharp thing nipping at her jugular, he slapped the tape back onto her mouth and wound it around her wrists. Then he gave her a shove, past the fallen body of the guy who'd wanted five hundred dollars.

Shocked, she staggered a few steps and tried to run. He moved up alongside her and tripped her. Hitting the pavement with her hands bound was an interesting experience. He yanked her up by her wrists, raising the interest level even further.

The tape muffled her shriek of anguish. Once he had her on her feet, he leaned in close and spoke.

For the first time, she glimpsed his face. But she'd known: Garner, of course.

"Next time, I'll cut your throat just like his. Now walk."

She obeyed, wondering wildly where they were going, and if anyone would find her.

And if she'd still be alive when they did.

The alley let out between the senior center and a driveway with a fence running along it, adjacent to the massive old wood-framed Baptist church.

Back in New York, the night sky never really went black. But in Eastport, a hundred-plus miles from the nearest city's light pollution, the night sky prickled with stars.

And up here, away from all the commotion on Water Street, everything was quiet. Garner hustled her roughly along the fence-lined driveway to where it ended at a garage. The house the garage belonged to was dark except for a dim porch lamp, its glow not even reaching the yard. No one home . . .

"Hurry up." Garner put a foot in the small of her back and shoved. She fell forward over a lawn chair onto the cool grass and rolled hard to the right, hoping to find some hiding place, a low bush or maybe a picnic table.

If she could just get away from him for a moment, she could get the tape off her wrists; she'd started yanking at it right away, so it was already down around the broad part of her hands. In darkness, her shoulders found the hollow at the foot of a huge tree, and she curled herself into it, praying.

But his footsteps followed unerringly. A thin flashlight beam pierced the darkness and found her. His hand shot out, its vicious grip on her ear agonizing as he dragged her up.

The blade touched her throat. "Through there." He let the flashlight beam rest briefly on a lattice screen at the rear of the yard.

Set up between two tall, bushy cedar trees, it gave the yard an illusion of privacy, she supposed as she scanned it hopefully. But if you didn't mind getting all scratched up by cedar boughs, it would be easy enough to push through to the next yard.

That is, if you weren't beat up and tied up. Squeezing her eye closed tight to protect it—the one that wasn't already swollen shut—she pushed between a tree and the lattice. On the other side, she might get a second chance to—

But the instant she was through, he was right there behind her. He grabbed her arm and the flashlight came on again, picking out an old, moss-covered brick path.

A garden path . . . suddenly she knew where she was. The Senior Center, the old church, and . . .

The old house loomed in front of her. He yanked her sideways with a tug on her wrist bindings, then stopped.

Her heart sank; she'd nearly had the damned things off. With a snort of irritation, he grabbed her hands, pulled them together, and wound more tape onto them, from forearms to fingertips.

Then he continued tugging her toward what turned out to be an old porch, its paint entirely absent in the flashlight's glow and its ancient decking splintered and broken.

And I thought mine needed work. The thing was a recipe for a broken ankle.

"Careful. Don't hurt yourself." She could hear the smirk in his voice. Unsteadily she made it up the first step, and then the second.

At the top she looked up at the old door. If I go in there, I'll never . . .

Hurling herself backwards at him, she didn't care if she fell or how. With a grunt of dismay, he landed beneath her, his knife clattering away, his hand scrabbling sideways for it.

He squirmed from beneath her and jumped up, but instead of trying to get up, too, she kicked both feet up and out at him, aiming for his knees.

Her heels hit his thighs, forcing an *mmph* from him but not fazing him. Instantly he was on her again, his clenched right fist coming around like a swung hammer to the side of her head.

Down and out. A prizefighting term, she recalled having heard Wade explaining it, somewhere over there in what once was her own other, much better life.

The one she was leaving.

She couldn't move, a lethargy so profound seizing her that she had to decide whether or not to take each separate breath. Even the headlights passing by just yards away, so that now she was within shouting distance of help, failed to motivate her.

Because for one thing, her mouth was taped. And for another, she wasn't sure she was even in her body anymore.

Garner kicked the door. It fell open with a shriek of rusty hinges and the crack of a breaking frame. Then he stood over her again.

When she didn't get up, he kicked her, but she didn't feel it, or not as pain, too disorganized by the punch to the head to be processing anything.

Sam, she thought. *Wade.*

Someone hauled her to her feet, shoved her forward at a tall rectangular dark opening. She didn't want to go through it.

A bad smell drifted from it: dampness, old dirt, and

mouse droppings mingled with a lemony whiff that was like Bella's spray cleanser. As he pushed her in, her thoughts fritzed in and out like sparks from a bad power cord.

Trying without success to seize on some shred of an idea and cling to it, she tripped and nearly fell over a deck board that was sticking up. Sharp splinters from the board pierced her skin.

Then another explosion from the direction of the waterfront shook the house. Inside, in the darkness still reverberating with the boom, plaster bits rattled down.

With a hand as strong as a metal claw, he helped her up again.

If you could call that help.

Inside, the air was thick with antique dust shaken loose by the explosion. The instant he let go of her, she tried to run, but he caught her and threw her to the floor.

Her face smacked the side of what felt like a porcelain sink on the way down, then struck the gritty floorboards.

Bella would have a field day in here. At floor level, the stench of mice and old dirt was even stronger, still oddly mixed with the sharp scent of spray cleaner.

She lay there trying to catch her breath. Across the room, he was fiddling with something; she couldn't see what.

Something heavy, by the door. But it was even darker in here than it had been outside, which seemed impossible, given that the house had windows, and if nothing else the streetlights in front of the place should be—

A battery lantern snapped on. Through the eye that wasn't swollen shut—yet, she thought with bleak realism—she could see the black plastic trash bags taped to the windows. At the sight, a bit of hope drained away; so much for any passersby accidentally glimpsing her predicament.

Heavy thuds from the doorway area drew her sluggish gaze back. By the lantern light, he was using a claw hammer to nail the door shut, using one of the broken boards from the porch decking to cover the opening, and the nails still sticking out of the board.

He wasn't doing a great job. Three out of the four big nails bent before he could hammer them home. But it would be enough to keep anyone else from pushing that old door open very easily.

In the unlikely event that anyone tried. The phone, though, I've still got the—

As if triggered by her thought, its ring sounded from her pocket. He dropped the hammer, strode across the ruined kitchen, bent, and pulled it out of her jacket pocket.

She didn't even have the strength to resist. Not that that came as a surprise; Victor the brain surgeon—the late great, she thought disorientedly—used to say the human skull was like a metal bowl full of water.

Smack the bowl, watch what happens to the water. Smack the head, same thing happens to the brain. The only difference being that the skull kept the brain from slopping out.

Lying there on the old floor, waiting for the newly arrived hideous waves of nausea to subside—yet another unpleasant consequence of concussion—she hoped her own brains hadn't begun leaking out of her ears.

But at the moment, she couldn't be certain. And if what good old Victor used to say was any guide, it would all get much worse long before it got better.

Great, Jake thought. The phone was still emitting the ringtone she'd programmed into it: the first thirteen notes of the "Anvil Chorus." It had seemed like a funny tune to put on an old-house-repair hobbyist's cellphone.

At the time. Garner switched the ringer off, dropped the device on the floor, and stepped on it. Crunchy bits of plastic flew, as did her last hope of summoning help.

From outside came the occasional distant rumble of a car going by, heading out of town on Washington Street. But most of the crowds were gone, even the vendors were heading home, and—

It hit her suddenly, what she wasn't hearing: sirens. No cop cars screaming in or ambulances howling out. Whatever happened on the barge must've created casualties.

But they weren't being transported up Washington Street, and that's how they'd have gone, on their way to the nearest hospital forty miles distant. Unless—

Unless nobody had survived it. She swallowed hard, tasting blood and fear. One of the few remaining sections of plaster in the old ceiling chose that moment to fall, crashing to the floor in a choking cloud of plaster dust.

The house must've shifted. In the massive vibration of all those fireworks exploding at once, it . . .

Garner frowned, shaking his head impatiently as if all the unexpected noise and disruption were almost more than he could bear. Then he squinted down, assessing her, yanked hard at the tape around her wrists, and tried pulling on the patch of it that he'd slapped over her mouth.

"Good," he said, and his mild tone of approval combined with the intensity of his dark eyes gave her the creeps, even through the pain of her injuries.

Inappropriate . . . the term didn't even begin to cover it. "Now you just wait for me. I'm going to go get cleaned up. After that, we're going to have a little chat, you and I."

Yeah, right, she thought, fully aware that her situation went way beyond sarcasm but unable to stop. Because right now, sarcasm was the only weapon she had.

It helped the sick feeling in her stomach to realize that at least she could still slap the taste right out of this wing nut's mouth in her imagination, and the first instant she got a chance to do it for real, she was going to—

Her fists clenched, flexing her numb fingers and stretching her wrists against their too-tight tape bonds, as she watched his shoes move away across the scarred kitchen floor.

The floor was also littered with trash and plaster,

and pierced along its exterior walls by old heat pipes, plumbing pipes, a drainpipe, a gas pipe—

She felt her eyes widen. All at once an alternative reason for her nausea occurred to her.

Correction: it slammed into her like a highballing freight train. Gas . . .

Now that she'd smelled it, it was obvious: the unmistakable rotten-egg stench of propane. Just a tiny whiff of it mixed in with the other bad smells, and only down here, by the floor.

Because as she happened to know after Bella insisted she learn all about it before trading their old electric stove for a new, gas-powered one, propane was heavier than air.

And that's why he hadn't smelled it. The leak must've just begun, maybe during the fireworks explosions. As if to confirm this, more plaster fell; at the same time, a low, ominous groan issued from somewhere below her, probably in the cellar.

No no no—but as fresh fright cleared the cobwebs from her brain, she realized it could be true.

The house must've already been in bad shape, some big beam rotted through or cracked, or maybe even cut when somebody was installing one of those pipes.

The notion that a beam was only as strong as its narrowest width had never penetrated some of those old do-it-yourselfers' heads, as she'd learned to her sorrow in her own old house.

But even as she tried battling panic with practical thoughts, a worse thought arose: that more than one beam had been cut, and not long ago, either.

That the house had been deliberately made unstable . . . Her wrists strained wildly against the tape again and her breath came fast, shuddering in and out through her nostrils uncontrollably.

Because she could suffocate with her face down here on the floor. Or the house, recently prepared for demolition—even as she thought it, she knew it must be true—could collapse on her.

Alternatively, it could explode if he switched that battery lamp on in here again. Or—she stiffened, listening—Garner could just come back and kill her himself.

Which, from the sound of his footsteps returning in darkness, he was doing right now. And she couldn't tell him about the gas, *or* the collapse potential of this old death trap, either.

Because he still hadn't taken the tape off her mouth.

He got her into the cellar by dragging her across the floor to the open doorway by her feet and pushing her through it. She hit the stepladder's top platform with her bound-together wrists and slid headfirst down the step edges to the bottom, landing hard on her chin and elbows.

"Look out below," he called down, and she rolled hard away, trying to hook the stepladder's leg with her foot. But before she could, he was beside her again.

Getting up, he brushed fussily at himself. The sharp smell of spray cleaner drifted to her nostrils again.

So that's where it came from, she thought. What she didn't smell here was the gas leak. Not yet . . .

But if it wasn't stopped, it would pool on the kitchen floor and eventually stream down through the open cellar door as if it were a liquid, which was just what it would behave like, filling the cellar.

Unless it got ignited first. She'd have told Garner about it, but he still hadn't removed the tape. And despite what he'd said about having a chat, she didn't think he was going to.

He planned to do all the chatting. She wished she thought it was all he was going to do.

But she knew better. . . . There was another lamp down here; he switched it on.

But nothing happened. Raising the lamp, he sent its yellow glow into the cellar's far corner; mice squeaked and vanished up into the walls, and she saw a shudder go through him.

There was something hanging around his neck on a thin strap, but she couldn't tell what. Then she saw the other thing, just over his head:

A massive old support beam, semi-round and with its sides still bearing the marks of hand tools and some century-old shreds of bark. But it bore a new mark as well: the unmistakable cut of a chain saw, like a thin slot running almost all the way through.

To get it ready to knock down all at once so the house lot could have a new, easy-to-care-for home built on it by people from away, someone had nearly severed it. They'd done the same to all the other beams down here, too, she saw as she scanned them with her one good eye.

But at least the bulldozer wouldn't be coming today. And her nausea had passed, now that she was breathing clean air again. Yet another low, agonized groan from the building she was trapped in, though, cut her relief short.

This old house wasn't just collapsing.

It was collapsing *now*.

He heard it, too, and a flash of uncertainty crossed his face as he ducked involuntarily, glancing up, frightened. But then the groaning stopped again, and he hurried over to where she lay, holding the lamp high to peer down at her.

Desperately, she used its light to scan the cellar's recesses for something she might use, or for some route of escape. Craning her neck as he hauled her up, though, she saw nothing.

Someone had cleaned this cellar, scavenging it for antiques or salvage before tearing the place down, probably, leaving only junk: a flattened garden hose coiled on itself like a deflated snake. A broken screen door, its old metal screen blackened and in tatters.

More mice skittered somewhere as he dragged her to her feet. "Do you remember me?" he asked in a conversational tone that was much worse than any threat because it was so insane. *This guy had more loose screws than Wadsworth's hardware store,* she thought.

"I'm the kid whose dad you killed. He asked you for help and you wouldn't help him."

It wasn't that simple, she thought, and then she spotted it: a thin line of light. Toward the front of the house . . .

No, the side. The streetlights reached that far, and the bulkhead doors were there, she recalled; she'd passed the house many times before now, and had seen them.

So that must be where the light came through. . . . "They shot him. The very next day, he disappeared on his way somewhere. They found his car later."

He gave her a hard shove. He either hadn't noticed the light leaking in through the cellar doors or didn't care. The latter, she thought; his lamp wasn't bright enough to be seen from outside.

And no one would be looking here anyway. Bob Arnold had already checked this house himself after she and Ellie had been inside; he'd think that was enough.

Garner held her up with one hand and propelled her forward with the other. Toward those cellar doors, as luck would have it, but it wouldn't do her much good being near them if she couldn't get to them, would it?

And he wasn't letting go. He'd hung the battery lantern from a hook nailed into one of the overhead beams—not the cut one.

Not that it really mattered. Low, grinding complaints and protests coming from all the beams, plus the crash of more old plaster upstairs, told her an important support beam had come undone somewhere. Sooner or later, the rest of the house would follow; its owners were figuring on later.

But her money was on sooner. As she watched, a beam resting on one big foundation stone shifted minutely, exposing fresh yellow wood. On the plus side, she still didn't smell propane. . . .

Yet. The battery lantern made a circle of dim light

on the dirt floor. "So first, I'm going to take a few pictures of you."

That thing around his neck on the strap was a camera, of course. "Don't worry, nothing salacious."

Yeah, right, that's what I was worried about. The thin line of light through the cellar doors was like the promise of heaven. If she could just get to the doors . . .

She looked around, puzzled. He had seemed so determined to get her here, but she still couldn't understand why.

Why here? But then . . . Then she looked up again, not at the beams but at what was fastened to them.

Which was when—with a drowning sensation of horror—she finally understood.

The moment he saw her spotting those big iron hooks nailed to the beam above her head was like Christmas, his birthday, and the first day of summer vacation all rolled into one.

Because he'd done it, he'd put that look of horror on her face. Made her feel like his father must have when he knew that the end was not only near but that it had arrived.

And that it was bad. . . . But now was no time for gloating. A few things still needed to be accomplished, fast. Before she got over being stunned at what was in store for her.

So first things first: he seized her wrists, cut the tape on them with a swipe of his pocketknife, and shoved her hands up through the clothesline nooses he'd suspended from the hooks.

Now she was held securely, perched on tiptoe to keep herself from having to hang by her arms. Next he set up his camera, stationing it on an upended crate he'd found shoved into a corner of the cellar earlier.

He'd brought a remote shutter-firing device for the camera; now with it clutched in his hand he posed gleefully next to her and pressed the button.

There, a record of his triumph. The cellar was still dark, damp, infested, and grimly filthy—stinking, too.

But right now, it was the only place he wanted to be. "You should have given it to him. The money, I mean."

In answer she kicked at him, wiggled, and angled her head at the cellar door opening he'd pushed her down through.

"No, no," he replied calmly, for there was no need for any agitation or anxiety now.

Not on his part, anyway. "I'm afraid you're not going to be going back up there," he said. "You might as well forget it."

The way he'd had to do.

Sometimes right after his dad died—after he was murdered, his mind shouted now as it had then; his mother hadn't shielded him from any of the details—he'd lie in bed at night trying to imagine it.

What his dad had been put through, what he must have thought about it. Steven's own small body had twisted into the various positions he supposed his father's must have been made to assume, ending with the slump-shouldered final one.

In that way he would put himself to sleep night

after night, his own slumber coinciding with what he imagined as the moment of his father's demise. In the morning, he would start over again:

Yes, Mother. No, Mother. By his scuttling obedience putting off her first screaming fit of the day, her first attempt to stab herself with kitchen scissors, her first drink.

Later, as a teenager, he got better at managing her. And as a grown man, better still . . .

Much better, he thought calmly as Jacobia Tiptree rolled her good eye and tried to speak from behind the tape on her mouth. She really did seem very worried about something. . . .

Good, he thought. As she should be. "My mother had a serious personality disorder," he said. "She'd do crazy things . . . take off all her clothes and walk out into the street. Call the police and say I was trying to kill her."

He shook his head, remembering, hiding a smile. They should have listened. . . . "It was okay while my dad was alive. He'd settle her down. Keep her," Steven added, "from doing things to me."

She kicked out at him and jerked her head at the door again. But it was only natural for her to protest.

He wanted her to, in fact. "But afterwards, it was another story." He heard his own voice harden. "Then no one stopped her."

Well, someone finally did, he amended silently. But by then it was too late.

"So, you see, it wasn't just his life you ruined. You

thought he wasn't worth fifty grand, and who knows, maybe you were right. After all, he was just another loser, wasn't he?"

She glared one-eyed at him. In response, he took yet another photograph of her. "For my collection," he confided.

But as he set the camera down, something small and soft fell from a beam above to his shoulder and skittered across his neck.

"Gah!" he exhaled shudderingly, flinging himself around to *get it off, get it off of himself*—

Clapping his hand wildly to his back, he found the mouse and flung it, saw it land in the lamplight and run squeaking into the gloom in the cellar's recesses. Gasping, he put his hands to his knees and tried to catch his breath.

Then he glared furiously at her. This was all her fault. His father's death, his mother's deterioration, his own emotional disfigurement. For that was what it was, surely; normal boys had normal emotions, they didn't grow up the way he had.

First terrified of their moms, then caretakers of them. Normal boys didn't live with their mothers long into adulthood, enduring a madness so profound, just being around it was toxic.

Until finally, after years of frustration and loneliness, of hearing her babbling and suffering her suspicions, he'd put an end to it all, and who could blame him?

And then, of course, he couldn't call anyone to help him with her body, since if he did, how would he explain . . .

No. He shook off those old thought patterns and addressed his prisoner again.

"The men who killed him? They tortured him first. To make an example of him."

She went very still. He let the moment lengthen, savoring it. "But," he added at last, "I'm not going to do that to you."

Her good eye rolled. Oh, thanks.

Even in the state she was in, he felt her sarcasm, and he had to hand it to her, she didn't cave in easily. There was some backbone there, some personal stamina.

"Well," he amended, "not a lot of torture."

Steven liked to think that at the end, his father had been at least that brave, too. But he knew better. The photographs his father's killers had taken had eliminated any such illusions.

"After all," Steven told Jacobia Tiptree sincerely, "I'm not a monster."

As if to prove it, he produced the final piece of equipment he'd brought along, stashed in his pack until now: a silver-plated .22 revolver and six bullets.

He'd had them for years. He'd known they were in his dad's dresser drawer, and as soon as he'd learned that his father was dead, he'd retrieved them.

At the time, it had been to keep his mother from killing him with them, in one of her then-intermittent attacks of paranoia. . . .

The stench around him was so intense, it interrupted his thought. God, but it really smelled terrible in this cellar. Rot, mice, and something else even worse: rotten eggs, maybe.

He wrinkled his nose, and at the gesture she began kicking and moaning urgently at him, trying to communicate something to him. Maybe she smelled the odor, too?

"Don't worry," he consoled her. "I know it's awful. But you won't have to put up with it for long."

Well, not too long. He brought the gun out where she could see it, slotting the bullets into the chambers.

"I've always loved this gun. Not only was it my dad's, but I also appreciate the simplicity of it."

He held it up. "D'you know how it works?"

Now he recognized the smell, the rotten-egg aroma of a gas leak. The pipes in this place were old, and even he could tell that the building itself was in bad shape structurally.

Especially that beam. And there was an old propane tank in the backyard. So it made sense, what had happened. In a way, it was even convenient.

He just didn't feel like dealing with the facts. "Pressing on the trigger pulls the hammer back," he said.

He held the weapon out so she could see it better. "When the hammer is released, it flies forward, striking the bullet and exploding the charge inside. It's that explosion in a confined space that—"

Drives the bullet forward, he was about to finish. Although in this instance, the bullet might end up being beside the point.

If he waited long enough, the spark from the gunfire would explode the leaked gas; not part of his original plan, but—

Well. It wasn't as if he had a lot to go back to, was it? He supposed that was why he hadn't done much about making a getaway plan: because deep down, he'd never intended to escape.

Overhead, something shifted with a low grating sound like a . . . well, he didn't know what, but it was big. And it wasn't good.

Grit and sawdust rained down into the cellar, at first just a little and then suddenly more. A lot more . . .

The ceiling overhead dropped suddenly about four inches, with an avalanche of debris following it. He coughed, unable to see in the sudden amber dust cloud filling the cone of lantern light.

A long, agonized creaking and crunching sound seemed to last forever; suddenly he was not quite so ready to die as he had been just moments ago.

The sound ended abruptly. There was complete silence. Then with a huge crack! the beam just over his head snapped downward, more debris pouring through and the adjacent beams moaning with the sudden added strain.

And then . . . nothing. The house shivered and was silent. Steven held the gun in one hand and brushed ineffectually at his face and arms with the other.

All quiet . . . but the smell of gas was stronger now. Much stronger.

Chapter 14

He hadn't figured it out yet, that with the partial collapse of the house, the cellar ceiling had dropped. That meant the beam she hung from had sagged; her feet were flat on the floor now.

Not that it was doing her any good. Her left eye was swollen shut, her right half-blinded by fallen grit.

Both arms were numb, and her neck was so stiff, she couldn't lower her chin.

On the other hand, the pair of clothesline nooses that he'd put her wrists into were slack now. She could've slipped out of them easily.

The question was, then what? The building was collapsing and the cellar filling with gas that would snuff her life out if she breathed much more of it even without an explosion. So the answer would've been obvious if it weren't for that gun he had: run.

He did have it, though. She kept her hands held high so as not to clue him in that she didn't need to, that there was plenty of slack to slip out of her bonds whenever she wished.

Although soon she wouldn't be able to for other reasons; already her neck and shoulder muscles felt as if lit matches were being held against them. Soon she'd be too stiff to move quickly.

Don't even think about lit matches. . . . A trickle of sweat ran down her face, into her good eye. The cellar blurred, only the line of light at the head of the cellar doors leading outside was still visible. When her vision cleared, he stood at the edge of the lamplight's circle with the gun's barrel pressed to his head.

The rest of the cellar was in darkness. His finger was on the trigger. "I could do it," he said in tones of discovery.

Please, she thought. Spare me your freaking drama.

He turned slowly, gun still raised. The instant his back was to her, she made her move, anguish shooting through her joints and ligaments after their long immobility.

I will never, ever make fun of Bella's rheumatism again, she decided as she rushed into the darkness. She couldn't see where she was going, but it had to be better than—

His outraged shout gave her another few instants of moving safely, unheard; when it faded she held herself very still in the gloom, waiting.

The bulkhead doors were perhaps twenty-five feet away; she kept her eye on the thin gleam leaking through them.

He plowed into something heavy, blundering in the darkness. "Filthy little brat, I'll get you, and when I do, by God I will make you so—"

Sorry, she finished for him silently. Something about his voice made her feel sorry for him now, too, though.

Because it sounded unreal. As if some other person's voice were saying the words, expressing resentments not his own.

A person even less sane than he was . . . It made her flesh creep. "I swear," he went on, "the first day I saw you was the last decent day of my life. . . ."

She crept sideways as his rant grew more intense. ". . . dirty, ugly, disgusting, sinful . . ."

Hey, watch it with the insults, she advised him silently.

She was so thrilled at not being strung up by her wrists any longer, though, she could almost overlook everything else.

Almost. Because that propane was still thickening, probably seeping through the floor by now as well as through the cellar door.

A string of profanities poured out of him as he searched for her, stumbling and falling, hauling himself up again. She crept away from his lantern, toward the cellar hatchway. Then:

"Don't worry," he crooned, "I'll get you." And at that, the hairs did stand up on her neck.

Because he was right. He had the lantern, and the reality was that the old cellar doors were too far away for her to reach without him shining its betraying beam on her, sooner or later.

Besides, the idea was to get out through those cellar doors, but for all she knew they could be locked, or even chained shut.

Or the partial collapse of the house could've jammed them. Still, what choice did she have? So until a better idea suggested itself, she went on creeping sideways toward the doors, her hands flat now on the damp, gritty wall behind her.

"I know you're here," Garner said quietly.

The smell of gas was a lot stronger again suddenly. In her mind's eye she saw the fireball of its ignition, superimposed on the explosions she'd already seen tonight.

Because of them, it was entirely possible that Wade and the rest of the downtown crew thought she'd gone home, while Sam and Bella believed she was still on Water Street.

In other words, maybe no one was even looking for her.

He raised the lamp, still holding the gun in his other hand. Behind him, the broken beam sagged. The lamp found her.

She froze as he smiled tightly at her, raising the weapon. "This isn't how I planned it," he began. "But . . ."

And pulled the trigger.

Nothing happened. Misfire, she had time to think, unable to believe her luck. That gun, unfired all these years . . .

But in the next instant a loud whuff sounded all around her. Through the flash, she saw the cracked beam snap, half dropping, the other half springing up before rebounding downward again.

The shock hurled her into the concrete cellar-door hatchway, under the slanted bulkhead doors. As debris began raining down she crouched reflexively, huddled up against the doors.

Crazily, the battery lantern was still on, casting a weird glow through the clouds of dust. Garner tried to run, but there was nowhere to go as more and more of the house fell into the cellar, one floor joist after another snapping and the old nails popping out with a series of reports like firecrackers.

Suddenly an avalanche of wreckage poured down. Through the dust, she saw a timber fall, heard him cry out again.

Choking dust filled the cellar, along with an occasional rustling slide of the loose plaster as it cascaded, the house still groaning and settling.

For now. Any instant, the rest of it could pancake down onto him and pull this end of the foundation in with it.

Right on top of her. That is, if I don't suffocate first. She reached up for the thin line of light coming tantalizingly through the bulkhead doors, then pressed her face to it, trying to suck fresh air through it.

Which was how she found the big, rusty padlock on it. Panic shot through her.

Okay. Just stop and think now. You didn't die in the blast and he's not holding a gun on you anymore. So . . .

So those were good things, ones that meant she still might escape. Still a chance . . .

Then she saw the flames flickering back there, near where he lay under the debris. The sight sent frantic energy through her; she forced her body harder up against the doors, now the only way out.

There hadn't been enough gas, and it hadn't been compressed enough, to blow the place to kingdom come, as Bella Diamond would have put it.

But what gas there had been had ignited the house, and more gas could be escaping right now, into some other more confined space. So . . .

Hurry. If she couldn't open the doors, maybe she could push through them, break the old wood they were made of, or—

"Help." She squinted in disbelief at the faint sound coming from behind her. "Help . . ."

Hardly even a word. More like a whisper . . . but it was there. Garner was alive back there.

Trapped, maybe, with flames rising behind him. As the dust cleared slightly and no more debris fell for the moment, she saw the battery lamp lying on its side on the dirt floor.

Still working, its yellow glow thickened to nearly

orange by all the dust in the air, but . . . a hand reached out, scrabbled for the lamp, and seized it weakly.

"Please . . . somebody . . ."

Oh, for Pete's sake, Jacobia thought in disgust. Her face was drenched with sweat and tears; the tape he'd slapped over her mouth hung soggily.

Rubbing the side of her face with her forearm, she rolled the sticky mess sideways until it peeled away from her lips. A hunk of skin went with it, and she tasted blood.

". . . help . . . help . . . help . . ." He sounded injured.

"Steven?" He went silent. "Steven, I'm coming to get you, but I need you to toss that gun out here first."

No answer. But just because it had misfired once . . . "I mean it, Steven. I'll come and drag you out of there, get us both to a safe place if I can. But not if I think you might shoot me."

More silence. Then came a groan, after which the weapon slid with a dull clatter across the dirt cellar floor.

She hustled down out of the bulkhead enclosure and snatched it up, then peered further into the dusty gloom. The lamp lit one small area of the cellar, and he wasn't in it.

"Steven, make a sound so I can find you."

Nothing. Maybe he'd lost consciousness. She crept forward and grabbed the lamp, held it high. Or as high as she could with the ceiling now a good four feet lower than it had been. . . .

A low moan came from her left, another ten feet or

so deeper in the collapsed recesses. Rushing forward in the shadowy gloom, she just missed impaling herself on a long, dagger-like splinter.

"Help me. . . ." His hand, filthy and blood-streaked, stuck out from beneath a heap of fallen brick.

It was part of the chimney, she saw with a chill. And if the chimney was down, the rest was sure to follow soon. She grabbed his hand; a thin scream of pain erupted from him.

"I'm sorry," she told him. But it couldn't be helped; he was no doubt badly hurt. Moving him could be agony for him.

Leaving him here, though, would be abandoning him to his death. And she couldn't do that—not quite.

Not and hope ever to be able to sleep at night again. "You and I, Steven, we're going to get out of here."

I hope. She pulled as much of the debris off him as she could, meanwhile hearing the old house parts disintegrating over her head: walls, floors, ceilings.

And the roof, and the rest of that chimney . . . a howl rose up from him as she hauled his shoulders out of the broken boards and heavy pine framing pieces.

Suddenly one of his hands came free. Then it shot out and grabbed the gun back from her.

He aimed it at her. And at this distance he could hardly be expected to miss. His finger tightened on the trigger.

But just then, over his head, the snapped beam sagged suddenly another alarming six inches. Plaster dust poured down, whitening his face and turning to red mud in the blood soaking his shirtfront.

"Steven," she said warningly, but he just smiled

dreamily at her. She kicked him and flung herself sideways as he fired, the sound deafening in the enclosed space.

Another gunshot ker-whanged off the stone foundation behind her, inches from her head; she flung the battery lamp toward him.

Still holding the gun, he staggered and collapsed, then vanished behind the fallen beam.

Not much more time . . . Any moment, something else would happen, something that would stop either of them from getting out of here. Grimly, she crawled back to the old bulkhead enclosure and up its concrete steps.

Try, try again . . . Putting her whole back against the cellar doors, she strained to stand upright. An old nail gave way, then another. One board in the door structure moved, partly loosened, then split lengthwise all at once.

Putting her face up to the resulting open slit, she tried shouting through the gap, but the silence she got for an answer said no one was around to hear her. Probably they were all still down on the waterfront, dealing with the fireworks debacle.

With a hideous creak, another old nail gave way, and then the board did. Fresh, cool air poured in, sharp with the smell of sea salt.

Salt and wood smoke . . . upstairs, the house was on fire.

"Steven!" Torn, she peered back down into the murky cellar wreckage and spotted him, still hunkered behind the fallen half-beam. In the failing lantern's weak gleam, his eyes were wide.

With hope, she thought at first. "Steven, just crawl toward me. We can get out, do you see? I've got the . . ."

But then she saw. He wasn't staring at her or at the escape route she'd forced nearly open. The flames now rising brightly behind him didn't seem to have captured his attention, either.

Instead, he was frozen with terror at something inches from his face. Perched on the fallen chunk of support beam, sitting up on its hind legs, gazing beady-eyed . . .

A mouse. As he stared, another one joined it, and another. In moments an army of them had appeared, running across the beam, leaping, and heading across the floor in a dark, squeaking wave.

Before she could move, they swarmed up the bulkhead steps and over her body, tiny little scrabbling clawed feet, furry bodies, wiggling and poking. . . .

A shriek escaped her, but all she could do was shrink into as tight and impenetrable a ball as possible, crushed into what little headspace there was, eyes and mouth clamped shut until at last the horrid living wave of vermin had passed.

When the last one had wiggled through the gap behind her, she dragged in an agonized breath, straightened, and shoved the next loose board off the door. In the next moment, her head popped out into the clear, chilly night.

"Help! Someone, fire, help!"

Above, the stars shone clear and bright in the indigo sky. A horn honked somewhere, and a dog barked. But if anyone heard her, they gave no sign of it, and no cars went by in the street.

Below, the fresh air hit the fire, whose light now filled the cellar, orange-and-red flames dancing behind the crouched form of Steven Garner Jr.

Rather, Garner and a mouse. Even from here, in the firelight she could see it was dead, its tiny form inches from his face.

Maybe it had been injured earlier in the propane blast. Or maybe it had suffered a teeny heart attack; she didn't care.

Garner went on staring at it, transfixed. "Damn it, Steven, I've had about enough of you."

Somewhere in the distance a siren began wailing, but she had no way to know if it was coming here. Wincing—somewhere along the way she'd sprained her ankle, and her head felt like bombs were going off in it—she made her way yet again back down the cellar steps and across the floor toward him.

Just not all the way. Because for one thing, she couldn't see the gun; where the hell was it?

And for another, as she approached, the beam still hanging over his head moved.

First downward. Then up again, maybe a half-inch. Clearly, it was getting ready to do something. . . .

To fall. And above it, the whole house waited to come down, too. "Steven. Do you hear me? Listen to me now. You have to come toward me. I mean it, Steven, there won't be any more—"

Chances. His gaze flickered at her. He seemed about to obey.

But then some crazed script in his mind started

playing again. "Don't," he whimpered. "Don't put it on me. I'm scared of it, I'll be good, please don't—"

His voice rose to a scream before subsiding in a pathetic whine. "I will," he whispered fiercely at her, "be good."

"Yeah, great. That's great, Steven." Dust filtered down from the fractured mess hanging hair-triggerishly above.

She backed cautiously toward the fresh air gusts puffing in through the bulkhead. Each time a breeze came in and down, those flames silhouetting Garner's form leapt higher.

Now she could hear the crackling sounds, flames munching the dry, stick-thin pieces of lath that had once supported plaster. A low whump! from above said the blaze had expanded upstairs.

Abruptly the cellar flames spiraled, inferno-like through the door above into the kitchen. He looked up sharply, seeming to remember who she was.

And aimed the gun at her. So there it was. She thought he'd fired three times, earlier.

One a misfire. No way to know if it would malfunction again, or if . . .

But there was no point thinking about that. "Look at me," she said.

He did. "You know, there's something I've always wondered," she told him, easing a little closer.

To him and the gun. Not to mention that damned fire, and an imminent old-house avalanche that would bury them both, now or in the very immediate future.

But if she could get near enough to fling that mouse

corpse away from him, she could still get them both out of here.

And she had to. She'd abandoned him to his fate once. But not this time.

Not again. "It's about afterwards," she said. "When you and your dad left my office that day, remember? Sunny and warm, that day. I remember you were wearing a baseball cap."

That day . . . it was the only subject in the world that still interested him. A tear leaked from his eye, drew a track in the grime on his face.

She eased closer, readying herself to grab him.

Crouched behind the fallen beam, he watched her approach. Oh, she thought she was clever. She thought she could fool him.

"Do you remember, Steven?" she asked. "Coming to my office with your dad? You must have other fond memories of him, too."

He could see her trying to hide her fear of the gun he held. The sight, and even more, what she'd just said, nearly made him chuckle.

He felt his lips curl back in fury. From the outside, he imagined the expression resembled a smile.

"You do remember," said Jacobia Tiptree, seeming pleased.

Yeah, I remember, he thought. Because of her, his father had been taken, the one who had controlled him, kept him supervised and confined.

The one who, alone among all the rest, truly understood his unusual son: what he was, and what he might do. . . .

The one, the only one, who'd kept him safe.

Yeah, he remembered, all right. He remembered every little thing about that day, and afterwards. He lowered the gun.

Stupidly, she crept nearer still.

Stupidly . . . and conveniently.

". . . because, Steven, here's the thing. If I made the wrong decision that day, I'm sorry."

His face didn't change. But then, she thought, why should it?

So she was sorry. Big whoop, as Sam might've put it if he was in as bad a mood as Steven looked to be at the moment. More important, though, was the situation they were in right now.

Leaking gas, collapsing house, a fire in the cellar, and . . .

Oh, yeah. An angry guy with a gun. "Steven, I realize you're still pretty mad at me. And I don't blame you. But we need to get out of here."

He watched her alertly. "Now, I'm going to turn around and go in a minute. But I thought . . ."

She moved forward again; he shrank back. "I thought maybe I could help you out of there first. And we could go together."

Still no change in his expression, a fixed smile that showed his teeth. Then it occurred to her that maybe it wasn't a smile.

That it was a grimace. The mouse corpse on the

dropped beam lay motionless, stiffening, she supposed, by the minute.

The battery lamp's glow kept fading. By its dying light she scanned the area around him, saw that he wasn't trapped.

Not physically. She should get out right this instant; the creaking and groaning overhead made that clear, as did the fire.

But . . . "Steven, when you and your dad left my office that day . . ." she began again.

Because if she could distract him, maybe then she could . . .

Before she could finish the thought, though, a grinding and crunching of metal from just overhead stopped her.

She cringed back with a shriek, breathing plaster dust; he didn't move. When the sound ended and the dust cleared, the old pipes crossing the ceiling overhead had fallen.

"Steven, did you go to a ball game? Did you have a couple of hot dogs for lunch? Or did he—"

Did your dad haul you along to the racetrack with the five hundred bucks I gave him?

Because that was the question she needed answered. Had she in fact been the last hope of a guy who was wising up, at last? Or had she been right? Had he taken the five hundred and blown it at the track, just as he would've gambled away the fifty grand if he had gotten it out of her?

She looked up. Steven Garner Jr. was still watching her.

Then from outside came the whine of . . . what? A distant engine, she realized, unable to place it at first.

Plane, she thought, puzzled, then remembered the military aircraft scheduled to visit Eastport airspace. The flyover . . .

Jet fighters, detouring on their way back to base to show respect for a fallen comrade and his grieving family—

The engine sound increased. Alarm pierced her; they didn't have minutes left, as she'd hoped.

They had seconds. "Uh, Steven? We've got to get out of here fast. . . ."

The plane was overhead. Its roar made the old house tremble. Dust sifted down; something crashed upstairs, glass breaking.

Windows, she realized; all the remaining—

Steven raised the gun he held. Gotcha, his smile said. She had a fraction of an instant to wonder if he really had been too frightened of the dead mouse to move.

Or if all along it had been a trap. "Steven!" she shouted, scrambling back. Stumbling and falling, getting up and calling him to follow, but he still didn't move, his smile unwavering.

A smile of triumph. The plane's sonic boom, when it came, was a thunderclap so loud that even underground, she felt it like a punch to the chest.

And so did the old house. The whole structure shivered, the sound wave's concussion rocking it on its foundation. Any window that hadn't already shattered fell out of its frame and broke; a river of bricks poured suddenly through the cellar door.

The attic pancaked thunderingly down into the bedrooms, and then into the kitchen and parlors: thudthudthud. The massive old beams in the cellar ceiling groaned. . . .

And snapped, one by one in a horrifying cascade over her head, roaring toward her. The last time she saw Steven Garner, he was steadying his aim, still grimly trying to draw a bead on her.

Then she hurled herself toward the bulkhead doors as behind her flames crackled and flared.

Ahead, dark night spread above the cellar doors' opening, a blessing if she could reach it. If . . .

Hand over hand, she hauled herself up the concrete steps. A wave of faintness made the world spin; she crawled through it. Behind her lay only silence and the fire, burning briskly.

A few inches more . . . She lay with her shoulder propped on the doorframe. Another try might do it, get her out of here and into the cool, dark night.

If the house didn't fall, if the fire didn't burst out over her. If the smoke, now thickening so much faster, didn't suffocate her.

And if the propane still leaking down there somewhere didn't explode again, this time for real. She got her arm up underneath her, pulled both her feet up onto the highest concrete step she could manage, and gulped in a few big breaths.

The task was to get her body over the doorframe, then roll away. A voice came from below. ". . . fifth."

Garner. Somehow the smoke hadn't killed him yet. He spoke again, coughing. "Alakazam . . . in the fifth."

"Steven?" she called again as she dragged her legs at last over the doorframe, landed hard on the packed earth outside.

Yes. Thank you, she exulted inwardly. Everything hurt. She steeled herself to roll away on the grassy earth.

To get as far as she could from whatever would happen next.

But then it hit her, what he'd said. Which was when she knew the answer to the question she'd asked him.

And one thing more. Why didn't I think of that? she wondered as the astonishing truth dawned on her.

But there was no time to think anything more. Flames burst from the bulkhead opening, spewed out, their heat caressing one side of her face.

A siren howled somewhere as her rolling body hit something. The cold, wet grass surrounded her, feeling icy on her hot skin. Blindly she clutched the grass and hung on hard to it.

"I'm so sorry," she whispered. "So sorry."

Then she began crawling again, until a sound made her look back. A high, thin howl, like a giant teapot whistling—

Fire exploded through the roof, a red fountain shooting at the sky. The house sagged hard; what was left of the front wall fell into the street in a shower of sparks.

She kept on crawling, deep into the thick bushes edging the yard. Sirens screamed up out front, beacons whirling and radios spitting. Help, she thought, and went on dragging herself toward them until, through the din, one sharp pop! came from the cellar.

Just one. But it was enough. A dull thud slammed into her eardrums, rattling her bones from within. She felt the blast in the earth she held to, clinging on with her fingers: a huge, low pulse of energy rolling beneath her.

The world erupted in flames.

Chapter 15

You know," Sam said thoughtfully, gazing out at the water, "sometimes I think maybe the universe is only an experiment. Like a trial run, sort of?"

Three days had passed since the events in the old house on Washington Street. Just that afternoon, they'd let her out of the hospital, one arm still wrapped in burn bandages and the other in a sling, her shoulder badly sprained.

In the light of the streetlamps running along the paved path by the water downtown, Sam resembled his father: tall, handsome, deeply skeptical. "So the big Whatever It Is can decide what to leave in and what to leave out," he said.

Jake smiled, then winced in pain at the slight movement. Her swollen eye had reopened, though it still looked like she'd gone nine rounds with a prizefighter.

And most of her hearing had returned. "Anyway, I don't get it," Sam said, changing the subject. "If his dad's still alive, why was he trying to get revenge at all?"

She looked down at her hands. "Sam, I told you. I'm not sure that his father is alive. The mob guys might really have killed him. Steven sure thought they did, I know that much. But—"

Alakazam in the fifth. "But it turns out you can look up old race results online."

Ellie had done it, after learning from Jake that Aqueduct and the Meadowlands were Garner's likeliest haunts, closest to the city. And the Meadowlands was a harness track. . . .

"Alakazam was a filly in her second season that year," Jake said.

Sam looked interested. "And she won? So like you thought, he took the money you gave him and—"

She nodded. "Bet it on a horse. Maybe he meant to take his son out, the way he said. But once he got money in his hands . . ."

Just like she'd thought he would do. "She was a long shot. The horse, I mean. Twenty to one."

And Garner was a photographer in his day job. He could have set up a picture, made it look like he'd been murdered.

"The thing is, he had a wife who was already mentally ill, a son who was heading that way also—"

Recalling the look in the little boy's eyes that day, she shivered. They hadn't changed, either, those eyes.

"—and some very bad guys after him," she finished, the real question still being why she hadn't suspected the truth before.

But in her heart she knew that, too, now. "Twenty to one," Sam repeated, and she watched him do the math in his head. "So if he bet it all . . ." He looked up. "Ten thousand. Not bad."

She nodded. "Not enough to get the loan sharks off his case. But it was enough to run with."

"And you think—"

Again she nodded, this time to hide a grimace of pain as she got up. "I don't know for sure, of course. No one ever heard from him again. But . . ."

But it was what she would have done. What I nearly did . . .

A husband who scorned her, a son who seemed to hate her, and a life she could so easily have left behind . . . I never suspected what Steven Garner Sr. did, because I didn't want to face how close I came to doing the exact same thing myself.

"Ouch," she murmured aloud, and Sam looked anxiously at her.

"You okay?" He got up and draped his jacket around her shoulders. She closed her eyes for a moment, feeling the warmth of his body still in it.

"Thanks," she said, holding back tears. So close . . . Out on the water, small boats bobbed, their running lights shedding red and white gleams on the waves.

"He was badly disturbed before anything happened to his father, though, you know. It wasn't only about what I'd done or not done."

After collecting his body out of the old-house wreckage on Washington Street, the New York police had shared more of what they knew of the house his mother had been found dead in: locks on the doors, bars on the windows, monitoring cameras.

Old ones, dating from Garner's childhood. They'd found a lot of medical bills and records, too—his and his mother's. "It turns out that he was in fairly intensive treatment, even as a child. And he was watched constantly."

It was the answer to why a man would bring his son along to beg for money to pay a gambling debt. Now she knew that he'd been terrified to leave the boy at home, for fear of what the child might do.

Or what his mother might do to him . . . "But when his father died—or went away, if that's what he did— that all ended. The treatment, the intense supervision."

Because his mother was sicker than he was. "So," she told Sam, "a short explanation is that he thought his father was murdered—"

Or couldn't face the idea that he hadn't been, that he'd simply run away.

"—and that it was my fault. That I deserved to suffer for it. So he made it happen."

Around them on the grass and perched on the massive granite boulders overlooking the boat basin, crowds had begun gathering. The Fourth of July fireworks—its first disastrous attempt had sent half a dozen men into the water but injured none—had once more been rescheduled, this time for tonight.

"But why now?" Sam asked reasonably.

She shrugged—ouch. "From what I can gather, he'd finally lost what little bit of self-control he had and killed his mother."

Her father looked up from where he sat nearby on a blanket with Bella. "And after that he had nothing else to lose?"

Jake nodded as a cheer went up; the fireworks barge had pulled away from the breakwater. "Uh-huh. Because you know, his mother might've been difficult— to put it mildly—but somehow they'd found some kind of a workable equilibrium."

Ellie White was on the blanket, too, with little Leonora squirming next to her, waiting for the show. "Without her, all he had left was his obsession about you?"

"I guess," Jake replied, not really knowing whether he had missed his mother or felt sad. And there was no one left to ask.

Sam crouched beside her. "Listen, I'm still really sorry I didn't come down and find you right away when—"

She shook her head. They'd been over it before. He just felt terrible about it. "Sam, there was no way for you to know. It was nobody's fault, what happened. Just bad luck, that's all."

"Here, put these on," said Bella, handing over a pair of the earmuff-style hearing protectors Jake usually wore while using tools, everything from sanding machines to claw hammers.

"You don't need any more loud noises in those poor ears of yours," Bella declared.

"Thanks," Jake said, taking them and putting them on, glad for the evening's darkness suddenly. It hid the tears she'd felt springing to her eyes way too regularly in the past few days.

Tears of gratitude for surviving, and for having this life and this family. And of sorrow for someone who, through no fault of his own, it seemed, hadn't had any of that.

Just then Bob Arnold arrived, looking disgusted; she pulled the headgear off. "Well, I'm done with that," he said, dusting his hands together. "State guys took that little bastard Jerry Finnegan away with 'em."

He caught Sam's interested look. "Finnegan," he explained, "killed the girl on Sea Street after she told him about her baby on the way."

There'd been an autopsy, Jake knew. Bob's face creased with distaste. "Too bad for him, his pals saw him do it. One of 'em gave him up to save his own butt."

"Oh," Jake breathed, beginning to understand. "But maybe the pal wasn't the only one who saw it?"

Because the Finnegan boy—ginger-haired and black jacket–clad, his scowling image rose in her mind—

had also been charged with placing a homemade bomb fashioned of wired-together M-80s plus a remote-controlled firing device on the fireworks barge, after his fingerprints had been found on part of it.

But Finnegan wouldn't have been daring enough to do that on his own. He'd have needed a reason; black-mail, for instance.

"Yeah," Bob said sourly. "Garner saw Finnegan beat the girl up that night. Lost his temper, beat her to death. Finnegan's pal says that later, Garner told Finnegan to create a diversion downtown, on fire-works night."

He sighed tiredly. "I guess Finnegan figured the simplest way was the direct approach. Had his bomb-building instructions and another radio con-troller he'd gotten off the Internet, did it just like he'd done before. Then he just sneaked the stuff onto the barge. Did it while he was supposedly unloading the truck."

He made a face, and a slapping-something-onto-the-side-of-a-barge gesture with one hand. "Bingo," he concluded.

But Ellie's brow knit skeptically at this. "I'm sorry, but that makes no sense to me. Why didn't he just—"

She applied a mother's time-honored ear protection devices, her own hands, to Lee's ears. "Kill Steven Garner?"

She took her hands off. "To shut him up. He'd al-ready done it once."

Which made sense to Jake, too, actually. But Bob just looked levelly at Ellie.

"Well, let's see," he began, tipping his head in pretended thought, then gesturing at Ellie to cover Lee's ears again.

She did, and Bob spoke. "Twenty-five-year-old guy, dressed like an older woman right down to the hat and stockings, wounds you and your friends with a hat pin, for God's sake, killing one of them, and you never even saw it coming.

"On top of which," he added, holding up a finger, "this guy also knows something very bad about you, that no one should. No one but your wounded friends. And while you're lying there, this guy tells you about it."

He signaled the end of ear protection time. "Kind of spoils your tough-guy self-image for you, I'd think. I think you'd have qualms," he finished, "serious qualms about crossin' the guy."

"Yeah," Ellie said thoughtfully. "Yeah, I'll bet you would, if you were Finnegan. Scared witless, maybe."

Bob nodded just as Lee lost patience and jumped up suddenly. "Where. Are. The. Fireworks?" she demanded, each word punctuated by a stomp of her small foot.

"Wow," Jake sighed, not meaning Lee.

The lab in Portland had traced the electronic communications from her laptop, discovering not much more than what they already surmised: that Steven Jr. had spent a lot of years messing around with computers, and in the process had become an expert at covering his online tracks.

And at computer fraud, too—all the equipment in

his pack and back at his home had been bought on fraudulent credit. Ellie settled her rambunctious daughter on her lap.

"The other thing I still don't get, though, is the gas explosion. I mean, there was a fire in there, for heaven's sake." In the Washington Street house, she meant. "So if there was going to be a blast, why didn't it—"

"Happen right away?" Jake's dad finished. "I can answer that one for you."

He'd been back to the ruins; Jake hadn't quite been able to bring herself to go yet. "The old propane tank out in the yard never got picked up by the company after the last people moved out," he said.

Out on the water, the barge jockeyed itself into position. A flare went up; several pleasure boats backed off prudently.

"So that's where the gas came from," he continued as Bella leaned in against him comfortably.

"What no one knew, though, was that the house was already scheduled to be demolished. Bulldozer. They were just planning to drive in and hit it. So—"

"So somebody prepped it," Jake supplied. "Went in and cut beams. Loosened it all up, to make it easier to—"

"Correct," said her dad. "Old place like that one. It's stood upright a long time, stands to reason it's not going to go over easy. Not unless you arrange for it to."

She nodded. Her own old house was a fine example of that. Two hundred years of everything mother nature could toss at it, including a few hurricanes . . .

And including me, she thought guiltily, recalling now with a twinge the long to-do list of maintenance chores waiting for her at home. That porch . . .

And dozens of other tasks. Yet there it stood. Her dad went on: "When a couple of vibrations from the fireworks blasts hit it, it was already primed to fall."

"Fire. Works. Fire. Works," Leonora chanted.

"Shh," Ellie told Leonora sternly, but she was laughing when she said it, so the effect wasn't very disciplinary.

"That busted a gas pipe," Jake's dad said. "The house settled and must have crushed it shut again. Only a little leaked out."

The first, smaller explosion . . . "Later, when the planes went over and the house shifted some more, the leak reopened. The gas collected, stayed where it was as long as nothing more got shoved around, but when it did, it just took a spark—"

A huge, long-tailed gold streamer rose up into the dark sky, its body casting off bright pinwheels. The boom followed.

A long oooh of delight rose from the crowd; Leonora just sat openmouthed, her eyes shining.

Fireworks, she mouthed silently, and at the next, a purple chrysanthemum with tongues of red flame licking from its center, the child laughed aloud.

After that, they all just sat watching, the succession of booming reports as the spectacle went on, making talk impossible.

An arm rested on Jake's shoulder, startling her. "Hey."

It was Wade. She leaned against him as overhead a

fire snake spiraled, spitting sparks. A flaming pin-wheel turned; then a white flash lit the night, and another. And . . .

When the fireworks were over at last, parents gathered up their children and belongings as older folks lugged lawn chairs back to their cars. Middle-schoolers, delighted to be downtown and on the street at night, roughhoused and ran in the parking lots, burning off some of their seemingly inexhaustible energy.

Wade eyed her judiciously. "Want to ride home with me in the truck?"

"You bet." She felt like the truck had hit her. Out of the hospital was not, apparently, synonymous with "all better." She even let him help her into the vehicle; when had that dratted passenger seat gotten so far up off the ground, anyway?

Instead of going straight home, however, he headed out Water Street to the north end of the island; where the street ended in a graveled circle drive, he pulled up and parked.

The water was dark, intermittently flared across by the turning beam of the lighthouse strobe on Cherry Island. Beyond, the hills of New Brunswick loomed, the sky behind deep indigo.

Wade rolled his window down; the fragrant night drifted in, smelling of sea salt, beach roses, and a bonfire of driftwood on the beach somewhere. Leaning together, they sat for a while in silence; she'd thought she wanted to talk.

But there wasn't anything to say. At last Wade started the truck again and drove slowly home through the soft, island-summer night.

Pulling in, he cut the headlights. Fireflies flashed at the back of the yard. "I want to have his remains sent home," Jake said, "when the authorities release them. And buried decently."

It felt like the least she could do, she who had so much. Helping her down, Wade nodded easily in agreement.

A few yards away on the porch sat Sam, Bella, and Jake's father, with the dogs, Monday and Prill, at their feet. As she crossed the lawn toward them, they all got up, even Monday, whose face opened prettily in a sweet, old-dog smile.

Lucky, Jake thought, climbing the porch steps with Wade by her side, as they all went into the house for the night.

If you enjoyed *Knockdown*,
please keep reading for a preview of the next
Home Repair Is Homicide mystery,

DEAD LEVEL

Coming in Summer 2012 from Bantam Books

PROLOGUE

Hours after inmate Dewey Hooper, seven years into a twenty-year sentence for manslaughter, escaped from the prison system's medium-security facility at Lakesmith, Maine, guard Jeff Rohrbach got his orders. He was to collect up all of Hooper's personal belongings, including books, papers, writings, drawings, and anything else that might give a hint as to the missing man's whereabouts.

Yeah, Rohrbach thought scornfully. *Like that's gonna happen. Guy decides to pull a runner, he's gonna leave clues. Little map, maybe, X marks the spot on it. Jeeze, you'd think some of these supervisors had never seen the inside of a prison before.* But:

Mine is not to reason why, Rohrbach told himself resignedly, stopping at the door to "D" corridor and turning his face up so that the guy watching the surveillance camera could see him. The locked corridor, called a pod, held a group of a dozen cells that constituted a prisoner's neighborhood.

While he was here, Hooper had been a good citizen of his neighborhood, or at least a relatively trouble-free one. Took his orders without backchat, no fights, no contraband discoveries. It was as if Hooper had been relieved, really, to have someone else telling him what to do for a change. Arriving for his shift this morning, Rohrbach had been amazed to hear that Hooper had taken the initiative to attempt an escape; that the inmate had actually made it out, Rohrbach thought, was just short of miraculous.

He waited patiently while the guard monitoring the camera opened the pod door's electronic lock: *ka-click!* when it opened, *ka-click!* again when it closed behind him.

Inside, the brightly lit corridor featured identical doors, each pierced with a small window. At this hour of the morning, the cells were empty, their occupants all out at various scheduled activities: work, school, exercise, and so on. Except for Hooper; what activity he might be engaged in this fine morning was still anyone's guess.

Rohrbach entered Hooper's cell, which looked just like all the others: a ten-by-fourteen-foot cubicle with white walls, a white linoleum floor, and a slot window too narrow for a man to get even half his face through, much less his body. The bed was a shelf built into the wall; the combination washstand and toilet was brushed steel, also built in. A desk-shelf with a molded plastic chair tucked under it was the only other furniture. The mattress on the bed was a thin blue plastic pad.

Brackets in the wall above the bed showed where another bunk could be hung, if necessary. There was nothing else in the room: no books, no pictures on the wall, no calendar. A blanket and a towel, neatly folded, were on the neatly made bed, atop Hooper's pillow. Cell and corridor smelled the same, like Clorox, sweeping compound, cheap air freshener, and men's sweat.

The cell's stark impersonality came as no surprise. Others on the corridor, in defiance of regulations, had taped clippings of newspaper stories, their kids' artwork, and other items that were personally important to them on the walls. But Hooper had been, Rohrbach recalled again grimly, a model prisoner, and when the order came down that all prisoner belongings should be stowed in footlockers, not displayed on the walls as if these were college dorm rooms, Hooper, unlike most of the other inmates, had complied at once.

Rohrbach thought the regulation was stupid. A comfortable inmate was a calm inmate, and a calm inmate was a safe inmate, in his opinion. And unlike the administrators who sat on their butts all day thinking up ways to make Rohrbach's job harder, when you worked among guys whose nerves were already severely on edge, the last thing you wanted was to make them even more angry, agitated, and resentful.

But that wasn't Rohrbach's call to make, either. His job was to root through that footlocker, dig out whatever Hooper-locating secrets it might hold. The idea that Hooper might've left a trail of breadcrumbs in the form of a map or a diary was still stupid; hell, the guy was barely literate as far as Rohrbach could tell.

On the other hand, it wasn't like they had anything else to go on. The prisoner had simply evaporated.

Gone like a fart in the wind, as the onetime head of another Maine prison had been known to say.

Rohrbach pulled the gray molded-plastic box from under the bed. Inmates couldn't have locks, so it opened easily. *Might as well ask a Ouija board where Dewey Hooper is,* Rohrbach thought. But when he looked inside the box . . .

"Holy mackerel," he breathed. Notebooks. The footlocker was filled to the top with notebooks, the kind prisoners were allowed to buy with their small work-detail earnings: tape bindings, no plastic or metal, cardboard covers removed in case weapons might somehow be fashioned from them.

Alert for sharp objects that might be rusty or contaminated—some inmates hid blades, needles, and other dangerous things in footlockers, and although he didn't expect any such problem from Hooper's belongings, you never knew—Rohrbach removed one of the notebooks and opened it.

A limp four-leaf clover fluttered out. As it fell to the floor, Rohrbach recalled Hooper's only idiosyncrasy: superstition. You could make the guy turn his cell into a plain white box, no problem, but don't try to make him walk under a ladder. Then, as what he was seeing sank in:

"Man, oh, man," Rohrbach said to himself, recalling again the passive little guy who'd seemed to live only for work detail, his eagerness for new assignments seeming to suggest he was enrolled in a training program for running a prison, not confined in one.

Rohrbach flipped quickly through the pages, then slowed, turning them wonderingly:

They were all the same. Page after page, over and over . . .

Day after day. Year after year. Hundreds of times, thousands of times . . . *I guess still waters really do run deep,* Rohrbach thought, and then a sound from the corridor made him turn.

It was Charlie Theriault, here for armed robbery, nine years into a seven-to-fifteen. "Hey," Charlie said.

"Hey," Rohrbach greeted the man in return. Charlie was all right. A little moody but not a problem. The inmate entered his cell, came out with his towel.

Rohrbach looked back down at the notebooks. "Charlie," he said, "do you recall her name? Hooper's wife, the one he—"

Killed. Beat to death. He didn't want to say it, though. Putting violent images in an inmate's head was never a good idea. And as it turned out, he didn't have to; Charlie remembered.

"Marianne," said Charlie, confirming what Rohrbach thought.

As he had expected, the notebooks gave no clue as to Hooper's whereabouts. What had been on his mind, though, through all those quiet years of him being a model prisoner—

Oh, that was crystal clear. *Marianne Marianne,* read the first line of the first notebook in childishly rounded cursive script, like the writing of a small boy. And the next line and the next, on both sides of the page.

Marianne Marianne Marianne . . .

Page after page, notebook after notebook. Year after year:

Marianne.

To remove screws easily, use a screwdriver bit and the "reverse" setting on your electric drill.
—Tiptree's Tips

Harold had Facebook, and LiveJournal, and Twitter. He had a BlackBerry, an iPad, an iPod, and a third-generation Kindle.

He had a pain, mild but constant, a fluttery twinge in the soft tissue just above his left eye, deep in the hollow where you'd put your thumb if you were going to try lifting him by his cranium. Sometimes late at night, in his tiny apartment in a grimly forgotten, perpetually unfashionable corner of Lower Manhattan, he would find himself Googling: *twinge, eye, flutter.* Or: *thumb, skull.*

When it occurred to him what that last pair rhymed with—*numbskull*—he stopped Googling it. But he couldn't forget.

Each weekday, Harold took the subway to his job at a video store a few blocks from Ground Zero, a place with a sale bin out front and a sputtery neon sign in the grimy window. Once it had thrived, but the only videos people rented nowadays were ones they wouldn't dare view on the Internet for fear of prison time.

The films didn't have brightly illustrated cardboard sleeves, or even titles. Furtive men—no women, in Harold's depressingly extensive experience—entered the store with money in hand, and asked without looking up at Harold for number 19, or number 204.

Harold wondered if they were ashamed of themselves, or if maybe they just didn't like seeing his eye twitch. If maybe *they* were creeped out by *him*. What he didn't wonder was what kind of unspeakably sordid images the videos contained; he needed the job too much for that.

But after three years in the store—the sputtering neon sign, the nagging eye pain, the worn black plastic cassettes or clear jewel cases that he wiped thoroughly with spray cleaner anytime one of them got returned—he also needed a vacation. So when the store's owner laid Harold off for two weeks due to cash-flow problems, he decided to go to Maine.

He'd never been, just seen pictures of the place. Probably Maine colors weren't as bright as they looked in the pages of magazines, with lighthouses as red-and-white-striped as new candy canes, and water as blue as . . . well, nothing in this life was ever really that blue, Harold felt sure.

But it didn't matter what it was like there. It was the *idea* of Maine that attracted him: clean air, not too many people. Forests you could walk into and not find your way out again, mineral-clear lakes, numbingly cold, where you could wade in and dissolve with a sigh, like a fizzy lozenge.

Not that he meant to; wade into one of those lakes, that is, and never wade out. But the idea of such wilderness—of surfaces that hadn't been handled and breathed on, or even looked at, by millions of people—spoke deeply to him, somehow, even though he had never experienced any such place himself.

So Harold left all his electronic gadgets at home and took a bus from Port Authority to Bangor, Maine, then a smaller one whose seats were made of hard plastic. As they wound out of Bangor, the driver drank Diet Coke and blared Top Forty on the radio propped up on the cluttered dashboard while the bus juddered along the twisty, crumbling two-lane blacktop.

Hours passed while Harold stared out the window at a world growing steadily more rural and less like anything he'd ever seen before: small wooden houses with garishly colored plastic toys in their rough yards, lobster traps stacked along unpaved driveways, boats sagging on trailers. Next came lengthy stretches where it seemed no one at all lived, the unfenced fields high and boulder-studded and the forests appearing darkly impenetrable.

At last they reached a small, desolate-looking intersection marked by an out-of-business gas station and convenience store. No sign, but the driver said it was the right place; hoisting his backpack, Harold got out and the bus trundled away, leaving him alone on the gravel shoulder, which was littered with hundreds of old and new filtered cigarette butts.

All around him loomed giant evergreens, their pointed tops etched on a fiercely blue sky. A big white-headed bird—a bald eagle, Harold realized; he'd never seen one of those before, either—sailed above.

The roar of a diesel engine shattered the silence as a log truck loaded with forty-foot tree trunks hurtled past, the smell of fresh pine sap sharp in its wake. Watching it go, he felt a sudden, drowning sense of isolation and loss, as if his old life had been torn away and had yet to be replaced by anything.

If it would be. Abruptly, he wished he hadn't come. Back in the city, he was always so surrounded and assaulted by crowds and clamor, it was easy there to pretend that he wasn't alone.

Here it was different. Turning, he heard the gravel crunch loudly beneath his feet. A big dog barked, somewhere on the other side of a line of trees. From the rotting eaves of the boarded-up convenience store, wasps drifted, each one materializing in the gloom at the nest's entrance, then launching itself.

Harold wondered suddenly what it was like in that

nest, in the insectile dark. But he didn't think he'd better try to find out. Just then a car pulled up to where the gas pumps used to be.

"You waitin' for a ride?" The car was an old, dark blue Monte Carlo with the word TAXI inexpertly stenciled on it in white.

The driver, a large, whiskery man wearing a fedora, chewed a cigar stub. Harold did not recall any cab driver back in the city ever waiting so patiently or looking at him so frankly, as if genuinely engaged in this interaction and curious about Harold's reply.

Harold hefted his backpack, which he had let down onto the cracked concrete pad that the absent gas pumps had once stood on. Ten minutes later, after crossing a causeway and traversing some of the most astonishingly beautiful geography he'd ever seen—trees, a long beach with legions of small birds striding stick-legged on it, a wide expanse of water, then more trees and water again—he reached the island city of Eastport, Maine.

"Here you go. That'll be seven bucks. A buck a mile," the taxi man explained around the cigar stub.

Harold blinked, still stunned by the beauty and variety of the fields, forested land, and reedy marshes he'd been whisked through, the ponds, pools, and tidal inlets he'd passed over.

Chomping the cigar, the driver eyed him wisely. "City boy, eh? Don't worry. You stay here, you'll get over it. Eventually," he added with a wink, taking the ten Harold handed him.

"Keep the change," said Harold. The Monte pulled away in a belch of gray exhaust fumes that the breeze, smelling strongly of salt water and creosote, snatched up and dispersed.

Leaving him alone, again, though here at least there were people going about their business: into the hardware store, the pizza shop, and the T-shirt-and-souvenir store all located in the three-story red-brick buildings directly before him. To his left loomed another brick edifice, an old bank now repurposed into an art gallery, with a fountain and a small terrace in front of it. There was an ornate metal park bench placed on the terrace, which he thought was a nice touch.

Right behind him was an old-fashioned diner. Through a small screened front window, he saw a long Formica counter and a series of red leatherette booths, and suddenly realized he was starving. He'd been on the road almost two days with only snacks and small bottles of juice to eat and drink, from the vending machines in various bus stations.

Turning to enter the diner, he got his first view of the bay, which even after all of the water he'd already crossed he hadn't realized was so very near. Seeing it on a map had been one thing, the letters printed over it spelling out *Passamaquoddy Bay*, which he guessed must be a Native American name. But being right next to it was another, especially since there was no one on it.

Or almost no one; dark blue with flocks of gulls hovering over it, the bay was narrow and extended a long way to his left and right, which he recalled from the map were north and south. A few fishing boats puttered, their wakes boiling white, engines puffing up clouds of diesel. The bay itself looked serene, though, not like the busy, commerce-clogged waterways at home.

He gazed for another moment, inhaling the salty air. But more delay than that, the pangs of his appetite would not allow. A whiff of grilled bacon drifted sweetly out of the diner's screen window, seized him by the nose, and drew him hungrily in.

Half an hour later he was sopping up the last bit of egg yolk with his last corner of buttered toast. The waitress was so free with the coffee refills, he thought she'd have left the pot if he'd asked. He washed the delicious mouthful down with a sip from his freshly topped-up cup and, sighing, leaned back.

He'd made it. He'd gotten here, all the long way to Maine's downeast coast, so far from the island of Manhattan and, as he had already begun realizing, so utterly different from it.

And he felt . . . fine. Scared, a little, and still not sure how he was getting away with such an adventurous, such a previously unthought-of, expedition. He didn't quite trust his success yet, he guessed. But so far, so good.

Two men slid onto stools at the counter. They were in their sixties, maybe, Harold thought from their work-bent postures, and they were similarly dressed in jeans, boots, and faded plaid shirts, with Red Sox ball caps on their heads. When they spoke, continuing a conversation that had evidently begun outside, their accents amazed Harold.

"Pretty fah from heah." The first man stirred sugar into his coffee.

"Fah," the second man agreed. "Nawt thet fah, tho."

They were saying that something was only somewhat far from here, Harold realized. He listened some more.

"State prison's just a hop, skip, and a jump from here, if you've got a car once you make it outside the fences." *Cah*.

"They didn't say he's got a car. In the newspaper." *Paypah*. "Maybe he didn't. Not then. He might by now, though. Have one, that is."

The second man drank coffee, then added, "He's not coming here, though. I know, I know"—he put his work-worn hands up to ward off objections—"this's where he's from originally. Killer like that, though, he does a runner"—*runnah*—"he'll hightail it to somewhere else, prob'ly. Somewhere he can blend in."

Somewheyah. "Prob'ly," the first man agreed, nodding sagely. "Like New York City. Hell, I guess most anyone you'd meet out on the street might be a killer, there."

You've got that right, Harold thought wryly, gathering from what he'd just overheard that a convicted murderer had recently escaped from the state prison and was on the loose. But that had nothing to do with him, he told himself reassuringly. All he wanted was a walk in the woods, and there was certainly nothing there, he felt sure, to appeal to a prison escapee.

He got up from his booth. The men had turned to discussing a hunter who'd gone out three days ago and hadn't returned. Old Bentley, they called him. Bentley Hodell; had heart trouble, poor guy. Had an attack out there, maybe—*mebbe*—out in the woods.

"Excuse me," Harold cut in. "Could either of you tell me a good place for a fellow to take a hike? Like, out in the forest?"

The men, who when they turned he saw to his surprise were not in their sixties at all, but closer to his own age, perhaps in their mid-thirties or even younger, gazed silently at him for a moment. During it, Harold saw traces of the fresh-faced boys they had been before hard work began taking its toll: bright blue eyes, open expressions, regular features.

"Not in a park, though," Harold added. "I want to hike in the real Maine backcountry."

The men looked communicatively at each other as if silently agreeing on a place to recommend. Then they told Harold about it, even borrowing the waitress's ballpoint to draw him a rough map on a paper napkin from the bright metal dispenser on the counter.

"Watch out for the killer," they added, but laughingly, and Harold decided that if they weren't worried, he wasn't, either.

Killah.